Dino's Story

Dino's Story

A Novel of 1960s Tuscany

The rain-soaked Basilica of Santa Croce in Florence, Italy.
Photo by Don Schaffer.

PAUL SALSINI

iUniverse, Inc.
New York   Bloomington

Dino's Story
A Novel of 1960s Tuscany

This is a work of fiction. The flood in Florence did, of course, occur, but all of the characters, names, organizations, and dialogue in this novel are either the products of the author's imagination or are used fictitiously.

iUniverse books may be ordered through booksellers or by contacting:

iUniverse
1663 Liberty Drive
Bloomington, IN 47403
www.iuniverse.com
1-800-Authors (1-800-288-4677)

ISBN: 978-1-4502-1080-5 (sc)
ISBN: 978-1-4502-1081-2 (ebook)

Library of Dongress Control Number: 2010901243

Printed in the United States of America

iUniverse rev. date: 02/23/2010

For Barbara
Jim, Laura and Jack

Also by Paul Salsini

Sparrow's Revenge: A Novel of Postwar Tuscany

The Cielo: A Novel of Wartime Tuscany

Second Start

Author's Note

When I wrote *The Cielo: A Novel of Wartime Tuscany*, I couldn't imagine that there would be a sequel, but the characters insisted, and *Sparrow's Revenge: A Novel of Postwar Tuscany* somehow materialized. Then they told me they had more stories to tell, and so *Dino's Story: A Novel of 1960s Tuscany* has now emerged.

Writing about Dino was enjoyable. I liked him when he was a baby in the first book and when he was a precocious ten-year-old in the second. Now, he moves from the village of Sant'Antonio and comes of age during a terrible event in Florence in 1966.

While "A Tuscan Trilogy" has ended, the characters tell me they have more to say and do, so I am planning to write a series of short stories that will continue their narratives. Perhaps that will be the next book.

Again, there are many people to thank for this one: My wife, Barbara, our daughter, Laura, and sons, Jim and Jack, for their support and encouragement; writers Martha Bergland and Larry Baldassaro for their helpful comments and suggestions, and, in Italy, once again my indefatigable driver/interpreter Marcello Grandini and my cousin, Fosca, who started all this by telling me how she and other villagers fled to a farmhouse in the hills during World War II.

THE MAIN CHARACTERS

In Sant'Antonio and Lucca:

Dino Sporenza, a young student
Lucia Sporenza, his mother
Paolo Ricci, her husband; Dino's stepfather
Ezio Maffini, a schoolteacher and owner of the Cielo
Donna Fazzini, his wife
Antonio Maffini, his father
Rosa Tomaselli, a neighbor
Annabella Sabbatini, a neighbor
Fausta Sanfilippo, a neighbor
Father Sangretto, the village priest
Francesca Casati, another student
Piera Casati, her mother

In Florence:

Roberto Sporenza, Dino's uncle
Adolfo Sporenza, Roberto's brother
Mila, Adolfo's wife
Penny Richards, a student from England
Raffaele, another student
Marie, another student
Ingrid, another student
Professor Mariotti, a teacher at the Accademia
Father Lorenzo, a Franciscan priest who runs a soup kitchen
Tomasso Nuzzoli, owner of a ceramics shop
Principessa Maria Elena Elisabetta Margherita di Savoia, a wealthy art patron
Sofia, a model and volunteer at the soup kitchen

PART ONE

Rooftops of Lucca, Italy. Photo by Gaby Thyssen @ Fotolia.com

Chapter One

June 1962

Years later, Dino wondered if his life would have been different if it were not for that disastrous incident with Saint Anthony.

Actually, it was the statue of Saint Anthony, and the incident occurred during the celebration of his feast day in the village named for him.

Everyone in Sant'Antonio had gathered in the little piazza in front of Leoni's *bottega* and Manconi's butcher shop for the annual *Festa di Sant'Antonio* on that blistering hot June 13 in 1962. Dino stood in the back, wondering why the procession to the church hadn't begun.

The women, even the widows who normally were entirely in black, wore colorful dresses and scarves. The men had brought out their ill-fitting suits, and the children were in their Sunday best. Everyone was very hot.

"Let's get going!" a man in the back yelled. "My collar is choking me!"

But first, the statue of Saint Anthony, brought from its honored place on the side altar, had to be placed firmly in an opening on the *portantina*, the platform that would be carried solemnly back to the church. Two men, Dino's Papa, Paolo, and Ezio, the schoolteacher, were having trouble.

"Lean it a little to the left," Ezio cried.

"No, to the right!" Paolo said.

"No, to the left!"

They didn't know why it didn't fit. It fit perfectly last year. Maybe all that rain in the last two months had warped the wood and changed the size of the opening.

Dino looked on silently, biting his lip and standing on one foot, then the other. Why can't they get it in?

"Maybe if we pushed a little harder," Ezio said.

His father, Antonio, joined the effort. "Let me help."

With Antonio and Paolo at his side, Ezio firmly took hold of the statue and tried to force it into the opening. Nothing.

"Oh, please," Dino thought, "what's taking them so long? This is stupid."

In the village of Sant'Antonio, Saint Anthony's feast day was celebrated more than Christmas or Easter. No one knew why the village was named after the saint, but he was popular all over northern Italy, and especially in this region of Tuscany. People believed that the church, which was dedicated in 1736, probably predated the village, which back then consisted of only a few scattered farmhouses.

Over the years, the village grew to almost a hundred people. Now, most lived a half mile from the church, which lay peacefully in a grove of cypresses.

"Don't push so hard, Ezio," Antonio said.

"If I don't push, Papa, it will never get in." Ezio stopped to wipe the sweat from his eyes.

Dino came closer. "Can't you hurry?"

More people gathered around the three men struggling to embed the statue into the *portantina*. Nothing so amusing had happened in the village since that stupid kid Bruno tried to climb to the top of the water tower and hung upside down by his belt for an hour until he could be rescued.

Ezio and Paolo took the jibes of their friends cheerfully, and at one point Paolo made an obscene gesture and mouthed a crude word. The women feigned horror and giggled.

Antonio had made the platform only three years ago, shortly after he moved from Florence to stay with his son and his wife, Donna, in their hilltop farmhouse, the Cielo. Having owned a carpenter shop in Florence, he was the likely person to build the new platform when the old one disintegrated.

He had taken a three-by-five foot piece of plywood and attached six-foot poles on either side. Then he took the five-foot statue of Saint Anthony down from the altar, measured the base and cut out a hole in the center of the *portantina* exactly to fit. And the saint had obliged. Until now.

Dino shielded his eyes and tried to look at the blazing sun, which was still high overhead. The new pimples on his face hurt. "Stupid, stupid, stupid."

"Push, Paolo, push," shouted the burly Rocco Mancetti, who owned the *gelateria* next to Paolo's *pasticceria* in nearby Reboli. "Show a little muscle!"

Paolo was laughing too hard to make any headway.

"You can do it!" Rocco yelled.

"How about you come and help me?" Paolo called back.

"No, no. You're strong enough."

"Shhh," Ezio said, "the priest is coming."

"Stupid, stupid, stupid," Dino thought.

Carrying the monstrance with the Holy Host inside, Father Sangretto slowly got out of his shiny black Fiat at the edge of the piazza and made his way to what was turning into a most unceremonious ceremony. Dino hurried up to him, bent his knee slightly and made the sign of the cross.

"I'm sorry, Father," he whispered. "There seems to be a little trouble. But I think they'll be ready very soon." He made his way back to the struggling trio. "Hurry. Father Sangretto looks very angry."

"Well, let him try to do this," Paolo said under his breath. "What does he know?"

"Papa," Dino said, "please..."

"Don't worry, Little Dino," Paolo said. "We've almost got it."

"Papa, please don't call me Little Dino anymore. I'm sixteen years old."

With renewed energy, Ezio, Paolo and Antonio each took hold of the marble statue, Ezio at the base, Antonio pushing down on the saint's tonsured head, and Paolo in the middle, putting his arms around the Baby Jesus that the saint held in his arms.

"One, two, three," Ezio said.

They pushed.

C-r-a-c-k!!!!

The sound of the splintering wood could be heard not only in the piazza but inside Leoni's as well. Nino Leoni ran from behind the counter to the window to watch.

The villagers gasped. Father Sangretto's face grew red.

Dino rolled his eyes.

Slowly, Saint Anthony eased down into the opening, stopping at mid-thigh.

Ezio turned around to reassure the onlookers. "It's OK. He won't go anywhere. Let's go."

He and Antonio grabbed the poles at one end of the *portantina*, put them on their shoulders and prepared to move. Dino joined his Papa at the other end.

For the last three years, the honor of carrying Saint Anthony along the winding gravel road from the village to the church had been given to these four: Ezio Maffini, because he was very popular as a schoolteacher; Antonio Maffini, because he was Ezio's father and the maker of the platform; Paolo Ricci, simply because everyone liked him so much, and Paolo's stepson, Dino Sporenza.

Antonio and Ezio were paired because they were tall and of the same height. Paolo and Dino were shorter and until this year of the same height as well. But something had happened since last June 13. Dino had spurted skyward, and was now a good four inches taller than Paolo.

The result was a lopsided arrangement, and Saint Anthony leaned very decidedly to the west.

"Crouch down, Little Dino," Paolo said.

"I am crouching. And stop calling me Little Dino!" Dino bent his back and his knees.

"Can we go now?" Ezio asked.

"Move!" Father Sangretto shouted from the rear.

In their haste, the four platform bearers grabbed the wrong ends, and although Saint Anthony was supposed to face forward, toward the church, this time he looked at the villagers who trailed behind.

Maybe fifty or sixty villagers followed the statue on the gravel road. First came six children, five girls in their First Communion dresses and a little chubby boy in a white shirt, brown pants and black tie. They tried as best they could to look solemn.

Behind them, Rosa Tomaselli held the arm of Dino's mother, Lucia Sporenza.

"Am I going too fast?" Lucia asked.

"No, no. I'm fine." Rosa refused to let a little arthritis in her knees stop her from doing whatever she had been doing for more than seven decades.

Annabella Sabbatini, limping because of her own arthritis, walked along with Fausta Sanfilippo, who more than twenty years later was still something of an outcast because of her Fascist activities during the war. Then came the others, neighbors and, with only a few exceptions, friends, loudly singing the "Ave Maria."

At the rear, Father Sangretto held the monstrance, covered with a white cloth, up high for a while but then his arms tired and he lowered it to his chest. The priest considered himself one of the finest singers in the region, and his baritone echoed off the stone houses and then, when they emerged from the village, off the olive and cypress trees amid the fields of grain.

Ave Maria, piena di grazia,
il Signore è con te.
Tu sei benedetta fra le donne
e benedetto è il frutto del tuo seno, Gesú.
Santa Maria, Madre di Dio,
prega per noi peccatori,
adesso e nell'ora della nostra morte.

After the awkward beginning, the procession seemed to be going well, solemn and yet festive. The villagers smiled at each other and at the children who were now scuffling along and no longer hand-in-hand.

C-r-a-c-k!!!!

"Oh, no," Dino whispered as he and Paolo, holding the poles in the rear, saw the opening in the *portantina* splinter even more. Slowly, Saint Anthony began to fall through, inch by noisy inch.

The children screamed and pointed, the women gasped and the men laughed. Father Sangretto was so engrossed in singing that he didn't even notice.

C-r-a-c-k!!!!

The saint was now in danger of falling right through to the gravel path. But the Baby Jesus stopped the descent. That part of the statue was wider than the rest, and so the statue came to rest with Saint Anthony looking down on the child's head and outstretched hands in beatific adoration.

For years, people had smiled when they saw the Baby Jesus in the church. With eyes that seemed a little crossed and its mouth open, it seemed to be crying out for help.

"Help me!"

The voice was high and shrill, and the villagers stopped short. "Did you hear that?" Rosa clutched Lucia's arm tighter. "Did you hear that? Did Baby Jesus say something?"

"No, Rosa, of course not," Lucia said. "It's only Paolo acting silly. Stop that, Paolo!" she shouted.

A stream of giggles ran through the procession.

"Help me!"

Ezio looked over his shoulder and laughed. "Paolo, how can you make your voice so high?"

Paolo wouldn't stop. *"I'm falling!"*

Dino was mortified. "Papa, please stop that."

"Help me!"

"Papa! Please!" If he hadn't had the platform on his shoulder, Dino would have run from the scene.

Paolo knew it was time to stop the joke, and the procession moved along without further incident. Barely suppressing their laughter, the villagers finally made it to the church, up the stairs and into the dark interior, lit only by red votive lights and a bank of yellow candles. Ezio, Paolo and Antonio quickly rescued the statue from the *portantina* and returned it to the side altar across from the centuries-old painting of Saint Francis shaving the head of Saint Claire. Except for a few scratches on his brown tunic, Saint Anthony had survived the ordeal.

Dino, limping because his back and legs ached, hurried into the sacristy and donned a black cassock and white surplice. Reluctantly, he would be the altar boy for the Mass because there weren't any other teenage boys in the village. Dino once suggested to Father Sangretto that a girl be enlisted as an acolyte, but the priest's fleshy jowls began to quiver.

"A girl! A girl!" he shouted. "We can't have a girl up at the altar. Holy Mother Church would never allow that. And I won't either!"

His voice softened. "The reason boys serve as acolytes, Dino, is so that they can appreciate being near the sacred altar and think about becoming a priest, as I hope you are."

Dino fervently wished the priest would stop bringing up that subject. He did not want to be a priest.

The women took their places in pews at the front, and the men stood in the back. Father Sangretto was known for his quick masses, and it was over in little more than a half hour. Dino tore off his cassock and surplice and fled the church so he could avoid seeing the priest. And he didn't even look back at the scarred statue of Saint Anthony.

Chapter Two

After the Mass, everyone went down into the musty but cool church basement. Since Sant'Antonio lacked a school, this was the gathering place for happy occasions like the *festa* and for lunches after funerals. Rosa and Annabella had decorated the place with streamers and flowers and placed white paper on the three long tables in the middle of the room.

Every parish had a festival on its saint's feast day, and it was customary for people from all over to attend each one. So the basement was filled for the *Festa di Sant'Antonio* and Father Sangretto hoped that the money raised from admission tickets could repair a rapidly growing hole in the church roof.

Watching all the hugging and kissing and shaking of hands, Dino stood along the wall. Everyone is so old, he thought.

But before the meal came the annual pageant on the life of Saint Anthony put on by the First Communicants. Wrapped in a brown towel, the little chubby boy portrayed the saint, and the tallest girl was the narrator, describing how Saint Anthony was born in Portugal in 1195, became a friar and moved to Assisi. Waving their arms like fins, the other girls enthusiastically took part in the main scene, Saint Anthony preaching to the fishes at Rimini.

Nine years ago, Dino was that little boy in the pageant, though not as chubby. Now he was taller than his Papa and so skinny his Mama kept forcing pasta on him.

"Eat! Eat! You've got to put some meat on those bones. It's not healthy."

Two things hadn't changed in nine years, his freckles and his ears. Dino hated his protruding ears so much that he took to wearing a band around his head at night. It didn't help. He was also embarrassed that when he blushed, his freckles turned darker and his ears to bright red.

It was now almost 5 o'clock and time to eat. Rosa brought her usual ravioli, six dozen this time.

"How could we ever have a feast without your ravioli?" Lucia said as she removed the red checkered cloth that covered them.

Rosa had gotten used to such compliments. "*Allora,* you wouldn't have a feast," she said.

First came the *bruschetta* with tomato and basil, then slices of boiled ham and salami, then Rosa's ravioli, then thin cuts of veal and beef, then a spinach salad. Like all Italian meals, the pace was leisurely, with good times for conversations between each course.

Three hours later, after the apples and pears and torte had been passed around, Ezio convinced his father to get out his concertina, which Ezio had secretly brought along in the trunk of his car. From the lovely ballads *"Colombo che sul poggio"* and *"Maremma amara"* to the lively tongue-twisters *"E voi Caterinella"* and *"il baco Gigi,"* Antonio's firm tenor filled the room with traditional songs of Tuscany.

Ezio and Donna noticed that Antonio glanced shyly at Rosa when he sang a ballad, and that Rosa blushed and looked away.

"Say," Ezio said, "is something going on between those two?"

"So you finally noticed?"

"You think my dad is, what, smitten?"

Donna smiled. "Yes, Ezio. I think he's smitten."

"I can't believe it. After all these years? He's seventy-seven years old."

"So?" Donna said. "Rosa is about seventy-three, I think. Love happens at any age, you know. Look at us."

"Yes." Ezio smiled and hugged her. "Look at us."

Tables were pushed to the side and the children danced and then chased each other around the room. Women took their awkward turns on the improvised dance floor. Men gathered around the bar and ordered beer and grappa.

In the kitchen, Dino was arm-deep in soapsuds washing dishes when Benedetta Mendicino came up behind him and put her hands over his eyes.

"Guess who?" she whispered in his ear.

"Benedetta Mendicino."

"Oh, you're no fun, Dino. How did you know that?" she squeaked. "I thought I'd fool you."

Ever since fourth grade, Benedetta had made her feelings about Dino known, sometimes blatantly. He tried to avoid her as much as possible.

"I'm busy, Benedetta."

Benedetta pretended to frown, making her upper teeth protrude even farther. "You're always busy, Dino. Oh, OK. But I'll be in the piazza tonight. I'll see you there, OK?" She ran her fingers down his back and went back to the music.

"Don't count on it," Dino muttered. He finished the dishes and returned to the dancing. All of the girls were acting silly, jumping around instead of dancing. He wouldn't want to dance with any of them, even if he knew how to dance, which he didn't.

Carrying a bowl of leftovers, Lucia found Dino in a corner. "Dino, I'm going home. I've left your grandmother alone too long."

"Me, too." Dino said.

On the walk home in the now cooler countryside, Dino regretted not being nicer to his mother sometimes. She's had such a hard life, getting pregnant with Dino during the war, losing his father in a gunfight, raising her son alone until she married Paolo. And now, caring for her sick mother.

At home, Lucia went into her mother's upstairs room. Ever since her husband had died, Gina Sporenza mostly stayed in bed, overwhelmed by depression, a bad heart and severe stomach problems. The doctor said he couldn't do anything more for her. Lucia always tried to amuse her, and tonight related the events of the day.

"And then, you know what, Mama? The funniest thing happened. When Father Sangretto blessed the statue after the mass, the top of the holy water sprinkler came off. It flew right off! And it landed right in the middle of Saint Anthony's head. Right in the middle!"

Lucia could swear that Gina smiled a little.

Across the hall, Dino dug out his book on Michelangelo. Final exams at the *liceo artistico* in Lucca were next week, and he didn't feel ready. Worse, he didn't feel interested. Lately, he had been restless, unable to concentrate. He didn't know why.

Paging through the book, he examined the photos of the ceiling of the Sistine Chapel, the Last Judgment, the tomb of Julius II, Moses, the Pietà, the David and the Unfinished Statues. Dino stopped at the picture of The Waking Slave, wondering why Michelangelo had not finished it. He kept the book open to that page.

Ever since he was a boy, Dino liked to draw, and now he enjoyed it even more. He didn't know why, but he seemed to express himself better in drawing pictures of flowers and trees and buildings and sunsets than in actually talking. The images seemed to flow from his fingertips, expressing things that Dino could not express in words.

"Why are you always so quiet?" Lucia would ask him. "Why don't you talk more?"

Dino had no answer.

Taking out a piece of paper and a charcoal pencil, Dino tried to copy the photograph of the statue, but became frustrated and threw the paper away.

He wandered around his room, looked out the window, and then lay on his bed staring at the ceiling. He got up and opened the *mangia dischi* he had received last Christmas. It played little discs, which the owner of the record store said were called "45s."

Dino still had only five records. His favorite was by the new young composer, Fabrizio De André. He sat on the edge of his bed, pretending that he, too, had a guitar, and sang along to the mournful lyrics.

E fu la notte
la notte per noi
notte profonda
sul nostro amore.
E fu la fine
di tutto per noi
resta il passato
e niente di più.

It was the night
the night for us
deep night
on our love.
It was the end of
everything to us
The past remains
and nothing more.

He lay on the bed again. Those songs that Antonio played tonight were all right for Antonio and old people. But Dino was young. He was sixteen. What did Antonio and Rosa or even his mother and Papa know about the torments of love? A couple of years ago, he was little. Now, so many changes had occurred in his body that he didn't understand. Worse, he had so many worries and doubts that he couldn't talk about with anybody.

Dino picked up the book and looked at the photo of The Waking Slave. It was in the Accademia Galleria in Florence. He wondered if he would ever see it or any of the other wonders of Florence, a city everyone said was the cultural capital of the world. Restless, he paced between his bed and the window. He'd probably never get to spend any time in Florence. He was stuck in Sant'Antonio. Stupid village.

Chapter Three

June 1963

Word of the tumultuous *Festa di Sant'Antonio* of 1962 had spread so far that people from villages all over the region gathered the following year hoping for a repeat. They were disappointed.

Antonio and Ezio had built a new *portantina* for the saint, this time binding two pieces of plywood together, and for extra protection they tethered the statue to all four ends. Saint Anthony and the Baby Jesus didn't have a chance to escape.

The pageant on the life of Saint Anthony had only four First Communicants this year, and so there were fewer fishes in the Rimini story. But Rosa brought her usual ravioli, again six dozen, and Antonio played the concertina and got up the courage to sit next to Rosa, who smiled. Benedetta Mendicino unsuccessfully tried to get Dino to go to the piazza.

After washing the dishes, Dino left the *festa* early and went for a walk. Evenings were his favorite times now, and he had discovered a path that led to Mansagrati where a chapel dedicated to Saint Zita had been built. He knew that the saint's body was under the altar of a church in Lucca, but that didn't interest him. What he liked was to sit outside and sketch the chapel from different angles and at different times of the day. The chapel seemed to take on a life of its own, and Dino had drawn or painted a dozen versions in just a few months, most of which he had thrown away, but Ezio and Donna liked one large painting so much they asked to keep it.

After drawing, he liked to go inside the chapel and just be away from everyone else, everything else. Tonight, he opened the creaky door and sank into one of the heavy oak pews.

He was seventeen years old now and painfully aware that he had never had a date with a girl, had hardly ever talked to a girl. There wasn't anyone in Sant'Antonio, certainly not Benedetta Mendicino, and there wasn't anyone on the bus to the high school in Lucca. When the other boys and girls on the bus giggled about their adventures, he looked out the window.

But lately he noticed this girl in his Renaissance art history class. She had long blond hair tied in the back. She had freckles, just like he had. She was small, maybe a foot shorter than he was, and had thin arms and fragile hands. Her eyes were a watery light blue. She rarely said anything in class, but she seemed to be studying very hard. He liked her paintings very much and wished he could find the words to tell her that.

Twice, he could have sworn she smiled at him.

Her name was Francesca. He thought that was the most beautiful name in the world. Sometimes, in class, he looked at her back, two rows ahead of him, and wrote her name over and over in his notebook. "Francesca. Francesca. Francesca."

But why was he even thinking about her? Why would she be interested in a boy from a village? A boy who was even quieter than she was in class. A boy who had never had a date with a girl. A boy with big ears and pimples. He left the chapel and went home.

A few days after the *festa*, the telephone rang.

"Dino!" Lucia said, putting her hand over the receiver. "Father Sangretto wants you to come to see him."

Dino waved his hands frantically. "No!" he mouthed. "No!"

"He'll come right away," Lucia said into the phone. Then, ignoring her son's glare, "Well, what could I say? You're right here. Go."

Father Sangretto had come to Sant'Antonio in 1945, right after the war. At first, villagers wondered why a priest who had served in a large parish in Prato would come to their village, especially when his mother, brought along as his housekeeper, observed that compared to Prato, Sant'Antonio was "so terribly small." There was plenty of gossip when the priest erased the bloodstains on the rectory office floor, left when the saintly Father Luigi was killed by the Germans at that very spot a year earlier.

It didn't help that the priest was only five feet tall, and that his girth made up for his lack of height. He tended to stutter when he got excited.

Dino had to wait in the office for a half hour while the priest and his mother discussed what they would have for dinner when the bishop came next week. Dino didn't know where the priest got his Cuban cigars, since the government controlled the imports, but the office reeked. The heavy crimson drapes were always closed and huge portraits of agonized saints covered the damask walls. Dino felt suffocated and hoped he could get out of there quickly.

Dino knew what Father Sangretto wanted to talk about, but he had no intention of becoming a priest. For one thing, he couldn't see himself getting up in front of people and talking. And he didn't think he was such a good Catholic. He went to Mass most Sundays with his mother, leaving his Papa home to do chores. He used to be a member of the Catholic Action organization, but didn't like the other teenagers who were members. They talked too much.

Father Sangretto liked to talk, too.

"The *festa* was good, wasn't it?" he said, loosening his collar as he eased himself into the plush chair behind the desk. "I don't know how much we took in, but I know it was more than last year. Wish we had a crowd like that every year."

"Yes, it was fun."

"And Rosa's ravioli…oh, my." The priest patted a belly that threatened to burst the buttons on his black cassock. "I could eat them every day."

"Yes."

The priest took off his glasses. "And how's your *Nonna* doing, Dino?"

Dino shrugged. "She's the same."

Since she rarely came out of her room, Dino had little contact with his grandmother. And since she had been ill since he was little, he felt that he barely knew her.

"Dino, you have to understand, Gina has lived a long and good life. She went through the war, she brought up all those children, her husband was sick for so long. Now she's going through many struggles. I know it's hard on your mother and Paolo. But soon your grandmother will be with your *Nonno* again and with Our Lord and all the saints forever. We must keep her in our prayers."

Father Sangretto made the sign of the cross and leaned back.

"Dino, I want to talk to you about your vocation."

Dino slumped in his chair.

"I know you have one, Dino. I've known that ever since you were a little boy. You were so earnest when you received your First Communion, so devout. I could tell even then that you were destined to become a priest. I saw how you looked when you prayed, and I thought, this boy is going to be such a wonderful priest. Don't you agree, Dino?"

"Well, Father..."

"Dino, you have the patience, the understanding, the knowledge that are so necessary. You're going to make a wonderful priest, I know it."

Dino tried to make his legs more comfortable. They still hurt from carrying the platform at the *festa*. He was even taller than Paolo now and had to crouch even more.

"But Father..."

"But? Oh, Dino, I know you have a lot of questions about this. We all go through that. I remember when I was going through what you are now. I wondered and I worried so much. What order should I join? Should I be a parish priest? Should I be a teacher? Should I be a missionary, maybe to Africa? The Holy Mother Church gives us so many choices. But, Dino, Our Lord will see you through this. All you have to do is ask Him, and He will show you the path you should follow. I promise."

Dino squirmed in his chair again.

"Father, I just don't think I have a vocation. Sometimes I look at girls, and I think..."

"G-g-g-girls? Girls?" the priest's voice rose. "You mean girls like Benedetta Mendicino? Stay away from girls like Benedetta Mendicino, Dino. They will lead you down the path to, well, I won't say it. Maybe if her mother would take her to church once in a while…"

"No, Father, I'm talking about, well, nice girls. There's one in my class at Lucca and I keep thinking about her."

"Oh, Dino, I knew you shouldn't go to that *liceo artistico,* where all you learn about is art and you paint who knows what. I know what kind of students they have. They're wild, aren't they? What kind of clothes do they wear? What kind of music do they listen to? Do they ever go to church? I know what's going on. I see it on the television. I read it in *l'Osservatore romano.* The Vatican tells me."

Father Sangretto paused and his face reddened. At sixty-two years old, and after too many cigars and pasta dinners, he lost his breath more often now.

"Oh, Dino, you should have gone to the *liceo classico,* where you would learn Latin and Ancient Greek and history and philosophy. No, you should have gone right to the seminary after you finished the elementary school. But, no, your parents wanted you to wait. I don't know if I'll ever forgive them for that."

Dino had heard this complaint many times. "Well, part of it was the money, Father."

"Oh, money. People can always find money if they want something bad enough." The priest fingered the box that held the receipts from the *festa.*

"Father, if I really had a vocation, would I be thinking about a girl?"

Father Sangretto sighed and got up and went to the bookshelf behind him. He took out a large folder labeled *Azione Cattolica Italiana.*

"You were a member of Catholic Action, right?"

"I was, but I, well, I dropped out."

"Y-y-y-you should have stayed in, you know." The priest's face was getting redder. "You wouldn't be questioning your vocation or thinking about girls if you had stayed in. Now then. Just last week I was reading a publication they put out, and I found this editorial comment on a letter they'd received from a reader. Listen to this."

The priest put his glasses back on and began to read:

"Let us now answer Vittorio, who writes from Turin: 'One of the members is acting like a rebel. He's just made a habit of going to the

movies with some girls in his class at school. I have tried many times, using good manners, to make him understand that this must stop, but nothing doing. What am I to do?"

Father Sangretto looked up. "And here's their reply."

"Did you ever ask yourself why he acts like a rebel? I think he's trying to cope with a need for affection. Quite conceivably a good reason for this may be that his family does not satisfy that need. This is another reason why you ought to be close to him, to be patient and understanding, as well as intelligently firm."

The priest put the leaflet down and looked hard at Dino. "Isn't that good advice, Dino? You see, it's just like you and me. I've tried to be close to you, I've tried to understand your feelings and to guide you along this path to your glorious future in the priesthood. Now I won't comment about whether your family satisfies your needs. It seems to me they don't care much for the church. If they did, they would come to services more often, don't you think? Yes, your mother comes most Sundays, but your stepfather, well…"

For the first time in his life, Dino resented what this man across the desk was saying. He knew it was a sin to question a priest, but how could this man doubt the love and devotion his parents had for him? Dino knew that Paolo loved him as if he was his own son, and if Lucia was overly protective, he knew she adored him and he could not have asked for better parents.

He glared at the priest. How dare he say such a thing?

"Dino," the priest said, "how often do you think about this girl?"

"Well, sometimes."

"Sometimes at night, when you're in bed?"

"Sometimes."

"D-d-d-dino! You're not doing anything impure, are you?"

When Dino blushed, his freckles brightened and his face became red all the way to the shock of blond hair that fell on his forehead.

"Of course not, Father!" Dino was not about to tell a priest what he did in bed unless it was in a confessional.

"Good. I know you wouldn't do anything like that. I know that. You're a good boy, Dino. What do you think about?"

Dino wanted to end this conversation. Soon. But he felt he had to answer. "Father, I just think about how pretty she is, how nice she is."

"Ah, but Dino, you know that thoughts can be sinful, too. And one thing leads to another very, very fast."

Father Sangretto sighed again and turned more pages of the folder, slowly at first, and then faster.

"Ah. Just what I was looking for. This was written by Father Giuseppe Nebiolo, a holy priest who was the national assistant to the youth movement of *Azione Cattolica Italiana*. Truly, a holy man. Listen to this. It's how he says a young man should think."

It was a long section, and the priest cleared his throat and began.

"My great ideal of love tells me that I am to collaborate with God in the creation of life. Thus I want to make my body strong, healthy, well-developed. Thus I shall avoid all sins against love, as well as the nervous torment of an immature attachment, because they would disturb the harmony and integrity of my forces. My great ideal of love tells me that I will have to preserve all my spiritual richness for the companion destined to me. Thus I shall avoid all strain on my purity so as to be able to tell her one day that I preserved my body from the facile seductions of evil. My great ideal of love tells me that it can reach the height of its greatness only in the sacrament of marriage."

Dino interrupted. "Love? Marriage? Father, I'm seventeen years old! I'm not thinking about marriage."

His face now as crimson as the drapes, Father Sangretto rose from his chair and leaned forward, his hands on the desk. His voice rose as well. "Dino, listen to me. As I said, one thing leads to another, and we must stop this now."

"But Father…"

"No buts, Dino. You cannot think about this girl, this girl in your high school. If you do, the next thing you'll have impure thoughts about her. Then you will get together with her and I don't want to think of what would happen then. But you can't, Dino. You are not destined for marriage, you are destined for the holy priesthood!" The priest was shouting now. "I know that. God knows that. You cannot defy God in this way! Do you understand?"

"But Father…"

"Y-y-y-you must stop these kinds of thoughts now. D-d-d-d-do you hear me? Now!"

"Father…"

"Remember, Dino. 'Avoid all strain on my purity.' That's what the holy priest said. Do you understand?"

"Father…"

The priest wiped his face with a white handkerchief. He came around the desk and took Dino by the shoulders. His voice was softer now. "Good. Now go into the church and say the rosary. Three times. God will help you, Dino. Pray hard."

Dino rushed out of the door and ran back home. He had no intention of saying the rosary. And he had no intention of becoming a priest.

Chapter Four

Fall 1963

In August, along with almost every other shop owner in Italy, Paolo closed his *pasticceria* in Reboli for two weeks. Then, since Rosa had volunteered to look after Lucia's mother, he, Lucia and Dino drove over to Viareggio. Like everyone else, every year they fled to the sea to avoid the heat, and, like everyone else, every year they vowed that they would never go back. Half of Italy seemed to be on the beach.

Dino spent most of the first two weeks under a beach umbrella reading Alberto Moravia's novel *Two Women* for the third time. His mother thought it disgusting. "Rapes and violence! Why don't you read some nice stories?"

Dino turned his back and the page.

Two days before they were to return home, Dino was at the pizza stand when a girl next to him dropped some *lire* that she'd gotten in change. Dino dug around in the sand and found the coins, dropping his *Two Women* in the process.

"*Grazie*," the girl said, as Dino restored the book under his arm. "Oh, you're reading the Moravia. I love that book. Did you see the movie?"

"No, we, I mean our village, don't have a movie theater. I mean our village *doesn't* have a movie theater." Granted, it was hot under the blazing sun, but why couldn't he get simple words out? And why was he sweating so much?

"Really? Where do you live?"

Dino knew she wore a white bathing suit with red dots but he didn't dare look below the shoulder straps. "It's a tiny village near Lucca."

"I have friends in one of those villages. What did you say the name was?"

"It's called Sant'Antonio. Really, you probably never heard of it."

"Sant'Antonio. No, I guess not. My friends live in Piazzano."

"I know where that is, just a few miles to the southeast. I mean the south*west*." Why couldn't he think straight? She had a small heart-shaped birthmark on her shoulder.

"Actually, they're not my friends, but my girl friend's friends."

Dino had never taken part in such a stupid conversation. Maybe her eyes were blue under those big sunglasses.

The girl put her hand on his book. "I cried and cried when they were in Rome. That poor mother, and that poor daughter."

"I liked the part," said Dino, suddenly animated, "where the mother sews everything she has into her dress."

"And then they flee to the South."

"Yes."

"I can't imagine living through a war like that," she said.

"No." Why were his baggy swimming trunks suddenly tight?

"I can't either," she said. "But my father did. He was a partisan."

"So was mine!" Dino said. "But he was killed. My stepfather was a partisan, too. They served in the same *banda*." He couldn't believe he said four sentences.

"Really? That is so interesting."

"Yes," he said.

She put her hand on his arm and he jumped back. "Say," she said, "would you like to sit over there on the bench and we can talk some more. It's really hot here."

He followed her down the boardwalk. She had such a fascinating walk, swaying from side to side. Her swimsuit was very tight. Under one of the few trees on the beach he learned that her name was Olivia, which he thought was beautiful but not as nice as Francesca. She lived near Milan and her family came to Viareggio every year, too. She would be a second-year student at the University of Milan in the fall.

That means, Dino quickly noted, that she was at least a year older than he was.

"What about you?" she asked. "I don't even know your name."

"It's…it's Dino."

"Dino? That's your full name?"

Now he was really blushing. "Well, it's actually Aldobrandino. But nobody calls me that. It's a terrible name."

She repeated his name several times. "No. No. I think it's a beautiful name. It sounds like a musical instrument, or a symphony or something."

She did not seem concerned that Aldobrandino was still in high school. She said she had friends in Lucca, too, and sometimes went to visit them. Dino hoped that was an opening for him to ask her to visit him, but she started talking about films.

"I love the film of *Two Women*," she said. "Sophia Loren is so great in that. And I love all of De Sica's work. He's a genius! I think *The Bicycle Thief* is the saddest film I've ever seen, even more than *Umberto D.* That poor man, that poor boy. Lately, he's been doing these comedies like *Yesterday, Today and Tomorrow,* which I don't like so much. I wish he'd stick with neorealism. I love all the films that were made after the war. Rossellini. Fellini. Visconti. Did you ever see Visconti's *Ossessione?* I think it's one of the great neorealist films, but a lot of people dismiss it. I don't know why. Have you ever seen it? Oh, I guess not."

Dino couldn't think of anything to say. He had heard of the directors, vaguely, but had never seen any of those films. Sant'Antonio, he didn't have to remind himself, did not have a theater.

"Well," Olivia said, finishing her pizza and wiping her red lips with the paper napkin, "I should get back. My Mama and Papa will be worried. Maybe I'll see you tomorrow?"

"Um, well, um, sure. I hope so."

Dino watched her as she walked away. He had never seen a girl walk like that.

That night, lying in bed, he couldn't get Olivia out of his mind. The way she talked. The way she knew everything. But mostly her hair, her skin, her bathing suit, her walk. He wished he had his own room so that he could relieve his tensions, but his Mama and Papa were sleeping in the bed under the window.

The following day was the last for the family at the beach. Dino spent much of it hanging around the pizza stand. He acquired a sunburn, but did not see Olivia, although he looked all up and down the beach. Just as Lucia and Paolo were taking down their umbrella and packing their towels, he saw her walking near the ocean. She was holding hands with a tall, dark-haired boy and laughing. Dino grabbed his things and walked away.

"What's the matter?" Lucia called after him.

"Nothing. Let's go home."

Sant'Antonio seemed even smaller when they returned. To avoid his mother's constant hovering, he took to hiking in the hills, sometimes to the Cielo, sometimes to other farmhouses. He liked looking down at his village. It looked like the toy houses he played with as a boy.

"Where do you go all the time?" his mother asked at the dinner table one day. "What do you do?"

"I just go for walks."

"All by yourself? Dino, I don't think it's good for you to be so alone all the time. You think too much."

"Mama, I think too much? How could I think too much?"

"I don't know. But I'm worried about you."

"Don't worry, Mama. I'm fine."

"Let the boy alone, Lucia," Paolo said.

"Dino, sometimes I wish I knew what was going on in that head of yours."

"Lucia," Paolo said, "he's seventeen years old. What do you think is going on in his head?"

Before he knew it, Dino had to start preparing for classes in his final year at the *liceo artistico.* He had mixed feelings. What was he going to do when he graduated? His teachers, impressed with his work, kept urging him to study art in Florence. That would mean he would be surrounded by the greatest art in the world and could finally leave Sant'Antonio. But Florence seemed so big, so overwhelming. He didn't want to think about it.

Returning to classes in Lucca also meant that he would be able to see Francesca again. Maybe this time he could talk to her. He didn't know what he'd do if she had a boyfriend.

He did indeed see Francesca on the first day of classes. She was in his charcoal drawing class, at an easel across the room. For days, he worked on a drawing of a bowl of flowers, not making much progress because he kept looking across the room. His teacher, a wisp of a woman named Professor Maria Ponzo, finally told him to hurry.

"Dino, Dino, Dino," she said, gripping his arm. "Other years you did so much good work. What's happening this year? Are you all right?"

"I'm fine, Professor."

"*Bene,* but we need to get some of your work together for the Christmas show, you know."

Dino kept his eyes on Francesca and took hope in the fact that he never saw her talking to another boy.

Two weeks before Christmas, Ezio and Donna drove down from their hilltop farmhouse for drinks and conversation before they all set out for the Christmas party and art show at Dino's high school in Lucca.

The subject, at first, was what so many people in the world were talking about in late 1963.

"Did you hear," Paolo said, as soon as they had settled on the porch he had just completed on the back of the house. "They've established a commission to investigate it."

"Yeah," Ezio said, "but they won't find anything. Who's going to talk now?"

"Everybody knows it was a conspiracy," Paolo said. "Oswald could never have done that on his own. He had to have help. That's why Ruby killed him."

"You guys," Donna interrupted. "Can't you stop talking about a conspiracy all the time? I think he did it on his own. Just a crazy guy."

"A crazy guy who happened," Paolo said, "to have spent a lot of time in Russia."

"Yeah," Ezio said. "Everyone is going to blame the Communists again."

Lucia brought out a tray of beer and white wine and a Coke for Dino. "I wish you'd stop talking about this all the time. That's all people talk about. At Leoni's. At Manconi's. Let's just pray for his poor soul. He was a great president. The whole world loved him. His poor wife. Those poor little children."

"Yes," Donna said, "I wish we had a president like that in Italy."

Dino didn't take part in the conversation. He liked John F. Kennedy very much, and after his death he read the newspapers and watched the news programs on television, but he had no thoughts on how or why he was assassinated. Sant'Antonio seemed so far removed from the rest of the world.

"Let's change the subject," Lucia said. "Ezio, how do you like the new porch?"

"Great job, Paolo," Ezio said, slapping his friend's back. "Too bad it slants so much."

"What the...? It does not! Oh, you're joking! You damn..."

Paolo attempted to throw Ezio off the porch, but Lucia stopped him.

Although the temperature had dipped into the 40s, it was one of those perfect Tuscan nights and no one seemed to mind the cold. The new porch provided a vast view of mountains in the distance and the first stars emerging.

Paolo pointed. "Look, you can almost see your farmhouse."

"Today, I don't know if I want to see it," Donna said. "Work, work, work. We finally finished knocking down the last of the olives and took them to the mill. Now maybe we can relax for a few weeks."

Ezio put his arm around his wife's shoulders. "You know you love the Cielo, Donna."

"I know. I just like to complain sometimes."

A dog barking in the distance broke a long silence. Donna sipped her wine and put the glass down.

"You know," she said, "I miss that mimosa tree over there."

"I do, too," Lucia said, looking pointedly at her husband.

"Well, I needed some wood for the porch," Paolo said. "And anyway, it was too shady back here in the summer."

Ezio knew he should change the subject. "We're looking forward to seeing your drawings and paintings tonight, Dino. You must be very proud."

"They're all right," Dino said.

"I'm sure more than all right," Ezio said. "You know you were the best art student I ever had."

Dino put his Coke bottle to his face so no one could see him blushing. "I think it's time we should go," he said.

"Let me check on Mama, and then we will," Lucia said.

With little traffic, the ride from Sant'Antonio to Lucca took only thirty minutes on this Friday evening. Workers had already gone home and it was too early for the three restaurants along the way to get busy. The most popular one had decorated every wall with shirts of famous Italian soccer players.

After Cappella, there were no other villages, and rows of cypress trees loomed over the roadway like sentries in the bright moonlight. In the back seat, Dino was squashed between Lucia and Donna. In the front, Ezio and Paolo grumbled about the Italian soccer team's third-place performance leading up to the World Cup. Still, they'd been able to watch the finals on Paolo and Lucia's little television set for the first time, amazed that the game came all the way from Chile.

Paolo pulled up to the high stone walls that surrounded Lucca. This was as far as they were permitted to drive. Dino went on ahead to his school while the others walked through the Vittorio Emanuele gate, turned north to via San Paolino, past the Church of San Paolino and then south on Via Burlamacchi. With Christmas only two weeks away, Lucca had strung blue and white lights across many of its streets, and shop windows were ablaze with displays of candy, cookies and wine. On almost every corner, venders hawked roasted chestnuts, which Lucia forbade Paolo to buy. "They may be rotten and you'll get sick."

The *liceo artistico* occupied two floors of a sixteenth-century palazzo, and candles gleamed in every window. Evergreens and lights trimmed the stairs and hallways, and a good crowd, mostly parents of students, had already gathered in the reception room on the third floor. The students' paintings hung on the walls and their sculptures were displayed on tables.

It was hard not to notice Dino. He was by far the tallest, and skinniest, student in his class, and his freckles were even brighter under the glaring spotlights. He stood behind a table, pouring wine into little paper cups.

Professor Ponzo swooped over to greet Lucia and Paolo. With jet-black hair, huge gold earrings and a dark blue-and-green dress that flowed down to spiked heels, she looked in her early seventies, but it was hard to tell with all the makeup. She had taught at the school for forty years.

"Ah, Signor Ricci, Signora Sporenza, it's so good to see you again! Thank you for coming to our little Christmas party, it gives us a chance to meet our students' lovely parents and to show off their good work. And such good work they are doing, just look around you, over there and there and there. I do my little bit, but every year they seem to be getting better and better and I don't know where they will end up, but I know they are all very talented. Very, very talented."

Lucia drew the professor away from the others. "And Dino? How is he doing, professor?"

The professor looked at Dino and then away. "Ah, yes, Dino. Well, I have to say…how should I put this?"

"Is there a problem, professor?"

"No, no, not a problem, not a problem at all. Nothing to worry about."

"But…?"

Professor Ponzo glanced at Dino again, but he was busy pouring wine for Paolo, Ezio and Donna. "I have to say, and please don't make too much of this, that his work in the last months hasn't been quite up to the same standards as last year. No, please note. Dino is one of the finest students we have had at the *liceo artistico,* and his work is still very fine. And he has set such high standards for himself that it is difficult to even consider anything not quite positive."

"But it's still not quite as good as last year?"

"Maybe, Signora Sporenza, something happened over the summer? Dino has always been such a quiet student and now this year he has been even quieter. I'm sure it has to do with being seventeen years old, and you know what all that brings. It's as if he is preoccupied with something."

"And his work?"

"Well, look at that drawing of the bowl of flowers. My God, any one of my students could have painted that. And those two paintings over there. Last year, they would have been bright, bold. They would have gripped the viewer. You would want to know more about that landscape and that portrait. You would want to know more about the painter. Now, well, they're nice, in fact they're better than many other students', as you can see. But, you know what we like to ask the students? 'Is this you?' I don't think these are Dino."

Lucia thanked the professor and shook her hand. She returned to the table where hungry students were devouring an array of antipasti, breads, cookies and cakes before their parents could get near.

Lucia noticed a young blond girl who seemed to be taking a long time putting things on her plate as she stood before Dino. Dino, blushing furiously, held out a wine cup for her to take. His hand was shaking. The girl took even more time in choosing what she would like, then smiled at Dino and took the cup. Briefly, they both held it, and they looked at each other.

"*Grazie,*" she said softly.

Dino mouthed something and grinned, a grin Lucia hadn't seen for months. The girl smiled and walked away.

Since Dino stayed to help with the cleanup, he would take the last bus back to Sant'Antonio. Paolo and Ezio were again in the front seat and Lucia and Donna were in the back on the return trip. Lucia was smiling. "Did you see that little scene with Dino and the blond girl?" she asked.

Paolo and Ezio didn't know what she was talking about.

"I did," Donna said, reaching over to pat Lucia's hand. "I thought it was sweet."

"I did, too," Lucia said.

"Lucia, do you think Dino might be in love? Is that why he's been so quiet?"

This sent Paolo into a round of laughter. "Love? Little Dino? Little Dino doesn't even know any girls!"

"Well, Paolo," Donna said. "He knows at least one."

"And don't keep calling him Little Dino," Lucia said. "You know how he hates that."

St. Zita's Chapel at Mansagrati, Italy

Chapter Five

Christmas 1963-Spring 1964

Encouraged by the only word Francesca had ever spoken to him, Dino set out on a mission. During the Christmas recess, he told his mother he needed to go to Lucca to look for some art supplies, but he was really looking for Francesca Casati.

On many school days in the fall, he had followed her as she walked up Via Veneto after the last class, staying far enough behind so she wouldn't see him. Then he turned onto Via Fillungo just behind the old Roman amphitheater and on to a side street. But, just as she put the key into the green door in the brick apartment building, he hurried back to catch the bus to Sant'Antonio.

Now, he didn't know why or how or what he was doing, but he knew he had to be somehow close to her. He zipped up his jacket and tightened the long woolen scarf around his neck against the brisk, chilly wind.

Ignoring the stands with post-Christmas sales of scarves and purses in the market at San Michele in Toro, he crossed into the amphitheater, now converted to shops and restaurants. The sun brightened the gray stone pavement, and a large Christmas tree stood at one end. He was soon on the right street.

Now what? He stood in a doorway across from the green door and waited, for what he didn't know.

He began to pace. Although it was midmorning, no one was out except for an occasional woman pulling a shopping cart full of groceries. Whenever that happened, he pretended to scrutinize the frieze above the doors up and down the street.

He paced some more. This was silly, Dino thought. He should go home. He was cold.

A small orange-and-white cat scampering from stoop to stoop briefly gave him something to watch. But then it disappeared.

He was getting hungry. He walked to the end of the street and then went back to his post.

The cat returned, jumped in front of the green door and sat down. That was interesting.

Suddenly the door opened. Seemingly in answer to his prayers, Francesca emerged.

"Marcellina! Marcellina! Naughty!"

But Marcellina had already fled from the doorstep and headed straight toward...Dino.

There was no place to hide and Francesca was soon in front of him.

"Dino? Dino Sporenza? What are you doing here?"

Predictably, Dino's face reddened and his mouth opened, but nothing came out.

"Dino, are you all right? You don't live here. I know you live in Sant'Antonio."

"You do? You know that?"

Now it was Francesca who blushed.

"Yes. I saw...I saw...I saw it on a list somewhere."

Dino knew that students' records were kept private and that Francesca could not have known where he lived—unless she asked someone.

Marcellina was now rubbing against Francesca's legs, demanding to be picked up. Francesca opened the green door and shoved the cat inside.

Minutes later, they were inside a *bar* in the amphitheater, each of them ordering an espresso, which Dino paid for.

"I can't believe you were waiting outside my door," Francesca said.

"No, no. I was just walking down the street in order to get to…to get to…" He had to take off his jacket because it was suddenly very warm in there.

"Oh, sure." She smiled. "Just walking down the street. It's OK, Dino. Actually, I'm glad. There have been so many times I've wanted to stop and talk to you in school."

"Really?"

She looked down at her cup. "Yes. You probably haven't noticed, but I've watched you in medieval history and Raphael and Renaissance and other classes, too."

"Really?"

"Yes."

"And," Dino said, "you didn't notice me watching you in charcoal drawing?"

"Actually, I did."

They both stirred their coffee.

"You know," Dino said, "I don't know much about you."

It turned out that Francesca had never had a boyfriend and she and her mother lived alone, except for Marcellina, in a small third-floor apartment. Her father died after a heart attack fourteen years ago, and her mother, not well herself, made a scant living as a clerk part time in a toy shop on Via S. Andrea.

Lingering over one espresso after another, they talked about how difficult the classes were at the *liceo artistico,* how Professor Ponzo was so silly, and, with the superior knowledge of high school students, the relative merits of contemporary artists.

"How could anyone consider Pietro Annigoni a good example of a modern artist?" Dino wanted to know.

"He's just a portrait painter," Francesca scoffed. "I mean, Queen Elizabeth? The Pope?"

"Right," Dino said. He was so nervous, his knees were shaking and his teeth were chattering. He had never realized that her eyes were so blue.

They talked about the books they'd read, and Dino told Francesca about a few television programs he'd watched. He said he really liked the Perry Mason shows from America. Francesca said she wished she had a television. Before they knew it, it was 1:30 and the *bar* was closing.

"Oh, my God," Francesca said. "I have to get home. My mother will be frantic."

"I have to get home, too," Dino said. "You think your mother will be frantic. You should see mine."

He walked her home, where there was an awkward shaking of hands, and then fled to the bus station. But he was whistling.

That was in December. In January, Lucia noticed a major difference in her son, and even Paolo commented that when Dino helped out in his *pasticceria* on Saturdays he whistled a lot, smiled even more and patiently waited for customers to make their difficult choices among the pastries. But when he was asked about this transformation, he simply blushed and smiled.

"You're in love, right? It's that girl at the Christmas party, right?" Lucia said one day. "It's all right. I approve."

"Oh, Mama," Dino replied, and ran up the stairs to his room.

In February, Dino no longer took the bus that left Lucca right after classes but the later one, at 8:30, which meant there was little time for questioning when he got home. He said that he had to study in the school library.

He and Francesca spent the time in her apartment, allegedly studying, but mostly whispering, with her mother always nearby. Since Dino was the first boy Francesca had brought home, he underwent careful inspection every time he walked in the door. But he passed.

They began to hold hands when they walked to her home and even sometimes under the table as they jointly read a book on art history. By the end of the month, Francesca was standing on her tiptoes and giving Dino a peck on the cheek when he left.

In March, they had their first date. Lucia gave her reluctant approval, but Paolo slipped Dino a few thousand extra *lire* so he could buy Francesca a *gelato* afterwards. Francesca's mother warned her that she'd better be home by 10 o'clock.

They were going to a new movie, the first Dino had ever seen. Beforehand, they studied the reviews of *8½,* so they came out of the cinema bursting, somehow both relating to Marcello Mastroianni's character.

"That was about me!" Dino exclaimed over strawberry ice cream in the *gelateria.*

"And me!" Francesca dipped her plastic spoon into her pistachio.

Remembering what a critic had said, Dino declared, "It's about the creative process. That's just like we're doing in school."

"And how," Francesca said, also quoting, "we have to deliver something personal and profound, just like Professor Ponzo makes us do."

"And how we try to find personal happiness in what we do," Dino said. "Oh, Francesca, if you only knew how much I want to...I don't know...break out..."

"Break out of what, for goodness sakes?"

"Francesca, I live in this tiny village. I don't have anyone to talk to about what I want to do, what I want to be. My parents wouldn't understand. Sometimes I don't know what I want myself, but I know I want something more than to live in Sant'Antonio all my life. When I come to Lucca, I feel like I'm in a big city, but I know this isn't really very big. I..."

Other customers, filling the shop after the film, began to notice the young man who was speaking so loudly.

"Dino, settle down. You're getting ice cream on your shirt. And you're making me nervous."

Dino lowered his voice. "Francesca, you know that book we have for class, the one with the pictures of Michelangelo's statues? There are those four unfinished statues in the Accademia Galleria in Florence, where the David is. I keep looking at the picture of one of those statues. The Waking Slave. He's this person bursting out of the marble as if he can't stay confined in there anymore. Francesca, that's how I feel. I feel like I want to burst out."

"And then?"

"And then?" Dino looked perplexed. "And then, I don't know...I just don't know...But I think about Florence and all the treasures and I dream about being there and studying there. I don't think I'm a good artist, far from it, but being in Florence, well…maybe I could get better."

Francesca twirled a strand of hair with her fingers and thought for a long time. "Dino, you take art much more seriously than I do. I like to paint, but I don't have any big dreams. I've never thought of actually being a painter. And I like living here in Lucca. I imagine I'll live here all the rest of my life."

"And do what?"

"Get married. Have kids. Take care of my mother when she gets old. If there isn't anything else, I'd still be happy."

Now Dino was getting upset again. "Francesca, don't you know that things are changing? Women are starting to work. Your mother works. Even my mother has talked about working after…well, after she doesn't have to take care of my *Nonna* anymore."

"I don't know, Dino. I guess I don't have much ambition."

"Francesca, don't say that! You are such a good artist, better than me. You should be one! You would be great! Wouldn't you want to go to Florence to study? Professor Ponzo says I should go to the Accademia di Belle Arti. Why don't you come, too?"

"The Accademia? Oh, I'd be too frightened."

"You don't think I am? But, Francesca, I want to try. I really want to try."

Francesca smiled. "Well, I'll think about it."

Dino didn't know what to say. They walked slowly to her doorstep, where Francesca kissed Dino and gave him an extra long hug.

"Don't worry, Dino. Things will work out. And you know how much I care for you."

The other passengers on the bus wondered why this tall, skinny, freckle-faced kid seemed to be talking to himself all the way from Lucca to Sant'Antonio.

In April, Dino upset Paolo by saying he couldn't work at the *pasticceria* in Reboli on Saturdays anymore because he had to go to Lucca. To study.

"Right." Paolo said.

Francesca's pecks on the cheek had turned into passionate kisses as Dino left each night. They longed to do more, but with her mother nearby, that was impossible.

One night, over pizza in a trattoria in the amphitheater, Dino said casually that his pastor kept telling him he should become a priest. He waited for her reaction, but she seemed merely curious.

"I thought you'd laugh," he said.

"You don't know me very well, do you?"

"You're not surprised?"

"Dino, you are a kind and gentle person. I've seen how you help other students in class. Why wouldn't you want to be a priest?"

Francesca herself went to church only at Christmas and Easter. Her mother refused to go, angry at God for taking her husband so early.

"I used to go to Mass every day," Dino said. "I was a member of the *Azione Cattolica Italiana*. I went to confession every week."

"You sinned that much?"

"No. I never had anything to confess. I just went to confession. And I served at Mass. I don't do any of that anymore."

"Did you ever think about becoming a priest?"

"I guess I did. I was pretty much a lonely little kid. I didn't have any friends. There aren't any boys my age in the village. Well, one day after Mass, the priest saw me and asked if I wanted to be an altar boy.

"I thought that was a pretty important job. To be up at the altar and help the priest. So I'd get up early, go to church, put on my cassock and surplice and think I was the biggest kid in the world.

"About a year later, the priest, Father Sangretto, called me over after Mass and said, 'Dino, have you ever thought about becoming a priest?' Well, it had never occurred to me. Here I was eleven or twelve years old, I didn't know what I was going to do, I didn't even think about it. Oh, sometimes my Papa or Ezio, my teacher, would ask me, and I said I loved to draw and paint, but that was about it.

"Well, the priest said I should think about it, and then when I was fourteen, he wanted me to go to the seminary but my parents said no. They said I had to think about it some more, and anyway, they couldn't afford it. Father Sangretto said that becoming a priest wasn't our choice, it was God's decision."

"God's decision?"

"Yes. I guess I was so naïve I didn't even question what he meant. He was a priest!"

"When did you stop thinking about it?"

"Last summer."

"Why?"

"I kept thinking about you..."

"Really?"

"Yes, I've been thinking about you for that long. So last summer when the priest told me again that I had to become a priest—had to, mind you—I told him I was thinking about you and didn't want to be a priest. He got all upset. Said I shouldn't be thinking about girls. Said I had to follow God's plan. That got me thinking. I realized that the only reason I had thought about becoming a priest was because he told me I had to. That's no reason to become a priest."

"Dino, want to know something?"

"What?"

"I'm glad."

"Me, too."

In May, Professor Ponzo told her students to prepare for their annual art show. She selected two works from each student, and told them to build frames for the paintings and platforms for the sculptures. On the afternoon before the show, Dino and Francesca thought it would be best to frame their paintings at Francesca's apartment.

Francesca's mother had been called in to work, so it was the first time Dino and Francesca were alone in the apartment, if you didn't count Marcellina running across the table where they were working and then sitting squarely in the middle of one of Dino's paintings.

The two were painfully aware that they were alone, Dino furiously cutting wooden slats for the frames and Francesca feverishly working on the mats. Neither said anything. In fact, they avoided looking at each other.

But then Dino backed into Francesca as he fitted a mat into a frame. Francesca touched his arm. He looked at her. His heart was pounding. And then there was no stopping.

Francesca's bedroom was decorated in a dark rose, and she had painted a row of bright red roses on the walls just below the ceiling. She closed the shutters and the room was dark. Because neither of them had ever done this before, they fumbled with their clothes and quickly crept under the covers. She kissed him first, and he held her close. They hugged, they kissed. Their lovemaking was tentative and awkward. And very serious. At one point, Marcellina attacked Dino for what he was doing to her mistress.

When Francesca let out a little cry, Dino quickly stopped, but she urged him to continue, and together they rode the waves of excitement until their passions were spent.

"Are you OK?" Dino asked.

"I'm fine. Just fine." She kissed his cheek.

Afterward, they lay for a long time, just grinning at each other.

Dino started laughing.

"What?" Francesca asked.

"I was just thinking of how a year ago I was such a pious little kid. Even Father Sangretto said I was such a good boy. He should see me now."

"What would you tell him?"

"I'd tell him that I'm happy. Very, very happy."

"I am, too, Dino."

Dino and Francesca arrived at the art show a little late and tried to avoid the looks of their classmates and teachers. Lucia, Paolo, Ezio and Donna got there just in time for Professor Ponzo's elaborate greeting to the parents. Later, she swooped over to Lucia and told her how much Dino's work had improved in the last months.

"If I had to put these paintings next to the ones Dino showed at Christmas, well, I would not believe they were by the same student. Look, look! The colors. The tone. The depth. I can look at these new paintings and I want to know more about the artist. As I told Dino the other day, 'This is you.' You can be very proud of your son, Signora Sporenza."

"We are, Professor."

"And I hope you'll be able to send him next year to the Accademia di Belle Arti in Florence. It's the best art school in Florence, and he will do very well there. Mark my words."

"We're trying," Lucia said. She and Paolo had discussed Dino's future many times and still could not figure out if they could afford to send him to Florence. Anyway, he would have to be accepted first.

Lucia moved to the table where Dino towered over Francesca as they poured wine into little paper cups and passed out cookies. Both were grinning and seemed to glow.

"Well, Dino," Lucia said, "you look very proud. Your paintings are very good, even Professor Ponzo said so. Now, can you introduce me to your friend here?"

Dino made an awkward introduction and Lucia shook Francesca's hand. "Very nice," Lucia said. Dino was glad his mother approved.

On the ride back to Sant'Antonio, Dino was lost in thought, retracing the events of the afternoon minute by minute, hug after hug, kiss after kiss, and finally their lovemaking, over and over.

"You're thinking of how well you did in the art show, aren't you?" Lucia said.

"What? Um, yes, of course," Dino replied.

In his room later, he put on the record by Fabrizio De André and sat at his desk with a paper and pencil and, although he had never done it before, decided to write a song. It was influenced more by Fabrizio than the ballads sung by Antonio.

In the garden
I found a flower
In the garden
A beautiful rose
In the garden
I lost my heart
I will always love
The beautiful rose.

Dino knew it needed work. He also knew that he suddenly liked writing songs. And that he was in love.

Chapter Six

June 1964

There were three reasons to celebrate on this June 5 in 1964. It was Dino's eighteenth birthday. He was about to graduate with high honors from the *liceo artistico*. And he'd just been accepted by the prestigious Accademia di Belle Arti in Florence. After much worrying, Lucia and Paulo agreed that Dino could go to school in Florence, but it took them many nights at the kitchen table to figure out how they would afford it. Paolo finally told Dino they would send him a certain amount twice a month, enough for food, school supplies and the rent on a room. Dino's uncle, Adolfo, had found space in the basement of their sixteenth-century apartment building, once a palazzo, on Piazza Santa Croce.

Shyly, Dino took the congratulations of his family, neighbors and friends as they toasted the boy, now man, over dinner in the backyard where a gorgeous day under the Tuscan sun now stretched into a starlit evening.

Lucia made chicken cacciatore, Rosa brought over ravioli—"*allora,* only three dozen"—Annabella her signature chocolate cake and Fausta a spectacular bouquet of poppies from her garden. Bearing wine and grappa, Ezio and Donna and Ezio's father, Antonio, drove down from the Cielo. As usual, Antonio found a place next to Rosa, a move silently approved by everyone there, including Rosa.

Dino himself sat at the end of the table with Francesca at his side. Lucia had insisted that she attend, since Dino seemed to enjoy studying with her in her apartment on so many afternoons.

"Such a lovely little girl," Lucia had told Rosa earlier in the day. "And they look so cute together."

Rosa frowned. "Do you really think they're just studying every afternoon?"

For a woman who was *non sposata*, or unmarried, when she had Dino, Lucia seemed shocked. "Well, of course they are! Dino wouldn't do anything like that."

She did not know that after that initial fumbling experience, Dino and Francesca had occupied many afternoons perfecting their art of lovemaking since the toy shop where Francesca's mother worked had fortuitously changed her hours to the afternoons.

Lucia also invited Francesca's mother, Piera Casati, to Dino's party. "Francesca is graduating from the high school, too," Lucia told Paolo, "and she has no other relatives besides her mother. So Piera should celebrate."

With the introductions over, the villagers questioned Piera all about her life and her work. Piera was born in the same apartment where she lived now. She moved back after her husband died to take care of her parents, who eventually died as well. Without any inheritance, she had found the job in the toy shop. The pay wasn't good, but it was all she could find. She wasn't complaining, but she hoped Francesca would have a better life.

Dino looked up to say that Francesca was a great painter and he hoped she would pursue that career. Piera smiled. "Well, I would like to encourage that, but I don't see how Francesca could possibly support herself as a painter."

Dino and Francesca had been arguing lately about the fact that she hadn't applied to a university, especially the Accademia di Belle Arti. He felt she should at least study art even if she wouldn't make it her career. Francesca said she just didn't want to. So that meant that this would probably be their last summer together.

With so much good food and talk, the meal went slowly, and after the cheese and fruit, there were the presents. The neighbors brought little things they found at Leoni's, and Antonio gave Dino a fine penknife. Ezio and Donna presented Dino with a small framed photograph of Michelangelo's The Waking Slave.

"How did you know that I like this sculpture so much?" Dino asked, somewhat overwhelmed.

"You mentioned it once or twice," Ezio said.

"Or three times," Donna said, smiling.

If Dino was expecting a Vespa from his parents, he was disappointed. Lucia gave him a woolen sweater "because it's going to get cold in Florence" and a raincoat "because it's going to rain a lot." She hoped he didn't see her wipe a tear away.

Dino liked the sweater but couldn't imagine wearing a long yellow raincoat.

Paolo went into the house and brought back a guitar that he found in a second-hand shop in Lucca. Its body was battered and its strings were loose, but Dino held it like a newborn baby.

"How did you know I wanted a guitar?"

"What boy doesn't want a guitar?" Paolo said. "No, what young *man* doesn't want a guitar?"

Paolo said he used to play and would help Dino learn a few songs. Dino immediately started strumming as best he could.

Then Dino opened Francesca's present, wrapped in gold paper with a pink ribbon.

"Wow! This is great! Now I'll know everywhere to go and what to see in Florence."

"Well," Francesca said, "I was going to get you a new guidebook, but I found this one in a used store. It's from 1958, but Florence doesn't change, right?"

Dino leaned over and kissed her hair.

"And," Lucia said, "I have something for Francesca in honor of her graduation. Will you permit me, Signora Casati?"

"Of course."

Francesca opened the little box and immediately put on the pearl pendant, on a gold chain, around her neck.

"It was my grandmother's," Lucia said. "I know she'd want you to have it."

Francesca got up to kiss Lucia.

Under a sky that was now dense with stars, the Tuscan hills shimmered in the distance. Over beer and grappa, the conversation drifted from one topic to another, mostly about all the changes that were starting to sweep across the United States, Europe and even into conservative Italy. Women wanting rights. Rock music. Drugs. Protests against war. A new frankness in films. And now, with Vatican II, changes even in the Catholic Church.

"I don't like some of the changes," Fausta declared. "Now I've heard they'll be saying the Mass in Italian rather than Latin. And the priest will be facing us. I don't want to look at Father Sangretto. And I don't want Father Sangretto looking at me!"

"I'm not going to look at him," Rosa said.

"And," Fausta continued, "then I heard that we'll be shaking hands with everyone. During the Mass! I don't want to shake hands with everyone! I go to church to pray, not catch everyone's germs."

"Fausta, Fausta," Annabella said. "Things change. Everything changes."

Fausta held her hands firmly in her lap. "Well, I think the old ways are best."

"*Allora*," Rosa said. "Everything's changing. Look at Dino here. Going off to Florence. In the old days, boys wouldn't go off to big cities. They'd stay at home with their Mamas and Papas."

"Yes," Lucia said, "tell that to Dino."

Dino rolled his eyes.

"And it's dangerous there now," Fausta said.

"How do you know that?" Paolo asked. "Have you ever been there?"

"No, but I've read about it," she said. "People play loud music into the night. There are drugs now that do terrible things to you. And there are," she lowered her voice, "naughty girls."

Ezio, who had grown up in Florence, said, "Well, Florence is a big city. There are some bad things, but look at all the good things, the art, the museums, the churches, the culture. Dino will learn so much there."

"Yes," Lucia said, "I'm afraid of what he'll learn there."

Dino remained quiet, but reached over to clutch Francesca's hand. He had been thinking about paintings and sculptures and hadn't realized there were drugs and "naughty girls" in Florence.

Fausta was on a rant. "And furthermore, there are all these beggars who rob people. For no reason."

"Maybe because they're poor," Ezio said.

"That's no reason," Fausta said.

"Adolfo and Roberto don't seem to mind," Dino said. As soon as he said it, he wanted to take the words back. Rosa, Annabella and Fausta looked down at the table, Ezio and Donna looked up at the sky, and Lucia burst into tears. Francesca started to ask a question, but Dino kissed her on the cheek.

"I would like to visit Florence," Rosa said quickly, "but I wouldn't want to live there. I just want to stay in Sant'Antonio."

She might have added "with my Antonio" because he now put his arm around her shoulder.

"It's happening all over," Piera said. "In Lucca now we lock our doors, even though we're on the third floor."

The villagers of Sant'Antonio could not believe this. "I never lock my doors," Annabella said. "All the people are nice here. Nothing is going to happen."

"I lock my doors," Fausta said.

Dino remained silent. These were things he hadn't thought about before. Poor people? Beggars? He still struggled with his feelings about leaving Sant'Antonio and going to Florence. Sometimes, he felt he had to get away from people who got so concerned about a few changes in the church. Who cared? But when he looked around the table, he knew that he loved these people very much and would miss them.

Then Rosa's face grew red as she denounced "those politicians in Rome" who were trying to make divorce legal.

"Can you imagine? Divorce? In Italy?"

"No, no," Antonio said. He gripped Rosa's hand.

"It will never happen," the other women declared.

"It's all right," Ezio said. "The Christian Democratic Party will never let such a law pass in Italy."

"*Allora*," Rosa said. Seeking to lighten the conversation, Paolo asked what that common, everyday word really meant.

"*Allora*,'" he said. "Italians use it all the time. Why?"

"I think it means something like 'well,' or something like that," Donna said.

"It doesn't really mean anything," Ezio said. "People just use it to fill in time."

"I like it," Rosa said as Antonio moved even closer to her. "*Allora*."

"You know," she said, "this is almost like the old days, when we all got together. *Il Gruppo di Cielo*.

"*Il Gruppo di Cielo?*" Piera asked. "What is that?"

And so the story was told again. How people from the village were ordered to evacuate during the German occupation in the summer of 1944. How the priest, the beloved Father Luigi, found them farmhouses to stay in the hills. How Rosa and Annabella and Fausta and Lucia's mother with all of her children, along with others from the village stayed for three months in the old farmhouse called the Cielo. It was the very place where Rosa grew up and where Ezio and Donna lived now, having restored it after it had been abandoned for years.

And how Ezio's band of partisans had been in the area and had fought the German invaders, and how not all of them, including Dino's father, had survived. Piera didn't know that Paolo wasn't Dino's real father.

"Oh, Dino," Piera said, "I'm so sorry."

"It's all right," Dino said. "I never knew him."

Dino might have dismissed the thought of his father, but in truth there were times when he thought a lot about the man whose name he bore. This was especially true when he walked up the hill to the little plot near the Cielo where his father was buried. There was only a small headstone, but sitting on the grass there, Dino felt a little closer to the man who hadn't even left a photograph behind. But then Dino always thought about Paolo and how good a father he had been to him for so many years.

Dino sometimes asked his mother if he was like his father. Lucia always said she never got to know him well enough, but that whenever Dino went off on his own, he seemed as headstrong as his father.

The silence was interrupted when the phone rang and Lucia ran inside. She had a habit of talking so loudly on the phone that everyone outside could hear her voice, if not her words, through the open window.

"Adolfo? *Ciao!* What's the matter? Are you all right? Oh, that's all right then.... *Sì....* *Sì....* *Sì....* No!...No!...No!...Of course I remember him...No...No...In August?...Three of them?...All right, all right.... Look, Adolfo, we're celebrating Dino's birthday right now. I'll call you back tomorrow, all right? Yes, I'll tell him. You're sure you're all right? Tomorrow, *Bene?* Love you! *Ciao!*"

"Oh!" Lucia said, emerging from the house. "I have news! Guess what? Colin Richards is coming. Sometime in August. Adolfo didn't know the dates."

"Who's Colin Richards?" Dino asked.

Another story about the Cielo. While the villagers were trapped in the farmhouse during the war, they took in a sick and exhausted British soldier who had escaped from a prison camp. Colin Richards. They hid him in a secret room and fed him what little food they had. Eventually, he was well enough to flee.

But he had kept in touch, writing occasionally to Lucia's brother, Adolfo, in Florence.

"Dino, you weren't even born when Colin was at the Cielo," Lucia said. "And now he's coming here! Can you imagine? And he's bringing his wife and their daughter. They're going to fly to Pisa, rent a car and stop here in Sant'Antonio before touring around Italy for a while. Then they're going to bring the daughter to Florence. And guess what, Dino, the daughter is going to study at the Accademia di Belle Arti. Isn't that wonderful? Dino, you'll know someone there."

Dino looked up at Francesca. Francesca looked away.

"Well," Lucia said quickly, "I'm sure there are a lot of students there and you may not ever see her."

"Oh, my goodness," Rosa said. "Colin Richards! I thought we'd never see him again. Such a nice boy. So sick when he came here. Colin Richards!"

"Can you believe it?" Lucia said, "And now with a wife and a daughter who's all grown up."

"I still have the pictures he sent," Rosa said. "I have them on the mantel. The one from his wedding. His wife, what is her name?"

"Um, Bertha? Bridget? I can't remember."

"So pretty, so delicate. And then the picture he sent later, with their little girl. I remember, her name is Penelope, but they call her Penny. That's an odd name, isn't it?"

What Rosa, along with others around the table, really wondered was how parents in England could leave their daughter in a foreign country. It was bad enough that Dino was going off to Florence, little more than two hours away. What could these people in England be thinking?

"Oh," Lucia said, "Something else. Colin wrote that he wants to see everyone who took care of him at the Cielo."

"Well, of course!" Rosa cried. "But there aren't many of us left, are there? *Santa Maria!*"

Piera asked who else was at the farmhouse.

"Oh, so many," Rosa said. "All dead now and in the cemetery. Dante, our wonderful schoolteacher. Maddelena and Renata, those silly sisters, Vito and Giacomo, those crazy cousins…"

"And the Contessa," Lucia said.

"Who wasn't a countess," Rosa said.

"And Francesco, my husband," Annabella said, pulling out a handkerchief. "He was killed right outside the Cielo. It's as if it were yesterday."

"And Maria. Dead five years now," Paolo said.

"And now my Marco," Rosa said. "Just four years ago." Antonio hugged her closer.

"And I suppose soon, Mama," Lucia said softly, looking at the window on the second floor. "She's barely with us now."

For a long time, no one around the table spoke.

"Now," Rosa said, "where will they stay? My goodness, his wife. From England! She's probably rich, probably used to staying in nice places."

Ezio and Donna said it together: "Of course! They'll stay at the Cielo!"

Ezio said the secret room had long been expanded and wasn't a secret anymore, but there were at least two extra bedrooms.

Rosa pulled out her handkerchief and wiped her eyes. "We haven't seen Colin for so long. We'll have to show him everything. The first day we can go to Lucca. Then one day we have to go up in the hills...I wish my legs were better...then we can drive to the coast..."

"Rosa," Lucia said, "let's just wait until they get here and then we can decide. Mainly, we just want to see Colin and his wife and his daughter. We have so much to talk about."

As everyone carried chairs back into the house, Francesca stopped Dino. "You look worried," she said.

"I guess I hadn't thought about all these other things about Florence. When I look at the guidebook, that's one Florence. I guess there's another Florence that's not in guidebooks. Now I really feel like I'm just a kid from a tiny village."

Chapter Seven

July 1964

Francesca was curious about Dino's mention of his uncles at his graduation party and kept asking him questions. He tried to ignore the questions, and he was successful until the end of July when she was sure the uncles must be involved in some sort of criminal activity. Otherwise, Dino would talk about them.

"No, no, no," he said. "It's nothing like that."

So in a long walk around the top of Lucca's walls, he told her the story as best he could.

"But let me say first," he said, "that we've never been really sure of what happened."

"It started," Dino said, "nine years ago, in 1955. Ezio and Donna were getting married in Pietrasanta. It wasn't supposed to be a big wedding, just in the city hall, but all of Ezio's friends and some of his former pupils from Sant'Antonio went, and his father, Antonio, came from Florence. With all of Donna's friends, and her father's friends, the reception at the Casa del Popolo, the Communist gathering place, was filled.

"Roberto and Adolfo were there. Adolfo had just finished his studies at the University of Pisa and was planning on moving to Florence and look for some sort of teaching job.

"Roberto had been living in Florence for some time and he was having a great time. He'd hold a job for a few months, quit it and spend his time drinking with his friends, going to movies and, yeah, picking up women, many of them from France or Germany.

"Adolfo is four years younger, he's about twenty-eight now, but he has always been the more serious of the two. When they were kids, Roberto was always getting them into trouble. They were at the Cielo during the war and their baby sister was very sick. Even though they weren't supposed to leave the farmhouse, they snuck down to the village to get medicine for her. They were almost shot by the Germans. But the medicine didn't work. The baby died.

"Anyway, they were always really close, best buddies. They'd do anything for each other. When Roberto went off to Florence and Adolfo went to Pisa, they sort of went their separate ways, but they were still close and they called each other all the time.

"Well, at the wedding, Roberto got to talking to Antonio. Antonio had this woodworking shop on Piazza Santo Spirito in the Oltrarno in Florence.

"But Antonio was getting on in years, his wife had died during the war, so he was alone. He had wanted Ezio to take over the shop, but Ezio didn't want to. Didn't have the talent, he said, and anyway, he loved teaching.

"Roberto told Antonio that when he was a kid he liked to make things with wood. Birdhouses, scooters, even games. Well, Antonio asked him to come around and see if he wanted to work in the shop. Roberto did, he liked it, and he did well. He had to learn a lot, but Antonio taught him, and then he took him on as a partner.

"So when Antonio decided to retire, Roberto took the place over.

"What's the problem, you're asking. I'm getting to that.

"As soon as Roberto took over the shop, he knew he was in trouble. He was very good at making door frames and windows and moldings, but he had a terrible time keeping customers because he was so bad at keeping the books. He'd charge them more than he estimated, he gave them the wrong change, he didn't get things done on time, he was terrible.

"So, since Adolfo had come to Florence and was still looking for work, Roberto asked him to take over the management part of the business. And since Roberto was living in the back of the shop and it was a pretty big room, he asked Adolfo to move in there.

"Soon, Adolfo was accusing Roberto of not coming to work on time and smelling of beer when he did. And Roberto said Adolfo should be out getting more customers instead of adding up figures all day. They had terrible rows.

"One day, a pretty young girl came in. She wanted Roberto to repair this huge ornate picture frame that was a family heirloom. It had the wedding photograph of her grandparents. He said he would. And he did a pretty good job of it. The girl was happy with it. Roberto found an excuse to have her come back, and pretty soon they were dating.

"Adolfo didn't meet her until after a few weeks when the girl came into the shop again. Roberto wasn't there but Adolfo was. Well, Adolfo and the girl, her name was Mila, got to talking. Then they were laughing and having a good time. Then Roberto came in. He saw what was happening and took that girl out of the shop so fast.

"But it didn't end there. Mila kept finding excuses to come back to the shop. She brought another picture frame to be fixed, but she really wanted to see Adolfo. She was making payments on the picture frames once a week and every time she said she wanted to see Adolfo rather than just leaving the money.

"Then one night Adolfo took Mila to a movie. Didn't ask Roberto, just took her. Roberto was furious and there was a terrible fight. First in the shop and then right in the piazza in front of Santo Spirito. They were hitting each other and then they were rolling on the ground. Finally, some men from the other shops pulled them apart.

"A few days later, Adolfo moved out. Found a little apartment on the second floor of an old palazzo on Piazza Santa Croce about a mile away. He got a job in the restoration room of the *Biblioteca Nazionale*, the National Library, and he didn't go back to the woodworking shop. Mila broke off with Roberto, and she and Adolfo became more serious.

"It seemed like Roberto went crazy after that. Didn't take on any new work. Went out drinking every night. One night he went to Mila's apartment building and yelled and banged on the door. The neighbors had to take him away.

"Well, about eight months later, Adolfo told my mother that he and Mila were going to get married. My mother knew there were some tensions between her brothers, but she didn't know how serious they were. She talked to Adolfo pretty often, but not Roberto, and she was worried about him.

"On the night before the wedding, Roberto went to Adolfo's place near Santa Croce. He started throwing rocks at his window. Adolfo yelled at him to go away. Roberto wouldn't. Adolfo went down and they started fighting. This was even worse. They hit each other and yelled and cursed. They rolled around and chased each other. They got all the way to the Arno and they were fighting on the wall in front of the *Biblioteca Nazionale* and suddenly Roberto fell in. Right into the river. And this was at night and it was cold. He couldn't swim. He was thrashing around and finally two guys jumped in and pulled him out. He was wet but all right.

"The *carabinieri* came and wrote up a report and there was a big article in *La Nazione* the next day. "Two Brothers Try to Kill Each Other." The family was so embarrassed.

"Well, Adolfo and Mila still got married, but it wasn't much of a celebration. We all went. Roberto didn't attend, of course. And now my mother hardly hears from him. She keeps trying to call, but he doesn't answer. As far as we know, he still lives in the shop, but we don't know if he has any business. We knew he always liked to drink with his friends at night, but now we've heard that he drinks a lot more. But that's about all we know.

"Mila got a job at the Casa del Popolo in Florence, but neither of them makes much money. And Adolfo? Well, he may have gotten married, but we don't think he's very happy. You know why? When Roberto fell into the river, Adolfo didn't try to save him. Just stood there. Didn't make a move. At least that's what the people there said. Maybe he was in shock, maybe he was confused. Or maybe he just refused. Nobody knows, and maybe he doesn't know either. So now maybe he's carrying all that guilt around. My mother says he's depressed. He doesn't talk to her very often either. Mila says he's very withdrawn, doesn't talk much at all.

"We don't think Adolfo and Roberto will ever get together again, not even speak to each other. And they're only a mile apart.

"And the family never talks about this. Everyone is very, very ashamed. You know, it's the old Italian thing. If you don't talk about it, it didn't happen. My Papa said once it's like the story of Cain and Abel. That's why I've never mentioned my uncles."

Francesca took a long time to absorb all this. Then she stopped, near the turn of the wall, and faced Dino. "Dino, you're going to be staying with Adolfo in Florence, aren't you?"

"I'll have my own room in the basement, but I guess I'm taking some meals with them."

"Do you think you'll see Roberto?"

"I don't know. My mother wants me to find him."

"Dino, your family doesn't expect you to try to solve Roberto and Adolfo's problems, do they?"

"What? No! No, I'm going to Florence to study and to paint. I don't know anything about that stuff."

"Good. You can't solve other people's problems, Dino. You're going to have enough to do in Florence."

"I know."

He thought he'd make one more try. "Want to come with me?"

"Florence is too big for me, Dino. Do you think it's too big for you?"

"I don't know, Francesca, I don't know."

Chapter Eight

August 1964

When Colin Richards pulled up in front of Lucia and Paolo's house in his rented Fiat 1300, you would have thought he was the captain of the local soccer team that had just won the championship.

Lucia and Paolo ran out, with Dino trailing behind. Rosa and Annabella emerged from neighboring houses. Fausta came out, too, but she stood silently in the back. Colin could hardly open the car door before he was engulfed with hugs, kisses and tears. Rosa wouldn't let him go.

"Colin, Colin, Colin," she kept saying, pinching his cheeks. "You're still such a handsome man."

"Whoa," he said, "I'm not a returning war hero, you know. I'm the one who had to escape from the country."

A tall and lean twenty-three-year old when he fled the Cielo, Colin was now a husky forty-two-year old with a few more pounds around his middle and considerably less hair on his head.

"But wait," he said, freeing himself from Rosa's arms. "I want you all to meet Bridget, the love of my life."

Colin extricated his wife, and Bridget stood shyly at his side. In a flowered yellow dress and a white hat at the back of her head, Bridget looked like she had just materialized from an English garden, which she had only yesterday.

"And this is Penelope," Colin said, opening the rear door of the car. Clutching a large book bag, Penny stepped gracefully from the car and stood at the side. She wore a long-sleeved white blouse, a long navy skirt and a serene smile. She had dark curly hair, which she wore short, and large sunglasses. Her skin was pale and she had broad shoulders. What impressed Dino most was that she was tall, almost as tall as he was, not short like Francesca. He couldn't take his eyes off her.

"*Buongiorno.*" Her voice was firm, deep, confident. "Forgive me, but I'm trying out my Italian. I hope it's not too bad."

Pleased that she had made the effort, everyone shook her hand and then trooped into the house. As they crowded in front of the television set in the living room, introductions had to be made. Colin had never met Paolo, who was serving in a band of Resistance fighters near the Cielo while Colin hid in a tiny space inside. And, of course, Dino hadn't been born.

The villagers were relieved that Colin had remembered the Italian he had learned during his stay in Italy, bolstered by *Learn Italian in Thirty Days* records he had borrowed from the Liverpool library.

"What a time to come to Italy," Paolo said. "August is always hotter than hell. We just got back from the seaside, and it was hotter than hell there, too. We're never going to go again."

"It's not like Liverpool," Colin said. He loosened the collar of his sweaty shirt.

Despite being a little odorous, Colin went up to each of the women to give thanks that were long overdue. Warm hugs and kisses for Lucia, Rosa and Annabella. Finally, Fausta. She looked into Colin's eyes and burst into tears.

"It's all right," he said, putting his hand on her shoulder. "It's all right. You were just doing what you thought was right at the time."

Fausta pulled out a handkerchief. "Oh, Colin. You don't know how many sleepless nights I've had. To think that I almost went off to tell the Germans you were in that little room. I can't imagine what I was thinking. But I'm not that person anymore, really I'm not." Her lips trembled.

"It's all right, it's all right."

"I'm so ashamed, Colin, so ashamed."

"Really, Fausta, it's all right now." Colin held her hands for a very long time. He took her handkerchief and wiped her tears.

Colin looked around. "Not everyone's here. Lucia, your mother?"

Lucia explained that Gina was ill and sleeping upstairs. "She doesn't come down anymore."

"I'm so sorry. Such a lovely woman. Lucia, before I left the Cielo, Roberto said he would write to me, and he did for a while, but not anymore. Is he OK?"

Lucia hesitated. "I'm sure he is. I think he's awfully busy."

"The first thing I'm going to do when we get there is call up Adolfo and we're going to take him and Roberto to the finest restaurant in Florence. I know they'd like that, right?"

"Maybe not," Lucia said.

"They're both very busy," Paolo said.

Dino stood in the back through all of this, never taking his eyes off Penny, who was studying every person in the room as if she was going to write a report about them. Who was this girl?

Gathered around the kitchen table and a spread of tea and cookies, the women remembered the days of Colin's captivity in the Cielo.

"Remember, Colin," Rosa said, "how we used to have English lessons every day, and you taught us silly words?"

"Silly? Things like *pantaloni* is 'trousers'?" Colin said. "You never know when you'll have to use the word."

Colin summarized the last two decades of his life in a few sentences. After running from the Cielo, more for the sake of his protectors than his own safety, he traveled north through Italy and almost made it to the Swiss border before he was again captured by German troops. He stayed in a prison camp until the end of the war and then returned to Liverpool.

"I got a job in construction, but I hung around this pub for so long, the owner finally asked me if I wanted to buy it. So I bought it and I built an addition and now it's one of the most popular pubs in Liverpool. Richards' Retreat, we call it. People come from all over."

"You have a pub in Liverpool?" Paolo was amazed.

"And we have a great band. Rock and roll, they call it. Everybody thinks of Liverpool as the Beatles. Heard of them?"

No one except Dino had. "I've heard a couple of their songs on the radio," he said. "I don't know…they're different. Maybe I should hear more."

"They're going to be really big," Colin said. "But blimey, we knew the Beatles when they were still the Quarreymen. Don't get me started on the Beatles. We tried to get them to play at our place but, no, those blokes said they were too good for us. Too good for us. We've got our own band now. Great band. Plays every Saturday night. Just as good as the Beatles, even better. People love it. But hey, Paolo, you should come to England and come to my pub. You'd like it."

It had never occurred to Paolo to travel anywhere beyond Italy, or even Tuscany, and from the look that Lucia suddenly gave him, it was clear that he never would.

"I don't even know where Liverpool is," Annabella said, "and you came from Liverpool to Florence? Who can believe it?"

Few around the table could. And who, they wondered, would leave her family in Liverpool hundreds of miles away to come to Italy to study.

Rosa was the only one who dared bring up the subject. As it always did when she was upset, her voice rose several levels. "Penelope, I wonder. How old are you?"

"Signora, I was seventeen on my last birthday, in May. Why do you ask?"

"I'm just curious. You know that you'll be away from your parents for a long time."

Penny put down her cup of tea. "Signora, I've been wanting to come to Italy since I was about ten years old," she said in impeccable, if book-learned, Italian. "First, because my father told me how beautiful it is and having been here only a few hours, I can see why he loves it so much. For years I've been teaching myself the language, which is so much more beautiful than ours.

"And then I started studying the Italian painters and sculptors. I mean, England cannot compare to the geniuses you have produced. I am always overwhelmed when I look at the books about Italian art. My teachers, when I was young, encouraged me to draw and paint, so that's what I did. They said I had some talent, and they said I should come to Italy and study the masters here, go to the museums and the churches and see the works first hand. And of course that meant Florence most of all. I researched other universities, but my dream has always been to attend the Accademia di Belle Arti.

"Yes, I know I'll miss my mother and father, but an artist has to make sacrifices. Sometimes artists have to break out from the place where they've been all their lives."

Penny picked up her cup again. It was as if she had just delivered a speech to the Italian Parliament. No one could respond. The girl flattered them with her knowledge and love of Italy so why shouldn't she study in Florence?

Dino could not believe what she had just said and almost dropped an almond biscotti in his lap when she looked at him.

"Dino," she said, "I hear you're going to be studying in Florence, too. Where?"

"Um," he said. "The Accademia di Belle Arti."

"Really?" Penny said. "Why, that's wonderful! Perhaps we'll be in some of the same classes and we can study together."

Dino wiped his forehead with the back of his hand. "Um. Um. Yes. Yes, we should."

"Well," said Paolo, getting up from his chair, "it's getting late. I know Ezio and Donna will be expecting you for dinner."

Colin, Bridget and Penny promised to come back the next day. Dino walked Penny to the car, opened the door and smiled at her when he closed it. He went right up to his room. Francesca...Penny...Francesca... Penny. Sant'Antonio...Florence... Sant'Antonio...Florence. He couldn't get to sleep.

Darkness was just settling in on the long, winding drive up the hill from Sant'Antonio to the Cielo, and Colin had trouble recognizing anything. Another problem was that it had been almost twenty years since a very weak and sick Colin had found his way to the Cielo and he hadn't been aware of his surroundings. Spreading chestnut trees now towered ominously on one side, then olive groves on another and then vineyards that stretched on and on. But there were vast spaces where the evening mist had not yet enveloped the dusky distant hills.

"Look, Penny," Bridget said. "Isn't this beautiful? Nothing like we see in England."

"I can't believe I'm here."

Colin was having trouble getting used to driving an Italian car on an Italian road so he wasn't watching the scenery.

"On this road I don't have to worry about driving on the right or the left," he said. "There's not enough room for two cars anyway."

"Lord help us if another car comes down the hill," Bridget said, her fists clenched.

And then the Cielo loomed ahead of them. Ezio and Donna had cleared out brush and trees so that the golden walls of the farmhouse, alone on the hilltop, seemed to glow in the faint moonlight. Colin had tears in his eyes.

"I remember when I first came here. I was so sick, and they took me in, they took me in without even asking questions."

Ezio and Antonio had recently painted the exterior walls, but they had done even more inside, changing and enlarging rooms and opening the first floor into one large space except for a bedroom in a corner. The first thing Colin wanted to see was the little room off the kitchen where he had been hidden. The room was no more, now part of the kitchen and containing a new stove.

Colin looked around. "But where's the place where all the wine and grappa were kept?"

Ezio lifted a rug and then the trap door. "See down there, we still keep our wine and grappa there."

"And a good supply, too. I could use some of this in my pub."

Ezio led his guests on a tour, showing them the bathroom that had replaced the outside *cesso* first. "I didn't mind using it, but that was the first thing Donna wanted."

Heavy red drapes matched the bedspreads in the bedrooms upstairs. Dressers and chairs had been purchased from the market in Lucca. Framed portraits hung on the walls.

"People think they're our family, but we don't have any family pictures," Ezio said. "We just found these in junk shops."

When they returned downstairs, Colin suddenly put his hand on his wife's arm. "Look at Penny."

Their daughter stood before the fireplace, absorbed in the painting over the mantel. Her hands were folded behind her back, and her eyes glistened.

Bridget edged to her daughter's side. "Do you like it?"

Penny was so engrossed in the painting that she didn't hear her mother.

It was a large painting, almost four feet wide and more than three feet high, and held by a simple oak frame. The dominant oils were a dark blue, a deep green and ivory. A starlit Tuscan sky hovered in the background. Evergreens and olive trees sheltered a small white building in the lower right. It had a tile roof and two arch-shaped windows. There was also an arch over the door. But the most striking thing was that it seemed to glow from the interior, not brightly, but enough to show that something important was alive inside.

In small letters in the lower left, "The Chapel."

"May I ask what this is?" she said.

"Of course," Ezio said. "It's from a place near here called Mansagrati. It's the chapel dedicated to Saint Zita. You wonder who that is. A lot of people do. Well, she lived in the thirteenth century in Mansagrati and from what I have read, she was just a servant girl but very holy. I don't know why they made her a saint, but there's a legend that one day she went off to help someone when she was supposed to be baking bread and that her employers found angels making the bread for her. A nice story, but who believes it?"

Penny smiled. "And those initials in the corner? A.S.?"

"That's Dino, Dino Sporenza." Ezio said. "You just met him. His real name is Aldobrandino. That was his father's name. Nobody calls him that, of course, but Dino thinks it sounds more professional than 'Dino.'"

"Aldobrandino," Penny murmured. "It sounds so musical. I like it."

Chapter Nine

Fall 1964

Since classes at the Accademia di Belle Arti were to begin in the first week of October, September was a time for farewells. As often as they could, Dino and Francesca spent afternoons in Francesca's darkened bedroom while her mother was working. Piera Casati needed the extra money that longer hours at the toy shop would bring, though she knew full well what was happening in the third-floor apartment behind the old Roman amphitheater. She had some long talks with her daughter, who assured her that everything was "all right."

That depended, of course, on the definition of "all right." She and Dino had improved their lovemaking to the point where they were no longer awkward or nervous, and Marcellina now watched stoically, if disdainfully, from a corner of the bed. But every time Dino and Francesca looked at the calendar above the bed, they knew that their time together was running out.

"This is the end, isn't it?" Francesca said on their last afternoon together as she pulled the sheets up around her neck. "We're never going to see each other again."

"No, no," Dino said in a voice that was far from reassuring.

They stared at the ceiling.

"I knew it wouldn't last," she said.

Dino could not say otherwise.

"I'll try to come back often, maybe even once a month."

She cradled her head on his arm. "You know you won't. You'll be off in Florence and you'll be busy with all the work you'll have."

What she really meant was that he would be busy with a new girl, maybe that girl from England. Francesca knew that Penny was now in Florence, but Dino brushed off the many questions she had about the girl.

"She seemed all right," he said when the questions persisted. "I hardly talked to her."

"Is she pretty?"

"No...well...no..."

"What does that mean?"

"She...well, she looks English."

"Dino, how do English people look? What a strange thing for you to say."

"I don't know. Different. Just different, I guess."

The conversation went nowhere after that. Dino said that he'd try to write Francesca often, though he wasn't specific when, and that he'd surely be back home for Christmas. Francesca said she would write, too.

After getting dressed, Dino and Francesca had their last private dinner together in what had become their favorite trattoria in the old amphitheater. There were just two other diners in the place, which was lit only by candles on the tables. They stared at the menu, they held hands, they ate their pasta, and they hardly said a word. Afterwards, he walked her home, where their kiss was long but gentle. Both parted with tears in their eyes.

The next afternoon, Dino walked to Mansagrati and sat for a long time in Saint Zita's chapel. He didn't pray much anymore. He rarely went to church. He avoided Father Sangretto, who now seemed more sad than upset when he saw him. But for reasons Dino couldn't understand, he still found a peace in this small space that he didn't experience anywhere else. He wondered if he could ever find a similar place in Florence.

In less than twenty-four hours, he would be in Florence. He couldn't believe it. He thought he'd be jumping up and down with excitement, but there were so many mixed feelings. Apprehension. Exhilaration. Anticipation. Loneliness. And, yes, fear. He thought of The Waking Slave. Did he feel like he was breaking out of a stony prison? He didn't know, and he worried about what the next few days would bring.

That night, there was the inevitable gathering of the remaining members of *Il Gruppo di Cielo* to wish Dino goodbye. Judging from the tears, shed even by Paolo, you might think Dino was going across the continent, even to Liverpool, instead of to Florence.

There were toasts and hugs and kisses. Ezio and Antonio, who were the most familiar with the city, warned Dino that food could be very expensive, that he should buy clothing only at the outdoor markets, that he should walk and never take the bus, that he should not gawk like a tourist and that he should always keep his wallet in his front pocket, not his back.

"The beggars are everywhere now," Antonio said. "And they know who's a tourist and who's new to the city. They use their kids. The beggars ask for money and the kids pick your pocket and run off before you even know it."

Donna said that Dino would be just fine, but Rosa, Annabella and Fausta said they would worry every day he was gone. Lucia added to his general apprehension by once again bursting into tears.

"Mama," Dino said. "I'm eighteen years old. I can take care of myself."

To which Lucia replied, "Yes, you're eighteen years old. That's the problem."

And then Paolo reminded Lucia that he was fighting in the Resistance when he was seventeen. When the evening ended and the guests had to leave, there were more tearful hugs.

Since Adolfo had weekends off at the *Biblioteca Nazionale,* Paolo decided to go to Florence on Saturday. He got up at sunrise and knocked on Dino's door. "Time to go!"

"OK, Papa!"

Paolo sat at the desk chair as Dino packed. "You know, Dino, we haven't really been very close all these years."

"Don't say that, Papa. I think we've been very close."

"Dino, I want to tell you something. Your father was my best friend. We did such crazy things together, you wouldn't believe it. And I'm not about to tell you now." Paolo smiled. "But I would have done anything for him and he would have done the same for me. When he was killed, I thought my life was over. I really didn't want to go on. Then your mother and I started seeing each other and talking about him, and how we missed him, and how he was so funny. Over the months, your mother and I became very close. We grew to love each other.

"Dino, I guess I've never told you this, but I didn't marry your mother because she was pregnant with you and I wanted the baby to have a father. I married her because I loved her. But then when you arrived, I loved you so much. I'm not good at expressing my feelings, Dino, but I just want you to know that I love you, and I'm going to miss you. I know you're not Little Dino anymore, and I guess I feel kind of bad about that."

Paolo brushed tears from his eyes, and Dino hugged him for a long time.

"I love you, too, Papa. And I'm going to miss you."

"All right," Paolo said. "Let's get going."

Dino had a large suitcase containing clothes, books and the framed photo of The Waking Slave. His *mangia dischi*, records and guitar were separate.

Lucia seemed to take a long time frying eggs and warming up the bread from last night, and Dino gulped the food down. Now that it was morning, he was eager to get on the road. She also packed a bag of sandwiches and fruit in case they got hungry.

"Do we know how to get there?" she asked.

Paolo pulled out a map from a kitchen drawer. "Sure. I just go around Lucca and take A-11 to Florence. Simple."

"Not just to Florence, but to Adolfo's. He said it's on Piazza Santa Croce."

"We'll find it," Paolo said. He showed her a map of Florence city streets. "Look, it's right over here."

"Florence can be tricky, you know. A lot of one-way streets."

"It's right on the map. I'll find it."

With Dino's suitcase and the *mangia dischi* tucked in the trunk, their Fiat 1500 eased down the narrow driveway, Paolo and Lucia in front, Dino in the back with his guitar. Rosa, Annabella and Fausta held their aprons to their eyes and shouted from their doorsteps.

"*Buon viaggio,* Dino!"

"*Buona fortuna!*"

"*Ritorna presto!*"

And Paolo shouted back, "*Mille grazie!* But Lucia and me will be back before sundown!"

Dino looked out the back window at the rapidly disappearing village and closed his eyes.

Paolo had driven to Lucca many times, but he had rarely gone on to Florence. Once on the *Autostrada,* he quickly remembered the habits of Italian drivers, who had apparently never heard of speed limits. Paolo stayed in the slow lane, but then drivers came so close behind him that he could almost feel the cars against his back bumper. Then he would speed, and so would the drivers behind. He tried slowing down, very slowly, forcing the other drivers to jam on their brakes, scream and then try to pass him.

"Don't mind them," Lucia said, her own hands shaking. "Just drive at your own speed."

Paolo felt sweat warming his cheeks and hands. "Stupid Italian drivers," he muttered.

The exit signs went by fast: Montecatini Terme, Pistoia, Prato, and then *Firenze.*

In the back seat, Dino held the map and gave directions. "Get off on Viale Guidoni. Good. Now turn right and follow Via Forlanini. Good. Now Via di Novoli. Good."

"See," Paolo said. "We're getting there."

For some reason, Dino expected the Duomo and the Palazzo Vecchio to suddenly appear, just like in the photographs, and they would be in the heart of Florence. Instead, miles of factories and suburban enclaves encased this western extension of the city, part of Italy's industrial revolution after the war, and the traffic became intense. He didn't feel like he was in Florence.

"OK," he said, looking up from the map. "That little river is called Mugnone. Now get on Viale Francesco Redi. OK, good."

"This is easy," Paolo said, wiping the palms of his hands on his pants legs.

"Now swing to the right to Via Belfiore. We're going to hit Piazzale di Porta a Prato."

That's when things got more difficult. Paolo hadn't counted on the hordes of people, the roar of Vespas, the whine of ambulances and police cars, the heat of the morning sun and the humid air that enveloped the city even on this October day.

He was hopelessly lost as soon as he got to the Piazzale di Porta a Prato and didn't know how to maneuver around it.

"Where am I? Where the hell am I?" he shouted as he narrowly missed an elderly woman crossing the street.

"*Cretino!*" the driver behind shouted.

Lucia put her hand on his arm. "Maybe you should stop and ask someone."

"How can I stop? How can I stop? There's no place to stop! Where are the street signs? Where the hell are the street signs? What kind of a city is this?"

"Look above!" Dino shouted. "They're up high on the buildings."

"Well, how the hell can I see up there when I'm driving?"

Lucia and Dino took over the responsibility of looking at the signs, immediately discovering that street names changed from block to block.

"Please," Lucia cried, "slow down and ask someone."

Reluctantly, Paolo jammed on the brakes when he found a storekeeper emptying garbage into the street.

"*Scusi! Dov'è* Piazza Santa Croce?"

"Piazza Santa Croce?"

"*Sì*, Piazza Santa Croce!"

A line of cars beeped loudly.

"Ah," the storekeeper said. "Santa Croce. *Sì, è bella!*"

"*Sì*," Paolo shouted over the din of car horns. "*Dov'è? Dov'è?* Where the hell is it?"

"Ah, *Sì*." The man pointed up the street. "Via il Prato, then Via Curtatone, then Lungarno Amerigo Vespucci."

"*Grazie*," Paolo said as he wiped his forehead with the back of his hand.

Once on the Lungarno, the busy highway on the north side of the Arno, Paolo was still driving too slow and the object of numerous obscenities and fists in the air. Paolo returned them in kind.

They couldn't see the Arno down below, but Dino imagined that it was calm and green in the morning sun. Across, he thought he saw the crown of Santo Spirito.

"Look, Mama. I think Roberto lives over there by that church."

"Dino, once you're settled, you go and find your uncle. Hear?"

Dino ignored the command. "Can you believe it? We're in Florence, Mama!"

"I can believe it," Paolo said under his breath.

Dino became more and more excited. Reality had set in. He remembered every photograph from the guidebook Francesca had given him. "Look, there's Ponte Santa Trinità! It's as beautiful as the book said. And the Ponte Vecchio! See all the shops, Mama? If we stopped and got out we could buy some earrings for Rosa or somebody."

"I'm not stopping for anyone," Paolo said.

"And there," Dino pointed. "That's Ponte alle Grazie! Here's where we should turn, Papa."

Soon, Dino spotted a rare parking place on Borgo Santa Croce, and Paolo quickly pulled in. "We'll walk," he said, mopping his forehead. "Wherever it is, we'll walk."

Dino carried the suitcase, Paolo the guitar and Lucia the *mangia dischi* as they walked toward the magnificent Basilica of Santa Croce. Dino stopped and stood motionless. The church. The statue of Dante. The huge piazza spreading out in front of it. Everything he had seen in the photographs was right there. The only difference was that photographs were taken in the bright sun. Now, an overcast sky robbed the setting of its beauty.

"Let's go," Paolo said. "People will think we're tourists."

"And try to rob us," Lucia said. "We'll come back. Let's go find Adolfo and Mila."

They had the address, in a high building that was once a palazzo right on the piazza. Paolo rang the buzzer. No answer. He rang again.

"Maybe they've gone out," Lucia said.

"He said they'd be home, right?"

Dino thought of throwing rocks at the second-floor window, but that reminded him of what Roberto had done, and he didn't like that reminder.

"Well, let's wait," Paolo said. While Lucia and Paolo sat on a bench, Dino wandered around the piazza but mainly stood transfixed by the façade of Santa Croce.

Paolo worried about the increasingly overcast skies.

"They say it rains a lot in Florence in October," Lucia said.

"It's even worse in November," Paolo said. "That's when the Arno floods."

Dino couldn't sit still. He paced around the piazza, studying all the buildings, then sat down and got up again. After a half hour of watching kids playing soccer, residents walking their dogs and shoppers going in and out of stores, they saw a slight young woman turning the key in the lock of Adolfo's building. "That must be Mila," Dino said. "Mila!"

"Dino?"

Mila had met Dino and his parents only at her wedding, and since it was such a subdued occasion, they didn't talk much. It was clear now, though, that she was relieved that they had come.

Lucia hugged her. "Oh, Mila. How are you? You look pale. You've been working too hard. Here, let me help you with those groceries. Paolo, Dino, take some of these bags."

The halls that once sheltered royalty were dark and the steps were steep.

"Be careful," Mila said. "There are holes in some of the steps."

The smells of baked cod and fried tomatoes drifted from splintered doors along the way. When they arrived on the second floor and Mila turned the key, there were more smells. Dank. If darkness had a smell, this would be it.

"Adolfo doesn't want me to open the shutters, not even during the day," Mila said as she flipped a switch for the sole light on a wall. "It gets so musty in here."

"You have a nice place," Lucia said, though she was thinking just the opposite. A threadbare couch and a stack of books sat under a window. A small table to the side. A chair in need of repair. A worn rug that once had colorful flowers on the floor. That was it.

"I thought Adolfo would be up, but he must still be sleeping," Mila said, urging her guests to find a place to sit.

"Mila," Paolo said, "is Adolfo all right? When I called him to get directions, he sounded, well, like he was far away, thinking about something else."

"He gets that way sometimes. He…"

Mila turned her back. She went into the tiny kitchen and started unpacking the groceries, her shoulders shaking. Lucia went up behind her and took her in her arms.

"Mila, Mila, I'm so sorry."

"It's all right. I'll be all right."

"You poor girl."

"No, I'm OK. I'm used to it now. I love Adolfo very much. I just wish I could help him. He doesn't want to talk about it. And, then, you know, sometimes I think it's all my fault. If I hadn't been so foolish, first one brother and then the other…"

"Oh, don't be silly, Mila," Lucia said. "Those two boys, they've always been headstrong, ever since they were little. They always wanted their own way."

"Mila?"

The faint voice from the bedroom was hoarse and hesitant. "Mila?"

"We're in here, *caro*."

When her brother was a little boy, Lucia remembered, he was rambunctious, always smiling and laughing and full of energy. The figure that emerged from the bedroom was gaunt and unshaven. His eyes were sad and his words almost inaudible.

"Lucia, Paulo, Dino. All the way from Sant'Antonio…"

"Adolfo!" Lucia cried.

Tears streaming down her face, Lucia rushed up to hug him. "Adolfo…Adolfo."

"Lucia," Adolfo said quietly. He shook Paolo's hand, then Dino's. No one said anything.

Mila offered to make something to eat, but Lucia said they had sandwiches in the car and ordered Dino to go and get them. There wasn't much conversation around the little kitchen table when he returned. Although Adolfo hadn't asked, Lucia told him that their mother was failing and that he should come to visit her.

"Maybe," he said.

"I really wish you would, Adolfo."

"Maybe."

"Are you all right, Adolfo?"

"I'm fine, Lucia. Don't worry about me. I'm fine." He stared out the window.

Then Lucia finally asked the question that was burning in her mind. "I was just wondering...have you heard anything of Roberto?"

Adolfo abruptly got up and went back to the bedroom. Mila whispered, "No, we haven't."

A crack of thunder sent Paolo to the window. He and Lucia really had to start going back, he said, worrying how he would get through Florence and find A-11 again in the rain.

"First," Mila said, "let me show Dino his room. You can see we don't have room here, but the landlord says there's a nice space in the basement near the boiler. It will be nice and warm."

Part Two

The Uffizi Gallery and Palazzo Vecchio (the Old Palace) in Florence, Italy. Photo by Cat @ Fotolia.com

Chapter Ten

October 1964

Lucia cringed when she saw the basement room, and even Paolo shuddered. But Dino said, "Look at how big this is!"

In the nineteenth century, when the granddaughter of an ancient duke lived in the palazzo, the huge space was used for storing horse equipment, and a faint equine odor remained. The most recent owner had thrown up partitions and rented it out to students.

Another art student had lived there until graduating in July, Mila said, and reminders were still around. Posters of recent films—*La Dolce Vita, Rocco and His Brothers,* and, Dino noted, *Two Women*—covered cracks in the stone walls on one side. On another, the student had started a mural showing what looked like a bloody medieval soccer game right in the piazza outside, but it was unfinished.

A large table dominated the room. Dino thought it would be great for studying. He piled most of his books on one corner and placed another under an unsteady leg. Mila had donated a worn chair with a broken arm. Lucia immediately said she would mail Dino a large afghan made by her mother.

And then there was the bed. Lucia, Paolo and Dino had stared at it for some time before Mila explained. It consisted of a long plank, the kind that would hold a statue of Saint Anthony, with a thick cotton mat on top. But instead of legs, it rested on four wine cases so that it was more than a foot off the floor.

"You're wondering why," Mila said. "Well, this room is situated in the part of the building that's near the river. You know the Arno hardly ever floods. It hasn't flooded since, well, for a long time, 1944, I think. That's twenty years ago. But, the landlord is very cautious, so just in case, he put the bed on these boxes. No need to worry."

Dino avoided his mother's stare.

Mila also said that although the boiler was just outside the room, sometimes it didn't work quite right, so she would give Dino a *scaldino.*

"What's that?" Paolo asked.

"You don't know a *scaldino?* It's been around Florence forever. It's this little iron pot and you put hot coals in it. You can keep it on your lap when you're studying or reading. You can even take it to bed. We have two of them and we use them a lot in winter. It gets cold in our place."

"You take a little pot with coals and put it in your bed?"

"It's very safe. Really. And there's a pile of coals right around the corner in the boiler room."

Another worry for Lucia all the way home, even more than the dust in the corners and the cracks in the walls.

Mila pointed out the tiny room next to the boiler room. It had a rusty sink on the wall and a large hole in the floor. A roll of toilet paper was next to it. Mila saw their confused looks.

"You've never seen a squatter? You'll get used to it. And you can take baths in our place, Dino."

Lucia turned her back so that Dino wouldn't see her holding her nose.

"We'd better go," Paolo said. "It's starting to rain harder. We'll never get out of here."

It was such a hurried departure on the doorsteps that Dino couldn't tell if there were tears or raindrops on his mother's face.

"I'll call you tomorrow, OK?" Lucia said.

Paolo held Dino's shoulders. "Take care of yourself, son."

Dino put his clothes on the back of the chair, his guitar in a corner and his *mangia dischi* and his records on the table, then spent the rest of the day reading his guidebook about Florence. About Michelangelo and Raphael and Donatello, about the great museums, the Uffizi and the Pitti Palace, and about the Medici and the history of Florence. He turned the page when he came upon photos of the Arno, knowing that it was just a short distance from where he sat.

He stood on his chair, pulled aside a dirty curtain and looked out the window high on one wall. Across the piazza, he could see the feet of passersby slogging through the rain. Big men's shoes. Delicate ladies' shoes. Canvas kids' shoes. And dogs! Did everyone in Florence have a dog? A few came to his window to sniff, and one attempted to do something else until it was dragged away by its master.

If he pressed his head against the window and looked to the right, Dino could look far down the piazza where the steps of the basilica were hazy in the rain. Santa Croce. He couldn't believe it was so close. A few hours ago, he was in his village. Now he was in Florence!

He started to laugh. He remembered a stupid book by E.M. Forster that Francesca had found for him when she learned he was going to Florence. It was about this stupid English girl and she had a room with a view. She had a silly name…Lucy…Lucy something. Yes, Lucy Honeychurch.

"This is my room with a view," he thought.

And then he thought of another English girl who wasn't silly at all.

When it was too dark to see out of the window, he got under the thin blanket and sheet. Except for vacations in Viareggio, he had never spent a night away from home. He should have been thinking, "I'm in Florence, I'm in Florence." Instead, he wondered if his Papa and Mama got home all right. He thought about Sant'Antonio and Leoni's and Manconi's and the church and the statue of Saint Anthony. He thought about his room at home and his grandmother. He thought about Adolfo and Mila and how he would get along with them.

He could hear rain hitting the cobblestones outside his window and yelling and laughter from the piazza. He tried to think about Francesca and even though it had only been two days since he'd seen her, he had to force himself to remember whether there were freckles on her forehead or just on her cheeks. But he remembered everything about their afternoons in her darkened bedroom. Then he thought again about Penny and wondered how many boyfriends she'd had in England.

Briefly, he wondered what he would do if he fell in love with a girl here. He couldn't bring her back here, that was certain. Well, there was little likelihood that he would meet, much less fall in love with, a girl here. He was from a tiny village. His ears were too big.

Finally, he went to sleep, awakened in the middle of the night by a scratching sound in the walls. He was too tired to investigate.

The basilica's bells woke Dino at 6 o'clock, and he had trouble realizing where he was. Then he saw a hint of sunlight coming through the curtain.

It was too early for Adolfo and Mila to be up, so he opened his guidebook and planned his day. Finally, the realization took hold. "I'm in Florence! I'm in Florence!"

Mila was making coffee and Adolfo was seated at the table when Dino opened the door to their apartment two hours later. Though still unshaven, Adolfo looked a little better this morning and even made some conversation. He told Dino about his work repairing and restoring medieval books in the *Biblioteca Nazionale*, a job he not only loved but was becoming quite good at.

"The only problem is that the work is in the basement, and being so close to the Arno, it gets very damp. I wear a sweater all the time, even in summer."

Mila also told Dino about her work at Casa del Popolo, the Communist meeting place. After the war, it had become the main gathering place for old partisans, but now it also served the whole neighborhood with community services.

"There's a priest nearby who has a *cucina popolare*, a soup kitchen, so he gives people food and we give out clothing and other things. You're going to find out, Dino, that this is one of the poorest areas in Florence."

When the telephone rang, everyone knew it was Lucia.

"*Ciao,* Mama. Yes, I slept well. No, I wasn't cold. Yes, Adolfo and Mila made me a good breakfast. Yes, I'm going out today. Yes, I'll be careful. Yes, I'll wear my sweater. *Ciao,* Mama."

Five minutes later, he was out the door and across the piazza where the rain had stopped but puddles remained. He stood before the giant statue that was photographed on the cover of his guidebook.

"Dante Alighieri l'Italia." An eagle stood at the famous poet's side, four lions at the base. Impressive, but why did he look so angry? Was he that angry in life? Dino had tried three times, without success, to get through *The Divine Comedy.* Maybe someday when he was older he would understand it better. Then he thought that Penny had probably read it and understood every word.

He looked at the façade of the church and remembered exactly what the Forster book had called it. "A façade of surpassing ugliness."

Stupid book. How could anyone write that? It was just as beautiful as the Church of San Michele in Lucca, which he could, and did, gaze at for hours.

People were going into the church, and he followed them up the steps and across the green, brown and white marble. Inside, he thought of Lucy Honeychurch again. This was where she had her meeting with the Emersons, and he remembered again exactly what that silly girl had called it. A barn. And cold. He vowed never to think of that book again.

The church was huge. The nave seemed to stretch for miles, with the high altar far in the distance. The floor was filled with flat tombstones for long-forgotten medieval royalty and the sides with altars and tombs and monuments. He had to catch his breath and get his bearings. Where to begin?

And then he saw it. To the right, close to the entrance. He almost knocked an elderly woman over as he rushed to it. He consulted his guidebook.

"Tomb of Michelangelo Buonarroti. Considered the most beautiful of the sixteenth-century tombs in Santa Croce, it was designed by Giorgio Vasari and executed between 1564-1574. The *Pietà* above was frescoed by Giovanni Battista Naldini. The Bust of the artist and the Statue of Painting, on the left, are by Giovanni Battista Lorenzi. The Statue of Sculpture in the middle is by Valerio Cioli. That of Architecture on the right is by Giovanni Bandini called Giovanni dell'Opera."

Despite his years studying Italian artists, Dino didn't recognize any of the names, but it didn't matter. He was standing before the tomb of the greatest artist in history. The man who sculpted the David, the man who painted the Sistine Chapel, the man who created the *Pietà* at Saint Peter's in Rome, the man who…Dino couldn't remember them all. And the man who almost finished The Waking Slave.

Standing rigid, his feet apart, his hands holding his guidebook behind his back, Dino remained immobile for almost an hour. He lost track of time. Tour guides, holding their umbrellas aloft, had to direct their little processions around him. One loudly asked him to move, but Dino didn't even hear him.

Then, Dino wandered to other tombs, of Machiavelli, Galileo, Ghiberti, Rossini. There was even a monument to Dante, although Dino knew he was actually buried in Ravenna. But he kept returning to Michelangelo.

He knew he should visit the chapels to see the Giotto paintings and the Della Robbia altarpieces, and, oh yes, go to the Refectory for Gaddi's Tree of the Cross and Cimabue's Crucifixion.

He would save all that for another day. Dino also put off a walk along the Arno, perhaps a visit to the Uffizi and the Pitti Palace and the Piazza della Signoria and the Duomo.

He was both exhausted and exhilarated as he returned to his basement room. He had stood before the tomb of Michelangelo. And although he had vowed not to think about that book again, he remembered one other thing. Lucy Honeychurch hadn't even mentioned Michelangelo. Stupid girl.

Chapter Eleven

October-November 1964

Dino thought the Accademia di Belle Arti might be in an ornate grand palazzo surrounded by formal gardens and fountains. Instead, he found it on Via Ricasoli, heavy with traffic and not far from the Duomo. It was a plain two-story building, distinguished only by a long colonnade with delicate arches. A row of expensive Vespas and bicycles stood outside, and Dino immediately thought that he would be the poorest student there.

Inside, he found the place to register for his classes and then, since this was Italy, he stood in line. Then he stood in another line. Then another, and another for the rest of the day filling out forms and getting his class schedule straightened out. In high school, he didn't have any choices on what classes to take. Here, he could chose from among a few, though as a first-year student he had to take the required courses. Introduction to Medieval Art, Raphael, Life Drawing. Dino wondered about the last one.

All the other students were laughing and talking. Dino looked around for Penny, but she was nowhere to be seen. He climbed the huge ornate staircase and looked down the halls. He stepped into the library and stood frozen by the sight of bookshelves reaching to the vaulted ceiling, long inlaid tables, busts and statues. He could never study there because he wouldn't get anything done. Dino knew that Cosimo de Medici had left a powerful legacy, but he never thought he would see it first-hand.

He walked down the hall and into the courtyard where students lined the walls talking about their classes. Next to a pillar on the other side, Penny was saying something to a boy, a boy even taller than he was, with black curly hair. He was smoking a cigarette. The boy said something and she laughed. She said something and he laughed. Dino couldn't bear to watch anymore, and walked quickly into the hallway leading to the classrooms.

With all the paperwork to fill out, professors to meet, tours to take and orientation sessions to attend, Dino slowly immersed himself into university life during the first weeks. Several times, he thought he should go next door to the Galleria dell'Accademia and see the David. But he knew that in order to get to Michelangelo's most magnificent statue, he would pass his unfinished works, including The Waking Slave. Dino didn't understand why, but he could not bring himself to see the real thing, at least not yet.

When classes started the following week, Dino found that getting used to university life was far more difficult than he had expected. In high school in Lucca, everything was scheduled. One class followed another and you knew where you were supposed to be and what you were supposed to do every minute of every day. The teachers asked the students questions and there were tests and examinations.

Here, the professors lectured. And lectured and lectured, talking for the full class period. Students were supposed to take notes and do research on their own in the various subjects, and instead of having regular tests and examinations, the professors gave individual oral examinations at the end of the year. Dino panicked. How would he know how he was doing if he wasn't tested? How would he remember everything by the end of the year? Used to a structured schedule, he didn't want this much freedom.

After a lecture on Raphael one day, Dino and Penny tried to discuss the artist's work during his Umbrian period. Dino had little to say, but Penny gave a long account of how Raphael began as an apprentice to Pietro Perugino "who had such a great influence that it is impossible to tell their works apart because they both applied their paint thickly and used oil varnish and..."

She could have gone on, but Dino stopped her. It was only the second week and he was sure he was going to fail the class.

He also couldn't find a place to read and study and found himself wandering around the building looking at the statues, some of them ancient originals and some plaster reproductions. He missed one of his art and architecture classes because he couldn't tear himself away from the library. He knew there were manuscripts by Galileo—Galileo!—somewhere here, but as a student he couldn't look at them.

As the weeks went on, he sometimes felt confused and lost. For so long he had wanted to break out from what he considered the stifling life of Sant'Antonio. Now that he had the freedom, he didn't know what to do with it. The other students were so worldly in the way they talked and acted. The boys joked and slapped each other on the back and the girls whispered in little groups. Everyone seemed to know one another, and they lived near the university. Since he was way off near Santa Croce, he didn't gather with them at night at a nearby coffee house or a jazz club near the Duomo.

He took to picking up something to eat at a cheap pizzeria so he could delay going home as long as possible. He didn't want to eat with Adolfo and Mila because he knew they didn't have much money. Adolfo's job at the *Biblioteca Nazionale* didn't pay much, and Mila's clerical work at the Casa del Popolo paid even less.

He also felt a certain sadness when he was with Adolfo and Mila. They were pleasant enough, and Mila told Dino that Adolfo seemed more cheerful when he was around. But Adolfo often seemed like he was in another world, a past world that he didn't want to remember but couldn't forget.

"Adolfo!" Mila would cry when he wouldn't answer a question.

"What? Oh. Sorry."

Dino still felt bad about the rift between Adolfo and Roberto, and he didn't know what to do about it. So after a few words with Adolfo and Mila every night, he edged down to his basement room to study. He filled notebook after notebook and then had trouble reading his writing. He was exhausted.

Penny became his only friend, if he could call her even that. But even Penny baffled him. She could be sweet and tender, but at other times she was so sophisticated that he felt like the naïve kid from an obscure village that he knew he was. Granted, Dino's experiences

with a young woman had been limited—Francesca was the only
one—but he just didn't understand Penny. She both confused and
fascinated him.

She had found a place to live two streets over from him, and on
Tuesdays and Thursdays, when they had the same class schedule,
they arranged to walk to the university together. Penny was living
with two other students in a fourth-floor apartment. The three girls
had to share a single bedroom with each other and a bathroom with
four other students across the hall. But she had the same greeting
when she ran down to find him waiting at the steps.

"Can you believe it, Dino? We're in Florence!"

Her enthusiasm was contagious, and they smiled all the way to
their first class of the day. That happened to be Professor Mariotti's
life drawing class in the studio. Dino was surprised that students in
their first year would be instructed to draw nudes from live models.
He thought they'd start with a vase of flowers or something.

He tried to look away when the model came in for the first time.
He thought the woman might be voluptuous and older, like one of
Renoir's figures. Instead, she appeared to be about twenty-three or
twenty-four. She was short like Francesca, but that was the only
similarity. A mass of black curls surrounded a round olive-colored
face with dark eyes, high cheekbones and full, ruby-red lips. Smiling
slightly, she looked all around the room, then dropped her crimson
kimono, focused on a far doorway and settled on a couch surrounded
by students and their easels.

Dino had never really seen a naked woman before. Francesca's
bedroom had always been so dark there was a lot of fumbling. This
woman's breasts were round and full, not like Francesca's. When
the model stretched one arm along her side and the other behind
her head, his face turned almost as bright as her fingernails. He
noticed that the other boys had the same reaction, and there was
some snickering until Professor Mariotti pounded on his desk with
a pointer.

"There will be none of that!" he shouted. "Get out your paints
and brushes."

After that, the model might as well have been a vase of flowers,
except for the times when she moved. Then Dino realized that she

was indeed alive, and that night, he went to sleep thinking about her smile, her breasts, her thighs, her fingernails.

On the Saturday of the second week, Dino and Penny decided to tour Santa Croce together. It started out badly.

"Come over here," Dino said as soon as they entered and he led her to the right. "Look! Can you believe it?"

"Yes, I saw that when I came here before. Magnificent sculpture, isn't it?"

"But Penny...don't you realize? It's him! Michelangelo's in there!"

"Oh, well, I suppose so. I mean his body probably was, once. Now it's just a pile of ashes, don't you think?"

"But Penny! We're standing before the tomb of the greatest artist who ever lived!"

"Oh, I know that. But Dino, it's just a tomb. He didn't do that sculpture. Somebody else did." She consulted her guidebook. "Vasari, that's who it was."

"But Penny!"

"I guess I'm not so excited about tombs, Dino. I mean, look all around here. Machiavelli, Galileo, Ghiberti, Rossini, Dante..."

"Dante's body isn't there," Dino said. "It's in Ravenna."

"Well, anyway, this all seems like a big giant cemetery to me. Look at the floor. All those old counts and knights buried in there. Now we just walk on top of them and don't think anything about it."

Dino didn't know what she was saying. All he knew was that she wasn't as excited to stand before Michelangelo's tomb as he was.

"Penny," Dino said, "did you ever read the book *A Room with a View*?"

"Read it! I devoured it! I love that book."

"Oh."

"Have you read it?"

"Yes," Dino said. "It was OK."

"I think I read it three times. In fact, I brought a copy along just so I could compare what I see with what Lucy saw. Sometimes I think I'm Lucy, having an adventure in Florence. Liverpool can be so confining, so old-fashioned. Here, I'm meeting and seeing people who are so unlike the people there. You Italians are so in love with beauty. You're so free! You love life so much! I want to be like that, too."

"But Lucy went back to England and married an Englishman."

"Well, yes, I suppose I will, too. But while I'm here I'd like to have a fling with an Italian."

Penny marched along then, with Dino following behind. He couldn't see if she really meant that or if she was teasing him, and he was more confused than ever.

"Let's go see the high altar," he said.

"It's called the Maggiore Chapel," Penny said, again consulting her guidebook. "All these altars are called chapels."

"I know that," Dino said. He was becoming sullen.

They were silent for much of the time as they walked along, making their way to the Giottos and the Gardis, the Donatellos and the Bancos. They couldn't comprehend it all. Their eyes glazed over.

"Just like I was saying," Penny said. "It's like a museum."

Then they reached the Medici Chapel off to the right from the main basilica. Plain white walls, a towering arched ceiling, a few sculptures on the sides. And above the simple altar covered only by a white cloth was a delicately carved, blue and white Della Robbia, Madonna with Child. Dino and Penny sank into a wooden bench and although no one else was around, they whispered.

"I could spend the rest of the day here," Penny said.

"Or a week," Dino said.

"After all those important works of art that we're supposed to know about, this simple chapel is such a contrast. You know, we don't go to church much in England. My parents don't believe all that stuff. One time we were on holiday and went to the cathedral at Canterbury. I thought there were lots of nice stained-glass windows, but it seemed like a museum. Santa Croce seems something like that, too. All the artworks. And the tombs."

They didn't say anything as they went back into the main church and down the long nave to the exit. As they passed Michelangelo's tomb, Dino asked Penny to look at it again.

"Do you feel anything?"

"Can't say that I do. Well, maybe a little. Now I can write home and say I saw Michelangelo's tomb."

As they went down the steps to the piazza, Penny suddenly stopped. "Oh, my God. You know what we didn't do? We didn't go to the museum to see Cimabue's Crucifixion. Professor Guidotti said we had to see it. He said Cimabue had such an influence on Giotto and Duccio but that the Renaissance artists overshadowed his work. Professor Guidotti will kill us if he knew we'd come here and didn't see the Cimabue."

"We won't tell him," Dino said.

They decided to walk along the Arno. The river was green and churning on this chilly October day. Dino remembered that Roberto had fallen in right here, in front of the National Library. He also realized that he still hadn't tried to find his uncle.

Dino put his hand on Penny's arm. "I know I want to forget about that book, but remember when Lucy and George were standing by the Arno and George says he feels like something tremendous has happened? He wasn't referring to the murder that just took place, but what was happening inside himself. Penny, that's how I've been feeling ever since I got here. That something tremendous is happening to me, too. I don't know what it is, but something is."

Penny stared into the roiling river. "I guess I've been thinking the same thing ever since I got here, too. I'm not sure, though."

They walked east, avoiding bicyclists next to the river, and stopped before the monument to the Battle of Mentana.

"Every time I see this," Penny said, "I don't know what to think. The soldier looks so fierce, his rifle outstretched like that, and yet there's always pigeon poop on his head."

"Another monument to war," Dino said. "Actually, this one remembers Garibaldi's fight to unify the country."

"I'm going to have to study my Italian history more," Penny said.

They walked to the Ponte Vecchio and admired all the rings and bracelets and necklaces in the shop windows. But, as usual, the bridge was crowded with students, some of them playing guitars and singing, with beer bottles at their sides. A sweet odor pervaded the area.

"What's that smell?" Dino asked.

Penny laughed. "You don't know that? It's pot, silly."

Again, Dino felt like a boy from a village. "I'll walk you home," he said.

But Dino wasn't ready to go to his basement room just yet. This would be the day he was waiting for. He walked briskly up Via Verdi and around Piazza G. Salvemini, then faster up Via Fiesolana, left on Via degli Alfani and, finally running, north on Via Ricasoli. There was only a half hour left before the Accademia gallery would close, and all the tourists had left.

His heart beating wildly, Dino purchased a ticket and entered. After a couple of turns, he could see Michelangelo's David towering in the far gallery. It was colossal, taller and more powerful than he had ever imagined. He would come back soon and just stand in front of it.

Now, what he really wanted to see was at the left of the entrance.

Not much was known about The Waking Slave. Michelangelo was commissioned to design a tomb for Pope Julius II in Saint Peter's in Rome. But after Julius died in 1513, the contract was changed, and what was to have been a monument with some forty figures was greatly reduced. Michelangelo finished the giant figure of Moses for the tomb, but left other figures unfinished. Four were brought to the Accademia.

Dino remembered what Michelangelo had written about the statues. He would outline the figure on the front of the marble block and then work from this side. Only the torso had emerged from this block, and Dino could see chisel marks.

Dino stood alone before the statue until a guard told him he had to leave. He knew he wasn't old enough or experienced enough to find great meaning in what Michelangelo was trying to do, but he did remember what the master had written: "Liberating the figure imprisoned in the marble," he wrote.

That was it. A slave, or any person, becoming alive.

Chapter Twelve

November 1964

Adolfo and Mila told Dino to be prepared. The first week of November always brought rain. Heavy rain, constant rain, and biting cold.

"We call it "*la pioggia di novembre*," Mila said. "Florentines just live with it. You'll get used to it, too."

The rains started November 4, and Dino wore his birthday sweater both day and night. When he went out, he put on the yellow raincoat and hoped no one would see him. Like everyone else, he carried an umbrella. Fortunately, he was tall and so didn't have to do the umbrella dance with other pedestrians.

At night, he got used to the incessant pounding of rain on the sidewalk outside his window. The slow stream of water in a corner worried him, and he stuffed newspapers and rags into the hole before opening his notebooks for more hours of reading, writing and memorizing.

On days when he didn't walk to school with Penny, Dino took to taking a different route so that he could experience the wonders of Florence, even in pouring rain. One day he walked down Borgo dei Greci to the Piazza della Signoria, feeling dwarfed by the Palazzo Vecchio and stunned by the copy of the David. His guidebook pointed out the marker where Savonarola was burned to death, so he followed some tourists and stepped on it.

"I'm in Florence!"

Another day he went up to Via dell'Oniuolo to walk around the Duomo and, holding his umbrella close, to examine Ghiberti's doors on the Baptistry. He'd never imagined the panels would be so intricate and beautiful. He especially liked the Esau and Jacob.

"I'm in Florence!"

On another, he took a side trip to discover the tombs Michelangelo had created for the Medici in San Lorenzo.

"I'm in Florence!"

Even at 8 o'clock in the morning and despite the rain, the streets were crowded with people going to work, gawking tourists, cars and trucks and buses. And dogs. Dogs everywhere. One little white one, with a black spot over one eye, was owned by the elderly woman next door and befriended Dino immediately as he left his building and walked through the piazza.

"Primo won't hurt you," Signora Alonzo said, pulling his leash so that the dog got off Dino's legs. "He's just being friendly."

"Hi, Primo!" Dino patted his head. Some day, he thought, maybe he'd get a dog. Then he'd have someone to talk to.

So much to see. He could never see it all in a lifetime. This made his university life bearable. Maybe he would never leave Florence, but he still felt pulled in another direction when he returned home and Mila told him there was another phone call from his mother.

"Yes, Mama, I like Florence very much. Yes, Mama, I miss Sant'Antonio."

After studying his notes again at night, he rewarded himself by picking up his guitar. He found that he had not only a natural talent, but also an ear for music. He could hear a song and play it on his guitar note for note.

"Maybe my ears are good for something," he thought.

He was now being influenced by a young singer named Gianni Morandi, who had a hit recording in "*in ginocchio da te*," which Dino played over and over.

Io voglio per me le tue carezze
si' io t'amo piu' della mia vita.
Ritornero'
in ginocchio da te

l'altra non e'
non e' niente per me.
Ora lo so
ho sbagliato con te
ritornero' in ginocchio da te

I want your caresses for me
yes, I love you more than my own life.
I will come back
go on my knees to you
anything else
is nothing to me.
Now I know
I made a mistake by betraying you
I will come back, go on my knees to you

Dino's version started:

Girl of my dreams
When will you come
Home to me once more?
I am waiting at the shore
Waiting waiting

Dino knew he had to spend a lot more time on this.

When he arrived at the university one day early in December, he saw throngs of students headed for the lounge, where the only television set perched on a small table at the end of the room. Dozens of students, along with a few faculty members, crowded on the floor, crammed into the couches and stood along the walls. The television set showed only fuzzy images.

"What's going on?" Dino asked the nearest student.

"They're showing some clips from California. A university, Berkeley or something. The students were having a protest, something about not being able to distribute literature at some tables."

"Why would they want to?"

"It was something about freedom of speech or something like that. Couldn't tell."

"What's freedom of speech?"

"I guess it's when people can say what they want anywhere they want to."

This was a new concept for Dino, and he didn't understand what this was all about. He had always imagined a university as a place where there was serious and thoughtful studying and learning, not a place for demonstrations by students. It soon became clear that some of the students in the room shared his opinion, but some did not.

"If they're students, why aren't they in their classrooms studying?" a boy on one side of the room yelled.

"If they're students, they should be questioning," a boy on the other side called out. "They should be questioning everything. That's what being a student means!"

"Question what?" the first boy said. "The fact that Michelangelo painted the Sistine Chapel?"

"Not that kind of stuff. But maybe if students in Italy questioned what the government was doing sometime, maybe we'd have a better government."

"Yeah," the student sitting next to him said. "Maybe we could get forms filled out in a week instead of three months!"

Dino had to agree with that. He watched the scenes of thousands of students converging around a police car and speaker after speaker standing on top of it. A guy with curly hair spoke the longest, but the translation from English was sketchy.

"You know who that is?" someone on the right side of the room asked. "That's Mario Savio. He's the leader of the demonstration."

"Savio? He's Italian?"

"His father is from Sicily, I think."

"Well, sure, from Sicily," another boy said. "What do you expect? They're all anarchists." Dino recognized him as the boy who had talked to Penny.

"Shut the fuck up, Raffaele!" a boy on the other side shouted. "You think anybody who has a brain is an anarchist."

"Don't tell me to shut up, you bloody Communist!" Raffaele started to lunge at him, but two other boys held him back.

Just as things were going to get ugly, the television screen showed students marching into a campus building, singing.

"I know that song," a girl said. "It's Martin Luther King's song. 'We Shall Overcome.'"

Some students started singing along in Italian.

"King is a Communist, too," Raffaele shouted.

That did it.

"And you're a bloody Fascist!"

Suddenly, the boys on the left got up and trammeled over cowering students to reach the boys on the right. One hit was thrown, then another and another and pretty soon a dozen students were punching each other.

Dino couldn't believe this and ran out into the courtyard. Moments later, Penny joined him.

"Are you all right, Dino?"

"Sure. I've just never seen people fight like that."

"I guess they're a bunch of hotheads."

"But over something that's happening in California?"

"Maybe they think it could happen in Italy."

At midmorning, the courtyard was cool and secluded. Except for a couple of cleaning ladies sweeping leaves, everyone else was watching television. Dino and Penny sat in silence for a long time. Occasionally, there was shouting inside the building and they knew the fighting had not stopped.

At one point, a dozen students chased another group right through the courtyard, screaming at each other. Four or five professors, waving books and rulers, emerged from the faculty lounge and chased the students. "Stop! Stop!" Dino and Penny recognized Professor Guidotti and Professor Mariotti having difficulty keeping up with the rest. Then the *carabinieri*, apparently called by the university administration, arrived and quickly cleared the area.

"I guess that's the end of the protest at the Accademia di Belle Arti," Dino said.

As they walked home after classes that day, Penny had a question. "Dino, I didn't know people still called each other Communists and Fascists here anymore. I mean, I know what happened during the war, that the partisans were mostly Communists and they fought the Germans and the Fascists, but I thought that was all over."

Dino had to remember what he learned in school, especially when Ezio had been his teacher.

"I guess it's never over. There are still people who think one way or another. There are still people who hate each other, I guess."

"That's terrible."

"I know."

No one in Sant'Antonio ever talked about being Communist or Fascist. Dino thought Ezio was probably a Communist, and since his Papa had fought with Ezio in a *banda* during the war, he must be a Communist, too.

Dino remembered the night when Ezio and Paolo might have had a little too much beer and grappa and Paolo said, "Hey, Ezio, how about we establish a Casa del Popolo in Sant'Antonio?"

"In Sant'Antonio," Ezio had replied. "A Communist meeting place here?"

"Sure. You could be the president and the vice president and the secretary and I could be the treasurer."

"Yeah, we'd have a lot of cash with just you and me as members."

The idea was so outrageous they stopped right there.

"Penny," Dino said, "you know that curly haired boy you were with before? He must be on the Fascist side. Is he...is he your boyfriend?"

"Raffaele? Don't be silly. I just talk to him sometime. We have two classes together. He's an interesting guy, and you know me, I'm here for the adventure."

What kind of answer is that? Dino thought.

That night, Dino stopped studying to stare at the ceiling. He was confused. Michelangelo and Ghiberti. Tourists and dogs. Communists and Fascists. All in Florence.

Chapter Thirteen

December 1964

Just before Christmas, Dino knew something was wrong as soon as he opened the apartment door because the television set was off. It had taken months of persuasion, but Mila had finally convinced Adolfo that they should buy a television set. They needed some joy in their lives, and this would be an early Christmas present for them.

When they came home from work, they made themselves a little dinner and sat with plates in their laps watching Perry Mason or the Italian variety shows or the news programs. For the first time in a long time, Adolfo showed signs of interest in what was going on in the world, and Mila smiled.

But tonight, the set was off and Mila was drying the dinner dishes.

"Bad news, Dino," Mila said. "Paolo called. Your grandmother died this morning."

Since Gina had been sick for so long and since he didn't really know his grandmother very well, Dino was neither surprised nor very upset.

"Oh, I'm sorry. How's Mama?"

"Paolo said she's doing okay. He said your grandmother just faded away. Your mother was with her. She called the priest and he came to give her the last rites, but it was too late so he just said some prayers."

"And Adolfo?"

"You know Adolfo. He keeps everything to himself. But I guess he feels bad, especially since he didn't go to see his mother when Lucia asked him to. He went to lie down and he hasn't gotten up yet."

"And the funeral?"

"Thursday. The day after tomorrow. We can take the 1 o'clock bus tomorrow to Sant'Antonio."

Dino said that he would have to miss two days of classes before the Christmas break, but that they were mostly review, and he could get Penny to take notes.

"Dino," Mila said. "There's something else."

Dino knew what she was going to say.

"When Paolo called, he said your mother would really like Roberto to come to the funeral. She said your grandmother would have wanted that more than anything. She hadn't seen him since, well, since…Have you ever tried to find him, Dino?"

"I've been so busy."

"I know, I know. But tomorrow morning, before we leave, do you think you could go over to Santo Spirito and look?"

Dino had no choice, though he knew it would probably be a fruitless search. After a breakfast of warm bread and coffee, he put on his yellow slicker and picked up his big black umbrella from the holder near the door. As usual, it was raining, but this time it was the cold drizzle that Florence endures in the middle of December.

He stopped at Penny's building and told her he would be gone until after Christmas. Penny herself was flying back to Liverpool in two days for a short holiday with her parents. She told Dino she was sorry about his grandmother and kissed him on the cheek.

Smiling and warmed by the kiss, Dino made his way to the Arno, murky and higher now with all the rain, then to the Ponte Vecchio and then over into the Oltrarno. Although he had been here for almost three months, he had been on this "other" side of Florence only once, when his class on the Medici toured the Pitti Palace to see the family's rich collections. But the students had just gone to the museum and then returned to their classroom.

Now, walking down Borgo San Jacopo, Dino thought he might be in a different city. The shops were closer together, the streets narrower. Two people could barely fit on a sidewalk, and he kept bumping into umbrellas. He turned onto Via Presto di San Martino and past one artisan shop after another, leather, furniture, plaster, ceramics. Then, another turn and he was in the Piazza Santo Spirito. He knew he should stop into the church designed by Brunelleschi, but there was no time. Three men, unshaven and in tattered clothes, huddled under an awning. A woman clutching a shawl over her head and holding a little girl on her breast approached Dino and asked for money. When he said he didn't have any, she glared at him and walked away.

The only thing Dino knew about Roberto's whereabouts was that he owned a woodworking shop on the square. He saw it on the left side. "Maffini." It still bore Antonio's name, even though he had sold it to Roberto years ago. The place looked even more forlorn in the rain. The door wasn't quite closed, but Dino couldn't budge it. He knocked and then pounded. No answer. Next to it, the window was dirty and cracked. When he peered into the dark room, Dino could see only a few tools buried in thick dust on the floor and boards propped against the wall. He could barely make out a door at the back, leading to what must be Roberto's room.

Dino went to the *bar* on the corner, where its only customer was a bearded man at a table in the corner reading *La Gazzetta della Sport.* The owner was also reading a newspaper behind the counter and did not want to be interrupted.

"Permesso?" Dino said, his voice cracking a bit. "Do you have a moment?"

The owner, a leathered old man with a drooping mustache, looked up but did not respond.

"I'm sorry to interrupt," Dino said. "Do you know anything about the shop three doors down, the woodworking shop?"

"The woodworking shop? No, nothing." He went back to his newspaper.

"Do you know if it's still open?"

The man didn't look up. "Hasn't been open for a long time."

"Excuse me again. Do you know anything about the man who owns it? His name is Roberto, Roberto Sporenza. He's my uncle."

The man lowered his newspaper and took off his glasses.

"Your uncle." His voice was kinder now. "Well, then, I'm sorry."

"Sorry?"

"Maybe you shouldn't be looking for him."

"I have to," Dino said. "His mother just died. We want him to come to the funeral."

"Well," the man said. "Last time I saw him, a couple of months ago, your uncle wasn't in shape to go to a funeral. Wasn't in shape to go anywhere."

Roberto, the man said, had suddenly stopped working a few years ago. Didn't take any new orders, didn't complete what work he had. He started drinking a lot and often lay sprawled on a bench in the piazza on sunny days. Children used to point at him and laugh.

"I'm sorry," the man said. "But I think it would be best for you and your family if you didn't find him."

"Thanks for the advice," Dino said. "But if you happen to see him, would you tell him that the funeral is tomorrow in Sant'Antonio? That's a village west of Lucca. That's where he's from. He'll know where it is."

Dino had crossed the piazza and was back on Via Presto di San Martino so he didn't see the bearded customer leave the *bar*, go down the street and pound on the door of the woodworking shop.

Carrying their bags, Dino, Adolfo and Mila barely got to the Florence bus station on time. The bus was crowded, and Dino had to stand, holding on to his guitar as the bus careened around curves on the way to Sant'Antonio. Rain poured in two broken windows.

When the bus stopped in front of Leoni's *bottega* in Sant'Antonio, they were aware that everyone knew of Gina Sporenza's death. The traditional death poster, *annuncio mortuario,* was tacked up at Leoni's and at Manconi's butcher shop next door, as well as on the half dozen telephone poles in the village.

In Memory
Gina Sporenza
Born 11 September 1905
Died in the early hours of today 19 December 1964
Sadly missed by daughter Lucia Sporenza,
son-in-law Paolo Ricci, sons Adolfo and Roberto,
daughter Sister Santa Anna della Croce,
grandson Dino Sporenza.
Mass 10 o'clock 21 December 1964
Church of Sant'Antonio

How strange, Dino thought, to see his name in print on a poster. At first he didn't know who Sister Anna della Croce was, and then remembered she was Adolfo and Roberto's younger sister, Anna, who had long been living in a cloistered convent north of Florence.

A black wreath hung on the door of Lucia and Paolo's house. Inside, neighbors, mostly women and old men, filled the living room, talking and helping themselves to trays of sliced meat and cheeses. Dino, Adolfo and Mila found Lucia and Paolo in the kitchen, washing dishes.

"Oh, my boy, my boy, my Dino!" Lucia smothered her son with her tears and kisses. Paolo hugged him and shook his hands as Lucia turned to her brother. "Adolfo! Adolfo!" More tears.

"*Ciao,* Lucia," Adolfo said, kissing her but averting his eyes. Lucia held his hands for a long time.

"You came alone? Just you three?"

"Yes," Mila said.

"Well," she said, "you can go upstairs. There are others there now."

The shutters were closed in Gina's room on this gray day and a dozen red votive lights cast dancing shadows on the walls. Annabella and Fausta were on one side of the bed, Rosa and Antonio on the other. Antonio's arm was around Rosa's shoulder. The women were reciting the rosary softly.

On the bed, Gina lay in a plain pine casket. Lucia had dressed her in the white peasant blouse and long red skirt she had worn years ago. Her hair had never turned gray, and Lucia had curled the golden locks as best she could and put extra rouge on her cheeks, just as she always liked. Her hands were folded across her chest, entwined in a rosary given by Rosa. Dino thought the coins on her eyes made her look like an owl he had seen in a Florence shop.

Adolfo put his hand on Gina's shoulder and began to sob. Mila held his arm and they stood beside the bed for a long time, then stepped back and sat next to Rosa. When Dino looked at his grandmother, he couldn't help but think of what Penny had said about Michelangelo's ashes in his tomb at Santa Croce. He hadn't seen many dead people. His grandfather, Pietro. Maria, who had lived next door. Rosa's husband Marco.

Dino didn't want to think about death and stood in a corner. After the rosary, there were the customary remembrances. Rosa said she loved to watch Gina and Pietro walk hand in hand down the street before they were married, and even afterwards.

"They were such lovebirds," she said.

Annabella remembered how lonely Gina was when Pietro went off to war and then, when he returned, how she cared for his devastated body and mind for so many years.

"She never complained," Annabella said. "She loved him so much."

Fausta said she was sorry she criticized Gina for not silencing her children when they were all at the farmhouse during the war.

"I never had children," she said, "so I didn't know anything about it."

When Dino went back down to the living room, everyone had the same comment: "Dino, you've grown so much!" This, even though many of them had seen him a few months ago.

"Dino, we miss you here," one elderly woman said. "Why don't you come back more often?"

"Dino," another said, "why did you have to go so far away?"

"Dino," said a third, "young people should stay in their village. You're coming back soon, *va bene?*"

Dino smiled and sat in the only vacant chair, between his mother and a woman who turned out to be Gina's distant cousin from Gallicano. Although she had not seen Gina for forty years, she wiped her eyes incessantly.

"She had such a wonderful family," the woman said.

"Yes," Lucia said, holding Dino's hand. "So many children. Besides me, Roberto, Adolfo, Sister Anna and little Carlotta."

"Carlotta?" the woman said. "I don't remember her."

"She died in the war. At the farmhouse. She was only three months old."

"Oh my." The woman wiped away more tears. "And I'd forgotten all about Sister Anna until I saw her name on the *annuncio mortuario.* I haven't seen her here."

"She couldn't come," Lucia said. "She's in a very cloistered convent."

"She couldn't even come for her mother's funeral? *Santa Maria!*"

"She joined the nuns when she was just fourteen," Lucia said, "and we haven't seen her since. We went to the ceremony where she took her vows, but she was behind a screen and we couldn't tell which one she was in those black dresses. She's in one of those places where they don't go out, just pray all the time."

"I know a place like that," the woman said. "They pray and they make honey and they sell that."

"I think they make communion wafers where Sister Anna is."

The woman wiped her eyes again. "Adolfo seems so sad to me. I hope he's happy. But what about your other brother, Roberto? I haven't seen him here either."

Lucia looked toward the door. "He's very busy in Florence. He has a woodworking shop and you know, at this time of year..."

"He didn't come for his mother's funeral either? *Santa Maria!*"

"Excuse me, I see some people I need to talk to." Lucia abruptly left the room, leaving Dino to answer unanswerable questions from Gina's distant cousin.

The next morning, Dino, Adolfo and Mila sat silently as Lucia fried eggs and Paolo set the table.

"Adolfo," Lucia said, "I know you don't want to talk about this, but, please, when you get back, can you see if you can find Roberto and talk to him? Please do it for Mama's sake. Please?"

Adolfo waited. "Lucia, I've thought about this and thought about this. Right now, I just can't."

"Maybe someday?"

"Maybe someday. I don't know."

While the others were cleaning up, Dino left the house and went down a familiar path. The little chapel dedicated to Saint Zita hadn't become any smaller because it always was tiny. And Dino was surprised to find that he still felt the same way as he sat on the wooden bench, at peace. He closed his eyes. Florence seemed a long way away.

Men from the funeral service had arrived when Dino returned home, and the lid on Gina's coffin was nailed shut. With the help of Paolo and Ezio, who had arrived with Donna, it was carried down to the living room. A spray of flowers from Fausta's garden lay on top as Antonio, Ezio, Paolo and Adolfo shouldered the coffin and lifted it down the steps and onto the street.

A few dozen people had already gathered outside, all of the women dressed in black, the few men in their suits. Lucia and Dino and Mila came first, then Rosa and Annabella and Fausta and Donna. Praying the rosary, they followed the coffin down the narrow street and on to the church, passing the cemetery with its newly dug grave next to Pietro's. Father Sangretto blessed the coffin before it was placed in front of the altar.

Dino went into the sacristy and pulled on the black cassock and surplice he had worn only a few years ago. Now they were even shorter on him. In a telephone call the day before, Lucia asked the priest if Dino could serve at the Mass. He agreed, but said little to the boy when he arrived. "What a waste," he muttered under his breath.

Father Sangretto's sermon was, predictably, short. It was basically one he could have, and had, given for anyone in the village. He said Gina was now with her husband, Pietro, and daughter, Carlotta, and that if we obeyed God's laws we would all be with her in Heaven. Looking at Lucia and Paolo, he said it was very important that people attended Mass because they never knew when they would be called by God, too.

At the end of the Mass, as Dino held the incense burner, Father Sangretto came down from the altar and gave the final blessing over the coffin. With the priest occupied with his prayers, and everyone else facing the altar, only Dino saw the shabbily dressed man swaying against the wall in the rear of church, his hat pulled down over his face. When the priest had finished, the man disappeared.

Chapter Fourteen

December 1964-January 1965

Adolfo and Mila took the bus back to Florence right after the Mass, not even staying for the lunch in the church basement. "I don't want to answer any questions," Adolfo said.

Because of Gina's long illness, the lunch was not entirely sorrowful and it gave the villagers another opportunity to express their condolences to Lucia, Paolo and Dino. Again, the frequent question was: "Where was Roberto?" Lucia mumbled an answer and changed the subject.

At home afterwards, Dino cornered his mother in the kitchen.

"I think Roberto may have been at the Mass."

"What?" She dropped a dish into the soapy sink.

"When I was standing at the end, facing the entrance, there was this man leaning against the back wall. He had his hat pulled down so I didn't see his face, but it may have been Roberto."

"Are you sure?"

"No. I haven't seen Roberto since the last time he came home when I was about ten, I think. But it could have been him."

"What did this man do?"

"He was just there. I guess he looked kind of nervous. He was swaying back and forth. When I looked up again he was gone."

"Why didn't you stop him, Dino? Why didn't you stop him?" Lucia was frantic.

"How could I stop him? I was holding the incense next to Father Sangretto. And anyway, he was gone."

Lucia picked up another dish, then looked up. "Did you tell this to Adolfo?"

"No."

"Good. Dino, when you get back to Florence, look real hard for Roberto, all right?"

"Yes, Mama."

With the funeral wreath still on the door, Christmas was a subdued affair at Lucia and Paolo's house. Dino put the *presepio* on the mantel, arranging the little figures of Mary, Joseph, the Christ Child, the shepherds and the wise men just has he had every Christmas for as long as he remembered. That was the only decoration in the house.

He spent a lot of time in his old room that had suddenly grown smaller like the rest of the house. Maybe he should have brought some books home to study, he thought. Instead, he reread Ezio's memoir of serving as a partisan during the war, *A Time to Remember.* He found the most interesting parts were about his father and Paolo in Ezio's *banda,* and tried to imagine his father and stepfather as young men looking for adventure. He wondered what crazy things they did. Then, twenty years after the war, Dino tried to imagine himself as a partisan, fighting and sabotaging the Germans. He could not.

Sometimes, he went for walks around the village, but he didn't like to tell the elderly women who stopped him why he left Sant'Antonio. He had been away less than three months but Sant'Antonio looked so different. Leoni's and Manconi's had always seemed such wonderful places to visit. Now they were just little shops. Even the houses seemed smaller, especially his own. He didn't know why these things were so different.

One morning he walked up the hill to the Cielo and sat for a while next to his father's grave. He brought his guitar along and pretended he was playing for his father. Then Ezio came out and they both sat there for a long time.

"You know, Dino," Ezio said, "I still miss your father."

"I wish I had known him."

"You would have liked him a lot. And he would have liked you. And he would have liked those songs. He loved music. He was a great guy, your father." Ezio looked into the distance.

Early each morning, Dino went to the Saint Zita chapel. Frost thickened the grass under his feet, and one morning he woke to find a thin blanket of snow covering everything. He couldn't remember the last time it snowed.

At night, he stared out the window at the starlit sky. So much had happened since he looked at those stars in October. Florence, the Accademia, Penny, the search for Roberto. Sometimes he felt guilty that he had never written to Francesca. He had started a letter a couple of times but gave up, excusing himself by thinking that he didn't know how to write letters. He also justified it by the fact that Francesca hadn't written to him.

Undoubtedly, the highlight of the Christmas season was the dinner at Rosa's on Christmas eve. Forsaking her usual ravioli, Rosa had made a huge pot of the traditional *baccalà*. Not only was this the custom in Italy, it wouldn't have been Christmas without *baccalà* at Rosa's. The planks of cod had already soaked for twenty-four hours, and Rosa added olives and plum tomatoes. With crusty bread, this was more than enough for those who had gathered around her table, Lucia, Paolo, Dino, Ezio, Donna, Antonio, Annabella and Fausta.

Rosa and Antonio went around pouring red wine into her Christmas glasses and, despite Gina's death, it was mostly a merry occasion. Everyone wondered why Rosa wore her best blue dress, the one she wore only for weddings and funerals, and why Antonio had his best, well, only, suit on. Both were flushed and a little giddy.

"Rosa," Annabella wanted to know, "have you and Antonio been drinking some of this wine all day?"

"Wine?" Rosa blushed even more. "No, no, of course not."

"What's going on, Papa?" Ezio asked. "Something's going on."

Rosa and Antonio looked at each other and Antonio put his arms around her.

"Well...," Rosa said. "No, you tell them."

"Me? No, you." Antonio said.

Rosa cleared her throat. "Well, all right. Antonio has asked me to marry him, and I've said yes."

The room erupted with cheers. All of the women gathered around Rosa, kissing and hugging her. Ezio embraced his father and kissed him on both cheeks, which were wet with tears. Even Dino kissed Rosa and shook Antonio's hand.

"Oh, my," Annabella said.

"Oh, my," Fausta said.

"Oh," Lucia said, "I wish Mama would have been here to see this. She'd be so happy."

"I'm sure she's watching us right now," Paolo said.

Rosa was beaming. "Well, it's not every day that a seventy-five-year-old woman gets an offer to marry a handsome man, and I'm glad I took it."

"And," Antonio said, "it's not every day that a seventy-nine-year old man has a chance to marry a beautiful woman."

There was talk then of Rosa's late husband, Marco, and of Antonio's wife, Marita, who died shortly after the war.

"Marco and I had a wonderful, wonderful marriage and I will thank him every day for making my life so happy," Rosa said. "For so long, I had thought I was never going to get married, and then this kind and generous man came into my life. And you know what? Marco was so much fun. He liked to tell me jokes. He took me dancing! Imagine! Me, dancing!" She paused to dab her eyes with a handkerchief. "Marco loved me so much, he was my rock during the war. I was so frightened at the Cielo. Oh, my. And then, well, you all know what happened after that. He just seemed to fade away, he..."

Antonio put his arm around her and stroked her hair. "There, there."

And then it was his turn to pay tribute to his late wife. "Marita was such a lovely woman, I don't know why she ever chose me. I'm just an ignorant carpenter, and she was so refined. She took me to the museums and the churches and she pointed out all these things I had never noticed. And then when we had Ezio here, well, all she could think about was bringing him up to be a good boy. And he did turn out that way."

"With your help, Papa," Ezio interrupted.

"And then when I left her to go with the other partisans, Marita was so brave. But the war killed her, the war killed her. She just faded away, too."

It was the longest speech Antonio had ever given in his life. Rosa kissed him on the cheek.

Donna hugged Rosa and Ezio hugged his father. Everyone agreed that Marco and Marita would approve of this union.

Toasts were made with wine and grappa, the happy couple was teased, and everyone wanted to know when the marriage would take place.

"He just asked me today," Rosa said. "There's no hurry. Anyway, I have to get a new dress."

"Well, of course!" everyone shouted at once.

"But you should know," Rosa said, "that we're not going to wait until a wedding ceremony to be happy. Antonio is moving in here tomorrow."

"Rosa!"

"What? Are you shocked?" Rosa asked. "It's almost 1965, people do this all the time!"

"Not in Sant'Antonio!" Fausta said. She was indeed shocked.

"Do it!" Ezio and Paolo said together.

"You might as well move in, Antonio," Donna told her father-in-law. "You've been staying overnight three or four nights a week anyway."

This was news to most of the villagers, and Rosa and Antonio looked like teenagers who had been caught in a hayloft.

"Look," Rosa said, "We want to have every minute of every day together, starting right now."

No one could argue with that. It was agreed that Ezio, Paolo and Dino would move Antonio's belongings to Rosa's on Christmas day.

"Right after Mass," Rosa said, "but we won't tell Father Sangretto."

Everyone went to Mass on Christmas day, and the church was crowded. Pointedly, Father Sangretto said he wished attendance was this big every Sunday.

Two days after Christmas, with the funeral wreath finally down and Antonio moved in with Rosa, Dino took the bus to Lucca. Now taking an architectural class, he looked at the massive churches differently, and with more appreciation. The church of San Michele did not remind him of a wedding cake anymore, and when he went inside to see the Madonna and Child by Della Robbia he compared it to the similar version in Santa Croce.

He walked past the Church of San Paolino and then south on Via Burlamacchi. Perhaps it was because the day was overcast, but to Dino, Lucca's blue-and-white lights looked faded and the candy boxes in the shop windows seemed old and dusty. Even the venders selling roasted chestnuts looked tired.

When he came to the old Roman amphitheater, he thought briefly that he might walk up Via Veneto and Via Fillungo and see if there was any activity, like maybe an orange-and-white cat, around a green door. But he thought better of it. He wouldn't know what he would say or do if he saw Francesca.

Instead, he tried to see if anyone was in the *liceo artistico*. Surprisingly, the old palazzo seemed smaller now. On the second floor, he found the student art show still in place. He didn't think any of it was very good, and he was fingering a bust of a young woman when Professor Ponzo swept into the room.

"Dino? Dino Sporenza? Oh my God, is it you?"

Now that he was no longer at the high school, she could reach up and embrace her former student. Then she asked so many questions about Florence, the Accademia, his teachers, his classes, and his paintings that he barely had time to answer one before she was on to another.

"Oh, Professor," Dino said, "the Accademia is so much harder that the *liceo artistico*. I'm going to fail, I know it."

Professor Ponzo held his arms tightly. "Dino, don't talk like that. You've only been there a few months. It takes time to get used to the system. You'll be fine, I know you will. Oh, Dino, we miss you here. This year's students...well, you see what they do."

"Well, they're young..."

"No excuse. They are as old as you were when you were here."

Although no one else was in the room, Professor Ponzo lowered her voice. "Dino, do you ever see Francesca? I do wish she had continued on with her painting, but I suppose she had to find employment. She's working in the stationary shop on Via Sant'Andrea, you know. I stop in there every once in a while. And I've seen her in the pizzeria near the amphitheater. Her friend looks like a nice boy, I don't know who he is, but he didn't go on to university either. But then many young people nowadays have to find..."

Dino didn't hear what else Professor Ponzo had to say. He suddenly wanted to go home, and so he took an early bus back to Sant'Antonio.

On the morning he was to return to Florence, Lucia got up extra early to pack a lunch. Ham sandwiches, apples, pears, biscotti, which she put in a brown paper bag.

"Mama, this is enough for three days," Dino said as he finished his breakfast of eggs and bread and milk.

"Well, then, you can eat it over three days." Lucia was already in tears.

Paolo sat across the table, and it was clear that he had something to say.

"Dino," he said finally, "I want to talk to you about something. You know, things haven't been going so well at the *pasticceria*. It's always slow in the shop in winter, but this year, it's been so cold, people don't want to come in and buy the pastries."

Dino feared that Paolo was going to ask him to drop out of the university.

"So I have to tell you something. You know that money we send you every two weeks so you can pay your rent and buy other things? Well, I'm afraid we're going to have to cut back. Way back. We'll send what we can, but I don't know how much. We'll have to go week by week. I'm sorry."

"Oh, Dino," Lucia said, putting her hands on his shoulders. "I'm sorry, too." She leaned down and kissed his hair.

Dino suddenly did some math in his head. He had to pay for his room and his lunch every day and there were always things to buy for his classes, textbooks, notebooks, paint, brushes, paper. And he liked to treat himself to a movie every two weeks. He figured he had enough in the little wooden box under his bed to last two or three weeks. He would need thousands of *lire* every week if he was going to stay in Florence.

"Um," was all he could say.

"We were thinking," Paolo said. "Maybe you could get a little job?"

"I guess," he said. "What do you think I could do?"

"Maybe Adolfo could find something at the library?" Lucia said. "But not if you didn't have time for your studies."

"Adolfo told me once," Dino said, "that the library doesn't allow students to work there."

"Then maybe Mila knows of something at Casa del Popolo?"

"She always says how they can't afford workers but they need a lot of volunteers."

"Or a shop? How about a shop?" Paolo said. "Or maybe a pizzeria or a trattoria? Don't you have friends who work in those places?"

Dino said one of Penny's friends worked in a trattoria. It was that Fascist he didn't like. He didn't want to work with him.

"It's all right," he said. "I'll be fine. I'll get a job. Somewhere. Don't worry about me."

"Oh, Dino," Lucia said. "We're so sorry."

Dino kissed his mother. "Mama, I'll be fine, really. Lots of students work. I can, too."

But on the bus to Florence, he still didn't know where that would be or how he could still find time to study.

Chapter Fifteen

Spring 1965

The first job Dino found was as a temporary replacement for a janitor at Santa Croce. As the man mopped the floor of the church one day, he tripped on the tomb of a medieval knight and broke his foot. He would be out for six weeks.

Except for helping out in Paolo's *pasticceria,* Dino had never held a job before, but this was simple work. Three nights a week, after he had spent a couple of hours studying, Dino swept the floors, mopped and dusted. He liked being in the cavernous, vaulted church after all the tourists had gone. But he hadn't counted on all the distractions and kept hearing from a supervisor who told him to work faster.

Mopping from left to right near the high altar, he examined Donatello's wooden crucifix in the Bardi di Verni Chapel, then Daddi's frescoes in the Palci Becaldi Chapel, Gaddi's enormous Legend of the True Cross in the main chapel and Giotti's frescoes of Saint Francis in the Bardi Chapel. His pail needed refilling four or five times, and his head was swimming.

Dino especially liked to linger at Michelangelo's tomb, examining each figure above the monument in silent wonder. He still could not believe that he was in front of the master's crypt, no matter that it just contained ashes. After he lingered too long one day, the supervisor began yelling: "Move on or quit." Dino asked for another location, the Medici Chapel, but then he lingered too long before the Della Robbia.

He was transferred again. This time it was to the Museum. That was dangerous because Dino could have spent all night exploring Gaddi's huge Last Supper and the Tree of Life fresco above it. There were so many characters, it seemed like everyone in Heaven was there. But if he stayed too long he wouldn't have time to stand before Cimabue's Crucifixion. Gazing at the tortured face of the Christ, he knew now what Professor Guidotti had said about the painting being such an influence on Giotto and Duccio. It seemed that every time Dino lingered before the Crucifixion, his supervisor would arrive and tell him to speed things up.

Besides all the famous works of art, though, Dino was equally impressed by the sight of a young priest who walked through the church several nights a week, sometimes with a guitar on his back. Each time, he stopped to talk to each of the janitors and seemed to know them all. Dino had never seen such a friendly priest, and he almost dropped his broom when he saw the priest put his arm around a young cleaning woman who was crying. A priest who laughed out loud in church? And who put his arm around a woman?

The priest was tall and slim and what Dino noticed first about him were his brilliant blue eyes. Sometimes, the priest wore an ordinary shirt and jeans instead of his brown Franciscan robes, and Dino wouldn't have recognized him except for his tonsured head and sandaled feet. Dino tried to avoid the man, but one night as he was carrying his mop and pail to the storage room, he ran into the priest, literally.

"Whoa!" the priest said.

"Oh, sorry, Father."

"That's all right. My shoes needed some cleaning, anyway." The priest was grinning. "You're new here, aren't you?"

Dino acknowledged that he was a temporary replacement for Signor Costa.

"Ah, yes," the priest said. "Poor Signor Costa. Got to watch out for those medieval knights. They'll get you every time, even if they're dead. Sorry, I'm Father Lorenzo. And you are?" He stuck out a ruddy hand.

"Dino, Dino Sporenza. I'm a student at the Accademia. Just trying to make some money here."

"Well, you're not making much, I'm sure."

Dino had to agree. He was getting 500 *lire* an hour.

Father Lorenzo went on to ask Dino about his classes, where he was from and how he liked Florence. He said he ran a *cucina popolare* near the church and Dino should stop in if he ever ran out of money.

"My aunt works at Casa del Popolo," Dino said. "She said there was a priest who ran a soup kitchen. That must be you."

"Yup. We give them food for the body and sometimes the soul. They give them everything else."

Dino noticed the long fingernails on the priest's right hand, just like his own. "Father, I've seen you with a guitar. Do you play?"

"Well, I try. I try to get the folks who come to the soup kitchen to sing with me after they eat. But I have a such terrible voice they probably think I'm trying to get rid of them."

Dino said he'd received a guitar for his eighteenth birthday and really liked to play.

"I've even tried to write a few songs, but they're pretty bad."

"Really? Hey, you should come by sometime and we'll have, what do they call it in America? A hootenanny!"

Dino couldn't believe he was laughing with a priest.

Father Lorenzo shook his hand again. "Well, good to meet you, Dino. Good luck with your studies. Stop by if we can help, and bring your guitar. And watch out for those medieval knights!"

The priest moved on to greet another janitor nearby, leaving Dino confused, but smiling.

The job ended after Signor Costa returned to work a week early, stumbling on crutches and mumbling about medieval knights. Dino had been able to survive with his meager earnings but little more.

It was just as well. Dino needed more time to draw, to read and to study the notes he diligently took in class each day. He tried to establish a system so that when the big oral exams came at the end of the year he would know which notes were more important. After studying each night, he tried to think about other things, but that got him thinking about girls. He picked up his guitar and played sad songs.

Dino didn't tell his mother, during her frequent calls, that he was out of a job, but after three weeks, he was running out of money again. He had to find another job. Walking home along Via dei' Neri, near the Arno, one night, he passed a music store he had never noticed before. In the window was the most beautiful thing he had ever seen. A Gallinotti guitar.

Hands behind his back, Dino stood with his mouth open. He had heard of Gallinotti guitars but never imagined that he would see one. Pietro Gallinotti was one of the world's great guitar makers, winning prizes all over Europe, and many great artists used his guitars. And here was one right before him, more beautiful than Dino could have imagined. He'd read that Gallinotti guitars used German spruce for the top and Honduran mahogany for the back and sides, and even in the dim lights of the window in the early evening, it seemed to glow from inside.

Dino tried to see if there was a price anywhere on the guitar or the window.

"Of course there isn't a price," Dino thought. "No one could afford one of those."

He took one last wistful look and walked on.

In contrast to the simple display of the music shop, Nozzoli Ceramics next door was an avalanche of dazzling Florentine pottery. Dino had never seen such a mammoth display of dishes, bowls, cups, saucers, pitchers in the shape of roosters, flowerpots, mugs, canisters, clocks, centerpieces. They crowded the shelves, covered the walls and spread out on the floor.

He almost missed the little sign in the corner of the window. "Stock boy wanted immediately."

"Well," he thought, "I can't work there. I'd break everything the first day."

But then he thought of the Gallinotti, and pushed the door in. Very carefully.

There was no sign of life until he saw a tiny fluffy gray ball wedged between a stack of dishes and a huge pitcher. It was not until it stretched that Dino realized it was a cat, the smallest he'd ever seen. He thought of an orange-and-white cat in Lucca.

"Hello? Anyone here?"

With all the delicate, and breakable, merchandise on display, Dino expected an equally fragile old woman to emerge from behind the beaded doorway at the rear. Instead, a huge husky man, who must have been more than seven feet and some two hundred and fifty pounds, was suddenly behind the counter. The man's head was bald and shiny except for white marks that Dino thought must cover old wounds.

"Finding what you want, son?" His voice was remarkably soft and gentle for such a big man. "We're having a sale on these frames over here. Do you have a girl friend? Nice frame for a picture of your girl friend?"

Dino explained that he wasn't in the shop to buy anything but was answering the notice on the window. He jumped when he felt a movement against his leg and found the cat rubbing furiously against it.

"Bella, Bella! Stop that. Don't worry, son, she's very friendly, she's just saying she likes you. Tiny, isn't she? People say she's the smallest cat in Italy, but I think just in Florence."

Dino lifted the cat gently, and it fit in the palm of his hand, but it started crying.

"Everyone says she sounds like a baby," Signor Nozzoli said. Dino put it down.

While Dino kept a wary eye on Bella, Signor Nozzoli explained that the job would entail opening boxes from a supplier, stocking the shelves, keeping inventory and eventually waiting on customers.

"I'm not sure how long the job will last," the man said. "My son had been working here, but he's off with his mother in Corsica and I have to hire boys." Dino thought it strange that Signor Nozzoli's voice cracked when he said this, and his hands, which were blistered and bruised, were shaking. Then he took out a big red handkerchief and loudly blew his nose. Dino bent down to stroke Bella, whose baby sounds could probably be heard on the street outside.

Having regained his composure, Signor Nozzoli told Dino the hours and the pay. Dino would get 650 *lire* an hour and work three hours four nights a week and six on Saturdays. Dino quickly added that up, realizing he'd make 11,700 *lire* a week. He could imagine another wooden box under his bed, besides the one that he needed for his expenses. This would be labeled Gallinotti. Dino told Signor Nozzoli that he could start the following Monday.

When Dino excitedly told Adolfo and Mila about his new job, they had an immediate reaction.

"Tomasso Nozzoli! Don't you know who he is? He's *il Toro*, The Bull!"

Dino confessed that he had never heard of the man, and Adolfo explained that Nozzoli was one of the great players for the Santa Croce team in the annual *Calcio Storico.*

"What's that?"

"You'll find out. And you'll find out about *il Toro.* It's in June."

It was now only late April. Buoyed by his weekly earnings and an occasional splurge in his parents' contributions, Dino whistled when he walked to school and to the shop. He went to see his favorite movie, *8½,* for the third time at a vintage movie house. He thought how he had seen it for the first time with Francesca and what stupid comments they had made afterwards.

Without telling Adolfo and Mila, he went back to Santo Spirito to look for Roberto. He thought it strange that the boards against the wall had been removed, and it looked like the floor had been swept. The door was now closed and locked, but the owner of the nearby *bar* said he knew nothing.

Dino was also becoming more confident in his classes, taking better notes and knowing where to find more material. In his drawing class, Professor Mariotti spent almost an entire period showing the details of one of Dino's paintings to the other students. With, as usual, his topcoat over his shoulders and his shock of white hair flowing, he thrust out his cane to the figure of a seated girl.

"See the lines here?" he said. "See how they flow from this section to this, sometimes dark and sometimes light? Now this is what you should be trying to achieve. Some mystery. You don't have to be so explicit. Let your subject come alive on its own."

A boy in the back of the room started talking, and the professor waved his cane at him. "That will be enough, Giorgio. Should we look at your work next?"

Giorgio didn't think that was a good idea, and the professor moved on. Then, after class, Professor Mariotti told Dino to meet him in his office. Dino was certain he was about to be reprimanded, but didn't know why.

"Why are you nervous, Dino? I've got good news!"

Each year, Professor Mariotti said, he chose an exceptionally talented student to join the Cellini Society. The society, founded by aristocratic art patrons, dated from the mid-eighteenth century. It was founded to encourage young artists, but now was mostly a group of elderly men who gathered occasionally to drink expensive wine and exchange gossip.

"You are privileged to be asked to join," the professor said. "I hope you know that."

"Thank you, sir."

"I'll let you know when we meet again."

Dino was in such a good mood after that class that he went down to the Arno and started to compose a new song on his guitar.

Work at the ceramics shop was actually fun, and before entering and after leaving the shop every time, Dino checked to make sure the Gallinotti was still there. He had yet to build up enough courage to actually enter the music shop and examine it.

In one of their conversations while stocking shelves, Tomasso Nozzoli told him that he had been a partisan during the war north of Florence, and Dino told him about his own father.

"You can be very proud of your father," Tomasso said, putting his arm around Dino's shoulders. "Too many young men gave their lives for this cause."

Twice, Dino was put in charge of the shop for a few hours while Tomasso Nozzoli went to practice for the *Calcio Storico*. The event was weeks off, but it seemed like the competition would be even greater this year. Dino tried to get Tomasso to talk about it, but the man just shrugged, blew his nose and changed the subject.

Then, five weeks into the job, bad things started to happen. Rearranging a shelf, Dino dropped a hand-painted plate that sold for 44,000 *lire* and it smashed to pieces. Dino tried to put the bits together but Tomasso threw them away. "These things happen," he said.

Then Dino tripped over Bella and a 38,000 *lire* sugar bowl fell to the floor. "Please be more careful," Tomasso said, his voice strained this time.

Finally, Dino slipped on the stairs to the basement and dropped an entire box of dinnerware. He didn't dare estimate its cost. "I guess you'd better find another job," Tomasso said. "I'm sorry." His soft voice contained more regret than anger.

Dino was sorry, too. He had managed to put only 25,000 *lire* into the Gallinotti box, not enough to buy even part of a string.

Chapter Sixteen

Spring 1965

Unable to find another job, and with the *lire* in the box under his bed fast dwindling, Dino was feeling depressed when Penny slipped him a note during Professor Guidotti's class the following week. "Want to come to my place Friday night? I'm inviting a few friends. We're going to listen to Beatles records! Bring your guitar."

Dino read the note over and over. He was almost nineteen years old, and he had never been to a party. He had never even been invited to a party. Like most young people in the world in the spring of 1965, he knew about the Beatles, how they were a sensation in England and how they caused a smash on an American television show, but he hadn't seen their movie, *A Hard Day's Night,* when it played last year, and had heard only a few of their songs on the radio. He didn't know what to make of them. He looked over at Penny and nodded.

Penny told him to arrive at 8:30, so of course he did.

"Shit," he said to himself as she opened the door and he looked into the room. "I'm the first one."

"Hi," she said. "You're the first one. But that's all right. Just put your guitar in the corner. The others will be here soon, I'm sure."

Penny's apartment was small compared to his basement room, just one big space divided off by bookshelves and partitions. The furniture consisted of a worn-out couch, two folding chairs and three wooden boxes that could double as tables or chairs. Three bunk beds were in one corner. The bathtub dominated the tiny kitchen.

Penny's roommates were making sandwiches on a cutting board. Ingrid was from Germany and also in her first year at the Accademia. She was tall and broad-shouldered. Marie was from the south of France. She was small and shy and wore her hair in bangs. Dino thought she might be a dark-haired version of Francesca. Dino thought he might like to talk to her some more.

They asked a few questions of Dino, like what classes he was taking and who his favorite professors were, but didn't seem to wait for his answers. That made him more nervous, as if they didn't find him interesting enough to talk to. The three girls giggled and talked over their work, and Dino found a wooden box in a corner and read a magazine.

Finally, around 10 o'clock, others came, all at once. Five boys and three girls who obviously had stopped at a nearby *osteria* first. The boys all wore tight jeans and open shirts that showed chains and medals. The girls also wore jeans, white blouses, thick makeup and scarves around their necks. Singing and yelling, two of the boys had beer bottles in hand, though Penny pointed out that she already had a supply on ice near the refrigerator. Raffaele was among them. He seemed to have had more to drink than the others.

With a dozen people in the apartment, there was hardly room to move. Dino shrank back into the corner next to his guitar and fiddled with his hands. One of the students pulled out a pack of cigarettes and soon every one in the room was smoking, except Dino. He had never smoked, though Paolo did sometimes. He didn't like the smell and, anyway, he couldn't afford it.

Soon the room reeked of cigarettes and beer. The talk got louder about people Dino didn't know, films he hadn't seen and places he'd never been. He desperately wanted to go home.

"All right, it's time," Penny announced. She held up the *Meet the Beatles* album. "Aren't they adorable?" She passed the cover around.

"Look at that hair," one of the girls said. "All four of them. You guys, why don't you wear your hair long like that?"

"Looks kind of faggy," one of the boys said.

"They look like they have mops on their heads," a second boy said.

"Which one is which?" a girl asked.

"That's John Lennon," Penny said, pointing to one of the photos on the album cover. "That's Paul McCartney, that's George Harrison and that's Ringo Starr. I'm in love with Paul McCartney."

"Just play the record," a third boy said.

Everyone found a place on the floor, some girls sitting on the laps of their boyfriends. Dino gave up his box in the corner and stood nearby. He had yet to say "Hi" to any of the newcomers.

Penny recited the song list: "It Won't Be Long," "All I've Got to Do," "All My Loving."

"That's my favorite," she said, then continued, "Don't Bother Me," "Little Child," "Till There Was You"...

"Enough," one of the boys said. "Just play the record."

Penny lifted the cover off the turntable and delicately put the record down. For young Italians used to the sentimental crooning of singers like Gianni Morandi, Johnny Dorelli, Domenico Modugno and Bobby Solo, this revolutionary quartet from Liverpool was a revelation. They weren't used to this modern sound, these crisp harmonies—or the energy. Although the students didn't understand all the words, they certainly felt the emotions. This was a new kind of music that for all its innocence was also sensual and sexual. Reared in conservative households, the students found that the songs expressed a kind of freedom and adventure they never knew existed.

No one spoke when Penny played the first side or when she turned the record over.

Even at the end, the room was quiet. Some girls were so teary-eyed their mascara ran down their cheeks. Then the boys started talking about the music as if they knew the difference between a major sixth chord and a seventh. As the night progressed, more beer was consumed until the case was almost empty and the air became even thicker with cigarette smoke. Penny opened the only window, but that didn't help much.

She played the record over and over, until it seemed everyone could sing along with every song even though they mangled the words.

All my loving I will send to you.
All my loving, darling I'll be true.

And

To-night, to-night,
Making love to only you,
So hold me tight, to-night, to-night,
It's you, you you you - oo-oo - oo-oo
You oo-oo

"All right," Penny said, "now let's listen to this other album. She held up *A Hard Day's Night.*

"Oh, aren't they cute?" one girl said. "Look, there's twenty pictures of them." She looked closer. "Or are they all the same guy? I can't tell."

"They sure think a lot of themselves," a boy said. "They put their pictures on every album."

"Well," the girl responded, "you would, too, if everyone in the world was singing your songs."

Penny put the record on and soon everyone was singing, even if only an approximation of the words.

It's been a hard day's night, and I've been working like a dog
It's been a hard day's night, I should be sleeping like a log

Raffaele had become increasingly drunk and leaned out the window.

"Raffaele!" Penny cried. "Do you know what you're doing? Throwing up on those people out there? We'll be evicted!"

"It's been a hard day's night, I should be sleeping like a log," he sang, and promptly lay down on the floor and fell asleep.

Two of the boys got up on the wooden boxes, tried to pull their short hair down over their foreheads and pretended to play imaginary guitars as they sang.

"What we need," said Marie, "is someone to play a guitar so we can all sing along with it. I wish we had a guitar right now."

"Dino brought his!" Penny screamed.

"Who's Dino?" three students yelled out.

"He's standing right there," Penny said.

Through all of this time Dino hadn't paid any attention to what anyone was saying. For the first time, he felt connected to the Beatles' songs and he began mouthing the lyrics. His fingers itched to be playing the chords.

"Dino!"

"Uh, what?"

Penny poked him. "Can you try to play one of the Beatles' songs?"

"Me?"

"Yes."

"I don't know. Let me try."

Red-faced, Dino tightened the strings, strummed a few chords and haltingly began to play. He stopped and started again. But soon this freckle-faced youth from a tiny remote village in Italy, a young man who at eighteen had had only one sexual relationship, played along with the sophisticated and experienced Paul McCartney from Liverpool, England.

I wanna be your lover baby
I wanna be your man

And:

Tell me that you love me baby,
Like no other can

"Go to it, Dino," one of the boys shouted.

"Man, you can really play!" another said.

Dino didn't look up. It was as if he was a fifth member of the internationally acclaimed quartet from Liverpool and he was playing before a rapt audience in a huge stadium. He had never felt this way before. He was in another world. The music had enlivened him, yes, but the response from those around him was more intoxicating.

When, at last, both sides of the record had been played once more, he put down his guitar. All of the students applauded, and two of the boys slapped him on the back. Another offered him a cigarette. He took it, but choked up on the first drag and put it out.

The other students went back to their smoking and talking and ignored him for the rest of the night. But walking home alone in the darkened streets at 2 o'clock in the morning, Dino had never felt so elated. His feet hardly touched the cobblestones.

He spent much of the weekend playing his guitar, either in his room or on the banks of the Arno. One day he ventured to the Ponte Vecchio where other students were also playing guitars, but at the last minute he couldn't bring himself to join them. Note for note, word for word, he remembered the songs he had heard at the party as if they were embedded in his hands. He even wrote a song that was virtually a copy of "A Hard Day's Night."

But when he put his guitar back into its cardboard case every night he had to face the hard facts. He needed a job. He would never be able to put any money in the Gallinotti guitar box. Worse, he feared that he would not be able to return after the summer break for his second year at the Accademia.

After almost a year at the Accademia, Dino found that he had a new perspective on his life. He still loved to paint. He could express ideas and feelings in his paintings that he could not, would not, ever voice in words. But maybe he also enjoyed music and the way it gave him a new form of expression. Or maybe there were other things out there he didn't even know about. The only thing he was sure of was that he wasn't sure of anything.

Michelangelo's statue of David in the Galleria dell'Accademia in Florence, Italy. Photo courtesy The Milwaukee Journal

Chapter Seventeen

Spring 1965

Although Dino scoured the streets, there were no "help wanted" signs in any of Florence's shop windows.

Then Penny had a suggestion as they walked to the university one day.

"Dino, have you ever thought about being a waiter?"

"Where? A restaurant or trattoria?"

"Well, where else?"

Dino said he would never do well as a waiter. He was too shy. He wouldn't be able to remember anyone's order. He'd give the wrong change. He'd trip like he did at the ceramics shop and drop the trays. And he needed the time to study.

"Oh, sure, make up excuses," Penny said. "But Raffaele says there's an opening at the place where he works, Trattoria Eleanora."

"Raffaele? You're still seeing Raffaele? After the way he behaved at your party?"

"I'm not *seeing* him. We talk sometimes between classes. No big deal. Anyway, I can find out about it if you want."

What Dino didn't want was to work with Raffaele. The Fascist. Smug. Thinks he knows everything. Drinks and smokes too much.

But the box under his bed was getting empty.

Trattoria Eleanora was known for its veal and fish entrees and fabulous desserts. A small storefront between a clothing store and a jewelry shop on Via del Corso, it attracted tourists from nearby

Piazza della Repubblica and the Duomo. It had at least three stars in many guides to Florence, and was especially popular among travelers from France and Germany.

Dino pressed his one good shirt, its sleeves now too short, and borrowed a tie from Adolfo for his interview on a Saturday morning. He waited for a half hour in the darkened dining room while the owner yelled on the phone in his office. Something about a bad shipment of cod.

Signor Michellini finally opened the door. "All right, come in."

Considering the stately furnishings in the dining room and bar, the office was a mess. Papers cluttered Signor Michellini's desk and the floor around it. Dino picked up some folders from a chair and sat down, holding the folders on his lap.

Signor Michellini was short, with a thin mustache and small goatee. His white coat was stained, apparently from making last night's dinner.

"All right," he said. "Any experience in restaurants or trattorias?'"

"No, sir, I'm afraid not."

Signor Michellini leaned forward. "You come here and look for a job and you haven't any experience! Don't you know what kind of clientele we have here? Don't you know our reputation for good service?"

"Yes, yes, I know that, sir, but if you could give me a chance…"

The questions and answers went on from there. Signor Michellini was not at all sure he should employ Dino, but the boy did seem earnest.

He picked up the résumé Dino had dropped off earlier. "Do you think I should I call your previous employer, Signor Nozzoli?"

"No, no, sir! I don't think that's necessary, sir." Dino said.

Signor Michellini leaned back. "Well, Dino, I already have. Who wouldn't want to talk to Tomasso Nozzoli? The hero of Santa Croce! *Il Toro*! He was very nice. Said you broke a few things, but they were accidents. And he said I should give you a chance."

Dino wiped his forehead with the back of his sleeve.

"All right. You will work Thursday, Friday and Saturday nights. From 6 o'clock to 11 o'clock. You will be paid 800 *lire* an hour. Plus tips."

Dino did some math in his head. The pay would be slightly less than at Nozzoli's, and he knew that in Italy, tips were very small or nonexistent.

"You can start Thursday night," Signor Michellini said. "You'll need a white shirt, tie and pants which we'll supply. We will take it out of your paycheck."

Dino calculated that he wouldn't be paid for three weeks.

"We'll assign another waiter to show you the ropes," Signor Michellini continued. "His name is Raffaele. You'll like him. Do what he says."

Dino felt his chest tighten. "Yes, sir. Thank you, sir."

Dino arrived at the restaurant at 5 o'clock on Thursday. It was locked. Signor Michellini arrived at 5:30, and the cooks and other waiters drifted in before 6. Raffaele was the last to arrive. He had slicked his hair to a shine that matched his black shoes. Dino heard him arguing with Signor Michellini when he was told to let Dino watch him that night.

"Just stay back," Raffaele warned Dino as they put on their short black aprons. "You're supposed to watch me, not breathe down my neck. Just observe. These are my tables. Don't say a word."

With Dino trailing at the required three feet, Raffaele swept into the dining room as if he owned the place. It took a minute for Dino to adjust his eyes because the room was so dark. Lamps with green shades barely lit the tables and dim sconces threw shadows on the walls.

When he opened the place seven years ago, Signor Michellini decided to out-Tuscan every Tuscan restaurant in Florence. The walls: burnt orange plaster. The paintings: dozens of bucolic scenes of cypress trees and farmhouses along with portraits of unknown royalty. The floor: large red glimmering tiles. Considering all this effort, Dino wondered, why didn't the place have more lights so everything could be seen?

At 8 o'clock, the restaurant was just beginning to fill up. Three other waiters took their places in other corners, and Raffaele, being the senior staff person, had the most advantageous spot in the quiet corner of the room. There were three tables under his command.

Only one was occupied now, by two German couples who were trying to decipher the menu in the dim light. One of the men passed a cigarette lighter around.

"*Buona sera*," Raffaele said in his most unctuous tone. "Welcome to Trattoria Eleanora. My young assistant and I are here to serve you." When Raffaele smirked, his eyes narrowed and his upper lip curled down. Dino could not understand why Penny even talked to him.

Before Dino knew what was happening, Raffaele convinced the Germans to buy a bottle of Brunello di Montalcino, one of the most expensive wines in the house. Dino followed Raffaele to the bar and then back to the table where the bottle was ceremoniously opened and the wine poured.

After that, Raffaele retired to the kitchen where he picked up a copy of *Panorama* magazine to look at pictures of naked women. Twenty minutes later, with Dino still trailing, he returned to the table to go over the antipasti menu. Dino noted that he started with the most expensive items.

"Ah, and now antipasti? May I suggest our wonderful *polpi piccantini alla griglia*? You don't know what that is? It's tasty marinated grilled baby octopus served on a bed of mixed greens. No? You don't like that? It's very good. How about steamed mussels? We have *cozze al guazzetto* served in a lightly spiced fresh tomato broth. No?..."

Raffaele went down the list, his smirk never leaving his lips. The Germans finally settled on *bruschetta*. "We like the way you Italians toast your bread," the smallest German said.

Muttering about "cheap German bastards," Raffaele went through the swinging kitchen door and out into the alley where he lit a cigarette.

"Aren't you going to give the order to the cook?" Dino asked.

"Listen," Raffaele said, wiping a tobacco speck off his lip. "Don't you know that Italy has a reputation for long leisurely dining? We don't want to spoil that reputation now, do we?"

That left Dino to stare at the three garbage cans, already overflowing with wasted food. He was desperately hungry.

Raffaele played the same game with the next courses. For pasta, he pushed the *ravioli pera alla giorgio* ("You must try our ravioli stuffed with pears and parmigiano!"), but all four chose spaghetti. For the main course, he was enthusiastic about the veal (*costolette di vitella alla griglia*) and the strip steak (*bistecca alla griglia*). Instead, one chose chicken breast, one grilled sausage and two eggplant.

Raffaele's smirk grew broader as he went through the kitchen and back to the alley for another cigarette before giving the cook the orders. "No wonder they lost the war," he said.

"Maybe they spent all their money on the wine," Dino said.

After two-and-a-half hours, with the Germans twiddling their fingers at the table, Raffaele presented the bill and collected the money. The tip was minimal, only 1,200 *lire*, which Raffaele pocketed.

"How did those bastards know about not tipping in Italy?" he muttered as he exited into the alley for another cigarette.

At the end of the night, when Dino went into the office to fill out his time sheet, he found Raffaele taking a cash box from a drawer. Raffaele quickly put it back and closed the drawer.

"What the fuck are you looking at, you stupid kid?"

Dino didn't say anything.

Dino was on his own the following night, and the starched collar of his new white shirt seemed even tighter. He was assigned the least desirable tables, next to the kitchen. Every time the kitchen door opened, the crash of pots and pans and the shouts of the cooks bombarded his diners.

The first customer turned out to be a girl he recognized from the Accademia who had brought her parents, visiting from Rome. The girl had never spoken to Dino at the university and she didn't acknowledge him now.

"Florence doesn't have the good restaurants that we have in Rome," she said loudly as Dino seated all three of them. "This is one of the better ones, but don't expect much."

With that as a start, there was nothing Dino or the restaurant could do to please the visitors. The gnocchi was lumpy, the linguine was stringy, the pork chop was overcooked, and the grilled vegetables not cooked enough.

Dino was relieved when they had vanished out the door, but they left no tip.

Three other sets of tourists followed, each with their own demands. Two from Chicago made a point of saying that the restaurants in Italy were not as good as their favorite in the Loop. Dino smiled as if he knew what the Loop was.

At 10:15, when all the other customers had left the restaurant, three middle-aged women came in. Members of a tour group from New York, they had gone off on their own to explore the seedier sights of Florence and apparently found them. Since he was the only waiter in the room at the moment, Dino was forced to seat them at one of his tables.

First, the women complained loudly that they couldn't read the menus in the dim light. Dino found the wall switch and turned on the ceiling chandeliers. Then they ordered martinis, "and make them doubles!" Then they decided to sing Broadway show tunes. Very loud and badly.

Dino tried to get them to order but they were more interested in him.

Putting her hand on his arm, the busty blonde looked at Dino and sang, "*The night is young, the skies are clear and if you want to go walkin', dear...*" Dino moved away.

"What's a nice young man like you going to do after work?" the redhead wanted to know. When she smiled, the makeup on her cheeks cracked.

"Want to come party with us?" the thin brunette said, her thick eyelashes in full motion. "We're staying near the Duomo." She pronounced it "Doe-wom-a."

Red-faced, Dino finally got them to look at the menu. They ordered an appetizer and fried squid and then dawdled over more martinis. When it was long past closing time, Signor Michellini ushered them out the door. They left no tip.

In the weeks that followed, there were a few more incidents that tested Dino's patience and abilities.

One night, he had to deal with four teenagers from France who had fled from a school trip. They spent a half hour deciding what to order while a line formed at the reception desk and Signor Michellini kept telling Dino to hurry up. When the group left, Dino found that two sets of knives and forks had also departed. Signor Michellini said he would take the cost of the cutlery from Dino's paycheck.

Another night, a couple from Madrid made their displeasure known throughout the restaurant when they were seated near the kitchen. The man, with steely white hair and rimless glasses, wore an expensive suit and a Bulgari watch. The woman, much younger, wore a fur stole even though it was a warm night. Even without Dino's suggestion, he had the strip steak (*bistecca alla griglia*), and she had the veal (*costolette di vitella alla griglia*). They topped it off with the Brunello di Montalcino and an expensive dessert. When he cleared their plates, Dino saw that they had left half of their meals, but only a small tip.

Dino became more and more alarmed by the amount of food left by patrons. Huge slabs of steak and pork chops, mounds of vegetables, half-plates of pasta. Since he was still waiting for his first full paycheck, he tried to sneak a bite or two after bringing the plates to the kitchen and was severely reprimanded by the cooks. "No eating the food! If the customer doesn't want it, it goes in the trash!"

Indeed, the trash cans in the alley were overflowing and had to be emptied every night.

Chapter Eighteen

Spring 1965

Despite the new work schedule, Dino developed a routine for Sundays. First, an early morning visit to the Medici Chapel in Santa Croce. He didn't go to Mass, but wanted to sit quietly before anyone else arrived, just as he did at Saint Zita's chapel. Each time, he found new details to admire in the Della Robbia.

Then breakfast with Adolfo and Mila, usually a quiet affair since the television set was on. Dino reminded himself each week that he should go back to Santo Spirito to look for Roberto, but he always found a reason not to.

Then a time for reading and writing in his room. Although he found that some of his professors droned on and on, he was even more confident now that he was learning the subjects. And there was so much to learn. He didn't know how he was going to pass the exams, but his professors seemed pleased. Professor Mariotti twice called him to the front of his class to praise his paintings, causing Dino to stammer and redden and rush back to his seat.

One Sunday, with reading completed, he decided to visit Father Lorenzo, who had waved to him across the piazza a few times over the months. At 4 o'clock in the afternoon, Piazza Santa Croce resounded with the sounds of children racing, street vendors hawking and fathers kicking soccer balls to their sons. A line started to form on the far end, and Dino knew Father Lorenzo's *cucina popolare* would soon be open in the basement of an old palazzo.

Before he came to Florence, Dino had never seen poor people. In Sant'Antonio, a few farm families lived in run-down houses, but they had plenty to eat if not new clothes to wear. No one considered them poor, least of all themselves. In Lucca, Dino saw a few old men in tattered clothes near the Casa del Popolo, but he figured they were probably veterans of the war and the Communists would take care of them.

Dino knew that the area around Santa Croce was among the poorest in Florence. Wearing threadbare clothing and often dirty, the poor begged for food and money on the streets and in front of churches. It was always a shock to come out of the grandeur of the basilica and find a woman crouched on the steps as she held a baby and a tin plate. Dino heard Raffaele say at school one day that the women carried dolls, not babies, in the blankets.

Dino remembered Fausta talking about the beggars in Florence, but that Ezio had said that maybe they begged because they were poor. Adolfo and Mila warned Dino never to give the beggars anything, which was not a problem since he didn't have anything to give anyway. But he smiled at them, and they often smiled back.

Dino joined the end of the line. In front of him, a woman of about twenty-five held a crying baby in a blanket while a little girl held on to her mother's skirt with one hand and sucked her thumb on the other. The woman had a large bruise under her left eye and she looked like she had been crying. Dino didn't know what to say, but thought he should say something

"Excuse me, Signora…," he said.

"Signorina."

"Oh, sorry. Um, do you live around here?" was the best he could come up with.

"I live where I can."

"Oh."

"I'd rather not talk about it."

"Oh."

Dino remained silent as the line slowly entered the hall. So these were poor people. People who had to come here to eat because they didn't have anything at home. Except for their clothes, and maybe a little dirt on their hands and faces, Dino thought, they didn't look any different from the villagers at Sant'Antonio. He noticed one young man, about his age, helping an elderly woman who was apparently blind. For a moment, Dino saw himself helping his grandmother.

Although there was little talk in the line outside, the hall itself burst with noise. Men and women hugged and kissed as though they hadn't seen each other in years, when in fact it was only yesterday. Three loudspeakers blared Italian melodies.

"*Benvenuto!*" a long sign on the wall said. "We are pleased you are our guests."

Basically, it was a soup kitchen, with huge pots of Tuscan bean soup and giant loaves of crusty bread. The line moved quickly and the diners sat down at long tables that were covered with white paper.

Dino found Father Lorenzo himself in the serving line, next to a girl with a mass of black curls and an olive skin. Dino knew at once that she was the model in his drawing class, and his face turned crimson. He thought she looked sexier in a long-sleeved white blouse and long blue skirt. The priest was scooping the soup into bowls with an iron ladle.

"Dino!" he cried as Dino held his bowl out. "You've come! Welcome!"

It had been four months since their conversation over a dripping mop in the basilica so Dino was surprised. "Father? You remember me?"

"Well, of course. At least I remember faces, if not always names. But yours I remember. It's a beautiful name."

"Thanks."

"This is my main helper, Sofia. Sofia, this is Dino."

"Hi," Dino said, looking away.

Sofia smiled, her dark eyes flashing. "Hi, Dino. Say, haven't I seen you in the life drawing class at the Accademia?"

Dino felt awkward saying that he saw her, too, but came up with, "It's a great class."

"Professor Mariotti is such a dear," she said. "I do enjoy the class. But I have to tell you, my arms go to sleep lying there. I have to shake them awake when I get up."

Dino started to say something but suddenly felt a wet nose against his hand and a large furry dark brown creature at his side.

Dino found himself stumbling. "Great dog." Terrific. He used the same word in two sentences. He wasn't as interested in the dog as he was in this fascinating girl. She had really long eyelashes. What must she think of him?

"Oh, that's Elvis," Father Lorenzo said. "The best watchdog we've ever had."

"Elvis?"

"Why not?" Sofia said. "She's big and very friendly and look at the way she wags her tail just like Elvis."

"She?"

"We named her before we looked very hard," Father Lorenzo said. He lowered his voice. "Don't tell her, though."

Sofia smiled and Dino wanted to ask her something, find out more about her. She was so fascinating. But then the priest noted that the line was starting to back up. "Look, have a seat over at the far table, and I'll join you as soon as the line thins out. Enjoy the soup!"

Dino hadn't intended to actually eat at the *cucina popolare*, but the soup certainly smelled good. The far table was crowded, and he found a place next to a grizzled old man whose crutch lay on the floor. Dino didn't want to look, but it was impossible not to notice that the man's left leg ended above the knee.

The man smiled at Dino and continued soaking his bread in his soup. "Well, young fella, you must be a student. We get a lot of students here these days. Your first time here?"

"Um, yes."

"Great place this is. Thank God for Father Lorenzo. We'd be out digging into trash cans at restaurants if it wasn't for this place."

Without prompting, the man gave his name as Angelo and said he hadn't been able to find work for four years. He said he had been with a partisan *banda* north of Florence during the war and came home to find his wife had left him for a shopkeeper.

"But I'm over that now." From the crack in his voice, that might not have been true.

Dino said his father was killed and his stepfather had been in a *banda* in the war.

The man put his hand on Dino's shoulder. "Don't ever forget the war, son. Do you hear?"

Dino promised he wouldn't as the man hobbled away. Others at the table had also finished and as they grouped in a corner to play cards, Sofia came by, ostensibly to take his plate although he noted that she didn't take others. He also noted her strong hands, so unlike Francesca's.

"Enjoy the soup?" she asked.

"Yes, it was great!"

Terrific. He'd used the same word *again*.

"I love coming here to help," she said.

"It seems like a great place." He grimaced.

"It is." Her teeth were so white when she smiled. "Well, come back for more! Let's talk!"

"Talk?"

"Yes! I want to know more about Dino! See you soon!"

And I want to know more about you, Dino thought. He liked the way she walked, not like that girl at the beach at Viareggio, more like a queen. Maybe, he thought briefly, he could volunteer at the soup kitchen sometime.

Dino wasn't alone for long. Wiping his hands on his apron, Father Lorenzo, with Elvis at his side, eased himself into the folding chair across the table. Elvis stretched out on the floor, resting her nose on the priest's sandal.

"Whew, what a night." Father Lorenzo fanned himself with a paper napkin. "We must have had three hundred people tonight. Every week there seems to be more."

After all of his one-sided conversations with Father Sangretto in Sant'Antonio, Dino found it difficult to talk to a priest who seemed, well, like just a normal person.

"Who are all these people, Father? Are they all from around here?"

"It used to be that they just came from here, near Santa Croce, because this is one of the poorest parts of Florence. But the poor are all over now. There are many near the train station and Santa Maria Novella. And in the Oltrarno. They come here often because there aren't many places like this elsewhere in the city."

Dino was silent, thinking of the poor he had seen near Santo Spirito when he looked for Roberto.

Father Lorenzo leaned down to pat Elvis. "You know, Dino, there are really two Florences. There's the tourist Florence, all the people who come from all over the world to look at the paintings, the sculptures, the churches and museums. Most of them are fine people, and we need them badly. Florence couldn't survive without them.

"But then there's the other Florence. The real Florence, where people go to work and raise their families and just live ordinary lives like—where are you from?"

"Sant'Antonio. It's a little village near Lucca."

"Ordinary lives like people do in Sant'Antonio. Really, no different, except that here people are surrounded by all these paintings and sculptures and churches and museums. But there's a difference. You know what it is?"

Dino did not.

"Here, some people can't make it. There's a real class system, and while some people are very, very rich, there are others who are very, very poor. The rich can take care of themselves, but what about the poor?"

"I guess that's why you have *cucina popolare.*"

"Yes. And there's Casa del Popolo. And the government agencies that help the poor with some necessities, but not much. Well, like Jesus says in Matthew, 'The poor you will always have with you.' But their numbers keep growing and growing."

Dino told the priest about the wasteful habits of his customers at Trattoria Eleanora.

"Father," he said, "it's terrible. You could feed everyone here for a week with what we throw away every night. We throw tons away. They don't even let us waiters eat it."

The priest leaned forward. "I know that. And everyone knows that. Yet we seem to accept it as nothing out of the ordinary."

"Can anyone do anything about it?"

"What?" The priest ran his fingers through his thick brown hair, stopping at the bald spot of his tonsure. "Sometimes I get very angry, but it doesn't do any good. Oh, Dino, let's talk about something else. How's your guitar playing?"

When Dino replied, the priest's voice could be heard two tables away. "The Beatles! You play the Beatles! Really!"

It turned out that Father Lorenzo had a friend in London who sent him the *Hard Day's Night* album and that he played it constantly. But, unlike Dino, the priest could not hear a song and instantly repeat it.

"I've tried, oh Lord, how I've tried, but it just doesn't sound the same."

Dino hesitated. "Um. If you want, maybe I could show you a few things?"

"Would you? Hey, Dino, that would be great. And if I learned a few, we could play them here. The people would love it!"

Dino had a hard time imagining Father Sangretto approving Beatles' songs for the next *Festa di Sant'Antonio.* Or playing guitar with Dino.

They agreed that Dino would stop in to see Father Lorenzo some Saturday morning, with his guitar, and the talk turned to Dino's studies, his life in Florence and what jobs he held since Santa Croce.

"Signor Nozzoli? You worked in Tomasso Nozzoli's ceramics shop? Did you get to know him? People think of him as *il Toro*, but he's really a very gentle fellow. Comes to my 9 o'clock Mass in the Rinuccini Chapel every Sunday. He always sits before Matteo di Pacino's fresco of Christ washing Mary Magdalene's feet. He's known as a hero around here, you know."

Dino said he wanted to know why.

"You don't want to know. It's a terrible thing, the *Calcio Storico.*"

"Why?"

"It's another side of Florence. A cruel side. Well, let's talk more soon, OK? And remember, you're going to teach me Beatles' songs. Come on, Elvis, time to lock up."

Dino knew he would be back, and one reason was Sofia. Throughout the room, diners were getting up, folding their chairs and kissing and hugging as they prepared to leave. Many stuffed extra bread into the pockets of their threadbare coats. Italian melodies still blared from the loudspeakers.

In the rear of the hall, custodians started to turn off the lights. Only a few men lingered at a table near the entrance. Dino noticed that one of them had pulled himself up and that he staggered out the door. The man was shabbily dressed and his hat was pulled down over his eyes.

Dino stood up. "Father! That man who just left. Do you know him?"

"That man? You know, he comes here maybe a couple of times a month. He's always been drinking too much, and we pour coffee into him. Then he has some soup and maybe takes a nap on the table, and then he leaves."

"His name? Do you know his name?"

"He's never told us his name. And you know we don't ask a lot of questions around here. He told someone once that he lived in the Oltrarno. Why are you interested?"

Dino hesitated. "I think he may be my uncle."

Chapter Nineteen

June 1965

Deep in a dream in which he was chasing Roberto along a rampaging Arno, and then up side streets and down narrow alleys, Dino thought at first the sound was thunder. Then perhaps an explosion. Or maybe an earthquake because it seemed like the ground was shaking. And all the while men were yelling and screaming at each other. The room was dark so he thought it must be the middle of the night.

Leaping out of bed, he tore open the curtain at the window but could see nothing but blackness. He ran upstairs to find Adolfo and Mila still in their nightclothes and sleepily making coffee.

"What's going on?"

"Stupid city workers," Adolfo mumbled. "It's 5 o'clock on a Monday morning and they've started already."

"Started what?"

"The bleachers."

"They've covered up my window! I can't see out!" Dino said. "And why are they yelling like that?"

"They're not yelling," Mila said. "They're Italian. They talk loud."

Piazza Santa Croce, she explained, was being transformed for the first game of the *Calcio Storico* next weekend. Bleachers would be built on all four sides, wire barricades erected, wooden goals set in place and dirt brought in to cover the entire area.

"Every year," she said, "I ask myself why we live in this place and have to suffer through all that."

"Not to mention the *calcio* itself," Adolfo added. "And it goes on for three weeks. The first preliminary match is next Sunday, then the other preliminary the following Sunday and then the final on June 24. That's the feast of Saint John, the patron saint of Florence."

"I wish we could afford to live someplace else." Mila poured coffee for the three of them and brought out crusty bread and jam.

Dino had two hours before he had to leave for school, so, clad in undershirt and pants, he sat at the kitchen table and heard the story of *Calcio Storico* over the sounds of yells and thuds and crashes from the piazza just below. Mila closed the windows and shutters but that didn't keep the noise out.

The event, Mila said, started in the fifteenth century when young noblemen played a game of football in elaborate Renaissance costumes in one of the piazzas, places like Piazza della Signoria or Piazza Santa Maria Novella.

"Actually," said Adolfo, who had studied Florentine history at the University of Pisa, "the most memorable game was in 1530 when some Florentines played in costume to show their scorn against imperial troops. Nobody quite understands why they did that. Anyway, it was played right here in front of Santa Croce, but the church wasn't even finished then."

The games continued every year for a long time, he said, but then they were discontinued. "They were resumed in 1930 by the Fascist government. So you can blame it on Mussolini."

The players, Mila continued, still wear colorful Renaissance costumes, tunics and pantaloons, "at least at the start." There are four teams of twenty-seven players each, from Florence's four quarters, San Giovanni, which wears green, Santa Maria Novella, red, Santo Spirito, white, and Santa Croce, blue. Two teams play the first day, two the second, and the winners of those two events play for the championship on the third, she said.

Dino finished the last piece of bread. "Are there rules?"

"Sort of," Adolfo said.

He explained that there are four-foot wooden walls at each end of the piazza. The players are supposed to toss the ball over the wall to score a *caccia*, or goal.

"I don't get it," Dino said. "This sounds like any game of soccer or football. Why is it such a big deal and why did Father Lorenzo say it was so bad?"

"Because," Adolfo sighed, "they don't just run and kick the ball."

"They punch each other," Mila said. "They wrestle. They butt heads. They choke each other. They get into fights."

"Terrible fights."

"One guy pushes another down and then there's a big *mêlée*," Mila said.

"The referees look the other way."

"They tear each other's clothes off."

"At the end of the game some of them are in their underpants," Adolfo said.

"Some of these guys get badly beaten up."

"Yet," Adolfo said, "they always come back the next year."

"If," Mila said, "they're still alive."

Adolfo added that he knew a well-respected businessman who refuses to go to the event and tells everyone to avoid it. "He says that it's much worse than the *palio* in Siena."

Dino said he didn't understand why anyone would watch such an event.

"Some people come just for the pageantry," Mila said. "Just to see the referees wearing Renaissance outfits, velvet caps with ostrich feathers and doublets and knickerbockers."

"But it's the procession through Florence beforehand," Adolfo said. "That's what brings out the crowds."

"And the tourists love it," Mila said. "Don't forget. Florence promotes this as a tourist attraction, not just an ancient rivalry."

The procession, they told Dino, starts from Piazza Santa Maria Novella on the other side of Florence and winds to Via dei Tornabuoni, going through Via degli Strozzi, and around Piazza della Repubblica. Then it goes to the Piazza della Signoria and finally to Borgo Santa Croce. The procession includes a young heifer bedecked in garlands.

"In years past," Adolfo said, "the winning team would get the heifer, kill it and have a big feast. Now, I think they just give the team some steaks."

"Anyway, people line the streets and everyone is shouting '*Viva Firenze!*'," Mila said. "'*Viva Firenze!*'"

Then they described the musicians, the mace carriers, the flag bearers and finally the referees and the players, all of them dressed in costumes carried down through the centuries. More than five hundred people sometimes participate, Mila said.

"And after the game?" Dino asked. "Do the losing players just crawl away and the winners get drunk?"

"Pretty much," Adolfo said. "Except that the players have these girl fans in the bleachers, and afterwards they rush down and kiss the winners. It becomes sort of an orgy."

"Sometimes I think that's why the players play," Mila said.

This was not, Dino thought, the dignified Florence of Michelangelo and Dante, unless one considered Dante's vision of hell.

Dino asked why Signor Nozzoli was considered a hero. Because, Adolfo said, the man was a giant but he was also gentle. He could knock the heads of two opposing players together, but he could also separate four or five men involved in a fight if he didn't think they should be fighting. "Everyone says what a great man Tomasso Nozzoli is. *Il Toro's* been the captain of the Santa Croce team forever, and Santa Croce almost always wins."

Dino wondered about one other thing.

"He seemed to get all upset when he mentioned his son. The kid must be very young."

"Massimo? He's probably twenty-two by now."

Adolfo and Mila then went on to tell the story of the young Massimo Nozzoli. In the *Calcio Storico* last year, Massimo was playing with his father on the Santa Croce team when he got into a bloody fight with two members of the Santa Maria Novella team. The men pummeled the boy badly, but instead of fighting back, he ran out of the piazza.

"Just ran out," Mila said. "Never came back."

"Tomasso has never been the same since," Adolfo said.

That wasn't the end of the story. The boy's mother brought him to Sardinia and he has never returned to Florence.

"Why does the mother live in Sardinia?" Dino asked.

"Rosaria? She left Tomasso many years ago and moved there," Mila said.

"Poor Tomasso."

"Well," Adolfo said, "it was partly Tomasso's fault. Everyone knows he had an affair with, what would you call her, Mila?"

"In the old days she'd be called a courtesan. Very wealthy. With lots of lovers."

Dino couldn't believe this. "Tomasso Nozolli? A lover?"

"People," Mila said, "say that Tomasso Nozolli and the principessa were really in love. But there's so much gossip in Florence, who knows?"

Dino would have liked to know more, but he was already late for his first class. "I guess I don't understand what *Calcio Storico* is all about," he said.

"Well," Adolfo said, "you can see for yourself on Sunday."

Before that, crashing noises and yelling awakened Dino every morning, and one day a fleet of dump trucks arrived to unload tons of sand, which was then spread throughout the piazza. It even drifted through Dino's closed window and onto his bed.

To avoid the turmoil, he stayed longer at school, and on the nights when he worked at the trattoria he didn't come home from school at all. When one of the other waiters got sick for two weeks, he had been able to fill in, thus increasing the *lire* in the Gallinotti box under his bed. He still visited The Waking Slave statue every week, but now he also made regular stops in front of the music store to make sure the guitar was still there. He was trying to come up with the courage to go in and ask the price.

On Tuesday night, after admiring the Gallinotti again, he looked into the ceramics shop next door and saw Tomasso Nozzoli lying far back in the overstuffed chair near the counter. His face was redder than usual, he had a handkerchief in his hand and it looked like he'd been crying. Tiny Bella nestled on his wide chest. Dino thought he'd better check.

"Signor Nozzoli?" The little bell rang as he closed the door.

"Dino!" Signor Nozzoli was clearly embarrassed.

"Is something wrong?"

"Wrong? Wrong? No, of course not. Nothing's wrong." The man blew his big nose and stuffed the handkerchief in his pants pocket.

"I just thought I'd stop in," Dino said, floundering for something else to say. "The shop looks nice."

Actually, it didn't. Plates were not aligned, and the display on the floor was scattered.

"Oh, it's all right. The new boy. Well, you know, Dino, he's not as good as you were in cleaning up and keeping order."

"But he probably doesn't break things either."

"Well, remember that big mirror on the wall? You see it's not there anymore."

"Broken?"

"A million pieces. I don't know. I guess I'm going to have to let the boy go. I'll think about it next week."

Dino said he must be awfully busy getting ready for *Calcio Storico*. With that, Tomasso's eyes watered and he pulled out his handkerchief again. Bella jumped down and rubbed her back against Dino's legs.

"I'm sorry," Dino said. "I didn't mean to talk about it."

"Oh, Dino, Dino. If you only knew how much I don't want to play this year. Every time I think about last year, and about Massimo, well, I..."

He blew his nose again. Dino crouched and rubbed Bella's ears.

"I know I have to play," the man said. "Everyone is counting on me. But my heart just isn't in it anymore. This is my last year, Dino. I'm never going to play again."

"Well, you've had a good career, you can be proud of that." Dino was stretching for something to say.

"*Boh!* What did I do? Punch a bunch of people. Kick them in the balls. Smack them on the head. Bloody their noses. A lot to be proud of, right?"

Tomasso blew his nose again, a sound so long and loud that it rattled the cups on the shelf above him.

"A lot of people say that even though you're called *il Toro,* you're also gentle, that you're the hero of Santa Croce. Even Father Lorenzo."

"Father Lorenzo. What a good man. He's a saint."

Dino stroked Bella's ears once more and said he should be going home.

"Maybe I'll see you in the game on Sunday," he said.

"I'll be there, son. For the last time."

As Dino closed the door to the shop, he saw Tomasso Nozzoli blow his nose once more as Bella jumped back into his lap.

On Sunday, the sun shown down on Florence as if ordered by the mayor, and the procession was everything that Adolfo and Mila said it would be. Taking a position on Via dei Neri, Dino thought that if it weren't for the Fiats and Vespas, he would be back in fifteenth-century Florence watching noblemen on horseback, flag throwers, trumpeters and drummers parading before the Medici. He might be wearing a dark blue tunic and light blue and white pantaloons. He would have a jaunty cap with a huge feather. He would play a guitar and bow and wave to the knights and damsels gathered on balconies above him.

This was Florence! This was why he came here! This was why he sometimes couldn't bear to think of Sant'Antonio and its little *festa.* And the statue of Saint Anthony.

And then a horse made a deposit right next to his shoes.

On the way to Piazza Santa Croce, he saw a woman in tattered clothes holding a baby. She was sitting on the street and begging. Dino found 500 *lire* in his pocket and placed it on her tin plate.

The stands were jammed with noisy spectators when Dino found a place in the middle of a row where everyone was wearing or carrying something blue. He figured this must be the Santa Croce section. As soon as he sat down, he felt a tap on his shoulder.

"Dino!"

Father Lorenzo was right behind him, wearing a crucifix over his blue shirt.

"Father! You come to these things?"

"Yes, I'm afraid so. It's happening at Santa Croce, so I figure I should be here. Besides, one of these years, I may have to give the last rites to one of the players."

"You're kidding, right?"

"Wait till the game starts, Dino. Wait till the game starts."

Santa Croce and Santo Spirito were matched in this first game. Dino watched the players, all of them elegantly dressed in bright tunics and knickers, stretch and bend on the sand-filled piazza that had been turned into a playing field.

Then Tomasso Nozzoli came into the piazza, and the crowd in the Santa Croce section went wild. Even some in the Santo Spirito stands cheered.

"*Il Toro!*"

Nozzoli doffed his cap, but then huddled with other players on his team.

Dino studied the cheering fans, many of them scantily dressed young women. Suddenly, he couldn't help but notice a man in the Santo Spirito section standing up, sitting down, standing up and sitting again, all the time waving a beer bottle and shouting.

"Father? Do you see that man over there, making the commotion?"

"Oh, *Dio.*"

"It's him, isn't it? The man who was at the soup kitchen that night."

"I'm afraid so."

Dino didn't know whether to stay still or run down behind the bleachers, to the other side and into the Santo Spirito section. He didn't have to make a decision. Two burly men in brown coats took the man by his arms and escorted him out of the bleachers.

A cannon fired, and the game began. Dino couldn't figure out what the six referees had to do besides look impressive in their velvet caps with ostrich plumes. One of them carried a sword, which appeared to be useless.

Dino wondered if this was really a soccer game. No one kicked the red and white leather ball, but instead, some players ran with it or passed it, and others wrestled, punched, kicked and threw each other to the ground.

In no time, tunics and undershirts were ripped off, much to the delight of the young women in the stands. Dino saw one of the Santa Croce players fall to his knees, blood pouring from behind his ear. Tomasso Nozzoli rushed to his side and knocked down a Santo Spirito player who was about to hit him again. Tomasso helped his injured teammate up and half-carried him to the sidelines.

Dino couldn't tell if anyone was actually scoring. He turned to Father Lorenzo.

"Yes, Santa Croce scored twice in the last three minutes. They're ahead."

Dino became dizzy trying to keep up. Two players down. No, three. No, four. Another fight on the other side. The fans were going crazy, and everyone was standing now.

"Go, Benito!"

"Hit him again, Fortino!"

"Hold him down, Luca!"

"Remember last year, Pino!"

Dino was forced to stand up, too, in order to see. What he saw he would never forget. In the middle of the piazza, a Santo Spirito player had pinned a Santa Croce player to the ground and was beating him on the chest. Then two more, then three Santo Spirito players pounded on the Santa Croce player.

"No!" the crowd in the Santa Croce section yelled.

Calmly, as if he were breaking up a schoolboy fight, Tomasso Nozzoli walked over to the fighting players. He picked up a Santo Spirito player and threw him on the ground, then the second and the third and the fourth. He looked out at the crowd, which was now silent. He waved his arm and made a slight bow. Then he picked up the Santa Croce player, brushed him off, held him up by the shoulders and whispered something into his ear before gently putting him back down.

And then Tomasso Nozzoli walked off the field.

"Tomasso! Where are you going?"

"Come back, Tomasso!"

"No, Tomasso, No!"

"*Il Toro!*"

Elsewhere on the field, the players on both teams stood silently, their uniforms in shreds and their hands behind their backs or their arms on each other's shoulders. There was not a sound from the stands.

A referee ordered the cannon fired. The game was over. For what it was worth, Santa Croce had won.

When he turned around, Dino saw Father Lorenzo leap down three rows and into the aisle leading to the entrance. Dino quickly followed him.

"I've got to find Tomasso," the priest said. "And I think I know where he might be."

Father Lorenzo ran behind the bleachers and to the entrance of the church, Dino at his heels. He forced the heavy doors open, rushed down the main aisle past all the tombs and turned to his right. There, in the Rinuccini Chapel, Tomasso Nozzoli sat before Matteo di Pacino's fresco of Christ washing Mary Magdalene's feet. There were tears in his eyes.

The priest stood by the man and Dino knelt at his side.

"Signor Nozzoli?" Dino whispered. "Are you all right?"

The man put his hand on Dino's head. "I'll be all right, son. Just give me some time."

Father Lorenzo put his hand on Dino's shoulder. "Well, Dino, now you've seen another side of Florence."

Chapter Twenty

Summer 1965

To his surprise and relief, Dino passed all of his examinations, answering his professors' questions with almost no hesitation. There was some awkwardness about his response to a question about Caravaggio's influence on the Baroque style, but the professor accepted it.

With exams finished, Dino made plans for the summer, and despite Lucia's constant pleas, he did not plan to go home to Sant'Antonio.

"Why not, Dino, why not?" Lucia was in tears when he finally returned her last telephone call.

"I want to stay here and work and save some money."

"But you need a vacation! You've been working so hard!"

"I can rest here in Florence, Mama."

"It's not the same. Here you could go for walks, you could visit with Ezio and Donna, you could see all the neighbors. Did you know Antonio is still living with Rosa and they haven't gotten married yet?"

"Good for them."

"Dino!"

Dino could hear her crying into the phone.

"Dino, we miss you so much! We haven't seen you since Christmas."

"I miss you all, too, Mama, and I'll be home for Christmas again. I promise. But I need to save up some money. Then maybe next year I won't have to work so hard."

"Dino, your Papa could pay you for working in the *pasticceria*. You'd like that, wouldn't you?"

Dino held the phone away from his ear, then returned it. "That would be nice, but it wouldn't be enough."

"Enough? What's enough? Dino, your Papa thinks you're saving up to buy a Vespa, and you know how he feels about that."

"It's not a Vespa, Mama."

"Then what, Dino?"

"I have to go, Mama. I've got a lot to do today."

Dino hung up the phone, said good-bye to Adolfo and Mila, and went out into the sultry June sunshine and headed for the Arno. Every time his mother laid what he called Catholic guilt on him, he needed to clear his head.

Dino had found that if he stared into the Arno long enough he could be mesmerized. He felt himself being carried along, under the Ponte Vecchio and Ponte Santa Trinità and the other bridges and out to sea and the vast oceans beyond.

It was true that he wanted to work through the summer and save money. He wouldn't have nearly enough to buy the Gallinotti, but every *lira* counted. But that wasn't the major reason. He just could not go back and spend the summer in Sant'Antonio. His mother breathing down his neck. The neighbors so curious about what he was doing. And nothing at all to do there. Absolutely nothing. He'd have to go to Lucca.

Lucca reminded him of Francesca. He wondered how she was, what she was doing. And who was this boy she was seeing? Maybe he should have written to her. And then he thought about Sofia. He needed to go back to the soup kitchen.

For someone who planned every day, every week, carefully, scheduling three whole months was exciting. In the mornings, he would play his records, now up to fifteen, and compose songs, now up to eight. In the afternoons, when the light was better, he would find a new place in the city and draw and paint.

Neither of these involved other people. After eight months, Dino still had no real friends in Florence, unless one counted Penny, and she had gone home to England right after classes ended. Dino still couldn't figure her out, and he wished she wouldn't be around Raffaele so much.

The plan went according to schedule. Each morning, after breakfast, Dino carefully took out a little record from its sleeve and played it. He had a couple by George Gaber, including *"Ciao ti dirò,"* which the record store manager said was inspired by Elvis Presley's "Jailhouse Rock."

One of his professors fumed about Presley one day in class.

"Elvis Presley will bring down America!" the professor, who was probably eighty years old, predicted. "His music appeals only to animal instincts. It's vulgar! It's obscene! It's depraved! America should never let his music out of the country. I tell you, if you young people like his music, then you're all depraved, too!"

"Professor," a girl in the front row asked, "have you heard any of Elvis' songs?"

"Heard them? I've heard enough about them so I don't have to hear them. Now. Let's get back to the cultural influences of mid-eighteenth century Milanese painting."

Dino couldn't help wonder how Father Lorenzo would have responded.

Dino didn't like Presley that much, so he didn't play the Gaber records very often. What he did like was Mina's recording of Gino Paoli's *"il cielo in una stanza."* The record store manager told him Paoli wrote the lyrics while lying on a bed in a brothel. "He looked at the purple ceiling and he thought that love can grow in any moment at any place."

Quando sei qui con me
questa stanza non ha più pareti

When you're here with me
this room has no more walls

Dino spent hours working on a musical phrase or a single line of a lyric. He tried not to be imitative, but a listener could hear the similarities.

When you are close to me
I can only think of you.

With the piazza cleared and back to normal after the *Calcio Storico*, sometimes he went outside to play his guitar, often joined by Signora Alonzo and her dog, Primo. Signora Alonzo smiled and hummed along while Primo wagged his tail.

"My Bernardo used to play the guitar before he got sick," she said one day. "Such wonderful songs. Now all I've got left is my little Primo."

"Hi, Primo!" Dino said, scratching the dog's ears. He still thought about getting a dog some day.

A young couple occasionally would sit on the bench opposite and hold hands while listening to his songs. But sometimes an elderly man in the neighborhood told him to cut out the racket or he'd call the *carabinieri*.

By noon each day, he was ready to make himself a bowl of soup or a sandwich in Adolfo and Mila's kitchen, and then grab his sketchbook and pencils. At the start of the summer, he had made a list of places he wanted to see and sketch. He'd start farther out from the central city, in places like Piazza della Libertà, where he could draw the colonnades, and the English Cemetery, where he could visit the grave of Elizabeth Barrett Browning. He wondered why her husband, the poet Robert Browning, was buried in London.

And he'd go up to Piazzale Michelangelo and sketch the copy of the David. He'd go to the Boboli Gardens, and soon the Egyptian obelisk or the Neptune fountain would emerge in his sketchbook.

One day, coming back from the Boboli Gardens, he diverted to Santo Spirito. Maybe, he thought, Roberto would finally be in his shop. The door would not budge and the floor looked like it had more dust but the shop was otherwise unchanged since Dino stopped by last. He tried the *bar* at the corner. The owner looked up from washing cups and saucers. No one else was there.

"Sir, have you seen anything of Roberto, my uncle?"

"Not a thing, son. Haven't seen him."

"Would you let me know if you hear or see anything?"

"Don't you think maybe you should be giving up?" the man said. "Look, I'm pretty sure you don't want to find him."

Dino wrote Adolfo's phone number on a slip of paper. "Please have him call us if you see him."

Work at the trattoria went on as usual. Raffaele kept his distance, ever since Dino caught him with his hands in the money drawer, and he noticed that Signor Michellini now kept the key to the drawer in his pocket.

With tourists flooding Florence, Signor Michellini gave Dino extra nights to work and gave him better tables to wait on. Many of the tourists came from Germany and England, as they had traditionally, but now they were from the United States and Canada, too. The Americans, Dino found, didn't know that tips were included in the bill and often left generous amounts of *lire*. The Germans and English either knew about it or were stingy.

Dino learned a few English words and tried them out.

"Welcome to Trattoria Eleanora," was always his greeting. "May I put you in your chair?"

Fortunately, the menu was now translated into English, so that when a customer read *Scaloppine di Vitello al Gorgonzola e Asparagi,* it was clear that this was sautéed medallions of veal with asparagus and a pinot grigio gorgonzola sauce.

Still, some customers just wanted to pretend they knew Italian.

"*Prego,*" one man asked nervously one night. "Where is the *gatto?*"

"*Gatto?*" Dino said. "I'm afraid we don't allow cats in the trattoria, sir."

"*Gatto! Gatto!*" The man was in distress. "I need the *gatto!*"

"*Gatto?*"

Another waiter came up and whispered in Dino's ear.

"Ah," Dino said. "You mean the *gabinetto*, the toilet. Of course, right through that doorway."

The man hurried off, followed by the chuckles of everyone else in the room.

What Dino hadn't learned enough about was Florence's annual infestation of mosquitoes. At first, he didn't think much about a few bites, but as the summer wore on, he encountered swarms of them ready to attack, especially near their breeding places on the Arno.

"The *zanzare!*" Adolfo said. "We learn to live with them."

Mila urged Dino to wear shirts with long sleeves and high collars, no matter how hot it was, and to go to the *farmacia* and get some lotion.

"And make sure your window is closed before you put on the light. Otherwise, they'll swarm right in."

"They'll still find you," Adolfo said. "They sit on your window sill just waiting for you."

It was true. One morning, Dino woke up scratching his arms, his neck and his legs and proceeded to count twenty-four welts.

"Shit! Shit! Shit!"

The bugs were especially bad in the evenings, so Dino almost ran to and from the trattoria. But they were also bad in the afternoons. Reluctantly going as far from the Arno as possible to draw, he discovered the little-known Parco di Villa il Ventaglio, a lovely park with chestnut trees, limes and elms, a little lake and a fifteenth-century villa. Since he was almost always the only person in the park, he could imagine once again, as he did in the *Calcio Storico*, being a nineteen-year-old guitar-playing troubadour in the Middle Ages.

In late July, Dino got a letter, a rare occurrence if he didn't count the weekly correspondence he received from his mother. He looked at the fine handwriting and stared at the stamp picturing the young queen of England, Elizabeth.

Dear Dino,

I'm returning on the thirtieth and Raffaele says we should all come to the coast the first two weeks of August. His uncle has an old farmhouse we can use. It's near Viareggio. Ingrid and Marie will be there and the other people from my party and I don't know who else. There will be tons of stuff to do. I'm going to bring NEW (!) Beatles records and Raffaele says he hopes his friends will bring some good stuff. Hope you can come. And bring your guitar! See you soon.

Love,

Penny

Dino didn't know what "good stuff" Raffaele's friends would bring but he read the ending over and over. "Love?" What did Penny mean by that? She'd never said anything like that to him. Was this some sort of English custom? Did she really mean it? Why did she use the word so loosely?

Dino tried to think of reasons not to go. He didn't like these people. He wanted to write songs and draw. He should do some reading for classes next year.

He did not have the excuse that he had to work. Like almost all other shops and restaurants in Florence and much of the rest of Italy, Trattoria Eleanora would close for the first two weeks of August so everyone could escape from the worst heat of the year, not to mention the mosquitoes, and go to the seaside.

And Penny said that Marie would be there. He hadn't seen her since the party. But thinking of Marie reminded him also of Francesca and Sofia. Women! He couldn't understand any of them.

Lucia was furious when Dino told her of the invitation.

"You can go off to the seaside with your friends but you can't come home to see us?" She was crying again. "The one year we're not going, and you go? Why can't you come home, Dino, why? I know why, you're seeing some girl and that girl is going to be there, right? Oh, Dino, why didn't you tell us about your girlfriend. What kind of girl is she? Where is she from? She's not a foreigner, is she? She's not from the South, is she? Is she a student, Dino? I hope she's a student. Is she a good student? And, Dino, does she go to Mass every Sunday? I hope you go to Mass every Sunday. Do you go to Santa Croce? That's such a beautiful church. And Dino, have you tried to find Roberto? Dino, can you answer me?"

"I'll call you when I get back, Mama."

Defying the mosquitoes, Dino took an extra long walk along the Arno that night.

Chapter Twenty-One

August 1965

Three cars were needed to take the travelers from Florence to Viareggio. Raffaele drove his father's 1964 Lancia Fulvia, with Penny in the front seat and Ingrid and two boys and another girl crammed in the back. A boy named Nicco drove a battered 1958 Fiat, with Marie in the front seat and three boys in the rear.

Another boy, Gregorio, was at the wheel of the final car, a 1960 Fiat. Another boy was in front and Dino sat in the back, between two girls who joked and giggled all the way.

"We like your freckles," one girl said. Dino's freckles suddenly got redder.

"You're very tall," the other girl said.

"And we know what that means!" the first said. They both screamed in laughter. Dino couldn't wait until they got there. His guitar was strapped to the top, and he worried about it the entire trip.

There was talk that four other boys were coming separately on their Vespas, and that they would be bringing some good stuff, but no one was quite sure. The girls were pleased that they were vastly outnumbered.

The group had gotten a late start. Nicco said he was hung over from a party the night before and Raffaele drove up at the last minute. He said he had to meet someone in Santo Spirito and the deal took longer than he thought.

Despite a flat tire on Nicco's car and an overheated engine on Gregorio's, and several wrong turns, they finally arrived at the old farmhouse. It was not near the seaside at all, but stood at the end of a gravel road about ten miles inland. A thick stand of chestnut trees spread north for several acres. The sun was just setting when the groups arrived, and the farmhouse looked serene and beckoning in the warm glow.

Then they went inside.

"They call this a farmhouse?" one of the boys said. "Looks more like a stable."

"Not even a stable," a girl said. "More like a pigsty."

"Looks like somebody had a party here," another girl said.

The place was one vast room with partitions at either end holding bunk beds. The kitchen consisted of a rusty stove, sink and refrigerator. A dilapidated couch occupied the space in front of a fireplace, and two folding chairs leaned against a wall. Empty wine and beer bottles crowded a corner. Scraps of vegetables and what looked like panini and pizza littered the dirty stone floor. Half-burned newspapers in the fireplace indicated that someone had unsuccessfully tried to light a fire, and the smell of old ashes filled the room. Electricity was at best unstable, with a wall light flickering on and off.

"Where's the bathroom?" a girl shouted. "I've got to pee."

Raffaele, who hadn't been here before but heard about the place from his uncle, said there wasn't an inside bathroom.

"But there's supposed to be a *cesso* outside the back door. Go look."

"I have to go to that little shack to do it?" the girl asked incredulously. "I'm not going to."

But she did.

They were hot, they were tired, they were dirty and they were hungry. Ingrid took charge.

"All right. Everyone listen. We're going to Viareggio. We'll go to a pizzeria for dinner. Then we'll go to a supermarket and get supplies for the week. All of us girls will take turns doing the cooking. You boys will do the cleanup. Any questions?"

No one had any. They piled back into the cars and drove down the hillside where they found a cheap pizzeria. Dino sat at the end of the long table and he kept an eye on Marie, but he didn't know the people the others were talking about and hadn't listened to the music they liked.

"Dino," Penny called from the middle of the table where she was the center of attention. "Tell us about the songs you've been writing."

"Um. Just some songs. I'm still working on them."

"Can you play them for us?"

"Maybe by the time we leave."

The conversation went back to the latest bands. After an argument about who owed how much, the group trooped down the street to a supermarket where they loaded up on groceries, mostly pasta, bread, and only a few perishables. Tired and irritable, they drove back and silently pulled sleeping bags from the trunks of the cars, spread them in no order around the room and went to sleep.

For a long while, Dino seemed to be the only one awake. He looked around the room to see if he could find Marie. She was in a corner, asleep. Before the week was out, he decided, he would talk to her.

He stared out the high window and into the moonlit sky. Trying not to wonder about the scratching sounds in the walls, he ran through the latest song he had written and thought maybe his room at Santa Croce wasn't so bad, even though it had scratching noises in the walls, too. And before he went to sleep he looked around the room at these students who didn't seem to care about anything but themselves, and he thought about the woman with the bruised face and the boy helping his grandmother and the man with one leg at the *cucina popolare*.

In the morning, there was a noisy line at the *cesso*, complaints by the girls that there was no place to wash their hair and grumbling by the boys that there wasn't enough to eat. Finally, they loaded blankets and beach umbrellas into the cars and headed for the beach.

It was only 10 o'clock, but hundreds of umbrellas left few open spaces. They found a space at the very end, near the garbage cans. Then they stretched out their towels and blankets and lay down.

Dino couldn't help but wonder what the point of all this was. Like probably everyone else at the beach—and there seemed to be thousands of them—they had slept all night and now they had come to the beach to sleep some more, only this time under a burning sun. That would be difficult, considering the flocks of screaming children and the pounding of waves. No wonder his parents had refused to come again.

He suddenly became aware that Marie was lying next him. Very close. He couldn't believe her bathing suit, little more than a few strings, really. That's what they must be wearing in France, he thought.

"Hi, Dino." When she smiled, one corner of her mouth went higher than the other.

"Hi."

She took off her sunglasses and smiled again. "Isn't it nice to be away from Florence and all those people and all the noise?"

"Yeah," he said, just as a little girl went screaming by, kicking sand into their faces. "Good to be here all by ourselves. Nice and quiet." He grinned, too.

"I'm glad you brought your guitar," she said. "I like the way you play."

"Thanks."

"Well, got to get my beauty sleep." She turned over on her stomach and away from him. Dino thought her back was as beautiful as the Venus in the Accademia. He stared up at the red and white stripes on the umbrella, aware that his swimming trunks had suddenly become tighter.

He wondered what it would be like to have a girlfriend again. From the few conversations he had with her, Marie seemed awfully nice. He wondered what his mother would say if he dated a girl from France.

For the rest of the day, he wished he had stayed at the farmhouse working on new songs. He could play them for Marie. He resolved not to come back to the beach again.

And he didn't. The next day, when the others took off, not even asking if he would be coming along, he pulled his guitar out from the corner and went outside. Although the heat was already becoming unbearable, he wandered into the chestnut grove. As he went in deeper and deeper, a cool stillness gradually replaced the oppressive heat. Someone had placed a bench in the coolest spot under an old chestnut tree. There, he played and sang one song after another. No one, except for a dozen greenfinches that settled on a tree branch, heard him.

After the sun had set, when the others returned, swaying and laughing and already sunburned, they waited impatiently for Ingrid to make pasta. Twice, she threatened to "throw the damn pot out" unless they "shut the hell up."

Since there wasn't a table, they sat on the floor, their plates in their laps, and washed down the overcooked and stringy pasta with beer and Chianti. Later, someone noticed Dino in the corner.

"Hey, Dino! Play us some of your new songs."

"No, play Beatles songs!"

Penny was upset because she'd forgotten her record player and her two new Beatles records remained in her suitcase.

"We don't need the Beatles," she said, her voice mushy from too many beers in the afternoon. "We've got Dino! Play some Beatles, Dino!"

Dino could not avoid playing. He tried to forget that anyone else was in the room. Instead, he was under a spotlight in the corner of a famous nightclub, and everyone listened raptly to his music.

All my loving I will send to you.
All my loving, darling I'll be true.

For once, the group was still, rapt in words they didn't quite understand but which they felt deeply. Eventually, they tired of the songs, so Dino didn't play any of his own. They wanted more excitement. Most of the boys and some of the girls held out their hands as Raffaele distributed thin slips of paper and then small contents from a plastic bag. He didn't offer Dino any. Fine, Dino thought, I don't want any anyway. Soon the cigarettes were passed around, and a sweet smell pervaded the room. Dino knew what it was. He had smelled it often enough on Ponte Vecchio. Giggles turned into loud laughter. Boys stumbled over one another. A few passed out.

Marie was the only other person who refused Raffaele's handouts. She was trying to read a French novel under the lone light on the opposite wall.

Dino pulled his sleeping bag to the farthest corner of the room. He didn't want to hear the grunts, squeals, moans and cries of the others, their clothes tossed aside, as they lay in various combinations of twos and threes in the bunk beds and on the floor. He tried to see where Penny and Marie were in all this, but with only a stream of moonlight, the room was too dark. He wished he'd stayed home.

One day was pretty much like another. Dino would get up when sunlight streamed in and go out to the chestnut grove to spend the day drawing or playing his guitar. Thankfully, no mosquitoes were in sight. At dusk, he returned and found some leftovers from the night before. Later, the others, who got up late and drove to the beach, came home. They were loud, even when they were having sex, except when they were too drunk or too delirious from pot.

Mostly, they ignored Dino, and he ignored them. He didn't mind, or at least pretended he didn't. It was good to get away from the trattoria, from his hot basement room, from the mosquitoes. Sometimes, he thought about Francesca and what she was doing. Sometimes about Sofia and Father Lorenzo and the *cucina popolare*. And sometimes about his parents. He'd call his mother when he got back.

He didn't see much of Penny, who seemed to be spending a lot of time with Raffaele. But one day, as she came out of the *cesso,* he stopped her.

"Penny. That note you wrote me to invite me here..."

"I'm glad you came, Dino. You should play the guitar more often."

"The way you signed it. What did you mean by that?"

"I don't remember. What did I say?"

"You wrote 'love Penny.'"

"So?"

"What did you mean when you wrote love?"

"Dino, Dino, Dino. It's just an expression. Did you think...? Oh, Dino, I'm sorry. Maybe you don't say things like that in Italy. We do it all the time in England. It doesn't mean anything."

"Oh."

"Oh, I'm sorry if I hurt your feelings. Truly. You know I like you, Dino. I like you a lot. You're one of the best friends a girl could ever have. How about playing guitar for us tonight, OK?"

Penny turned and went into the house. Dino went into the *cesso*.

Twice, Dino made attempts to talk to Marie. One morning, he asked about her hometown, Saint-Étienne. She said it was once the capital of France's bicycle industry but mainly it was known as the birthplace of Jules Massenet. Dino didn't know who that was.

"You've never heard of Massenet? The opera composer? *Manon? Thais?* No?"

"I'm afraid not."

"Pity." She went off to find her sunglasses.

Another time, after he finished playing one night, she told him she wished she could learn to play the guitar. Dino offered to teach her.

"That would be wonderful," she said. "Let's talk about it when we get back."

"Really?"

"Sure."

"Marie...I..."

"Dino, I like you a lot, but I don't want you to get the wrong impression. I've got a boyfriend back in France. We plan to get married after I graduate."

"Oh."

"Can we still be friends?"

"Sure."

On the day before the group was to return to Florence, everyone woke up when four Vespas roared right to the front door.

"Rocco! Arturo! Renzo! Silvio! It's about time!"

All four wore black leather jackets and caps. Lettering on their backs said *Ragazzi di Firenze*.

"Sorry we're late," Renzo, the stocky one, said. "We were real busy."

"Yeah," said Silvio, "there was a party."

"A really good party," Rocco said.

"And we brought some souvenirs!" said Arturo. He reached into his back pocket and pulled out two plastic bags. "We'll have some fun tonight."

Raffaele gave him a hug. "What a guy. We ran out days ago. It's been pretty grim around here."

The group decided to save the good stuff for the night and went off to the beach. Except for Dino, who wanted to complete one last song in the forest.

When the group returned from the beach that night, most sat in a circle in the middle of the floor. Marie stayed in a corner, trying to read her book in the dim light, while Dino remained in his usual quiet space. Raffaele went around the circle, passing out papers and the contents of the plastic bags, and soon the sweet smell spread through the room.

"Hey, I've got some left," Raffaele cried. "Marie? Want one?"

Marie shook her head.

"Who's that tall guy in the corner?" Rocco asked. "Ask him."

"Dino? Dino, my boy, want to feel better?"

All the others looked at him. Dino avoided Marie's stare and put his hand out. He was able to form a cigarette only because he had watched the others so closely.

Taking his time, and coughing only occasionally, Dino took deep breaths. He didn't feel anything and wondered why the others were starting to act a little silly.

"Dino!" Raffaele cried. "Enjoy!"

The others all watched for his reactions. Again, he wondered what all the fuss was about but also why his mouth and throat were getting dry. His heart seemed to be racing as well. Maybe he was getting sick. He tried to get up, but stumbled back to the floor. Maybe if he concentrated on something he would feel better. He tried to remember the words to the last song he had written. He couldn't remember. He wondered why Raffaele was walking into a wall. No, Raffaele was actually walking up the wall. How strange. Why did Penny have two dresses on? And why was Marie standing on her head?

Dino lay down. He put his arms over his head to try to stifle the loud bangs that came from under the floor. He looked up at the ceiling. Strange. There was a line of a lyric running across. *Cometomecometomecometome.* He reached up and tried to grab it. It floated away. He grabbed again, got hold of it and hung it on a hook on the wall. Then he let all the sights and sounds wash over him until he mercifully fell asleep.

He woke up with a throbbing headache. So did everyone else. He looked for the line of the lyric on the ceiling but didn't see it. He didn't see any hook, either. He thought Marie gave him a pitying glance as they packed, but then she turned her back.

No one spoke all the way back to Florence, and the two girls on either side of him fell asleep on his shoulders. Dino stared straight ahead.

That night, Dino called his mother.

"Mama? It's Dino. How are you?"

"Dino! We're fine, Dino. You've never asked before. Are you all right? Did you have a good time? How was the weather? Did you meet some new people? What did you eat? Did you get some rest?"

"I'm all rested up, Mama."

"Good. We miss you so much, Dino."

"Miss you too, Mama."

Chapter Twenty-Two

November 1965

Now in his second year at the Accademia, Dino had even more freedom about attending classes, and he used the time to do his own drawing. And sometimes he wrote new songs. Every week he found a new and exciting place to spend his afternoons. After all these months, he still pinched himself. "I can't believe I'm in Florence."

But he also found himself thinking about Sant'Antonio more often, and he wondered what everyone there was doing at that very minute. He even thought about Father Sangretto. He had mixed feelings when he stopped to look at The Waking Slave.

Sometimes, he thought he should visit the *cucina popolare* and see if Sofia was there, but after Marie told him she had a boyfriend, he was reluctant to risk another rejection.

Most tourists had left Florence, returning the city to its weary inhabitants. The rains started in October and steadily worsened. Twice, Dino noticed trickles of water on the floor at night, but they dried up during the day. For the first time, though, water seeped through the window and he had to stuff the cracks with rags.

The rains became heavier in November. It's "*la pioggia di novembre,*" Mila said.

Both Adolfo and Mila said that the rains were worse this year, and Adolfo warned that the basement of the National Library, where he worked, would be very vulnerable if the Arno overflowed.

"I don't know why they store all those manuscripts down there," he said one night as the three of them were watching the weather forecast on the television. "If the Arno floods, well, that's the end."

Dino walked along the Arno more often, worrying that it might be rising. So far, it had not. Like a Florentine, he decided he wasn't going to worry about the Arno. At least, not yet.

In his Michelangelo class one Tuesday, Dino looked up to see Professor Mariotti at the door, frantically calling him to come out of the room. Dino was sure his mother had died or something else terrible had happened.

"Dino!" the professor was flushed, out of breath and waving a piece of paper. "Look what just came."

Dino was now sure that the news was bad.

"It's an invitation! Dino, it's an invitation! Do you know how many people would die for this? Do you know, Dino?"

Dino did not.

Eventually, and in a rather convoluted fashion and with considerable waving of hands, the professor told him the details. Principessa Maria Elena Elisabetta Margherita di Savoia had invited the professor and Dino to her next salon, a week from Thursday night.

Dino had never heard of the princess, didn't know why he was invited and thought a salon was something to eat.

The princess, Professor Mariotti explained, was the most famous art patron in Florence and her salons were legendary. There were at least five other women, all of them of a certain age and some with dubious heritage, who held salons, the professor said, "but the principessa's is the most famous and hers is the most desired of invitations."

He went on to say that the princess had invited him and Dino as representatives of the Cellini Society, he because he was its president, and Dino because he was the newest and youngest member.

The principessa likes to have a great variety among her guests, he continued. There will be art critics and historians there, and respected professors--here he smiled knowingly--and surely some well-known artists. But Dino might also see the proprietor of a bookstore, the caretaker of the Florence Zoo, the manager of a tobacco shop and even perhaps--and here the professor grimaced--a journalist.

"Don't be surprised by anyone who is there," he said. "The principessa just wants good conversation. That's what her salons are, just a place for people to talk."

Dino was now terrified and tried to think of an excuse not to go. The professor would hear none of it.

"This is a great honor, my young friend. Someday you will tell your grandchildren about it."

When Dino asked to learn something about the hostess, Professor Mariotti hesitated, then decided Dino should know. He lowered his voice. Little was known about the principessa's early life, he said, but it was believed she was the daughter of a seamstress near Santa Croce. With flaming red hair, a bright smile, slim figure and, most of all, determination, she took a number of lovers as a young woman. Each of them, she proudly proclaimed, was better endowed, both financially and physically, than the last.

Her fame spread. She married an elderly count who, unfortunately, died after two years of marriage. This was followed by a member of the House of Savoy who also had the misfortune to pass on but had left her with a title and boxes of expensive jewelry. Her third husband was the love of her life, no matter that he was eighty-one when they married and eighty-four when he left her an estate near Urbino. Her fourth, and final, spouse actually lived for seven years after their lavish wedding in Santa Croce. When he died some thirty years ago, she inherited the palazzo facing the Arno where she has lived ever since. Gossips said that she continued her romantic liaisons for some years afterwards.

"You may even have heard of one of them," the professor smiled slyly. "Everyone says he was the love of her life."

Dino couldn't imagine, but then remembered something Mila had said. No, it couldn't be.

"But the time for romance for the principessa has gone," the professor said, sorry that he had no more gossip to relate.

He went on to say that the princess now suffers so terribly from arthritis in her hips that she is confined to the first floor, with the former solarium converted into a bedroom overlooking the Arno. All three floors above are vacant.

"She used to have a retinue of servants, but I imagine, like everyone else, she has fallen on rough times," Professor Mariotti said. "Now she has only Teressa, who is almost as old as she is but who would never leave her side. Poor Teressa. She has to carry the principessa around in her arms. It's lucky she weighs so little. But I have heard that sometimes the principessa uses a wheelchair."

The professor gave Dino the address and told him that the salon would begin at exactly 7:38 p.m. "No one knows why she has selected that time for the start of all of her salons, but some people think it is the time that her third husband expired."

His umbrella high because it was still raining, and with a suit jacket and tie borrowed from Adolfo, Dino walked down the Longarno on the appointed night, painfully aware that his jacket sleeves were too short and his tie too tight. He arrived at the palazzo at 7:30, finding a long line of men and women also holding umbrellas high. Some chatted in that elegant Florentine style and smoked cigarettes in holders. Others, less formally dressed, gathered in their own groups. Dino turned to run home but bumped right into Professor Mariotti.

"Ah, Dino, *buona sera*. You look…well…you look like a student. I'm sure the principessa won't mind."

The professor wore a sharply pressed black suit with white stripes, a black topcoat over his shoulders and a red ascot billowing over his ample chest. He had gathered his flowing white hair with a red ribbon at the back, and he smelled of cheap cologne.

At 7:38, the heavy oak doors opened, a liveried footman appeared, and the line quickly moved inside. An ancient woman Dino thought must be Teressa and a young girl took coats, and the guests entered the formal living room.

Dino almost tripped over the man ahead of him. He tried not to gawk, but couldn't help it. Scattered around the room were huge marble sculptures of nudes, both male and female, glowing under the lights of a dozen chandeliers. Some were copies, but Dino knew that many were original. He was afraid to get near any of them.

The walls stretched up a good eighteen feet and were covered in the deepest of red damask, expensive material, not like in Father Sangretto's office back in Sant'Antonio. There were dozens of paintings, small and large, square and oval, in gilded frames. Dino could not help but notice that the same woman seemed to have been the model for eight or ten nude paintings. In some she faced the artist, in some she looked over her shoulder, in some she reclined on a sofa. In all of them, her hair was a mass of yellow curls, her tiny eyes bright blue, her eyebrows plucked, her breasts small but firm. Dino wished she had modeled at the Accademia.

The professor pushed him forward. "Dino," he whispered. "Keep the line moving."

Some of those ahead of him found places on the ornate stuffed chairs and sofas or stood in groups of four or five, chatting and gesturing, under the statues. Two servant girls, in black dresses and white aprons, circled the room with silver trays loaded with tiny pieces of food that Dino didn't recognize. He politely declined when one girl held a tray out to him.

The principessa may have sought diversity among her guests, and the goal was reached. Some men and women were elegantly dressed in evening clothes, others looked like they had borrowed jackets or dresses for the occasion. Dino recognized one of the latter right away because the man, wearing a bright orange jacket, towered over everyone near.

"That's Signor Nozzoli. I worked for him in a ceramics shop," Dino whispered to the professor. "Is he...was he...I mean...?"

The professor smiled. "*Il Toro* has been a very good friend of the principessa for many years. A very good friend."

Now, the line had moved farther, and Dino and the professor found themselves in front of a tiny woman in a wheelchair. She wore a bright magenta dress, over which she had a red velvet jacket and around her neck a fuchsia stole. Two perfectly round red spots highlighted her cheeks, reminding Dino of the Venetian dolls in a shop on Via dei Tornabuoni. Her tiny feet were encased in scarlet bedroom slippers.

Looking down on her, Dino was fascinated by her hair, yellow curls barely hiding a pink scalp. Someone, perhaps Teressa, had dyed the end of each curl in red. When Dino looked at her face, he recognized the tiny blue eyes that seemed even smaller since her eyebrows had been plucked entirely clean.

The professor was talking. "And this is my gifted student, Aldobrandino Sporenza. We call him Dino."

"Ah, Signor Aldobrandino Sporenza." Her voice was so soft Dino could hardly hear her. "I do not like Dino. We will call you Aldobrandino. It is a pleasure to meet you."

She held out a porcelain hand, the fingers covered with diamond, ruby and sapphire rings. Dino thought it might break if he held it too long.

"And where are you from, Signor Aldobrandino Sporenza?"

"I'm...I'm from a little town called Sant'Antonio. It's near Lucca." Why was his throat so dry?

"Ah, Lucca, Lucca, Lucca. Maurizio was from Lucca. He took me home with him to his little apartment. He cooked lovely meals for me. He wouldn't let me do a thing. We made passionate love everywhere, in the parks, in the amphitheater. One night on top of the walls. Ah, Maurizio. He died so young. Do you see that painting over there? Maurizio did that. I was only twenty-three then. A long time ago..."

Dino feared she was falling asleep. "Principessa," the professor said, rather loudly, "it's a lovely painting. Let us leave you to other guests now." He grabbed Dino by the arm and led him to a group near a marble statue of Venus.

Standing behind the professor, Dino could hear only bits of the conversation. It was something about the works of Alberto Burri, an abstract painter whose work Dino was barely acquainted with.

"Have you seen what he's doing now?" one of the men asked. "He's using charred wood and burlap. Imagine! Charred wood and burlap!"

"Well," a tall woman in a mink stole said, "that may be better than his collages with pumice and tar."

Everyone began to laugh, and Dino moved to the edge of another distinguished group. Here, three men and two women, all balancing china plates and wine glasses, were dissecting the works of Emilio Vedova.

"I hear he's creating exciting painted things of wood and metal. They stand alone and are hinged," a woman said.

"I hope they're better than those L-shaped canvases he showed in Venice," a man said.

Dino edged to the far end of the room, where he could hear rain pelting the tall windows. He felt like he had when he was with the group at Viareggio. He desperately wanted to go home. Then he felt a large hand on his shoulder.

"Dino!"

"Signor Nozzoli!" Dino had never been so happy to see someone.

"It's good to see you again, Dino. You've made it. You've been invited to one of Principessa Maria Elena's salons."

"Um. Do you come to many of these?"

"Oh, a few. I've known the principessa for a long time. We are friends. Very good friends," Tomasso Nozzoli smiled. "But now I'm sure the principessa just likes to show me off, prove that she knows a lot of dumb football players as well as famous artists. I don't mind. I'd do anything for her. And this gives me a chance to get out. Forget things."

"I'm glad to see you, sir. Are you all right?"

"You mean after that little tussle in the *Calcio Storico*? Oh yes, that's all over. So are my playing days. Just taking care of the shop now, me and Bella. You should stop by sometime. Bella misses you." Signor Nozzoli blew his nose, causing most everyone in the room to look at him. "And you know, Dino, I miss you, too."

He patted Dino on the shoulder and then joined an oddly dressed group discussing recent articles and photographs in *Panorama*. Dino wandered to a corner where he hoped no one could see him.

No such luck. Wheeling quickly toward him, Principessa Maria Elena was suddenly at his side.

"Sit down here next to me, Signor Aldobrandino Sporenza. I need to talk to someone young."

"Thank you for inviting me, ma'am."

"You're bored, aren't you?"

"No! No! This is a wonderful party! Thank you for inviting me."

When she smiled, the red dots on her cheeks seemed to dance. "No, you can be honest. To tell the truth, I'm bored, too. I don't like many of these people. Oh, there are some exceptions, like Signor Nozzoli over there. But so many of these people are stuffy, self-centered, opinionated, pretentious bores. They talk about art as if they know what it is when actually all they know is what they have read in the art journals and they pretend the opinions are their own."

Dino didn't know what to say.

"I like the other people," she said. "The shopkeepers and the street cleaners and the lowly civil servants. This gives them a chance to tell their grandchildren they attended a salon of Principessa Maria Elena Elisabetta Margherita di Savoia."

She sighed and wiped her eyes with a tiny lace handkerchief.

"You wonder why I invited these people? Well, I give these little salons just so I can prove to myself that I can still do it. When you get old, my young friend, you find you have to keep doing the things you did when you were younger."

"But why?" Dino asked.

"Why?" Her laugh was like a tiny bell in the distance. "Just to prove that you're not getting old."

She put her dainty hand on his arm. "Getting old is a terrible, terrible thing, Signor Aldobrandino Sporenza. Here I am, in a wheelchair, not able to leave this dingy old palazzo. I can't even go up the stairs anymore. No, I just stay here."

"You have a beautiful palace, Signora."

"The only good part is when Teressa opens the curtains when I awake in the morning. If it's not raining, I can look across and see the buildings glowing in the sunlight on the other side. And I can hear the Arno swirling along. The Arno gives me hope. As long as I can hear the Arno, I can get up for another day."

"It's a wonderful river," Dino said. "I like to walk along it going to my classes."

The principessa held his arm tighter, and her eyes were pleading. "Walk for me, Signor Aldobrandino Sporenza. Walk for me along the beautiful Arno."

She smiled, and wheeled herself off to another group. Professor Mariotti returned to his side.

"Dino! What did she say? She's never talked to anyone as long as you!"

"Oh, I don't know. She said she likes giving these parties."

"Well, of course, she does. All the famous artists and historians and professors are here. We all adore her so."

"Yes," Dino said. "She's quite a lady."

He looked across the room and saw Tomasso Nozzoli crouched next to the principessa. He had his arm around her thin shoulders and they were laughing.

Chapter Twenty-Three

Christmas 1965

Dino kept reading the letter over and over as he waited in the Florence terminal for the bus to Sant'Antonio. It had come a week ago and he recognized the delicate handwriting on the Florentine stationery right away.

Dear Dino,

I obtained your address from your mother and I hope you don't mind that I'm writing to you.

I hope this finds you well. You must have such an exciting life in Florence. Sometimes I wish I had gone to university.

I understand you will be home for Christmas.

Best wishes.
Francesca

What the hell is that all about? Dino kept asking himself. Why is she writing after all this time? What is she trying to say? Does she still have a boyfriend? She doesn't mention him. Sometimes she wishes she had gone to university but sometimes she doesn't? And does she want to see me at Christmas? Was that a hint that I should see her? She doesn't say that either.

What the hell. Women!

Dino ignored the fact that he hadn't ever written to Francesca. He folded the fragile paper, replaced it in its envelope, and put it in his back pocket.

Dino had already had conflicting feelings about going home for Christmas. So much had happened since the last time he was home, last Christmas. Then, he couldn't wait to get back to Florence. Sant'Antonio was so stifling. Now, he didn't know. Sometimes he missed his parents and all the other people in the village. He knew he was just this kid from a village and maybe he shouldn't try to be anything else. Then he thought about all the things he had seen and experienced in Florence. How could he give all that up?

And then the letter came. Should he go to Lucca and try to see Francesca? Did he want to start that again? What were his feelings about her now? He didn't know. He felt like he was being pulled in so many directions. He thought of Sofia, and how fascinating she was, and how different she was from Francesca.

Women!

Finally the bus, crowded with Christmas travelers, left the terminal. Dino found a window seat and was soon joined by an elderly woman dressed in black who immediately pulled out her rosary.

As the bus entered A-11, the face of the city changed. No longer the glorious city of the Medici, it was simply another industrial complex. Dino leaned his head against the window and tried to sleep, but too many thoughts churned in his head. He looked out on the misty landscape, past Prato, Pistoia, Montecatini Terme.

Then a stop in Lucca, but it was outside the city's walls so Dino couldn't be bombarded by memories of the places where he and Francesca had gone.

Then Sant'Antonio. The bus stopped in front of Leoni's, decorated now with green and red crepe paper chains across the window. The small figures of a *presepio* rested in a cardboard stable in one corner. Dino remembered how he thought the figures of Mary and Joseph and the Baby Jesus were so big when he was a little boy.

Since it was raining, the old men who usually sat in front of Leoni's were at a back table inside playing a long-standing game of *scopa*. Dino wondered if they argued as much as the players he remembered as a child.

On the wall outside, a death poster, just as there had been last Christmas for his grandmother. This was for Signora Duccia Morino. He remembered her vaguely, an old woman who had a large mole on her right cheek.

Next door, where the smells of the hanging rabbits and pigs drifted outside from the butcher shop, Guido Marconi was arguing with a customer, his hands waving a meat cleaver in the air. Dino had always been terrified of the burly man.

Dino didn't bring his umbrella, so he hurried down the street to his home.

"Dino!"

Lucia engulfed her son, and her apron left his jacket covered with flour. "I didn't know which bus you were going to take, you never told me, but it's all right, you're here now. Are you hungry? I made some biscotti like you like them, crunchy, and we have some other cookies and candy, too. Don't tell your Papa about that or he'll eat it all. Sit down, sit down, you must be so tired."

"I'm fine, Mama. I've been sitting for two hours."

They sat at the kitchen table. Lucia's eyes filled with tears. "Oh, Dino, Dino."

"Mama, we've talked at least three times a week for the last year..."

"It's not the same. We've missed you so much. Oh, I have to call your Papa and tell him you're home."

Dino walked to the back of the house while his mother was on the phone. The backyard was smaller, too, and he wondered how that picnic table could hold so many people.

His mother's hand was on his shoulder. "Dino, have you ever found Roberto? Did you look for him?

"I looked for him, Mama. The shop was empty. A man said it was empty for a long time."

He didn't say that he thought he had seen his uncle twice, once at Father Lorenzo's soup kitchen and the other at *Calcio Storico*. No point getting a lecture on why he didn't pursue the man.

"I can't imagine where he is," Lucia said. "I wonder if that was really him at Mama's funeral. Does Adolfo know anything?"

"Adolfo never mentions him."

Dino hugged his mother, an embrace quickly ended when the door flew open.

"Dino!"

"Rosa!"

Kisses all over his face from Rosa, and then a hard handshake from Antonio, who had followed her.

"I thought I saw you coming down the street," Rosa said, "but I had to get Antonio to clean up. He's building another birdhouse. That will be eight in the backyard."

She put her arm around him and he bent down to kiss her.

Over coffee and cookies, Lucia and Rosa, with Antonio smiling but silent, brought Dino up to date on what was happening in the village. Annabella has had a cold for more than a month and people were worried about her. Fausta wasn't feeling well either and she missed Mass last Sunday. Father Sangretto has been giving more fire-and-brimstone sermons and people are starting to put less money in the collection basket.

Dino's mind wandered. He thought of the weeks at Viareggio and the pot party, of Principessa Maria Elena's salon, of the *Calcio Storico,* of Father Lorenzo's soup kitchen, of Sofia and Elvis, of Michelangelo's tomb, of Beatles' songs and of The Waking Slave...

"And ever since Signor Cardone passed away, Rufina has refused to come out of the house, and..." Dino said he had to wash up.

That night, Dino lay on top of his bed, looking up at the moon, which had now displaced the cloudy skies. He could no longer fit in the bed where he had slept since he was a boy. He stretched his arms and found that he could almost touch both walls. He missed his records and his guitar.

The Christmas eve celebration was again at Rosa's, who, of course, made *baccalà* with crusty bread. Annabella and Fausta sneezed into lacy white handkerchiefs and hoped no one would catch their germs. Ezio teased his father, pointing out that it was a year now since he and Rosa had gotten engaged, so why weren't they getting married? Rosa and Antonio blushed and Antonio said he was ready and Rosa said she needed to get a new dress but she was too busy to go to Lucca.

When everyone went to midnight Mass, Father Sangretto looked sadly at Dino before putting the host on his tongue. Dino noticed that Saint Anthony's statue still had scratches on its tunic, reminders of the disastrous procession now more than three years ago.

Dino went for long walks during his week at home, partly to escape from his mother's constant questions but mostly to try to put himself again in the place where he had grown up. Despite the cold and rain, he often stayed out for hours, sometimes sitting in Saint Zita's chapel, trying to sort things out in his head. He read Francesca's letter so often, it was now in shreds.

Convincing himself that he needed to go to Lucca to get some art supplies, he took the bus on the second last day of his vacation. After touring the churches of San Michele and San Paolino and the others, he hesitated, and then walked purposefully up Via Veneto and Via Fillungo. There, snoozing in the sun in front of the green door, was an orange-and-white cat. Marcellina opened one eye when he approached, then went back to sleep. He rang the bell. Again. Again. No answer.

Where did Professor Ponzo say Francesca worked? The stationery shop on Via Sant'Andrea.

No one was in the shop when he entered. He looked around and then opened the door to leave.

"May I help you?"

She was smaller than he remembered. Not just shorter, but thinner. Her long hair was tied up on top of her head. He'd never seen her hair like that before and didn't know if he liked it. She wore a pale pink blouse and a pearl pendant, the one his mother gave her for her graduation. He remembered unclasping the chain when they made love. Why was his heart beating so fast?

"Dino!" He could hardly hear her.

"Hi, Francesca."

His cold hands rested on the glass counter, hers on a box of Florentine stationery.

"I got your letter."

She blushed. "Yes. Well. I just thought I'd write."

"I came home for Christmas." Her skin was lighter than Sofia's, her breasts under her blouse were smaller but still lovely.

"Was Florence all decorated?"

"Yes. Some great decorations—"

"—maybe someday I'll go there for Christmas."

"Yes. There's lots of decorations."

He didn't know whether to leave or to continue this stupid conversation.

"Dino—"

"Why did you write, Francesca? It's been so long."

"I guess…I guess I just wanted to."

"But why?"

"I thought it would be nice to see you again."

"Don't you have a boyfriend? Professor Ponzo said you did. It didn't take you long to forget me, did it?" Dino's voice always cracked when he raised it.

"Domenico? No! No! He wasn't my boyfriend. We just went out a few times and had pizza. We never even kissed, we never, never… well, you know."

"Is he still around?"

"No! He took his Vespa and went to Milan."

"Do you miss him?"

"No!"

It was getting very warm in the shop.

"What about you, Dino? Don't you have a girlfriend? That English girl?"

"Francesca, Penny is not my girlfriend. I don't have any girlfriends. None." He hated to admit this.

"I'm sorry," Francesca said.

All right. Time for the big question.

"Francesca, do you miss me? Is that why you wrote?"

"Dino, sometimes I miss you a lot. But I know you've got another life now, and I'm not part of it. I know that's why you haven't written."

"I almost did. A couple of times."

"That's OK," she said. "I didn't expect you to. But you know how much I cared—care—for you. I would just like us to be friends. That's all. I guess that's why I wrote."

She turned her back so he wouldn't see her tears.

Dino was confused. "How can we be friends? I'm there and you're here."

"I don't know." She turned around again. "Maybe we could both write sometime, or you could come to see me when you're home and we could go out for pizza and talk about movies and artists and things like we used to? Would you like that?"

Dino wasn't sure of his answer, but he said, "Sure. That would be nice."

"All right then. I'd like that, too."

"Francesca, do you ever think you'd come to Florence? Maybe I could show you around."

Francesca smiled. "I think it would take a miracle for me to go to Florence. It's much too big for me. I'd be so afraid."

"But I'd be there."

"Yes. That would be nice."

Dino tightened the scarf around his neck. "OK. Well, I better be going."

"OK, Dino. It was good to see you." She went into the back room. Dino thought her shoulders were shaking.

On the bus home, Dino kept muttering. "Women. Shit! Shit! Shit!" He was terribly confused. He thought he had put Francesca in the past, but the sight of her pretty face, her small hands, her slim figure brought back so many memories. She was so different from Sofia, so shy where Sofia was strong, so modest that she undressed in the dark, while Sofia modeled in the nude. Could he be attracted to both of them?

Lucia and Paolo didn't understand why Dino was so sullen when he returned from Lucca and why he hardly touched the ravioli that Rosa had sent over.

"Let the boy alone," Paolo told Lucia as they washed dishes. "Who knows what's going on in his head."

"I know what's going on in his head," Lucia said. "He doesn't want to go back to Florence. He wants to stay here. I know it. I'm sure of it."

"Don't be too sure."

Since he had barely slept, Dino got up early the next day, put some crusty bread and an orange in his pockets and went for a walk. He stopped first at the chapel of Saint Zita, but it was still locked. Then, since he hadn't been to the Cielo on this visit, he found himself on the long and winding road to the farmhouse. Donna had driven the truck down to Reboli to pick up parts for the olive press and Ezio was at the table reading *La Repubblica.*

"Dino! Come in! We haven't had a chance to talk all week. Coffee?"

"Yes, please."

Over the years, ever since he was in Ezio's fifth grade class, Dino had developed more and more respect for his former teacher. He couldn't imagine being a member of the Resistance during the war or what he would have done if his own lover had been killed in a massacre. Everyone in the village rejoiced when Ezio met Donna, when they married and when they bought the farmhouse known as the Cielo.

"So tell me about your painting, Dino. What have you been painting lately?" Ezio poured Dino a cup of coffee, put out a plate of biscotti and sat across from him in front of the crackling fireplace.

"I've been working on a landscape looking across Florence to the hills. I've never really painted a landscape so big before. It's fun."

"And your music?"

"Still playing. I make up these stupid songs and sing them to myself."

"Dino. Listen to me. Don't ever say anything you do is stupid. I know you. Everything you do has some value. All right?"

"Yes, sir."

Ezio ignored the formality. "And how are you finding Florence now? When I was growing up there, I didn't really appreciate how wonderful and amazing it is. I guess I was too young. But you're not, right?"

"You know, sometimes I wander around looking up at the architecture and the sculptures and the paintings, and I bump into people. I have to say, 'Oops, I'm sorry. I'm just this little kid from Sant'Antonio and I've never seen such great pieces of art before.'"

Dino grinned and Ezio laughed.

"Dino, you don't have to apologize. No one—no one!—has ever been able to really appreciate the art and beauty of Florence. Just take it in one piece at a time."

"Like what?"

"Well, for example, take Ghiberti's doors of the Baptistry. Just look at one panel for a long time. Pick your panel and stand in front of it. Mine is the Adam and Eve. Such detail. Such a beautiful rendering."

"I think I like Esau and Jacob."

"That's great, too. So, do you have any favorite piece of art now that you've been in Florence more than a year?"

"The same as it was when I got there. The Waking Slave."

"Because?"

"I wish I could express this better. Michelangelo said the figures in his unfinished sculptures were trying to get out, be free. That's how I felt when I went to Florence. I know, I know, I'm supposed to love Sant'Antonio, and all the people here, and everything about it. And I do. But when I went to Florence I wanted to experience something much bigger. I wanted to do things. I wanted to be more than just this kid from Sant'Antonio."

"And now? You're putting this in past tense, Dino, if you don't mind your former grammar teacher telling you that."

"Signor Maffini…"

"Good God, Dino. It's been almost ten years since you were in my class. You can stop the "signor" stuff now, all right?" Ezio was grinning.

Dino blushed. "Sorry."

"Go on. I've taken my teacher hat off now."

"I haven't talked to anyone about this, um, Ezio. Not even my parents."

"Go on."

"It's just that, sometimes, not always, but sometimes, I just feel so, well, torn."

"In what way?"

Dino folded and unfolded his hands. "Well, sometimes, like I really am this kid from Sant'Antonio who doesn't belong in a place like Florence. Shouldn't even have gone there. People there are so, oh, sophisticated. They know everything. They can talk about art and architecture and sculpture. They know all the artists, some I've never heard of. They know food. They know wine. Hell, I work in a trattoria and I have to ask about wine all the time."

"So you think you should come back to Sant'Antonio, and maybe work in your Papa's *pasticceria* and marry a girl from here and settle down and have lots of kids. I saw Benedetta Mendicino the other day."

"No, no, no!"

They both laughed.

"And then," Dino said, "I think about how wonderful Florence is, all the art and museums and palazzi. Sometimes I feel like I'm in the Renaissance and it's all there for me to enjoy. And I think about Sant'Antonio and what it has. Just a statue of Saint Anthony."

"Well, let's try to forget about that day, shall we?" Ezio leaned back and laughed. "Dino, you said sometimes you feel this way. What about the other times?"

"The other times." Dino stretched his arms above his head. "Well, sometimes I really do miss Sant'Antonio. The people here seem more, I don't know, real. They care about each other. The other night at Rosa's, everyone was so concerned about Annabella and Fausta, and they just had colds. You'd think they were going to die in a minute."

"I'm sure people care in Florence, too."

Dino was excited now. "Ezio, I met this great guy. He's a priest, actually, but you wouldn't know it. He runs a soup kitchen in Santa Croce. Ezio, there are such wonderful people there…the volunteers…"

For a minute, Dino was going to bring up Sofia, but he needed to stay on the subject.

"And all these people who come to eat. They have nothing, Ezio, nothing. Father Lorenzo spends all his time there and he knows everybody and he'd give his life for any one of them."

"So he's not a priest like Father Sangretto?"

"Ha! No, not like Father Sangretto, not at all. I've never met a priest like Father Lorenzo before. In fact, I think I'm going to volunteer at the soup kitchen myself."

"Really! That's great! I'm so proud of you!" Ezio grinned. "You've really changed since you went to Florence, Dino, don't you think?"

"I don't know. I still am so confused. I'm going to be twenty next year and I don't know what I'm going to do with my life. I don't know where I want to live, I don't know what I want to be. Sometimes I want to be an artist, sometimes I want to be a musician, sometimes not either of them. I don't know. Something more?"

Others might have smiled, or even laughed, but Ezio did neither. Instead, he reached across the table and put his hands on Dino's arms.

"Dino, let me tell you a story. You know I grew up in Florence, but as I said, I didn't appreciate it much when I was there. I went off to school in Pisa and then I joined the Resistance. After the war I became a schoolteacher. How good I am as a schoolteacher I don't know."

"Signor—Ezio—you are an excellent schoolteacher!"

"We'll let that go. Anyway, I've lived in Florence, I've lived in Pisa, I've lived in the hills, and now I live here. You know what, Dino? It doesn't matter where you live. You're you. You make your own life. A city or a village doesn't change you. It just happens to be where you live. If you want to be an artist, fine. You could do that in Florence or in Sant'Antonio. If you want to be a musician. Fine. Do that anywhere you want. If you want to open up a soup kitchen, fine. Well, I guess we don't have a lot of poor people here, so you couldn't do that in Sant'Antonio. But there are places where you could. You know what I mean."

"I think so, but still…"

"Still?"

"I don't know. I just don't know."

"Mind if I give you a little advice?"

"No, of course not."

"Dino, I'm almost forty years old. You think I know the answers to any of this? Of course I don't. Some days I wonder what the hell I'm doing and what I'm going to do for the rest of my life. But I just live one day and then the next and then the next. Thank God I've got Donna and she feels the same way. We muddle along, but we enjoy what we are doing, and we love each other. So my advice to you is this: See what each new day brings, because every day will be different. Learn what you can in Florence because there's so much to learn there. But if you want to come back to Sant'Antonio, or go to Lucca, or go to Paris or to New York or anywhere in the world, then that's a possibility, too. The whole world is open to you, Dino, and you can do anything you want. You don't have to find the answers now. Just raise the questions and see the opportunities. You know, Dino, you may find something you've never even thought of. For now, just enjoy."

Dino shook Ezio's hand and was surprised when Ezio gave him a hug.

"I guess I've got a lot of thinking to do," Dino said.

"Don't think so much, Dino. Enjoy!"

When Dino boarded the bus back to Florence the next day, he still had more questions than answers. But at least now he knew the questions better. Except for the ones about Francesca and Sofia.

Chapter Twenty-Four

Summer/Fall 1966

Dino thought he might receive another letter on Florentine stationery in the months that followed, but none came. Twice, once in February and once just before Easter, he started to write one himself, but got no farther than "Dear Francesca." He resolved to put her out of his mind forever. And he did. Except at night and except when he thought about how different she was from Sofia.

Taking Ezio's advice, Dino tried to enjoy all the wonders of Florence and not worry about his own confusions. He stood before Ghiberti's doors of the Baptistry and after a couple of weeks couldn't decide if he liked the Adam and Eve or the Esau and Jacob panels better. He spent more time in front of The Waking Slave, trying to understand what Michelangelo was thinking as he was carving.

He was busier than ever, both in school and away from it. He finished the landscape of Florence, which not only won Professor Mariotti's high praise but also a nomination for prestigious all-university honors, rare for a third-year student.

"Dino, Dino, Dino," the professor whispered in his ear one day in a sketching class. Dino turned his head away from the garlic breath. "You have such great talent. Why don't you paint more? Why do you waste your time playing on your guitar? You're a painter! Paint!"

Dino smiled, but that night began writing a new song.

The months went by quickly. Once again, the *Calcio Storico* in June disrupted the lives of everyone on Piazza Santa Croce, but Dino went off to paint or play his guitar in distant parks. Father Lorenzo told him later that attendance was down because everyone knew *il Toro* would not be there. Tomasso Nozzoli himself stayed in his shop during each of the games, tidying up the displays and talking to Bella.

Dino again did well on his final examinations and despite his mother's pleas, he did not go home after classes ended in June. He needed to make some money, he told her, well aware that he had put only a few thousand *lire* in the box labeled Gallinotti under his bed. Working every night at Trattoria Eleanora, he had become accustomed to the oddities of the customers and had replaced Raffaele as the head waiter.

Early in the summer, Signor Michellini discovered Raffaele trying to pry open the drawer where the restaurant's money was kept. Signor Michellini called the *carabinieri*, who hauled Raffaele to court, which sentenced him to nine months in the Le Murate, the men's prison near the market of Sant'Ambrogio. It wasn't far from Dino's basement room, but Dino didn't plan to visit him. Penny went once, but found Raffaele so angry she came right home.

When the trattoria closed for two weeks in August, Dino declined Penny's invitation to join the group going to Viareggio. They only wanted him along so he could play his guitar, he reasoned, correctly. So he stayed in Florence, planning to endure the heat by staying in his room during the day and covering up as much as possible to avoid the mosquitoes on his walks along the Arno at night.

He told himself he didn't mind not having friends.

Then Mila convinced him to spend the two weeks volunteering at Casa del Popolo, where she worked.

"Poor people don't take vacations," she said.

Dino didn't know much about the Casa del Popolo, only that it was a meeting place for Communists and that it served the poor in the area around Piazza dei Ciompi, a short walk north of Santa Croce. Dino had often visited the artisans' shops and the flea market inside the piazza's colonnaded walls, but hadn't gone into the Casa itself.

He was surprised to find so much activity. In one room, a half dozen women sorted out clothing that had been donated for the poor.

In another, men and women arranged cans and packages of food. A hulking man unloaded gallons of water from a truck and stacked them in a corner. At the end, in a room decorated with Communist posters, elderly men argued loudly over their *scopa* and *briscola* cards. A game show blared on a television set, but no one was watching.

Dino was assigned to sort the clothing, separating adults from the children, and boys from girls. He couldn't believe what was donated. Some had barely been worn, others were in shreds.

"Look at this," one woman said as she held up a shimmering evening dress even Dino knew was very expensive. "It's never been worn, but who around here would wear such a thing?"

"Much too small for me," a busty woman said.

"I'll wear it the next time I go to the opera," another said. The dress was tossed into a box labeled "Resale" and it would eventually be taken to a small shop that provided a little income for the Casa.

When Dino tried to unfold a red plaid men's shirt, he found that it was missing a sleeve, half of its collar and all of its buttons.

"Why would anyone give something like this?" he wondered.

"Because," the busty woman said, "people think they're being so good if they give their junk to the poor."

"And the poor should be so very grateful for their great kindness," another said bitterly.

"The poor near Santa Croce at least."

The women were getting angry now.

"The Arno could flood us all out and nobody would pay any attention," one said.

"Right. Who do you think cares about the people around Santa Croce? The businessmen? All they care about is how much money the tourists bring in."

This was followed by a string of invectives that Dino had never heard, not even from the group at Viareggio.

One afternoon, Dino looked up from his table to see Tomasso Nozzoli, a big cardboard box on his shoulder.

"Signor Nozzoli! How are you?"

"Fine, just fine. The principessa asked me to deliver these things here."

With great care, considering the size of his hands, the giant of a man opened the box and gently lifted out one bejeweled dress after another.

"Wow!" Dino said. The women gathered round to finger the unexpected bounty.

"*Bene*," Tomasso said. "The principessa knows that you can't give these things away to the poor, but maybe you could sell them at the shop."

One woman held a flaming red silk cocktail dress against her and went over to a mirror.

"Oh, I almost forgot," Tomasso said, reaching to the bottom of the box. He pulled out a leather case. Inside, jeweled pendants mixed with diamond rings, pearl earrings and crystal tiaras.

"*Santa Maria!*" a woman cried. "If we sold all that we could operate the Casa for a month."

As the women clucked over the dresses and jewelry, Dino asked Signor Nozzoli about the principessa.

"Not well," he replied. "She's gotten a lot weaker in the last months. She's in her wheelchair all the time now. I go over there every day, it's not far from my shop, and try to get her to eat something, but she just nibbles. Teressa tries, too, and then the poor lady gets hysterical and has to go to her room."

"The principessa must like it that you visit."

"I don't know." Tomasso wiped his eyes. "Sometimes I think she doesn't want me around because she doesn't want me to see her like this. I think she's given up. She's starting to give away all her clothes and things."

"I'm sorry."

"You know," the big man said, "I've always loved that little lady. I'd do anything for her."

Dino saw Tomasso's eyes fill with tears and his shoulders hunch as he left the room.

After the two weeks were up, Dino stopped at the soup kitchen one morning to see if Father Lorenzo needed any help. Or maybe it was to see if Sofia was there.

She was!

"Hi," he said as he approached the serving table where she was ladling out soup. He thought the pale blue blouse complemented her olive skin.

"Hi," she said as she filled an old man's bowl.

"It's great to see you again," he said, and mumbled "damn" under his breath. Didn't he know another word? And why did he have to say that? He had finished the class in which she was the model.

"I've missed seeing you around," she said.

She did?

"Um, I guess I've been busy. But I'd like to come here more often. To see Father Lorenzo, I mean."

"That would be great," she said.

Wow. She said it, too.

Dino found Father Lorenzo in the storage room. The priest did indeed need help, and the following morning Dino stood by Sofia in the serving line as a volunteer, grinning.

"OK," she said, "you need to give each person a good helping of eggs. I'll serve the potatoes and they can pick up toast at the end of the line. They haven't eaten all night and they're hungry."

"OK."

"You can give the kids a little less, but they're hungry, too."

"OK."

Dino hadn't been paying much attention to what she was saying, since he was more interested in the way her eyes crinkled when she smiled. But he picked up a big spoon and began to serve the scrambled eggs. In the days that followed, he always managed to find the place next to Sofia but they were so busy they didn't get to talk much. Dino vowed that they would soon.

"We're getting more and more customers," Father Lorenzo said one night as they washed dishes after the last diner had left. "The poor are getting poorer."

"Father," Dino said, "Can I ask you something? Don't you ever get discouraged? Don't you ever want to just go back and be a parish priest or whatever you did before this?"

The priest smiled. "That's two questions, but I'll answer the second one first. No, I don't want to be a parish priest again. I mean, it was a wonderful and satisfying experience, but there are other men who can do the job just as well as I did, even better.

"As for the first question, sure, I get discouraged. Sometimes I go back to my room at night and I lay on my bed and I think, 'What's the use, Lord? Will it ever get better?' And how does the Lord answer? You expect me to say that He reaches down and tells me everything is going to be all right. Well, He doesn't. He doesn't say anything. And I go to sleep and I get up the next morning and I look out my window at the people lining up for the soup kitchen and I think, 'This is what I have to do. This is my job, and I'm good at it, and I can do it. Besides, there's no one else who will do it.' So I go down and I start another day. Maybe it's not going to get any better, but I know if I didn't do what I do, things might get a lot worse."

Dino said he wished he could feel like that.

Father Lorenzo put a soapy hand on Dino's shoulder. "Dino, give yourself a chance. You've got lots of time. What you're doing right now, right here, is very important. You're showing courage, you're showing bravery. You're showing it by doling out eggs and ham, even by washing dishes."

"Doesn't seem very brave."

"Dino, there are a lot of people who won't even look at the people we serve. You can see them all the time, hurrying away when a beggar approaches. No, what you're doing is sacrificing a little of yourself to come here. You can be proud of yourself for that."

Dino had to think about that.

"And, Dino," the priest continued, "someday you may be asked to do something more, maybe a lot more, and by doing this today you'll be able to do it."

Dino didn't know what the priest was talking about and remained silent. "What's the sacrifice in helping poor people?" he wondered.

They scoured out the sink and started mopping the floor.

"Dino," Father Lorenzo said, "you know what I worry about the most? What if something terrible would happen in Florence? Not another war. I pray to God we don't have another war here. But what if we had an earthquake? It happens in Italy a lot, you know."

The priest stopped mopping and stood still. His voice was rising now and Dino was sure there were tears in his eyes. "Or what if, what if...I can't even think about this...what if the Arno floods again, Dino? It hasn't really flooded since 1944. That's more than two decades ago. They've never fixed the dams in the north the way they should have, so it could happen, you know."

Dino changed the water in his pail and resumed mopping. "My uncle was worrying about that the other day. He works in the *Biblioteca Nazionale*. But most times when I walk by the Arno, it looks calm and peaceful. Except when it rains a lot."

"Calm and peaceful? Don't you believe it, Dino. Have you ever seen the Arno in November? And the rains? *"La pioggia di novembre?"* If I believed in an angry God, and I don't because I think He's a loving God, I might think that the Arno could be God's punishment. And if the Arno flooded again, many people who are barely able to survive now, who have terrible places to live, who don't have jobs, well, they'd be in far worse shape. They would lose their homes, everything, and they'd have no place to go. How would we care for them all? I don't know how we could do it, Dino, I just don't know."

Father Lorenzo leaned back against the wall, his eyes closed. Dino didn't know what to say. In silence, they emptied their pails, hung up the mops, locked the doors, and Dino went home.

That night, although the Arno was more than a block away, he thought he could hear roaring waters.

When classes started again, Dino was in his third year at the Accademia. He cut back on the nights he worked at the trattoria and instead volunteered more at the *cucina popolare*. He began to realize that it was not only to see Sofia more often, but also that he was getting to actually enjoy serving up the eggs and toast to the hungry patrons. He'd never felt that way about anything before.

In the last week of October, after the last diner had left, he finally summoned up enough courage to ask Sofia to sit down in a corner and talk.

"Well," she said, taking off her apron, "busy day. More people all the time."

"And there seems to be more young mothers and children," Dino said.

"The kids are so cute," Sofia said. "I can't wait to have some of my own."

"Really? You want more than one?"

"Lots, Dino, lots." She smiled.

They began to talk about themselves. Dino told her about wanting to leave Sant'Antonio but that he still had mixed and confusing feelings about where he wanted to live and especially what he wanted to do.

"It's not like I'm a kid anymore," he said. "I'm twenty years old!"

"Really? I thought you were older. I'm twenty-four and I thought you were my age."

"Really? Does it matter?"

"No, no." She looked him in the eye. "Dino, I think you're such a great guy, coming here to help all the time. I don't know any other guys your age who would do that. I really like that."

"Well, look at you! You do it, too."

"Yes, but I come from such a poor part of Italy, Dino. I feel like I should just do a little something."

Dino leaned forward as Sofia told her story. She was from a village in Calabria, "one of those places where you think the houses are going to fall down the cliff into the ocean any minute." Her mother died in childbirth and she was the only child. When she was seventeen, her father, who owned a tobacco shop, was aroused early in the morning by four big men and taken away. His body, with his hands tied behind his back, was found in a cave three days later. He had been shot in the back.

"It was the mafia," she said, as matter-of-factly as if she were talking about the weather. "They said my Papa owed them money, but he didn't."

After his funeral, Sofia took all the *lire* stashed under his mattress and took a train to Naples. Too noisy, too dirty. She stayed only two days, and went to Rome. Too crowded, too confusing. She took a train to Siena. Beautiful, but she couldn't find work. She took a train to Florence. She found part-time jobs as a seamstress in a dress shop, in a men's hat shop and, of course, as a model at the Accademia.

"With all three, I am doing all right. I've got a little apartment near Santa Maria Novella. I've been here six years now, and look, I can almost speak Florentine!"

Dino realized then that the reason he didn't quite understand every word she said was because of traces of her Calabrian dialect.

"You know," he said, "I've never even met someone from the south before you."

"I suppose you've called us *terroni*," she said.

"*Terroni*? I don't even know what that means."

"It literally means 'of the earth,' but it's very derogatory. It would be like saying 'nigger' in the United States."

Dino realized his life had been more sheltered than he thought. "Really? That's terrible."

"It's OK," Sofia said. "In the south, we call people north of Rome *polentoni*."

"Because we're supposed to like polenta?"

"Yes!"

"Actually," Dino said. "I hate polenta. All that mushy cornmeal. My mother makes it and I can hardly get it down."

They laughed until they had tears in their eyes.

"Say," Dino said, "next Friday is Armed Forces Day and I can get the night off. Would you like to go to a movie with me?"

"Really?"

"Sure."

"What movie?"

"There's *The Bible*. It's American, but it was produced by Dino de Laurentiis so it can't be all bad. There's supposed to be a great flood scene in it."

"Oh, I hate floods," Sofia said. "There was a terrible flood near my village and an old lady actually drowned. I'll probably close my eyes. But, sure, I'd love to go."

"That would be great." Dino said. He reached over to hold her hand. It was strong and firm, not like Francesca's.

"And, Dino," she said as they left the soup kitchen, "maybe afterward you could come to my apartment."

"And?"

"And talk, of course!" She kissed his cheek. All the way home, hoping against hope, Dino wondered if they'd do more than talk.

A few days later, Mila wondered why someone was calling so early in the morning, and was even more curious when she went down to the basement to wake Dino.

"It's 5 o'clock and you have a phone call from Father Lorenzo?"

Pulling on his pants and wiping his eyes, Dino ran up the stairs to pick up the receiver.

"Yes. Yes, Father. You're kidding! Are you sure? OK, I'll be right there."

Mila put the receiver back. "Something wrong?"

"Um, no. Nothing wrong. Gotta go."

Standing clear of the driving rain, Father Lorenzo was waiting for Dino at the door of the soup kitchen. "Now I'm not sure of this, but I think you ought to know. That man you thought was your uncle when you saw him in the soup kitchen last year? Well, some of his friends brought him here last night from the hospital. They said they didn't know where else to take him. They said he got into a fight a week ago and was badly beaten. He has three broken ribs and cuts and bruises all over. Yes, he'd been drinking. Heavily. Now, he needs a lot of rest. We put him in a little room in the back. Dino, this may or may not be your uncle, but I'll let you see for yourself."

Leading Dino through the winding, narrow corridor, Father Lorenzo noticed a growing stream of water.

"That only happens when it's been raining hard," he said. "Will this rain ever stop?"

Erected in the seventeenth century a few streets from the Arno, the old palazzo had been used over the years as a retreat house, a school, a leather workshop and a detention center for recalcitrant youths. The Franciscans had taken it over only three decades ago and it was used as a shelter during the war. Six years ago, Father Lorenzo was assigned to turn the space into a soup kitchen.

"Dino, one more thing," Father Lorenzo said as they reached the door. "The man doesn't seem to want to talk. He hasn't said anything since they brought him here. I think there are more things wrong with him than broken ribs. Go have a look."

Covered with a woolen blanket, the figure on the bed was curled into a ball. His heart racing, Dino lifted the blanket, and quickly stepped back.

The face was ruddy and bruised, the eyes tightly closed. A bandage, oozing blood in one corner, covered his forehead. The curly black hair was long and matted and dirty. Dino remembered Roberto as being tall, close to six feet, but this body seemed small. Yet, Dino saw something familiar, a thin scar running from his left cheek to his throat, visible even through the thick beard. He remembered that as a reminder of the time Roberto got into a bar fight that almost turned deadly years ago.

"Roberto?"

The man's eyes, bloodshot and quivering, opened slightly.

"Roberto?"

The man closed his eyes.

"Roberto!"

The man opened his eyes again and groaned. Dino leaned close.

"Roberto? You're Roberto Sporenza, right? From Sant'Antonio?"

The man closed his eyes. Tight.

"Roberto, it's me. Dino. Your nephew. Lucia's son."

Dino sat down on the edge of the bed. Staring at the man, Dino thought of how he had always looked up to Roberto and Adolfo. Roberto was twelve years and Adolfo eight years older than he was, and Dino always wondered if he'd ever be as smart and self-assured as his uncles. He admired Adolfo for going to the university in Pisa and actually completing the courses. But he couldn't help but envy Roberto and his carefree days in Florence—never holding a job for very long, spending days searching for girls on the Ponte Vecchio or the Piazza della Repubblica and his nights drinking and carousing with his friends.

Dino knew he could never be like Roberto, and he felt a tinge of regret.

Everything changed for the family when Adolfo and Roberto fought, and it was up to him now to see if anything could be restored.

"Roberto?"

No response.

"Can I tell you something?"

Nothing.

"My Mama, Lucia, she's very worried about you. Do you think you could call her? It's only a phone call. She'd like that."

The man didn't move. Was he asleep? Could he hear anything?"

"Roberto? Can I tell you something else? I'm living in Florence now. I go to the Accademia di belle Arti. I've gone to your woodworking shop looking for you, but you're never there. The man at the corner doesn't know where you are."

Nothing.

"Roberto, everyone in the family is worried about you."

Was he really sleeping?

"Roberto, I'm living with Adolfo and Mila on Piazza Santa Croce near the Arno."

Dino thought he saw the man wince.

"Would you like to see them?"

Nothing. Dino didn't want to leave, afraid that he wouldn't find Roberto here again, but maybe he was upsetting him. "All right, Roberto, I'll let you sleep, OK?"

Dino got up and edged toward the door.

"But I'll be back, OK?"

Adolfo and Mila were having breakfast when Dino returned from the soup kitchen. Mila burst into tears and went into the bedroom upon hearing the news about Roberto. Adolfo looked surprised and was about to say something, but then said he had to get ready for work and went into the bathroom. After Adolfo left for work at the National Library and Mila at the Casa del Popolo, Dino sat at the kitchen table and stared at the cracked linoleum floor, shaken and confused.

"Shit!" Now that he found Roberto, what was he supposed to do about it?

Later that day, his conversation with his mother was only partly inaccurate.

"Oh, Mama, I saw Roberto."

He could hear that she almost dropped the phone.

"Roberto! Oh, God in heaven! Where? When? How is he?"

"I saw him this morning, Mama."

"This morning? Did you wake him up?"

"Well, I guess you could say that."

"Oh, Dino, how is he? How does he look? Do you think he's been eating enough?"

"I couldn't tell, Mama. He was in bed."

"In bed? Is he sick? *Santa Maria*, is he sick?"

"Um, Mama, he was just sleeping."

"Does Adolfo know?"

"Yes, Mama."

"What did Adolfo say?"

"Adolfo had to go to work."

"Did Roberto say if he's going to come to see us?"

"I'm not sure, Mama."

"Is he working?"

"I don't know, Mama."

"So you didn't talk long?"

"No. I thought I'd let him sleep some more."

"That's good, Dino. That's good. He needs some sleep. But where is he staying?"

Dino had to think of an appropriate response.

"Um, Mama, he's staying with a priest."

"A priest! A priest! Oh *Dio,* thank you, God. My prayers are answered."

Part Three

The Arno River in Florence, with Ponte Vecchio in the foreground.
Photo by Masterlu @ Fotolia.com

Chapter Twenty-Five

Tuesday, November 1, 1966

Like other rivers that descend from mountains, the Arno begins as a simple little stream. At its start, it seeps out of Monte Falterona, far into the Castentine Forests about twenty-five miles east of Florence. The mountain is thought to be named for an ancient god who lived deep inside. For centuries, people in the area believed that if an earthquake awakened the god, they would all be drowned. The Etruscans, in fact, threw thousands of small bronze statues, depicting people and animals, into a lake, called Lake of the Idols, to keep the god happy.

Rushing down the mountainside, the Arno gathers size and strength and sweeps southeast near Arezzo, then turns west, flowing through the heart of Florence. Then it rushes on to Empoli and finally through Pisa, where it empties into the Ligurian Sea.

But before all that, there is a lake at Monte Falterona near the source of the Arno. It is called Gorga Nera, *or "black throat." Some people believe that it is bottomless and that one can hear mighty rumbles that can cause landslides and earthquakes. And floods.*

In 1966, heavy rains began falling in Tuscany in September. Soon, the Castentine area was saturated. The rains increased in October and November, and on November 2 alone, seventeen inches of rain fell in twenty-four hours on Monte Falterona. The snow on the mountain melted, and slushy rivers headed toward Florence.

On Tuesday of that first week of November, Dino slogged through puddles to the *cucina popolare*. Everyone knew that Florence could expect heavy rains in November, but this year they seemed especially hard. Hearing about the Arno's past flooding in November, nervous tourists kept a wary eye on the skies, but longtime residents were certain that the rains would stop and the Arno would recede. Dino now knew the threat of "*la pioggia di novembre.*"

Although drenched despite his yellow raincoat, Dino didn't pay much attention, singing to himself, "I've got a date with Sofia Friday night, I've got a date with Sofia Friday night. We're going to see a movie, we're going to see a movie. We're going to see *The Bible*, we're going to see *The Bible.*"

He wanted to add, "And maybe we'll make love," but he was afraid to. He had not made love since September 29, 1964, in Francesca's third-floor apartment. He remembered not only the date, but also the time.

Before joining the serving line, he went to Roberto's little room in back of the soup kitchen. Each time he visited in the last few days, Dino expected that his uncle would somehow have fled, and his bed would be empty. Each time, he found his uncle lying silently under the woolen blanket, staring into space through eyes that were finally becoming less bloodshot.

Dino brought him books to read. They were unopened. Lucia sent him a box of biscotti. The package was unwrapped.

After his first visit, Dino realized that he had gone too fast in bringing up the past. Roberto was not even ready to talk about his sister, much less his brother. In fact, Roberto refused to talk at all, and just remained silent. Dino didn't know if he still had the shop at Santo Spirito, didn't know if he had a girlfriend, didn't know how he got into a fight.

After one meeting in which Roberto was particularly sullen and withdrawn, Dino interrupted Father Lorenzo as he was cutting up onions for the night's fennel and onion risotto.

"Father, do you have any suggestions? I can't get him to talk, much less open up."

"I don't know, Dino," the priest said, wiping onion tears from his eyes. "We've had other cases like this. People aren't only physically injured, but they have been so hurt by something or so many things that they withdraw into themselves."

"Should I even come to see him? Sometimes it seems like I'm bothering him."

"Yes, yes, of course you should come. He hasn't told you to leave, has he? Well, then, he must like it that you're there. Eventually, I bet that he will start talking to you. Look, you're the only visitor he has. And more than that, you're family. You're the link to the rest of the family. He may not want to admit that now, but subconsciously, he knows he's got a lifeline in you."

"You're putting a lot of responsibility on me, Father."

Father Lorenzo grinned. "I wouldn't do that if I didn't know you could handle it."

Dino turned to leave when the priest called him back. "Dino? One more thing. Besides all of his injuries, I think your uncle is depressed. He's got a lot of time now to think. I don't have any idea what that kind of life he's led or if something terrible happened to him at some point. He may be very ashamed. But he'll have to work that out for himself."

"What should I do?"

"Say a prayer for him. Your uncle is in rough shape and needs all the heavenly help he can get."

The next day, in a long monologue and without interruption, Dino told Roberto about what he was studying in school, his work at the trattoria, his drawings and his music. He didn't mention Adolfo. With his eyes closed, Roberto seemed to listen to Dino's stories, but Dino thought he might just be asleep.

The one thing that did seem to arouse some interest was music, especially the Beatles. Despite the rain, Dino had brought his guitar along and tried his best to imitate the Beatles' sound. Roberto didn't say anything, or even hum or smile, but he tapped his fingers on the side of the bed railing.

Since Dino's knowledge of English was minimal, he had trouble understanding the meaning of the Fab Four's new hit.

We all live in a yellow submarine
Yellow submarine, yellow submarine
We all live in a yellow submarine
Yellow submarine, yellow submarine

"I don't understand a lot of the Beatles' lyrics," Dino told Roberto. "I think it's something about living in your own space. I don't know."

Roberto didn't respond. When Dino reported all this to Adolfo and Mila, Mila seemed upset and even angry, and Adolfo went to the window and looked out at the rain-soaked piazza. He said nothing, and Dino went back to his basement room.

On November 1, Dino couldn't believe the reason Penny gave for having a party. Her note, handed during the Caravaggio class that afternoon, said: "Come to my house at 9 o'clock tonight for a party. It's All Saints Day! And tomorrow's All Souls Day! Bring your guitar. There's going to be a surprise."

In Sant'Antonio, both November 1 and 2 were solemn church holy days. The first, known as *Festa di Tutti i Santi*, was a national holiday honoring all the saints in heaven, whether they were canonized or not. Everyone went to Mass. The next day, the Day of the Dead, *Il Giorno dei Morti,* was far more solemn. Rosa always led the women, Annabella and Fausta and Lucia—Donna always found something else to do—to the cemetery where they cleared the graves of relatives and polished the tombstones. Then they went home and baked cookies, either Bones of the Dead, *Ossa dei Morti,* a hard cookie made to look like a bone, or Beans of the Dead, *Fave dei Morti,* shaped like a fava bean.

No one would think of having a party on either day.

Making his way through the sodden streets that night, Dino barely glanced at the storefronts where Florence's merchants were sponsoring a British Week promotion. In shop windows from Santa Croce to Via dei Tornabuorni, Pinocchios, panforte and Madonnas were replaced by British flags, pub signs, little statues of royal guardsmen, replicas of Buckingham Palace and countless other paraphernalia. Dino thought it was all rather stupid. He wasn't interested in England or its kings and queens.

This time, Dino was not early, or even on time. When he arrived at 10:30, the tiny apartment was filled with cigarette smoke and the pungent odor of stronger stuff. Most everyone was there, except, of course, for Raffaele, languishing in the Le Murate prison because he had gotten four more months for bad behavior.

"It's nice to see you again, Dino," Marie said as she closed the door behind him.

"Great to see you, too." They smiled. Dino was pleased they could still be friends.

"Dino!" Penny cried as she rushed up to kiss him on the cheek. "You're finally here. I've been waiting for you to show my surprise."

She went into the bathroom.

Dino hardly recognized the figure that emerged fifteen minutes later. Penny stood in the doorway, her hands on her hips. She had big loopy earrings. She wore a flimsy white shirt that revealed a white bra. She wore high white boots. But most spectacularly, her white skirt was at least eight inches above her knees.

"Like it?" she asked.

The boys in the room hooted and howled, and the girls went up to touch the shirt, the skirt, the boots.

"It's the latest thing in England," Penny said. "There's a new designer, Mary Quant, who's all the rage, and she made up this skirt. It's actually called a miniskirt."

"I can see why," one boy shouted.

"Anyway, since this is British Week here, I had my mum send this to me."

"Thank you, mum!" another boy yelled.

Throughout the uproar, Dino stood in the back of the room, not knowing what to say. This was a different Penny than he had known. He didn't know if he liked her anymore.

"What do you think, Dino?" Penny asked.

"Um, I don't know. It's, um, different."

"Oh, Dino, I wanted you to like it. I waited until you came to show the others. I feel so different in these clothes."

Dino did not understand this woman. Sometimes so cool to him, sometimes coming on to him.

"Penny, maybe sometime we can talk, um, privately?"

"Well, sure! Let's do that. Come on, Dino, relax. Play us some Beatles!"

He knew now why he had been invited. But he played four songs and then put his guitar in a corner. The others were so involved in each other, in their beers and in their cigarettes that they hardly noticed.

As Dino was leaving, Penny said that she had gone to see Raffaele in prison.

"You should see the place, Dino. It's horrible. It's on the lowest level and there's water seeping in all over. Raffaele is furious. He wants so bad to get out of there, but he's still got two months left."

"He may have even more if he tries to escape again," Dino said.

"He's not that dumb," Penny said. "I don't think."

Actually, Raffaele was not that bright. After all, he was in prison because he tried to pry open Signor Michellini's money drawer. With a butter knife. During broad daylight. When the door was open. While Signor Michellini was in the next room.

But no one could accuse Raffaele of taking his punishment without complaints. At first, he yelled and screamed and pounded the bars of his cell door with a tin cup. "Goddamn it! What the fuck! Get me out of here, you fuckin' bastards!" were a few of the milder words he used. That got him an additional four months.

So he tried a more subtle technique. He had come to know one of the guards, Pietro, fairly well, and when one of his friends delivered some pot-laced candy or cigarettes or girly magazines, Raffaele made a habit to share his bounty with Pietro.

Pietro had been a guard at the prison for more than forty years. When not dozing at his desk, he liked to get to know the prisoners and to see what little gifts they could provide him in exchange for extra helpings of pasta or maybe even a grappa or two.

Pietro soon began to visit Raffaele frequently in his cell, and, at Raffaele's urging, tell him stories of the exploits of past prisoners.

"I imagine some of them have tried to escape," Raffaele said as he lounged on his cot and Pietro leaned against the wall near the toilet. There were puddles of water on the floor.

"Oh yes. But they never succeed."

"Why is that?"

"Because we always catch them."

"Always?"

Pietro thought for a while, enjoying his chocolate candy. Raffaele eyed him patiently.

"Well," Pietro said, "one guy managed to get out, but the *carabinieri* found him three days later."

"Really?" Raffaele offered Pietro another piece of candy.

"Yeah, the *carabinieri* always find them. Eventually."

"Yeah, the *carabinieri*. They're good. So how did this guy get out?"

Pietro paused. His head felt so light. "Well, see that window up there? All the cells have them. This guy found out that if you pry the lower right corner, it would come right off. You got any more candy?"

"Sure," Raffaele said.

After Pietro staggered off, to rest his head on his desk, Raffaele waited until dusk. Then he moved his bed just under the window. It was high, at street level. During the day, he could see the feet of the guards as they walked by.

Using the handle of his tin cup, he tried to pry the lower right corner of the window. It didn't move.

"Maybe he meant the left corner."

Nothing. He tried the right side again. Slowly, there was movement. Raffaele tugged and pulled and soon the window was on the floor.

Stretching, he pulled himself up to the window ledge, then, somehow finding the strength, he pulled himself through the opening so that his head, shoulders and upper body were outside.

"Fuck!!!"

Pellets of rain that felt like tiny knives pierced his body. Raffaele waited a minute, thinking he might endure the pain. Then he fell back down onto his bed.

"Fuck!!!"

Without even replacing he window, he curled up in the bed and for the first time since he was two years old, he cried.

In a stationery shop in Lucca, Francesca Casata looked out at the rain that had spread throughout Tuscany. No customers all day.

If business didn't improve in the next two weeks, her employer told her, Francesca would be out of a job. Maybe she should have gone to the university. Maybe she should move to Florence.

She opened a box of Florentine stationery and began to write a letter.

Chapter Twenty-Six

Wednesday, November 2, 1966

The earliest recorded flood of the Arno River in Florence occurred in 1117. While not much is known about that flood, the one that occurred in 1333 was described in detail by Giovanni Villani, a banker and diplomat, who wrote about it in his Nuova Cronica *(New Chronicles). The flood, he wrote, followed four days and nights of torrential rains throughout Tuscany. It was "as though the very cataracts of the sky had been opened."*

The Arno first submerged the Casentino plain and the entire upper valley of the river, Villani wrote. Then, joined by the flooding Sieve River east of Florence, it bore down on the city on November 4. All the city's church bells had been ringing all night, and there were terrified cries of "Misericordia! Misericordia!" as Florentines climbed to their roofs.

The waters reached the high altars of the Duomo and Santa Croce. They rose halfway up the main staircase of Palazzo Vecchio. They tore down three bridges, Carraia, Santa Trinità and Vecchio. The city was in chaos. Every well was polluted. Merchandise, wool, wine, furniture, tools, grain and acres of vineyards and fields were destroyed.

An Augustinian friar, Vallani reported, knew the reason for the flood. He had declared that it was God's punishment for the vices of Florentine nobles: They had enclosed the windows of their palazzos with glass.

Although it was Wednesday, and he usually went to Mass at Santa Croce only on Sundays, Tomasso Nozzoli was in his regular place in the Rinuccini Chapel fifteen minutes before the early morning service was to start. He attempted to read from the prayer book as Father Lorenzo said the Mass, but was distracted by the fresco of Christ washing Mary Magdalene's feet. Tomasso didn't go to Communion. After the life he'd led, he didn't feel that he should except, perhaps, at Easter.

Afterwards, he waited while the priest took off his vestments and came down the aisle.

"Father Lorenzo?"

"Signor Nozzoli! How good to see you!" Although Father Lorenzo was more than six feet tall, he still had to look up into the face of the former football player, still the hero of *Calcio Storico*. The priest shook his powerful hand.

"I wanted to come today to, well, I wanted to ask you something."

"Sure. What is it?"

Tomasso looked furtively at two elderly women in the back of the chapel and a young woman at the front.

"How about going to my office?" the priest said.

Hidden in a cranny of the giant cathedral, the office was little more than a large closet. Its only furnishings were a desk piled with papers, two rickety chairs and a crucifix on the wall. Tomasso looked at a chair and decided to stand, so the priest did, too.

"Father, I wonder if I can ask a favor?"

"Of course."

Tomasso looked at the floor for a long while and when he raised his head, his eyes were moist.

"It's about...it's about the principessa, Principessa Maria Elena."

"I've heard she's not well."

"No, not well at all."

Tomasso explained that the princess had become increasingly weak in the last months and, worse, seemed to have lost her will to live.

"I'm so sorry, Signor Nozzoli. I will pray for her."

"More than that, Father. Could you say a Mass for her? A special Mass for her?"

"Certainly. Of course."

"I just thought...I wasn't sure...I mean...well, you know about the principessa."

Like many in Florence, Father Lorenzo knew the principessa's reputation. He also knew of her old relationship with Tomasso Nozzoli.

"I mean," Tomasso continued, "is it all right to say a Mass for her? I mean, she was raised a Catholic, but I don't think she's been to church for a long time. And, you know, her life..."

Father Lorenzo smiled and put his hand on the big man's arm. "Signor Nozzoli, if we only said Masses for so-called 'good' Catholics, we wouldn't have much to do, would we?"

The priest took out a leather bound booklet from a drawer. "When would you like it?"

"As soon as possible."

Father Lorenzo looked at Tomasso's worried face. "It's that urgent?"

"Yes, Father, it's urgent."

"Well, this is Wednesday. I've got a Mass for Signora Antonelli tomorrow. I could change things around and say the Mass for the principessa on Friday."

"Friday. That would be good."

Tomasso reached into his back pocket for his wallet.

"No, no," the priest said. "None of that. It's an honor for me to do this. But one more thing. Usually, we announce who requested the Mass. Would you like me to mention your name?"

Tomasso's ruddy face reddened. "No, no, Father. Just say...just say...a friend."

As Tomasso walked back to his shop, pelting rain penetrated his jacket and he took refuge under shop awnings. Streets were already lined with green, white and red flags for the national holiday on Friday that celebrated Italy's defeat of Austria in World War I.

"If this rain continues, we're not going to be celebrating much," he thought.

Then he passed a cinema where the new film, *The Bible,* was showing. Tomasso looked at the poster of Noah's ark and the flood.

"And if this continues, we're going to have to build one of those."

Next door to his shop, he looked in at the music store. The Gallinotti looked odd in the midst of flags and posters honoring British Week.

"I hope Dino gets to buy that someday."

Since Tomasso saw no need to replace his fine ceramic pieces with "English junk," his sole concession for British Week was a Union Jack in the corner of a window. Bella greeted him with loud complaints about his absence and not being fed for at least three hours.

"Bella, Bella, Bella. Always hungry. How about some chicken from last night? There you go. What a day. Raining, raining. There you go, up on my lap. Just you and me now. Bella, Bella. Poor principessa. What times we had. What a princess. Wish I could go see her. She doesn't want me to. Ah, yes, Rosaria. Shouldn't have married Rosaria. Knew it wouldn't work out. But then we wouldn't have had Massimo. Poor Massimo. I miss him so much. Bella, Bella…"

Like Bella, Tomasso was soon dozing off, dreaming of long-ago happy times with Principessa Maria Elena Elisabetta Margherita di Savoia.

Rarely had the eighteenth-century palazzo been so cold. Years of neglect had caused cracks to develop in the corners and around the windows, allowing winds to whip through unhindered. Thick rugs did little to warm the frigid tile floors.

Bundled in three sweaters, a robe and an afghan, Principessa Maria Elena sat stoically in her wheelchair in her bedroom, looking out on the driving rain and shaking every time lightning crackled along the Arno. She thought she could hear the swollen river raging below, but that might have been her imagination. She did hear the church bells, though. It had been years since they had rung so often to warn of a flood.

Teressa frantically ran around the room, trying to stuff rags and blankets into the cracks.

"Principessa, please," she cried. "Come away from the window. There's nothing out there for you to see. Why don't you come into the salon? I can put some music on. Some Scarlatti? Or maybe an opera? Puccini? No, he's too sad. Well, we'll find something. Please, Principessa, come away from the window."

The principessa closed her eyes. Teressa smoothed down the pillow behind her head.

"Would you like some tea?" she asked gently. "I'll make you some nice chamomile tea. It will make you feel better, maybe you could take a little nap."

The principessa looked out at the rain again.

"Maybe if I read a book to you? You have so many, we can find something. A nice love story, one that you've always liked?"

The principessa reached out a shaking hand. "Teressa. I want to tell you something. Can you keep a secret?" Her voice was soft and shaking.

"Oh, yes, of course. But why don't we go into the salon and you can tell me there?"

"It's fine here. Come closer. Teressa, you've been with me for many years now, haven't you?"

"Oh, yes, at least forty. I've never counted."

"You know, I've never really paid you what you've been worth to me, for all that you've done for me."

"Oh, Principessa. You know I never expected payment. Just to serve you, just to live in this beautiful palazzo, that's all I ever wanted."

"No, no. That's not enough. And now we must settle things. Teressa, you know that box in the lowest drawer of my dresser."

"Yes."

"You know what it contains, right?"

"Yes, your beautiful tiara when you were a princess in the House of Savoy. You never wear it. Would you like me to get it and you can wear it now? Oh, Principessa, I'll do that right now, you'll look so beautiful…"

Teressa turned to run to the dresser.

"No, no, Teressa. I don't want it. What I want is for you to have it when I'm gone. I know you won't be able to wear it, but take it to my friend Signor Rossi. He has the jewelry shop over near the Medici Chapels. Ask Signor Tomasso to help you find it. He is such a good man."

The principessa paused to wipe a tear from her eye. "Signor Rossi will pay you a fortune for it, and you'll be set for life."

Teressa burst into tears. "Principessa!"

"No, no, no need to thank me. You deserve it."

"But Principessa, you're not going anywhere, why do you bring this up now?"

"Did you hear what I said, Teressa?"

"Yes."

"Good. Now go into the salon and put on some music. Puccini would be nice."

After Teressa had tearfully left, Principessa Maria Elena pulled out a small silver purse from under her sweaters and counted the pills. She had saved up twenty-six. She figured she would need thirty.

Rushing home from the Accademia, Dino was now counting the hours until his date with Sofia on Friday night...a movie...and maybe more. The wind was so strong that he had to hold on to his umbrella with both hands, and at Via Verdi, just as he entered Piazza Santa Croce, the umbrella turned inside out. Struggling to get it upright, he saw a sign on the corner building he had never noticed before. "On September 13, 1557, the waters of the Arno reached this height."

The sign was a little more than three feet above his head, which meant that floodwaters had reached nine feet in the piazza. He couldn't believe it.

"Adolfo! Mila!" Dino cried as he entered their apartment, his clothes dripping, his boots leaving muddy tracks on the cracked linoleum floor. "Did you know that there was a flood in 1557 and the water rose up to nine feet!"

"Everybody knows about the Arno, Dino," Adolfo said. "It floods all the time."

Dino had heard that the Arno had flooded frequently in the past but had no idea that it was that frequent.

"1333 was one of the worst," Adolfo said. "That destroyed bridges. And 1557. More bridges destroyed. And 1579. And 1589."

"And 1944," Mila said. "That was the last one."

"Until now," Adolfo said bitterly.

"We're going to have another flood?" Dino's face was ashen.

"Depends," Adolfo said. "Depends on how much rain falls up north where the Arno begins and if the dams can hold. If it's raining there like it has been here, and the dams don't hold, then the Arno will overflow here. And we'll have a flood."

"A big flood?'

"Don't know," Adolfo said. "The way it's been raining this week? Maybe. Those fools have never fixed the dams right. And after every flood they think, well, it's not flooding now, why should we do anything? And then it floods again."

"Sometimes they try to fix them, but it doesn't work," Mila said.

"This is insane," Dino said.

"You know, Dino," Adolfo said. "Italy has lots of natural disasters. So many earthquakes and landslides. They can't be prevented. But floods? By now somebody should have figured things out."

Dino wondered if the Accademia and especially the museum and its David and the Unfinished Statues would be damaged.

"Maybe a little," Adolfo said. "But the damage will mostly be in the low-lying areas. San Giovanni and Santo Spirito. Santa Maria Novella. And especially here, in Santa Croce."

"That means my basement room," Dino said.

"Yes," Adolfo said.

"And the church itself and the piazza."

"Yes."

"And the streets where Signor Nozzoli's shop and the music store are."

"Yes."

"And Casa del Popolo," Mila added.

"And Father Lorenzo's soup kitchen," Dino said.

"Yes."

"Where Roberto is."

Dino looked out the window. He hoped nothing would interfere with his date with Sofia Friday night. Forty-nine more hours.

The Duomo in Florence, Italy. Photo by the author

Chapter Twenty-Seven

Thursday Morning, November 3, 1966

The flood of 1333 claimed three thousand lives. Subsequently, the Arno flooded in 1334, 1345, 1500, 1547, 1557, 1589, 1646, 1676, 1688, 1740, 1758, 1884 and 1944.

Over the centuries, numerous attempts were made to harness the seemingly uncontrollable river. During the court of Cesare Borgia, two of Florence's most illustrious citizens, Niccolò Machiavelli and Leonardo da Vinci, developed a plan to actually change the course of the Arno. Machiavelli argued that if Florence diverted the river, it would deprive Pisa, Florence's archrival, of a dependable water supply. But in 1504, their plan failed after a flood destroyed much of their work. With their reputations damaged, Da Vinci moved to Milan and then Rome, and Machiavelli used his leisure time to write The Prince.

Two dams, at Lavane and La Penna, were constructed after World War II and became operational in 1957.

When Dino went to the *cucina popolare* Thursday morning, he found workers fighting a losing battle with puddles that had spread throughout the kitchen and dining room.

"Hey, Dino," Father Lorenzo said, "remember how you used to mop Santa Croce? You could get a job here."

"Want me to help?"

"Maybe later. Say hi to Sofia."

"Hi, Sofia." She had been working so hard that her face was flushed and the curls around her head were wet. Dino thought she looked particularly sexy.

"Hi, Dino. Remember we have a date tomorrow night."

"I remember." How could he forget? Thirty-two more hours.

While the mopping was going on, Sofia turned to organize other workers. "Franchino, please go to Amadeo's and get as many gallons of water that you can. We'll need it for the soup if something happens. Take Pepo with you. Gino, go to Giancarlo's and get as many packages and cans of beans that you can. Bonello, go to the bakery and buy up as much bread as you can. Doesn't matter if it's old. We put it in the soup."

Watching Sofia as she distributed *lire,* Dino marveled as how efficiently this twenty-four-year-old woman could take charge.

"Father," Sofia said, "what happens if the electricity goes out? You know how the lights are in this old building."

"The Lord and Guido will provide," Father Lorenzo said. "Guido, go to Santa Croce and take up all the half-used candles in the vigil stands. They just get thrown away. And see if there are any big candles lying around, if you know what I mean."

The priest smiled, and Guido did, too, as he picked up an umbrella and went on his way.

"Father," Dino said, "why is Elvis in the corner like that?"

"Well, Dino, it seems like Elvis met a very nice boy dog a few months ago. They had a nice talk, and more, and now we're all going to see the fruit of their conversation."

"She's going to have puppies? On the floor?"

"Dogs aren't particular, Dino. Now, go see your uncle."

"Is there any difference?"

"He seems to be getting a little better physically. He can go to the toilet now on his own, which is a relief for the bedpan workers. But he still stays in bed all the time."

Roberto's room was below ground level, with small windows near the ceiling. Except for two lights, the room was dark, lit occasionally by lightning flashes. Dino approached Roberto's bed cautiously because his uncle appeared to be asleep. In repose, his face was still alarming. Bruises dented his bearded cheeks. An eyebrow was tattered. The upper lip was cut. And there was that long scar from cheek to neck.

But it was still Roberto. Dino wondered if his eyes would ever twinkle again, if he would boast about his feminine conquests, if he would still drink all his friends under the table. But that, of course, was a reason he was lying here now.

"Roberto?"

No response.

"Roberto?"

Nothing.

Dino turned to leave, then felt a hand on his arm. Roberto said nothing, but his eyes were open, and he made a slight gesture for Dino to sit on the edge of the bed.

"Want me to stay?"

A light nod of the head.

"Feeling any better?

Dino couldn't tell if his uncle smiled or grimaced.

"Want me to read to you?"

Roberto shook his head.

"Father Lorenzo says you're able to walk now. That's great!"

Roberto shrugged.

"Hey. Want to get up and walk around a little? Get a little strength in those legs again?"

Roberto shook his head again.

"Come on, Roberto. It will be fun!"

Despite Roberto's unwillingness, Dino pulled the woolen blanket back and put his arm around his uncle's shoulders. He couldn't believe how thin they were. Gently, he turned him around so that he was sitting on the edge of the bed.

"OK, now. On your feet."

Leaning heavily on his nephew, Roberto eased to his feet, his body shaking.

"OK, now. One foot, then the other."

Roberto was so thin, his pajama bottoms kept slipping down. Dino guided his uncle to the door. That was as far as Roberto could go. Back in his bed, shaking and with the blanket up around his neck, Roberto closed his eyes. Now, Dino thought, he really would need some sleep.

Back in the kitchen, Dino asked Father Lorenzo if he had exhausted his uncle.

"No, that was fine, Dino. He needs to get out of bed. He's weak, or at least thinks he's weak. He needs the exercise. If he ever had to get out of here quickly, I don't know what he'd do."

As often as she had crossed Piazza Santa Croce on her way to Casa del Popolo, Mila had never seen so many huge puddles, large massive stretches of water, really. The rain had accumulated between and on top of the stones, forcing her to hop, skip and jump while trying not to jab other pedestrians with her umbrella. Along the side, the tall poles that on a hot June day flew the banners of the *Calcio Storico* were now emblazoned with the victory flags for the celebration of Armed Forces Day tomorrow, but unrelenting winds had already reduced some to tatters.

Mila ran up Via dei Pepi and crossed in front of Casa Buonarroti. Sometimes, she thought she should be more impressed, as Dino certainly was, that the house that Michelangelo built for his family was just a few streets away from where they lived. But Mila was more concerned with the people who were living in the neighborhood now.

She ran down Borgo Allegri to Piazza de' Ciompi, arriving at the Casa del Popolo just as the most violent lightning flash lit the sky. A half dozen workers were already cleaning, making sandwiches, setting up chairs in the television room and tables in the bingo room.

Mila had been at the Casa for five years now. The pay was minimal, but she and Adolfo were able to rent the apartment on Piazza Santa Croce. Mila hoped that one day they would be able to give her mother the grandchild she always begged for.

Mila shook her yellow raincoat and put her umbrella in a corner. "I'm never going to get dry."

"*Buongiorno,* Mila!" Franco was in his late thirties and the only staff member to actually live at Casa del Popolo. His parents had died when he was little and he lived in an orphanage until he was eighteen, though, in truth, he was not at all ready to go out on his own.

The nuns would shake their heads and whisper, "Poor Franco. *Ritardamento.*"

Casa del Popolo took him in, giving him a job cleaning and picking up. He had a cot behind the kitchen where he kept his growing collection of *Zagor* comic books, a hero most popular among young Italians. Once Franco started talking about Zagor's exploits in Darkwood, there was no stopping him.

"But, Franco," someone would say, "who cares about a hero who lives in the United States?"

"Not just the United States," Franco would reply. "Penn-syl-van-ia!" Franco loved saying the name although he had no idea where it was.

Four of the other staff members were former members of the Resistance, having kept the Germans at bay north of Florence during the summer of 1944 and even after Florence was liberated. Each carried the marks of their service. Alessandro's left arm was paralyzed, Nicolo could not see out of his right eye, Vincenzo's thumb and index finger were missing from his right hand and Ugo suffered severe back pains.

"*Buongiorno*, Mila!" Nicolo said as he dragged three folding chairs into the bingo room. "Is it wet enough for you?"

"I've never seen anything like this. Have you?"

"Not in my lifetime," Alessandro said. "But then, I'm only twenty-three."

"Yeah, right," Vincenzo said, slapping his friend on the back. "You mean sixty-three."

Church bells began ringing in the distance.

"I wish they'd stop ringing those damn bells," Ugo said. "We know it's raining. We know maybe we'll have a flood. We don't need the damn bells to tell us."

Perhaps Mila had inherited her mother's instincts. At the sight of snow, the prediction of heavy rains or the sounds of thunder, her mother invariably went to the corner market and stocked up on food. Then she filled buckets of water and kept them in the bathroom. She already had a supply of candles, pilfered over time from the nearby church.

"Now we're ready for anything," her mother would say.

Remembering that, Mila took charge. "Vincenzo, go to Giancarlo's and buy some cans of vegetables and meats. If Father Lorenzo's *cucina popolare* runs out, we'll have something here." She handed him ten thousand *lire*. "Carlo, go to the market and get some blankets. Don't pay what they're asking, get them down as much as you can." She handed him more *lire*. "Franco, take those old milk cartons and fill them with water. Hurry. And Ugo, go to Santa Barbara's and pretend you're lighting candles but take as many from underneath the stand that you can. Jesus will forgive you. Don't worry about it."

Well, she thought, even if there isn't a flood, they'll have some supplies on hand.

For all his sullen silences at home, Adolfo did enjoy his work repairing books at the National Library. He hadn't planned for that kind of career when he was at the university in Pisa. Greatly influenced by the family friend Ezio Maffini, he thought he would become a teacher. But there weren't any teaching jobs in Florence, and so he started at the bottom of the library, literally, since it was in the lower basement.

Adolfo had heard of the *Biblioteca Nazionale* even as a student. He knew that it was founded in 1714 when the scholar Antonio Magliabechi bequeathed his entire collection to the city of Florence. Those holdings were combined in 1861 with those of another library, the *Biblioteca Palatina*, founded by the Grand Duke of Tuscany, Ferdinando III. It now contained more than a million volumes, plus thousands of periodicals and countless atlases, maps, charts and engravings.

Adolfo found a biography of Magliabechi one day, and laughed out loud when he read it. How Magliabecchi could remember verbatim every book he had ever read. How he amassed a library of forty thousand books and ten thousand manuscripts and knew where every one was in his house. How he cared so little about his appearance that he didn't undress at night and so little about his health that a typical dinner consisted of three hard-boiled eggs. And how he constantly told jokes and made fun of the Jesuits and doctors. All this about a man who started out as a goldsmith and didn't become a librarian, under Cosmo III de' Medici, until he was forty years old.

For the last week, Adolfo had been occupied with a single large, leather-bound book from Holland, printed in 1793. It contained exquisite drawings of flowers. What Adolfo liked to do when he worked on a book like this was go to the vast reading room upstairs during his lunch hour and read what happened in Holland in 1793. He discovered that was the year that France declared war on Holland and managed to occupy the southern Netherlands. History, Adolfo knew, was just one war after another.

Early on this Thursday afternoon, between two tall tiers of manuscripts, the banter around the long table was over plans for the long Armed Forces Day weekend.

"I'm going to sleep," Dorothea said. She had spent the last few days gluing the binding of a seventeenth-century volume of verse. "Sleep and sleep and sleep. And I know I'll be seeing this damn book in my dreams."

"You're not going to get much sleep with all this rain and thunder," Maria said, smoothing out the pages of an ancient textbook

"I can sleep through anything." Dorothea pulled her sweater around her because the room was unusually cold and damp today.

Sandro said he wouldn't be able to sleep tomorrow because of the Armed Forces Day parade. "It goes right under my window. Who cares anymore that Italy beat Austria? I don't even know what war that was."

Carefully opening the pages of a hymnal dating from the 1600s, Enrico said he was going to a concert in the Hall of the Five Hundred in Palazzo Vecchio, "but I'll probably fall asleep before it's over."

Francesco said he planned to see *The Bible* because he liked films produced by Dino de Laurentiis. "I don't know, though. I could watch *La Strada* and *Nights of Cabiria* four more times and not get bored, but this is really an American film."

"Right," Sandro said. "You don't fool us. You just want to see Eve naked."

Francesco blushed and Sandro slapped him on the back.

"Don't get your hopes up," Enrico said. "I saw it. She has long hair all the way down her front. There's nothing to see."

"The critics said the flood scene was good."

"It goes on forever," Enrico said. "It seems like it really is raining for forty days and forty nights. The ark is nice, though, and the kids next to me liked all the animals. Where did they find those things? And John Huston is pretty good as Noah, but you think that flood will never end."

"Speaking of floods," Sandro said, "did you look at the Arno at lunch time? I've never seen it so high."

"The way it's been raining, I wouldn't be surprised if it reached up to the top of the retaining wall," Dorothea said.

"If it breaches that wall," Enrico said, "this place is done for."

Enveloped in his own thoughts, Adolfo didn't hear any of the conversation. He was thinking about his brother.

In Lucca, Francesca emptied a drawer on her last day of work at the stationery store. She looked at the envelope, stamped, sealed, but unmailed. "I don't know why I don't send it to him," she thought. "He must think I'm so stupid, the way I acted the last time. I wonder if I can find an excuse to go to Florence."

Chapter Twenty-Eight

Thursday Afternoon,
November 3, 1966

At 2.30 p.m. on Thursday, November 3, the Civil Engineering Department in Florence declared that there was "an exceptional quantity of water" and the city's drains were unable to cope. Suddenly, manhole covers popped off and powerful jets gushed in the air. Basements flooded around the Santa Croce and San Frediano areas. The first electricity failures were reported as fuses began to blow.

Surrounded by twenty-five foot walls, the Arno did not seem likely to burst through its banks in Florence, however.

Traffic in Florence Thursday afternoon was even worse than usual. Because the next day would be a holiday, some people wanted to get home early to enjoy the long weekend and others were fleeing the city for homes in the countryside. Cars lined up bumper to bumper around the Duomo and the side streets. Because of the rain, more people jumped on buses, where their sodden clothes and the cramped conditions created squalid smells.

With classes at the Accademia ending early, Dino was still counting the hours, now twenty-nine, and singing "I've got a date with Sofia tomorrow night," but he found unexpected obstacles on his way home. Besides the driving rain that threatened to upend his umbrella and the puddles that were becoming ankle high among the cobblestones, he encountered jets of water bursting out of manhole covers on Via Ghibellina and Via Verdi. Dino hopped between them, thinking this was sort of a devil's amusement park.

"What's going on?" he asked a workman who was losing a battle replacing a manhole cover.

"It's raining, goddamnit. Can't you see that, you stupid kid?"

"Um, is the city doing anything about it?"

"Besides sending stupid underpaid workers like me out to fix their problems? What d'ya think?"

"It seems worse here than over by the Accademia."

"That's on higher ground. Around here, all the basements are flooded. Now get the hell out of here so I can do some work."

Hesitating, Dino dared to ask another question. "Sir, what's going to happen if it doesn't stop raining?"

"Well, think about it. North of here, it's been raining hard for days, too. The dams at Levane and La Penna controlling the Arno will be threatened. If they break, then you're gonna see the Arno come over its banks and drown this goddamn city."

"Oh."

Dino fled when the handle on the worker's shovel broke, causing a torrent of profanities that momentarily drowned out the thunder. In Piazza Santa Croce, he was thinking so hard about his date with Sofia that he almost knocked over Signora Alonzo, who was clutching a frightened Primo in her arms. Knee-deep in water, she could barely move along until Dino picked both her and the dog up and carried them the rest of the way home.

"*Grazie,* Dino. *Grazie tante.* God bless you," she said as she pulled Primo into her doorway.

"Try to stay dry, Signora Alonzo. Let us know if you need anything."

Dino arrived at his basement room to find water three inches deep on the floor. In the room next door, the boiler was shaking and making terrible clanking noises. He grabbed his most valuable possessions, his guitar, his *mangia dischi* and his records, and the little wooden boxes under his bed. He piled some clothes on top and his Michelangelo book on top of that. Then he saw the *scaldino* under his bed. In his two years in the basement room, he had never used the thing even though Mila said it was perfectly safe. He should put an iron pot with burning coals under the blankets to keep warm at night? Dino would rather die of cold than be burned to a crisp.

He put the *scaldino* on top of his pile and, seeing that there wasn't anything left on the floor, he dashed up the stairs to Adolfo and Mila's apartment.

They had just arrived home, and were fumbling around the darkened rooms.

"Damn. The electricity has been going off and on," Adolfo said.

"And the batteries in the flashlight are dead," Mila said, glaring at Adolfo even though he couldn't see her.

Mila said she wished she had brought some candles from those just acquired at Casa del Popolo. "And maybe we'll need some food, too."

Dino had never been in a dangerous situation before. "What are we going to do?"

"We're going to sit back and wait till this is over," Adolfo said. "We've got enough food for tonight. We can get along without television for one night. We can go to bed early. And you can sleep on the couch tonight."

Dino eyed the couch, a lumpy creation that he found difficult to sit on and almost impossible to sleep on.

"Oh, and Dino," Adolfo said, "are you going to the soup kitchen tomorrow?"

"Sure. Why?"

"Just wondering."

An hour later, Dino tried to anchor his lanky frame between the various bumps and lumps on the couch. He could see flashes of lightning through the slats of the shutters, and he could hear the rain, the thunder, the clanging of church bells and the honking of car horns. Twenty-three more hours. Maybe.

As if he didn't have enough to worry about, Father Lorenzo suddenly had to cope with lights that dimmed and flickered throughout the soup kitchen, from the kitchen to the dining room.

"Don't anyone move," he cried. "Wait till we get some light in here or you might hurt yourself."

The priest stumbled into the kitchen and groped for the second drawer on the right of the ancient chest against the wall. Inside, he found two flashlights, not nearly enough to light the vast rooms, but a start.

"Manfredo, look in the bottom bin behind the big table. Yes, that one. Great! You found them."

Manfredo held up an armful of half-burned candles rescued from various churches in the area. Soon, with the help of the dozen volunteers who had braved the weather and had been cooking the evening meal or mopping the floors, candles were placed on every table and the room had a warm, if eerie, glow. Father Lorenzo threw open the doors to the line of bedraggled men, women and children ready for hot soup and pasta.

"Welcome!" he said. "A special treat tonight. We're dining by candlelight!"

A woman soaked to the skin under her cloth coat grabbed his arm. "Father Lorenzo, you never complain. Why is that?"

He kissed the thin graying hair on the top of her head. "What's the use of complaining, Guiditta? Doesn't do any good. Sorry, but I can't stay long. Have to finish building the ark."

He grinned, and she did, too.

The dining room was more than filled to capacity, and the smells of beef soup, basil and oregano mixed with the odors of bodies that were long in need of baths. Despite, or perhaps because of, the forbidding weather outside, greetings were warmer and hugs were longer as the line formed before the servers' pots.

"Father," whispered Sofia, soaked because she lost her umbrella, "I think we're going to run out of soup. There're so many more people here tonight."

"Run out? Never. Haven't you heard the story of the loaves and fishes?"

Father Lorenzo went into the kitchen and told the women making the soup to add two or three more gallons of water. "Add more spices, too. No one will be able to tell. Do we have enough bread? Pasta?"

Assured that the supplies were adequate, he grabbed a flashlight, excused himself and went down the long hall, now deep in water.

"Roberto!"

The beam from the flashlight in his eyes made Roberto wince.

"Roberto, it's freezing in here. Come into the dining room and have some soup."

Roberto kept his eyes closed and shook his head.

"Roberto, you've got to eat something. I don't think you've eaten all day. We have beef soup tonight!"

Roberto turned his head to the wall.

Reluctant as he was to do this, Father Lorenzo decided to take the tough approach.

"Roberto, I know you can walk. If you can walk to the latrine, you can walk to the dining room. Your legs are strong enough. You know that. The doctor says your ribs are better, and you need the exercise for your legs. If I bring the soup in here to you, you're never going to get up. So I'm not going to do that. You're going to have to come into the dining room if you want something to eat. OK?"

No movement.

"OK. *Bene.* I'll see you in the dining room."

Father Lorenzo turned and sloshed down the hall, leaving Roberto in the darkness. The priest could not see the tears that gathered in his eyes.

The lights were also flickering at Palazzo Tuttini, and Teressa looked everywhere for a flashlight. Not finding any, she had to sacrifice the tall thin tapers in the nineteenth-century candelabra on the massive wooden chest in the salon. She was just lighting them when she was interrupted.

"Teressa, come here! I have had the most wonderful idea!" Principessa Maria Elena called from her wheelchair in the bedroom.

Teressa carefully carried the entire candelabra into the principessa's bedroom and placed it on the bedside table. She hadn't seen her mistress look so happy in weeks, maybe months.

"Teressa, now get a piece of paper and write down everything I'm going to say."

Teressa found paper in a leather-bound folio and then was forced to use one of the most hated things around, a ballpoint pen.

"Teressa, I'm going to give another salon."

"Oh, Principessa! How wonderful!"

"Yes, it's going to be the best one we've ever had."

Teressa's tears blotted the paper. "That means you're feeling better, right?"

Ignoring the question, the principessa continued. "I'm going to have a special guest list."

"Oh, of course. The mayor, the bishop, the director of the Ufizzi, the director of the Pitti..."

"No, no. They're all too boring. No. This is going to be a very private salon. Very private."

"Just two dozen or so people?"

"No, no. Even smaller. Two."

"Two? Is that a salon?"

"If we call it a salon, it will be a salon."

Teressa was tired of playing this game. "And who will your two invited guests be, if I may ask?"

"First, Signor Nozzoli. My last lover and my best friend. I know you're surprised because I haven't been treating him very well lately."

"He keeps calling and I tell him that you're indisposed or something. I know he thinks you don't want to see him."

The principessa pulled her quilted blanket up under her chin. "Teressa, I just haven't wanted him to see me like this."

"But now you will?"

"I'll get myself ready. You'll have to help. I want him to see me like I was just one more time."

"Oh, Principessa, it will be more than one more time. You're going to be fine, I know it."

"We'll pretend."

"And the other guest? I can't imagine."

"Teressa, remember the young man who was at our last salon? Very tall and thin, with big ears and freckles?"

"Of course. The student at the Accademia. Professor Mariotti brought him. Some of the other guests were laughing at him."

The principessa smiled. "Well, I thought he was very sweet, and he's a friend of Signor Nozzoli's, so we will have a good conversation, the three of us. His name...his name...now I remember, was Aldobrandino Sporenza. What a lovely name."

"I think he goes by Dino."

"Yes. Invite them both. For Saturday night."

"Saturday night? This is Thursday, and we don't have much food in the house, at least not for a party, and the way it's been raining I don't know if I could go out tomorrow and get everything we need and..."

"Teressa, I know you'll take care of everything. Tomorrow morning, make the phone calls. Call Signor Nozzoli and he'll know where to find Signor Aldobrandino Sporenza."

"I'll try, Principessa."

"And you can tell them that they are invited to Principessa Maria Elena Elisabetta Margherita di Savoia's very last salon."

"Oh, don't say that, Principessa."

"Go!"

After Teressa had left, her shoulders shaking and tears flowing, Principessa Maria Elena took out the small silver purse from under her blanket and sweaters and counted the pills again. Twenty-seven now. There would certainly be enough by Sunday.

In her fourth-floor apartment, Penny pulled open the shutters and stared out at the downpour.

"Isn't it ever going to stop raining? What the fuck?"

"Hey," Marie said. "Let's not talk like some of your friends."

Penny collapsed on the broken chair. "Here we've got this whole weekend off and I was planning to do some shopping and how can I go out like this?"

"Well," Ingrid said, "you've got nice new boots. Why don't you wear them? You could wear your miniskirt, too."

"All right, all right," Penny said. "So I tried to make an impression. I guess it didn't go over very well."

"It went over well with the boys," Marie said. "Very well."

Penny slouched deeper into the chair. "I'm missing all the sales! This is British Week! Everything's on sale!"

"You can get them when you go back go England," Ingrid said. "They'll be cheaper there anyway."

"I can't wait until I get back to England! The sales are here. I want to go now!"

The rain continued to beat down as Penny put a Beatles record on the phonograph. She wondered briefly about Raffaele in the prison cell, then turned up the volume.

The National Library in Florence, Italy. Photo by Alberto Scardigi @ Fotolia.com

Chapter Twenty-Nine

Thursday Night, November 3, 1966

North of Florence, floodwaters poured over roads and bridges, cutting off the little villages and forcing people to the roofs of their homes. At the aqueduct, a workman named Carlo Maggiorelli, fifty-two years old, had arrived at 8 o'clock Thursday night, carrying a thermos of coffee, half a loaf of bread and a pack of cigarettes. In a telephone call to officials in Florence, he reported that "everything's going under." But he refused to leave; he was responsible for the plant. Later, his body was recovered in a tunnel choked with mud. He was the first victim of the flood of November 4, 1966.

Exhausted, Dino desperately tried to sleep. He rearranged himself a half dozen times on the couch, but each position was worse than the last. After a while, he dozed off, but then a muscle spasm in his right leg woke him. He could see his watch only when the lightning flashed.

11:48.

He turned over and put the pillow over his head to drown out the rain. But then his neck started to ache. He dozed off again, and woke with a start with an especially loud thunderclap.

12:24.

He sat up and wiped his eyes. He picked up his Michelangelo book from on top of his clothes pile, but didn't open it. It was too dark to read anyway. He lay down again.

12:52.

He began to shiver under the flimsy blanket. He got a sweater and put it over his shirt. Then he was too warm, so he took it off.

1:36. Eighteen and a half more hours. He hoped. What if they couldn't go on their date?

He had just drifted off when a violent explosion rocked the entire building and knocked him from the couch to the floor. Pictures on the walls, books from the shelves and vases on the mantel also crashed down.

"What the...?"

Dino was still on his knees, shaking his head and brushing off plaster from the ceiling when Adolfo and Mila rushed in.

"What the hell was that?" Dino yelled. "Did a bomb explode?"

Adolfo grabbed a candle and groped his way to the door. "It came from the basement. I'm going down."

"So am I," Mila said.

"Me, too," Dino said.

Holding on to each other in the hellish darkness, they stumbled about two-thirds of the way down the stairs when a foul smell forced them to cover their mouths and noses. The flickering candlelight revealed water pouring through the window but also water rising through the drain in the middle of the floor.

"What happened?" Dino said through muffled fingers.

"My guess," Adolfo said, "is that these ancient sewer pipes just can't hold all the rainwater, so the pipes are bursting. And the pressure caused the oil tank to break open. Looks like there's water and mud and oil about three feet deep down there."

They didn't have to ask about the terrible smell. The squatter had backed up and overflowed.

"Look," Dino said, "my blanket is floating on top of the mud."

"Dino," Adolfo said, "that's not just your blanket, it's the bed."

They huddled on the stairs, not knowing what to do.

"And it's still raining!" Mila wailed.

"If this continues," Adolfo said, "the Arno is going to overflow."

"What are we going to do?"

"Can't do anything." Adolfo led the way back up the stairs. Holding their noses, they slammed the door to the basement shut, hoping that would keep out the smell.

They stood by the window, the three of them, trying to see what was going on in the darkness that shrouded Piazza Santa Croce. Making out the giant statue of Dante Alighieri in the distance, they could only think of his *Inferno*. Water, mud and oil from other broken tanks flooded the once peaceful and now devastated square.

"Look at that!" Adolfo shouted.

"Oh my God!" Mila cried.

They watched in horror as a Fiat, parked just below them, jerked from its parking space, turned completely around, floated for ten feet and smashed into another car. Then a Vespa floated by on its side. A table and three chairs from the pizzeria down the street bounced in the waves. Another Vespa. Two more Fiats tossed like toy cars. Even in the dark, they could see litter everywhere. Garbage, newspapers, wine bottles, wrappers swept by. Through all of this, rain continued to pour down but failed to cleanse away the oil or dilute the putrefying smells.

With the darkness and the rain, Dino could not see the sign at Via Verdi that measured the flood of 1557 at nine feet. If this continued, would the waters in Santa Croce reach even higher? He stared out into the abyss, trying to see the white façade of the church at the end of the piazza. It was concealed in darkness.

Dino knew then that he would not have a date with Sofia tonight. And suddenly, it didn't seem to matter very much.

"Oh my God," Mila suddenly cried. "Franco's alone at Casa del Popolo."

"And Roberto's at Father Lorenzo's!" Dino said.

"Roberto," Adolfo said softly, as if to himself. He stared out into the mud and debris and hugged his wife.

"As soon as it's light, I'm going over there," Dino said. He tried to see Adolfo's face, but it was too dark.

Usually, Bella woke Tomasso Nozzoli because she demanded to be fed. She would kneed his blankets and if that didn't wake him, paw his neck and cheeks. This time, it was not because she was hungry that she clawed his shoulders and meowed incessantly.

Tomasso pushed her aside and tried to roll over. "Bella! You know you don't get fed until 6 o'clock."

The cat would have none of it, resorting to poking Tomasso's ear, the only thing protruding from the covers. He slowly threw off the blankets, got out of bed and switched on the light. Except that there wasn't any light.

"What the...?"

Groping through the drawers on his bedside table, he found his heavy-duty flashlight and pointed it at his watch. "Bella, it's 1:38. I fed you at 10 o'clock, you can't be hungry..."

And then he heard boxes crashing in the basement, crashes quickly followed by the sounds of breaking ceramics. With only socks on his feet, he slipped on the stairs and fell headlong almost to the bottom. Getting up, he was knee deep in water with big wooden boxes floating on top.

"Oh, *Dio!*"

The place was a shambles, with boxes crammed together in two feet of water. Tomasso saw that the drain was wide open. Filthy water was pouring out and rushing toward the outer wall. Tomasso tried to lift an oil drum out of the way. Too late. A seam on the thin shell burst open and thick brown liquid oozed out, spreading over everything.

With Bella perched on a shelf near the basement door and screeching in her loudest baby voice, Tomasso went to work. Carrying one box on his shoulder and sometimes another under his arm, he climbed the stairs. There was no place to put the boxes in the shop so he started a pile in the bedroom. Back down and up again. Five heavy boxes. Ten. Sixteen. Twenty-two.

The shop itself was not much better. Floodwaters from the streets had battered the lower part of the door and seeped throughout the store. Dishes, bowls, pitchers and picture frames lay in piles, broken into a hundred pieces. A tall shelf had crashed to the floor, destroying the delicate Florentine dishes Tomasso had purchased for a small fortune. He looked at it all and silently wiped tears from his eyes.

"What can I do? Oh, *Dio!* I can't do anything."

He went into the back room, collapsed on the bed and closed his eyes. His big body ached in every muscle and fiber. Bella, quiet at last, nestled under his arm. Soon he was snoring.

And then he woke with a start. He grabbed the flashlight and looked at his watch.

2:55 a.m.

"The principessa!"

At the Le Murate prison, the superintendent slammed down the phone and got on the intercom to his guards. It was the middle of the night and only a skeleton crew was on duty.

"Get in here! *Pronto!*"

In his thirty-two years as superintendent, he had never seen such a downpour. He wondered what the builders were thinking when they placed the prison in such a low-lying area. They knew the Arno flooded periodically, and they knew that the prisoners would be in grave danger. *Stupido!*

Fidgeting, the seven guards lined up in front of him, hoping it would be good news. The weather was so bad they would surely be sent home to their wives and children. Not yet.

"The mayor's office just called," the superintendent said. "The flood is the worst we've ever seen."

The guards agreed. There was more than a foot of water throughout the prison and inmates were cowering on their beds.

"It's terrible," one guard said. "They're screaming and yelling."

"One of them lunged at me through the bars and I thought he'd choke me to death," another said.

Just then a resounding thunderclap and long seconds of lightning flashes stopped the talk.

"All right, stop jabbering and listen to this," the superintendent said. "The mayor's office has given the orders. We have to free the prisoners."

Cries of "No! No!" went up from the guards.

"We can't do that. Don't they know who these prisoners are?"

"They're murderers!"

"Thieves!"

"Rapists!"

"Robbers!"

The superintendent pounded a phone book on the desk. "Well, what do you want? Leave them in their cells and let them drown like dogs?"

"Yeah," a few said, but most were confounded.

Then a new young guard had an idea. "Why don't we bring them up to the roof? If they want to stay there, fine. If they want to jump into the waters and drown, well, it's not our responsibility."

"Thinking like an Italian," another guard said, slapping the young man's back.

"All right," the superintendent said. "Do it!"

The guards hurried down the row of cells, unlocking each and ordering the inmates to climb the steel steps to the roof. "You're on your own up there!" they said.

The hundred or so prisoners pushed and shoved each other up to the roof, where they huddled in the pouring rain overlooking the Sant'Ambrogio market.

"Wait!" one cried. "Where's Raffaele? He's not here!"

"Raffaele's in lockup at the end of the hall," another yelled over the clang of rain on the tile roof. "He tried to escape."

"Pietro!" an inmate shouted to the darkness below. "Get Raffaele! Don't let him die down there!"

Pietro had just closed the prison door behind him.

"Pietro!" another prisoner called down. "Get Raffaele!"

"Don't let him die!"

"Goddammit," Pietro said as he tried to find his keys under his raincoat. Why should he bother getting that fool out of his cell anyway? Finally, he found the keys.

Sloshing though the rapidly rising water, he could hear Raffaele's screams as he made his way to the end of the long hall.

"Help me! Get me out of this fuckin' place! Where are you? Where is everybody? Fuck!!!" The voice was cracked now.

"All right, all right, I'm coming."

Then Pietro had trouble finding the right key for the cell door. "Stop banging on the bars, *stupido!* How the hell can I open the door if you keep moving it?"

It took both of them, pushing and shoving, to pry the door open against the waters, and then Raffaele tried to make a dash for safety, but instead he slipped and fell. Pietro pulled him up. Then Pietro fell. Together they tripped and floundered until they reached the stairway. Raffaele slogged his way up to the top.

On the roof, the other prisoners slapped Raffaele on the back but were too busy trying to find shelter under a caved-in part of the roof. Raffaele slid down to the edge and stared at the waters below.

Chapter Thirty

Late Thursday Night, November 3, 1966

The dam at La Penna and, farther south, the one at Levane, overflowed throughout the night of November 3. When the gates at La Penna were finally opened, they released more water than the dam at Levane could handle, and water poured down into the valley above Florence and then, racing at thirty-seven miles an hour, toward the city itself.

With no letup in the downpour outside, and with water rapidly rising in the dining room, it was obvious to Father Lorenzo that he couldn't send more than one hundred and fifty diners home after their soup and bread. For the first time, he invited them to stay the night.

"I don't know where you'll sleep, but we'll manage."

The priest was looking around when Sofia walked by with a huge pot of bean soup. "What about upstairs, Father?"

It seemed like an impossible idea. For one thing, the second floor had been used for storage for years, maybe centuries, and it was piled high with discards from the churches nearby. Broken pews, remnants of altars, hideous statues of saints. For another, it hadn't been cleaned in years because no one went up there anymore. And it had only one small round, stained-glass window. Now, without electricity, it would be pitch black.

"Great idea!" Father Lorenzo said. "Who wants to help?"

At least one hundred and fifty hands went up, some people holding up both arms.

"OK, Sofia, give everyone a candle until we run out. *Bene*. Now, all of you, form a line as best you can and follow me."

The door to the upstairs creaked loudly, and the stairs even more, as the line of men and women, some leading children by the hand, slowly tripped and shuffled to the second floor. Most had to wait on the steps because there wasn't enough room for them amid all the clutter.

Father Lorenzo grabbed a few of the strongest men and, by the flickering candlelight, the work began. The priest hauled a particularly gruesome statue of a bleeding Saint Sebastian and dragged it on top of a weeping Mary Magdalene. "You two behave now," he warned.

"All right," he ordered, "statues in the far corner, altar pieces over here. Stack the pews under the eaves."

It took more than an hour, but eventually a wide space was created in the middle of the floor. Sofia found some brooms, and a half dozen men and women soon had the floor respectable enough.

Father Lorenzo pushed one last pew against the wall and wiped his forehead. "There. It may not be the Royal Suite at the Villa Medici, but it's cozy, right?"

Without cots or blankets, the diners sank to the floor and arranged themselves as best they could so that feet were not in faces.

"Oh, one more thing," Father Lorenzo said. "Sofia, come help me. We have to move Elvis."

Together, they managed to lift the burgeoning Elvis from her corner, carry her up the stairs and settle her on a little rug away from everyone else. Sofia kissed the dog's head. "Be careful, little mother."

His shoulders drooping, Father Lorenzo looked around the room. *"Buona notte!"* But before he left, he paused in the doorway and closed his eyes. "Oh, God, please hold these poor people safely in your hands. Please don't let something terrible happen. Please protect them. Please protect us all." He made the sign of the cross.

There was one more thing to do. He raced down the stairs and into the far room at the end of the hallway. Roberto was kneeling in the middle of his bed, the woolen blanket wrapped around his shivering shoulders. Water had risen up to the mattress.

"Oh my, oh my," Father Lorenzo said. "Got to get you out of here."

The priest waded to the bed and helped Roberto on to his feet. "Yeah, it's cold, and your pajamas are getting wet, but we gotta get out."

Robert gripped the priest's arm. "Can't...can't...walk."

"Sure you can. One step, two steps. You can do it."

Eventually, they got to the stairs. Father Lorenzo had to practically drag Roberto up to the top. Tripping over the prone bodies in the darkness, he led him to a small open space next to two elderly women who were hugging each other to keep warm. Roberto crawled between them, and they covered him with the blanket.

"Pelegrina and Sabina will look after you. Get some sleep. You're safe now."

It was now 5 o'clock in the morning. Father Lorenzo crossed the room and went into the archway that led to the church. In the early morning light he could now look down at the streets below.

"Good God in Heaven!"

In Sant'Antonio, a thunderclap shook the house and sent Lucia bolt upright in bed. She grabbed Paolo, who was still snoring.

"Wake up! Paolo, wake up!"

He turned his head into the pillow.

"Paolo, something terrible is happening!"

Paolo turned over and slowly opened his eyes. "What? What's happening? Did lightning strike?" He was sitting up now, too.

"Paolo, I had this terrible dream, and you know my dreams always come true. I dreamt I saw Dino. He was in a river. It was tossing him all around. He couldn't swim. Why didn't you teach him to swim, Paolo? Why?" She shook his shoulders.

"Teach him to swim? I can barely swim myself."

"And the river kept rising, and he kept going under and he was drowning! He was drowning, Paolo!"

Paolo put his arm around his wife's shoulder. "Lucia, it was a dream. Nothing's happening to Dino. He's in Florence. He's with

Adolfo and Mila. I'm sure he's sleeping right now. Probably went out with his friends last night and had a few beers."

"No! No! Something terrible is happening there. We've got to call them. Call them, Paolo!"

"Lucia, it's 2 o'clock in the morning. I'm not going to wake them up because of a silly dream."

"It's not silly, Paolo. It's happening. I know it." She covered her face with her hands. Paolo had never seen her so upset.

Paolo sighed. No use to argue when Lucia had made up her mind. "All right. We'll call in the morning. When they're up."

"At 5 o'clock?"

"No."

"At 6?"

"No."

"7?"

"All right. 7 o'clock. Get some sleep, Lucia."

He put his head into the pillow again. Lucia lay back and stared at the ceiling.

Lucia could have called Dino at 6 o'clock or even 5 o'clock or even 2 o'clock. With Adolfo and Mila, he had remained at the window throughout the night, consumed by the sight of the rapidly rising waters in the dim light of Piazza Santa Croce. Occasionally, lights in the apartments across the piazza flickered on again, and he could see how the tide was rising up the steps of the cathedral. Surely, the waters wouldn't enter the church itself, would they?

"My God," he said, "the tombs could be damaged. Machiavelli, Galileo, Ghiberti, Rossini, and, oh, no, Michelangelo."

"More than the tombs," Adolfo said. "The waters could rise and threaten the Giottos and the Gardis, the Donatellos and the Bancos."

Dino thought about the graves of the medieval knights that he had mopped, about the frescoes of Saint Francis in the Bardi Chapel, the altarpiece in the Castellani Chapel, the paintings in the Baroncelli Chapel, and his favorite, the blue and white Madonna and Child by Della Robbia in the Medici Chapel.

"Well," he said, "thank goodness the church has moved Cimabue's Crucifixion to the museum. It can't get harmed there."

Next to him, Adolfo was thinking about the priceless manuscripts in the basement of the National Library. Close to the river, it would be the first to suffer damage if the Arno overflowed its banks.

"I don't know why they haven't stored more on the upper floors," Adolfo said. "There are thousands and thousands of things down there, ancient books and journals and periodicals. All the records from the unification of Italy onward. Maps. Atlases. So much more. I've been working on that flower book from Holland for days. I should have put it higher on the shelf when I left."

"That probably wouldn't do any good," Dino said.

"And Dorothea's book of verse, and Maria's textbook, and Enrico's hymnal and all the other works being restored. What's going to happen to them?"

"Good God!" Mila suddenly cried. "Statues! Paintings! Is that what you think about, Dino? And you, Adolfo! Flower books and hymnals! Who cares about these things? What about the people? What about the people who come to Casa del Popolo or go to Father Lorenzo's *cucina popolare*? What about them? They don't have anything now! We're having a flood, a terrible flood, for God's sake! These people are going to have even less, maybe nothing! What's going to happen to them? Where are they going to live? What are they going to eat? How can they ever find jobs again? They don't give a goddamn fuck about paintings and books! Shit!"

"Mila!" Adolfo had never heard his wife use such language in her life.

"Don't yell at me, Adolfo! This is serious. And what about those former members of the Resistance who help at the Casa? Alessandro and Nicolo and Ugo and Vincenzio? They live right here. They're not going to have their homes anymore. And poor Franco! Oh, poor, poor Franco. He can barely take care of himself as it is. What's he going to do all alone at the Casa?"

Adolfo took his wife in his arms as she burst into tears.

At Casa del Popolo, Franco couldn't understand why he couldn't make any headway mopping up the floor. The water had been coming through the walls all day and he'd been mopping ever since Mila and the others had left. Now, in the middle of the night, the water was coming up through the drain in the floor. He would have gone down to the basement but he never liked to go down there. Someone once told him strange creatures lived there.

"Gotta get this done, gotta get this done. People will be coming tomorrow to get clothing. Don't want them to get wet. Gotta get this done, gotta get this done."

Then Franco remembered his stack of *Zagor* comic books. He kept them under his cot behind the kitchen. The kitchen floor was deep in water.

"Ohhhhhhh, noooooooooooo!" he cried as he sloshed his way from the dining room to the kitchen and then to his cot.

He reached down and pulled out a sodden mass of paper, pages glued together, all the magazines covered with mud and water. Franco sat on his bed, his feet in the water, and held his treasures to his chest.

"Ohhhhhhh, noooooooooooo!"

Wrecked cars in front of Santa Croce. Photo by Swietlan Nicholas Kraczyna

Chapter Thirty-One

Friday Morning,
November 4, 1966

With the Armed Forces holiday on Friday, some revelers stayed up late on Thursday night, but most Florentines went to bed. Mayor Piero Bargellini had been the guest of honor at the American Chamber of Commerce dinner at the Palazzo Vecchio and then retired. Also asleep by midnight was Colonel Nicola Bozzi, the commanding officer of the carabinieri. Then, along with Florence's prefect and officers of the Civil Engineering Department, they were awakened in the middle of the night by calls about the rapidly rising Arno.

On the Ponte Vecchio, frightened by the water that was lapping ever closer to the street level, night watchmen alerted owners of the gold shops that lined the bridge's walkway. The merchants quickly arrived to gather their precious necklaces, earrings, bracelets and pins. Above them, in the Uffizi Museum's Vasari Gallery that stretched above the shops, museum officials formed a human chain to rescue priceless portraits.

At San Giovanni di Dio Hospital, the generator failed, the basement filled with water and the food supply disappeared as doctors, nurses and nuns carried two hundred patients to upper floors.

Behind the Cascine Park northeast of Florence, one of the Arno's tributaries, the Mugnone, burst over its banks, flooding the stables of the race course. Stable workers and owners arrived and saved some of the horses, but seventy of them were left to their terrifying deaths.

In another outlying area, a father, mother and their daughter, Marina, fled their home by using a wooden table as a raft. According to a contemporary account: "In the blinding rain they could see nothing, and the table collided with trees and telegraph poles. The man lost his grip and went under; he came up choking with mud and the oily water he had swallowed. He was overcome by dizziness and nausea, and fainted across the table. His wife had also been in the water, and she, too, had lost consciousness. The water tore the child from his arms. As the table was swept past an embankment, mother and father were saved. When the girl's body was recovered eighteen days later, they were both still in hospital, the father suffering from bronchial pneumonia, the mother in danger of losing her reason."

At 6:55 a.m., Lucia picked up the telephone, ignoring the frowns of her husband, who was still lying in bed.

"It will be 7 o'clock by the time it rings in Florence," she said, dialing a number she had long memorized.

Paolo turned over in bed. "They're probably still sleeping."

Lucia stared at the receiver. "I don't know why, but it's not ringing."

She hung up the receiver, picked it up and dialed again. And waited.

"I don't understand this."

"Give it time. Sometimes it takes a while."

"Not this long. Never this long. You try."

Paolo roused himself and picked up the phone. Lucia recited the number to him. Nothing.

"Well," he said, "I don't know. Maybe our phone is broken."

Lucia pulled the phone away from Paolo and dialed another number.

"Rosa? Did I wake you? Oh, I'm sorry. It's just that I've been trying to call Dino and there isn't even a ring there. It doesn't even ring! I wanted to see if our phone was working."

Lucia held the receiver away from her ear.

"Yes, yes, I know it's working now. Sorry to wake you. Come over later, all right? Say hi to Antonio."

She put the phone down. "Rosa's mad at me."

"I don't blame her."

Lucia started the espresso machine. "I still don't know why it didn't ring."

"Maybe the phone lines are out between Sant'Antonio and Florence. It's been raining a lot everywhere. Try again later."

"Paolo, do you think we should drive over there?"

"Lucia! What are you thinking? No!"

Despite the dark clouds and the heavy rain, dawn eventually arrived in Florence.

Still at their posts, Adolfo, Mila and Dino could not believe the sight that was now just below their second-story window.

"It was better when it was dark," Mila said. "I don't want to look at this."

But she could not tear herself away.

The water reached up almost to their window, far higher than the plaque that marked the flood of 1333. They were trapped, unable to go out until the water went down, and now the piazza was a sea of water and oil-soaked mud. Cars. A bus. Vespas. Bicycles. A small truck. Garbage cans. Tables. Chairs. Dolls. Toy trains. Pinocchios. All mired in water and mud and fuel oil that rose almost to the second-floors of the apartment buildings on either side. The base of Dante's statue was submerged, and he looked imperiously above it all, as if to declare that he had written about this hundreds of years ago. And it was still raining.

Dino was afraid to look to the east and the church. The waters covered the steps and clearly had invaded the entire building. He could have thought about all the precious paintings and sculptures, and even Cimabue's Crucifixion, but he could only think: "Michelangelo's tomb."

When Adolfo opened the window, all three stepped back in horror. First, the stench of oil fuel mixed with mud and debris was overwhelming.

"Shit!" Adolfo said.

Then, the noise. Floodwaters had short-circuited the wiring of the wrecked cars in the piazza, and car horns blasted continuously. And dogs, some of them howling, some of them crying piteously. Dino knew they must be trapped and would never survive. He covered his ears. And still the smell increased.

Now others were watching from their windows, as trapped as they had been by air-raid alerts and bombings during the war twenty years earlier. Occasionally, one neighbor would yell across to another. Some who had never spoken to each other before were now sharing stories of their jobs and even their spouses. Some who had exchanged unpleasant words about dogs or debris on the sidewalk now talked about how they needed to go to the grocery store or the *farmacia.*

"Well," Dino said, "it looks like this is bringing us all together at least."

"Don't count on it," Adolfo said. "These are Florentines. Very proud. Cold. Very independent. Next week they'll be complaining about their dogs again."

Dino wasn't so sure of that. This was a side of Florence he had seen only at Father Lorenzo's soup kitchen and the Casa del Popolo. A spirit of people caring for one another. He wondered how he could hold on to that.

Adolfo saw a friend leaning out from the next building. "Hey, Sebastiano!"

The man, in his early thirties, was in tears. "Maria's still in her room. She won't come out, she's so afraid. The baby is screaming, she's so hungry. The boy is yelling. I don't know what to do. I have to go out and get some food!"

His voice could hardly be heard above the blaring car horns, the yowling of dogs and the cries from others in buildings all around the piazza.

Mila looked down. "Oh, my God! Look what's floating down there!"

"It's Primo, Signora Alonzo's dog. From next door." Adolfo said.

"That dog was never out of her sight. Oh, the poor thing," Mila said.

"We've gotta go find her," Dino said.

"How can we go down there?"

"We have to, Mila," Dino said. Primo had now floated out of sight. "We have to go find her."

They pulled on their boots and ran down the stairs.

No one had slept well above Father Lorenzo's soup kitchen, least of all Father Lorenzo. Except for dozing for five minutes on a pew at the end of the room, he had not taken a break. A toddler cried for milk and he found some cold soup. An old woman complained that she was freezing and he put his own overcoat on her. A grizzled man shouted obscenities in his sleep and the priest shook him awake.

The candles had long since burned down, and for hours the room was in total darkness. When dawn broke, soft rays of light streamed down from the lone stained-glass window. Despite the torrent outside and the shambles inside, Father Lorenzo thought he saw God's grace shining through.

"It's a miracle that we're all still here," he whispered.

He groped his way through bodies that were starting to rise and move about. Roberto was still lying in the same position where the priest had left him. Pelegrina and Sabina sat at his side.

"*Povero sfortunato*," they kept murmuring. "Poor boy."

Father Lorenzo leaned down. "Roberto? Are you all right? Roberto?"

Tomasso Nozzoli tried to extricate Bella from the front of his shirt, but her razor-sharp claws dug even deeper.

"Come on, Bella, get down. I've gotta go."

He tugged and pulled. She dug deeper and her screeching almost drowned out the blare of car horns outside.

"Come on! Bella! Let go!"

The cat had now gotten one of his shirt buttons opened and had crawled inside, scratching his chest through his undershirt.

"OK. I can't waste time with you. You're gonna come, too. We have to go to the principessa."

Tomasso found his heaviest jacket, his thickest boots and a woolen cap he hadn't worn in years. With Bella ensconced against his chest, he stomped through the broken pottery on the floor and pushed the door open against the torrent of waters outside.

"Goddamn!"

Outside, he tried to survey the damage up and down the street. Shreds of plates and cups from his shop banged against the little Union Jack that was his sole contribution to British Week. Windows smashed on the meat market three doors down had released stinking masses of sausages, chickens and rabbits, which now floated amid chairs and tables from the trattoria across the street.

And next door, the window of the music store had been torn open. The Gallinotti guitar, in a hundred pieces, tumbled out.

At Palazzo Tuttini, Teressa ran back and forth to the windows fronting the Arno. She carried rugs and shawls and coats and pillows and tried to stuff them under the door frames, but the water still kept pouring in. It now was about a half-foot deep and it was rising.

"Oh my, oh my, I don't know what to do. The water keeps coming in and I can't stop it. And the principessa just lies in her bed there with her eyes open and staring at the ceiling. She isn't saying anything, and I thought she was dead but she gripped my hand and smiled a little. I wish I could carry her upstairs but I tried to lift her and she weighs a ton even though she is so tiny. I should go for a doctor but how can I go out in this weather? I'd never get back. And now we don't have much food and I tried to get her to drink but she won't drink anything. It's as if she almost wants to die. But she said she wants to have the salon on Saturday night, but how can we have a salon in this weather? Oh, I wish someone would come to help, I can't do this all by myself anymore, I'm an old lady, I should be in bed. Can't somebody come to help me? Oh my, oh my."

On the top of the La Murate prison, the hundred and more inmates huddled under the caved-in part of the roof overlooking the Sant'Ambrogio market. Four packs of cigarettes had lasted only a half hour and now they stood with their hands in their pockets, both frightened and angry.

Only one of them stood apart, near the edge of the roof.

"Raffaele, why are you looking down there?"

"The water's getting higher, Raffaele!"

"You think you can swim that? *Stupido!*"

Raffaele moved closer to the edge.

"Be careful, Raffaele!"

"Don't, Raffaele, don't!"

"You're crazy!"

"You're gonna drown, you dumb ass!"

"Don't!"

Raffaele covered his ears. He raised his arms, then dove into the turbulent waters. In a moment, he had disappeared, and on the roof the hardened criminals made the sign of the cross.

Chapter Thirty-Two

Later Friday, November 4, 1966

Florence's newspaper, La Nazione, *was in a building opened only a month before the flood and it contained some of the most advanced printing equipment in Europe. On Thursday night, the staff went to work preparing the paper for the following morning. It was printed before the basement presses were flooded, and it appeared on the streets at 7 a.m.:* "L'Arno Straripa a Firenze." *"The Arno overflows at Florence."*

The article went on to report: "The city is in danger of being flooded. At 5:30 this morning water streamed over the embankments, flooding the Via dei Bardi, the Borgo San Jacopo, the Volta dei Tintori and the Corso dei Tintori, the Lungarno delle Grazie and the Lungarno Acciaiuoli. Many families are evacuating their homes. The river banks at Rovezzano and Compiobbi were overtopped shortly after 1 a.m. The Via Villamagna and the aqueduct plant at Anconella were invaded a short time later, and certain areas of the city are in danger of losing their water supply. There are indications that the day ahead may bring drama unparalleled in the history of the city. At 4:30 a.m. military units were ordered to stand by to cope with a possible emergency situation."

Landslides blocked roads leading to Florence and the Autostrada was cut off. Still, no emergency was ever declared, and no alarms or sirens were sounded. There were no radio or television bulletins. However, the film director Franco Zefferelli was alerted by his sister, who lived near the Duomo. He flew to Florence and began filming a documentary shortly after dawn.

Waters reached the San Salvi mental hospital in the middle of the day, terrifying the fragile patients and destroying the drugs in the pharmacy that might have calmed them. Generators failed at the Meyer children's hospital, endangering sixty babies in incubators until more generators were found at Piazza Independenza in a display prepared for Armed Forces Day. Nine babies were born in Florence the night of the flood.

The city's clocks stopped at 7:26 a.m.

When the telephone rang at 9 in the morning, Lucia almost tripped over a rug getting to it.

"Ezio? *Ciao!*"

"Lucia?" Ezio said. "Are you getting a lot of rain there? It's pretty bad up here."

"No, we're all right. The little Maggia is overflowing, though. I don't think this rain will ever stop. But Ezio, I want to tell you I'm worried."

"About the Maggia?"

"No, about Dino. I've been trying and trying to call him, and the phone doesn't even ring. It's not our phone. I called Rosa. And you called here. Something must be wrong there, I know it. Adolfo must have done something. Do you think he hasn't paid his bills and they've disconnected him?"

"Lucia, haven't you heard? I've been listening to the BBC. The local stations aren't carrying anything. There's a terrible flood in Florence. The Arno overflowed this morning. It sounds terrible."

"Oh, *Dio!*" Lucia now regretted that she had ignored Paolo's desire to get a short-wave radio.

"There are crews working on it, but they're saying this may be the worst flood in Florence in history."

"Oh, *Dio!*"

"The city is cut off. No one can get in or out."

"Oh, *Dio!*"

"But I'm sure Dino and Adolfo and Mila are safe."

"Oh, *Dio!* How do you know that, Ezio? You're not there."

There was a long pause at the end of the line.

"I don't know, Lucia. I don't know."

Practically swimming because the water was so high, Dino, Adolfo and Mila splashed their way through the debris on the piazza to Signora Alonzo's building next door. All the windows on the first floor had been smashed open and floodwaters flowed freely into the rooms.

"Where does she live?" Dino cried.

"I think it's the one on the left. The purple door." Adolfo could barely be heard above the din of car horns blaring, church bells ringing, stranded people yelling and terrified dogs yowling.

They sloshed through the broken remains of the window that was next to the purple door. Inside, heavy chairs, a couch, a dresser and a desk crashed against each other.

"Help!" The voice was so faint only Dino heard it.

"Signora Alonzo? Where are you?"

"Help me!"

The voice seemed to come from down a long hall and in a far part of the apartment. A huge bookcase blocked the hallway. Dino pulled and pulled but it wouldn't budge.

"Maybe if you pushed it down?" Adolfo said.

With a strength he didn't know he had, Dino lunged at the bookcase, once, twice, until he forced it backwards. Dino crawled over it, followed by Mila and Adolfo.

"Please! Help me!"

They looked into the bedroom, a jungle of overturned furniture soaking in putrid water. No sign of Signora Alonzo.

"Help! Please help me!"

Dino led the others through a dark hallway. The kitchen was even darker.

"Help! Up here!"

Looking almost as small as her Primo, Signora Alonzo lay curled atop a cupboard that seemed perilously close to falling over. Her clothes were filthy, her white hair matted, her pale eyes moist. "Oh, *Dio! Io muoio!*"

"No, no. Don't be afraid," Dino said. "We won't let you die. We'll get you down."

Adolfo and Mila kept the cupboard from falling while Dino, being the tallest, reached up.

"There, Signora Alonzo. Don't be afraid. I've got you. There. Easy. Just grab on to my neck. Easy. There you go. Slowly. Down. Easy. I've got you."

Dino held the frail, whimpering woman in his arms like a baby.

"Let's get her out of here," Adolfo said. "Bring her back to our place."

Slowly, they half-walked, half-swam back to their building. Signora Alonzo clung to Dino's neck, and he held her close. Once inside, he lay her gently on the couch he had found so uncomfortable. She was so thin, she wouldn't notice the lumps. Her eyes were closed, but at least she had stopped shaking and Mila covered her with a thick blanket and made some tea. She had said only one word since her rescue: "Primo?" The others didn't answer.

"You saved her life, Dino," Mila said.

"Nah."

"Yes you did," Adolfo said. "Admit that."

"Nah."

"You're a hero, Dino."

It took a while for that to sink in.

Back at their window, Dino, Adolfo and Mila continued to watch the destruction below them.

"Oh, my God!" Adolfo cried. "Look at that!"

In a line, a stream of books and manuscripts, a few intact but most torn to shreds, floated by as if they were toy boats controlled by a young boy.

"They're from the library! The library has been flooded!"

"Can you just be a little patient?" Father Lorenzo shouted above the din. "It won't be long now. Really, I promise."

Those on the second floor of the *cucina popolare* were getting restless. They had spent the night on the hard floor in the dark, they had huddled all morning with only a little light, and they were cold and hungry.

Worse, there wasn't a toilet on the floor, and the large oil drum that had been used as a replacement was almost full and starting to smell very bad.

Father Lorenzo went down the stairs every hour or so, but always came back with no good news.

"The streets are still filled with water and mud," he said for the fifth time. "And it's still raining. We can't go out there yet."

Even he was losing his usual good humor. "Can you please, can you *please,* stop arguing? We will get out of this, I promise."

"We're sorry, Father."

"No, No. Don't be sorry. This has been a terrible night. We're all a little frazzled and exhausted. But we're here, thank God. We're all here."

In the middle of the room, he stopped again to see Roberto, who remained curled up with his knees against his chest. Pelegrina and Sabina were still murmuring *"Povero sfortunato,"* and wiping his forehead.

"Roberto?" the priest said. "How are you doing? Want to get up and walk around for a while?"

Roberto stirred and straightened out. "Father?"

"Roberto! You said something! What would you like? Maybe a cigarette? I think I can find one." The priest had a supply hidden in a back room.

"No."

"No? What then?"

Roberto closed his eyes. "Adolfo," he whispered.

Ingrid was reading a novel and Marie was writing a letter home, but Penny looked forlornly out the window.

"I can't stand this. I want to go shopping. I *need* to go shopping. It's a holiday and I don't have classes and I have some money from my allowance and I can't even go shopping. And they're having all these good sales. I can't stand being cooped up like this. I feel like Raffaele. In a prison."

"Penny," Marie said. "You're acting like a spoiled five-year-old."

"No," Ingrid said, "more like a two-year-old. Can't you see what's happening out there?"

"I don't care," Penny said. "I really want to go shopping."

Although his shop was only a few streets north, it took Tomasso Nozzoli almost an hour to reach Palazzo Tuttini. Floodwaters rose higher and higher as he approached the Arno, and he knew that the retaining walls had been breached.

He rang the bell and banged on the door for fifteen minutes before a frantic Teressa finally opened it a crack.

"Oh, Signor Nozzoli! I couldn't hear you! Oh, thank God you're here. Thank God."

She led him into the downstairs bedroom. Rugs and carpets had kept the Arno at bay, but water still stood six inches deep.

Teressa helped Tomasso take off his thick coat. "What's that noise? I thought I heard a baby crying? Where's the baby?"

"No, no, it's not a baby. It's my cat, Bella. She wouldn't stay home, so I brought her along. She's under my shirt."

Teressa did not like cats in the first place, and she certainly wasn't going to pat Signor Nozzoli's shirt front. "Come! Come!"

With six tapers in candelabra on either side of her bed, the principessa lay under the covers, her tiny head on a silk pillow. Tomasso thought she was dead and began to shiver.

Teressa put her hand on her shoulder. "Principessa? Look who's here."

The principessa opened her eyes and a faint smile momentarily broke the porcelain face.

Tomasso knelt at the side of the bed. "Principessa. It's me, Tomasso. Can you hear me?"

The principessa smiled again.

"She's very weak," Teressa whispered in Tomasso's ear. "She hasn't eaten in two days. It's as if she wants to die."

"No, no, Principessa," Tomasso said. "No, no." He was sobbing now.

"We've got to get her out of here," Teressa said. "We need to take her upstairs, where it's dryer at least and maybe a little warmer. But I can't move her."

Silently, Tomasso lifted the covers from the principessa's frail body. He put one arm around her shoulders, and another under her knees. Then he gently lifted her from the bed and, with Bella screeching because of this sudden intrusion on her space on Tomasso's chest, he carried her through the salon and up the long flight of stairs to the second floor.

Halfway, a silver purse fell out of the principessa's sweater.

"Wait!" Her voice was soft and cracked but insistent. "Please. Pick that up."

Teressa did as her mistress commanded.

Teressa had already made the bed, a huge ornate structure with golden angels decorating the headboard and a canopy of red damask. The principessa looked even smaller there.

"My purse?" she said. Teressa put it on the table next to the bed, but the principessa asked to hold it.

Tomasso held her hand. "Are you all right, my dearest? The love of my life?"

Teressa knew all about Tomasso's past relationship with her mistress. She didn't approve it then, and she didn't approve it now, but what was she going to do?

"I'll leave you then," she said. "I'll make some broth and see if she'll take it."

As evening fell, the rain finally stopped. Dino, Mila and Adolfo had remained at their window through the day, watching the wreckage in the piazza but keeping an eye on the sleeping Signora Alfonso.

"Say, Dino," Adolfo suddenly said. "Didn't you mention that you had a date with that girl from the soup kitchen tonight?"

"Mention?" Mila said. "That's all he's been talking about all week."

"Nah."

"Dino! It's Sofia, right?"

"Oh, all right," Dino said. "Yeah, we were supposed to go to a movie. *The Bible.*"

"Well," Adolfo said, "they won't be showing any movies tonight. Or tomorrow night. Who knows when?"

"That's all right, Dino," Mila said. "I'm sure you can go out with Sofia some other time."

Dino nodded. He didn't care about missing the movie. It was what might have happened afterwards that was important.

Car horns continued to blast, but Dino realized that the dogs' cries had faded and then stopped entirely. He knew exactly what had happened. There were still no lights anywhere because there was no electricity. In the dim light, Dino was the first to notice.

"Look! Over there, under that window on the right. The water was about a half-foot higher just a little while ago. Now it's dropping!"

"It's dropping!" Adolfo and Mila cried together.

And soon the cheer could be heard all over the piazza, even drowning out the car horns.

"It's dropping!"

The statue of Dante looking down at the wreckage in Piazza Santa Croce the day after the flood. Photo by Swietlan Nicholas Kraczyna

Chapter Thirty-Three

Saturday, November 5, 1966

After breaching its retaining walls on both sides, the Arno flooded the city on Friday. On the north side, it swept through the National Library, the Piazza Santa Croce and the church itself. Then it roared on to the Piazza della Signoria, covering the spot where Savonarola was burned to death, and on to Dante's House, the Uffizi, Palazzo Vecchio and the Badia. By 9:35 a.m. it reached the Duomo and the Campanile, where it tore off the precious panels from the Baptistry and flooded the church itself. Then on to the neighborhoods of Santa Maggiore and the Medici Chapel and San Lorenzo and Santa Maria Novella and San Paolino and on and on and on. At the Accademia, water inched up toward the David and the Unfinished Statues.

On the south side, in the Oltrarno, waters rushed past San Jacopo Sopr'Arno, Palazzo Guicciardini, the Palazzo Pitti, Santo Spirito and Borgo San Frediano. Florence had become an immense lake of water, mud and fuel oil covering, according to one estimate, more than seven thousand acres. The bridges connecting the two sides were impassable, turning Florence into two cities.

Plaques that recorded the height of previous floods were quickly covered with water and oil. In the Piazza Santa Croce, the water reached more than twenty-two feet, more than twice as high as the flood of 1557.

At nightfall, thousands of people were stranded on rooftops, waiting, often in vain, for rescue from helicopters. One elderly woman lost her grip and fell to her death.

Observing how the flood had ruined the lives of the poor of Florence, the writer Carlo Coccioli wrote in the newspaper Il Giorno, *"At the thought of the suffering inflicted upon the lives of those humble folk, my supposed understanding of God's will evaporated."*

Adolfo, Mila and Dino waited by the window until well past midnight, watching as best they could as the torrent outside subsided in the darkness and the waters slowly lowered, inch by inch. They were able to get Signora Alonzo to sip some broth and she slept fitfully on the couch, waking with a start every once in a while to murmur, "Primo."

After a few restless hours of sleep, Adolfo, Mila and Dino rose and began to get dressed. They were finally able to get out of the apartment. Two sweaters and three pairs of socks. Thick pants. Mila didn't have any pants but tried a pair of Adolfo's, tying them with a rope when a belt was too big. The heaviest boots they could find. Then raincoats and umbrellas, although spokes on all three were broken.

Mila propped a pillow under Signora Alonzo's head. "Will you be all right, Signora?"

The old woman nodded.

"Help yourself to whatever's in the kitchen. There's some old biscotti. Make yourself some tea."

They fled before she could ask about her dog.

Out in the piazza, they found the water to be about three feet deep, but that wasn't the only problem. They had to dodge the cars and Vespas and bicycles that were stalled in the mud. Some car horns still blared.

Too concerned about losing their footing, they went their separate ways without even saying good-bye or when they would be back, Adolfo to the library, Mila to Casa del Popolo and Dino to Father Lorenzo's soup kitchen.

When Adolfo got to the library, his worst fears were more than realized. The Arno had breached the river wall just in front of the mammoth building, pushing tons of mud into all the basement rooms and rising as high as six feet on the ground floor. All of the catalog, reading and administrative rooms were submerged. It was as if giant bulldozers had gone into the basement and disgorged hundreds of thousands of books, manuscripts and documents and dumped them all outside. Now, all these precious items ground against each other in a furious maelstrom. A few other library workers had also arrived, and they stood frozen, uncomprehending.

"Adolfo!"

It was Sandro.

"Can you believe it?"

"It's worse than the ninth level of Dante's hell."

Other workers arrived.

"I tried to come over here last night but I couldn't get out of my apartment," Dorothea said. "And I'm on the second floor."

"I was on the rooftop until 3 o'clock," Enrico said. "Finally a helicopter came. My apartment is ruined, but I came right over."

"I didn't want to leave my mother," Maria said. "She's still hiding under the covers. But I had to come here."

Maria put her head on Enrico's shoulder. Sandro and Dorothea held hands.

"How the hell are we ever going to clean this up?" Adolfo said. "We'll never be able to do it alone."

They clung to each other, unable to grasp the catastrophe unfolding before their eyes.

At the Casa del Popolo, Mila found Alessandro, Vincenzo, Nicolo and Ugo huddled just outside.

"You're here already?" Mila said.

"We just got here," Vincenzo said. "You don't want to go in there."

"It's that bad? We've lost the food, the clothes?"

No one answered.

"More than that?"

No one answered.

"Everything?"

Ugo raised his head. "It's Franco."

"Franco? Where is he? He didn't stay here all night, did he?" Mila tried to get through to open the door.

"Maybe you'd better not go in there," Alessandro said.

"Why in heaven's name not? Let me through!"

The men cleared a path. The place was knee-deep in water, oil and mud. Furniture, dishes, clothing, blankets lay tossed around. There was little left of Mila's precautions.

Mila slogged though the open rooms and into the kitchen.

"Oh, my God!"

Mila gently turned Franco over on his cot. It was then that they saw that this poor *ritardamento,* whose only joy in life had been his *Zagor* comic books, had gone to his maker clutching his hero.

A few streets away, Dino arrived at Father Lorenzo's soup kitchen just as a line of disheveled men, women and children filed down the stairs and out into the soggy street. He found the priest on the second floor, grappling with a smelly oil drum.

"Ah, Dino, just in time. I need to take this out back. Can you give me a hand?"

Dino didn't have to look to know what was inside. Trying his best to close his nostrils while wrapping his arms around the huge can, he and the priest edged down the steps and behind the building.

"I don't want to empty this here," Father Lorenzo said. "Let's put it on top of that Fiat. It's not going anywhere."

Without looking back, Dino followed the priest back up the stairs. "Father, all those people just now. Did they stay here overnight?"

"I'm afraid so. Couldn't let them go out in that. Maybe they should have stayed longer, but they wanted to go home."

Dino wondered what kind of homes they would return to.

"Remember what I said a while ago, Dino. How the poor will suffer the most in a tragedy like this. Well, it's happened, and they're going to suffer. They've lived in such shabby apartments and houses, and now they're probably all ruined. Where will they go? I don't know. I just don't know. They can stay here at night for as long as they want, but this can't go on forever."

Unshaven now for three days, the priest sank into a chair, stretched back and closed his eyes. Dino thought he might fall asleep.

"Father?"

The priest rubbed his eyes. "I'm all right. Just need a little sleep, that's all. Let's see, it's been, oh, forty hours or so."

"Oh, my God!"

"But, hey, I want to show you our newest guests."

On the tiny rug, Elvis lay prone, her belly sheltering five little furry creatures. Sofia was hovering over them.

"They came last night, right in the midst of everything," Father Lorenzo said. "Some priests would call this a miracle, that life goes on in the midst of tragedy. Well, I just think Elvis decided it was her time. But we love the little things, don't we?" He crouched down, patting one, then another.

"I've given them names, all after Presley songs," Sofia said. "This one is Hound Dog, of course, then Jambalaya, then this one is Shake, and this one is Rattle and this one is Roll."

"Jambalaya?"

"I know, it's a little hard to call, but we'll see."

Dino picked up the puppy and tickled its ears.

"Oh, Dino," Sofia said, "I really enjoyed that movie last night. Those special effects were spectacular! That flood scene was so real! I think I was soaking wet by the end of it. We should do that more often!"

Never known for a sense of humor, Dino was slow on the uptake. "Oh, right. Well, yeah, I guess."

"Some other time then?" Sofia said. "I suppose I could make a little joke about taking a rain check, but I won't. But you will take me to a movie sometime, won't you?"

"Sure! Of course! You bet!"

"Only next time," Sofia said, "how about a comedy? Maybe one on a desert island."

Dino looked hopeful. "And maybe afterwards we can go to your apartment and talk?"

"Of course!"

The priest got up. "There's more to see. Come over here."

Father Lorenzo led Dino to a far corner where two church pews had been pushed together to make an improvised bed. Dino recognized the priest's long black coat over a large lump. Father Lorenzo pulled back the collar.

"Roberto? You've got a visitor."

Dino looked at the priest. "You brought him up here?"

"Yes," the priest said. "But I'll let you two alone."

Dino stepped back, not knowing what his uncle would say or do. Roberto slowly sat up and edged to the end of the pews. He held out his hand to Dino.

"Come closer, Dino."

Dino crouched down as Roberto searched his face.

"You know," Roberto said, "you sort of look like Adolfo. He's got freckles, too. And big ears."

Roberto grinned, and Dino did, too.

"Haven't seen him in a long time, so I'm not sure, though."

Dino didn't know where this was leading, and was afraid to ask.

"You're surprised I'm talking like this, aren't you?" Roberto said.

Dino nodded. "I'm surprised you're talking at all."

"It's been rough, Dino. I've been a complete asshole. I know that now."

"But..."

"I know it. An asshole." He held his head in his hands. Dino reached over to touch him, but Roberto pushed him away.

"Don't, Dino. Don't try to be nice. I can't take that."

"But..."

"Something happened last night, Dino. I was lying on the floor in the middle of the room, feeling sorry for myself as I always do, and I looked around. Two old ladies were taking care of me, and there were all these people all over the room. Some of them were asleep, but a lot of them weren't. I could tell that they were staring up at the ceiling and wondering what was going to happen to them. This flood has destroyed them, Dino. They don't have anything left."

Roberto was almost of breath and had to pause. Dino looked down at the floor.

"And I was thinking. What am I doing here? I had money. I had a shop. And I threw it all away. Now I'm just like one of them. I'm just like one of them."

He wiped his eyes.

"Roberto," Dino said. "There's a difference, you know."

"What?"

"You have...you have a family."

"Yeah, sure."

"Well, you have."

"Who?"

"Me, for one."

Roberto put his hand on Dino's head. "You've been something, you know. Coming here all these months and I've been such an asshole."

Dino shrugged. "There's someone else, you know. Adolfo."

"Adolfo? Adolfo will never speak to me again. You know that. I know that."

"How do you know that?"

"Why would he?"

"Well, why wouldn't he?"

"Because I'm an asshole, that's why."

"Roberto," Dino said, "maybe Adolfo's been an asshole, too."

"No."

"Roberto, do you want me to tell Adolfo that you'd like to see him again?"

Roberto leaned back and closed his eyes. "I don't know. Do what you want."

All the way home, Dino muttered, "'Do what you want, do what you want, do what you want.' What the hell am I supposed to do? I don't know what I'm supposed to do. Blockhead! Shit! Shit! Shit!"

Penny had already left the apartment when Ingrid and Marie got up and ventured out into the muddy streets. Everywhere, people were silently using brooms, shovels, rakes, garbage can covers, boards, anything they could find, to clear the mud and debris from in front of their homes and shops. The girls felt helpless.

Marie hugged herself against the bitter wind. "What should we do?"

"I don't know, but we've got to do something. We can't just watch."

At the corner of Via Verdi and Via Ghibellina, they encountered an ancient woman, bundled in a ratty sweater and boots, pushing mud with a broken broom. She moved from her doorstep to the street, from the street to the doorstep in a fruitless battle. Every time she turned around, the mud would inch back. The woman sank against her door, sobbing.

Ingrid touched her shoulder while Marie gently took the broom from her gnarled hands. "Let us help," Ingrid said.

Tears streaming down her face, the woman looked up. "Oh, *grazie, grazie tanto.*" She sat in the mud, not understanding what was going on, while the girls took up the task, only marginally more successful in clearing the mess that had accumulated.

Ingrid bent down to pick up a ceramic pitcher, chipped and dripping with mud and oil but still intact.

"Look, Marie. This must have been in that shop down the street, the one next to the music store."

She wiped it off and handed it to the woman, who put it inside her sweater and clutched it to her breast. A faint smile briefly lit her worn face. "*Grazie.*"

They went to their favorite shopping street, Via dei Neri. This was where they had gone for bread and chicken and fruits and vegetables, where they bought shoes and leather purses, where Ingrid bought Elvis Presley records, and where Marie bought a necklace for her mother back in France.

Now it was unrecognizable, a sea of what Marie delicately called "gunk." Storekeepers and clerks carried the stuff from in front of their shops to the street, hoping that the city would eventually take it all away. They were mostly silent, these stolid people of Florence. They had survived the war. They had survived extreme hardships. They would get through this.

Up and down Via dei Neri, Ingrid and Marie assisted others. Two young women struggling with a cabinet that had wedged against their door. A mother and father trying to dig a baby carriage out of the mud. And then they saw two young men trying to upright an overturned Fiat.

"Look," Marie cried. "It's Gregorio and Nicco. From Penny's parties and the beach."

"Gregorio! Nicco!" Ingrid yelled. "What are you doing? You're not going to steal that car, are you?"

"No! No!" Gregorio grunted under the strain of the car's front end. "The owner is in that shop. He's got enough troubles. We just thought we'd help."

"You're helping?" Marie said.

"Well, aren't you?" Nicco said. "Say, have you seen Penny? She should be out here helping."

"Who knows where Penny is," Ingrid said. "Maybe she went to see Raffaele. He's probably in the best place in Florence right now. Those walls must be so thick. No flood is going to invade that prison."

Throughout the afternoon and late into the evening, the girls continued to help people they had never seen before. They weren't the only ones. They saw other university students, many of them from the Accademia or other schools, also coming out.

Finally, they ran into Penny. She was rushing down the street clutching what appeared to be a rag.

"Penny!"

"Ingrid! Marie! Look at this!" She held up the rag.

"What is it?"

"It's a Pucci! An Emilio Pucci! It's a silk dress, can't you tell!" She held it up against her. What was once a lovely cocktail dress, with green and yellow flowers, was now torn and filthy.

"You picked that rag up?" Marie said. "Why on earth why?"

Ingrid reached out but refused to touch it. "You're not taking that thing home, are you?"

"I know it looks pretty bad now, but I bet I can have it cleaned. I could even send it to my mother. They have better cleaners in Liverpool than they do here. Don't you understand? This is an Emilio Pucci! I'd never be able to afford this. It was stuck on a nail against a house. It must have come all the way from Via dei Tornabuoni. I can't believe it!"

"Penny, for God's sake, everyone here is destitute. They don't have food, they don't have water, they don't even have a place to stay. And you're thinking about a goddamn dress?"

"Oh, I know that. But, Ingrid, it's a Pucci!"

The principessa had eaten a little soup at noon and even had some bread with it in the evening. With Teressa's help, she was able to sit up against a pile of heavy pillows.

"Oh, Mistress," Teressa said, "you're looking so much better. Tomorrow, I bet you'll be walking around. The water is going down in the salon and your bedroom downstairs, so maybe you'll be able to go back down there."

The principessa looked at Tomasso, who had remained at her side throughout the day. "Oh, I'm fine here, Teressa. Signor Nozzoli is keeping me company. Why don't you lie down for a while. You must be tired."

Teressa did not get the hint, so the principessa made it more explicit. "Teressa, Signor Nozzoli and I have a lot to talk about. You may leave."

Reluctant to leave her mistress in the company of "that man," Teressa nevertheless gathered up the empty soup bowl and tray and went into the next room.

"She's a dear soul," the principessa said, "but I wish she wouldn't hang over me so much."

"I'll take over now," Tomasso said quietly. He had not let go of her hand since the morning. Her other hand rested on the sleeping Bella, curled against her hip.

"Oh, Tomasso. I'm so sorry. I was planning to have another salon. On this very night. But there would be only two guests. You and young Aldobrandino Sporenza. But we didn't get the invitations out. Anyway, it's too late now."

Tears fell freely down Tomasso's cheeks.

"Don't cry, my darling," she said. "Oh, my dearest. Remember the times we had? In the Boboli Gardens? Near San Marco? Along the river? Oh, my, we made love everywhere, didn't we?"

Tomasso laughed. "And we weren't ashamed. We got in trouble a couple of times."

"But the *carabinieri!* They were so kind. As soon as I told them who I was, they let us alone."

Tomasso wiped her forehead, which was glistening with sweat, and then kissed it.

"Do you have pleasant memories, Tomasso?"

"Of course. Don't you?"

"Yes, of course. Keep those memories, Tomasso. Keep them."

Tomasso kissed her hand.

"Now, Tomasso, could you hand me that glass of water? Thank you. And now go to my study, just across the hall. There's a book I'd like you to read to me. I don't remember the name. It has a blue cover. Maybe it's on the second shelf, maybe not. Look for it, Tomasso."

"Of course."

"Oh, and Tomasso. Kiss me again, please." He bent down, this big burly man, and gently kissed the lips of this tiny frail woman who had been his lover so many years ago.

As soon as she heard the door latch click, the principessa took out the silver purse from under her covers.

Chapter Thirty-Four

Sunday, November 6, 1966

Records after the flood estimated that 1,500 works of art in Florence were disfigured or destroyed. Of these, 850 were seriously damaged, including paintings on wood and on canvas, frescoes and sculptures. Among the casualties were Paolo Uccello's Creation and Fall at Santa Maria Novella, Sandro Botticelli's Saint Augustine and Domenico Ghirlandaio's Saint Jerome at the Church of the Ognissanti, Andrea di Bonaiuto's The Church Militant and Triumphant at Santa Maria Novella, Donatello's wooden statue of Mary Magdalene in the Baptisty of the Duomo, Baccio Bandinelli's white marble Pietà in Santa Croce and Filippo Brunelleschi's wooden model for the cupola of the Duomo, in the Duomo's Museum. Three panels were torn from Lorenzo Ghiberti's Gate of Paradise on the east side of the Baptistry and two from Andrea Pisano's panels on the south.

The greatest loss was the Crucifixion by Giovanni Cimabue, the Father of Florentine Painting, in the Santa Croce Museum. The water there rose thirteen feet and the painting was ruined.

At the National Library, the flood damaged 1,300,000 items, including the majority of the works in the Palatine and Magiabechi collections, along with periodicals, newspapers, prints, maps and posters. This was a third of the library's collections.

There was also extensive damage to the collections at the Opera del Duomo, the Gabinetto Vieusseux Library and the State Archives.

But more than all the art that was ruined, this was a personal tragedy that touched the lives of every Florentine. Twenty thousand families lost their homes, fifteen thousand cars were destroyed, and six thousand shops went out of business.

At least thirty people died; some reports put the toll at more than a hundred. Among them was a young inmate who drowned after he leapt from the prison roof.

Adolfo and Mila were in bed by the time Dino returned to their apartment after midnight, so he waited until Sunday morning to talk to Adolfo about Roberto. It was 6:30 a.m. and Signora Alonzo was sitting by the window, unable to grasp the destruction in the piazza. She had said little since she arrived two days earlier, and she probably wondered why everyone changed the subject when she asked about Primo.

Dino waited for an opportune time, but he knew that Adolfo and Mila would soon be leaving for the library and Casa del Popolo. Today, it made no difference that it was Sunday.

"I was talking to Roberto yesterday," he said quietly, not daring to look at Adolfo.

Mila stopped putting on the second of her sweaters. "Really? And he was talking, too?"

"Yes. For the first time."

Adolfo suddenly became absorbed in pulling on his boots.

"Well," Mila said, "what did he say?"

"He said he was just like all the other poor people at the soup kitchen."

"What does that mean?" Mila asked.

"I guess it means that he's poor. He doesn't have anything. It sounded like he was sorry he behaved so bad that he lost his business."

"So he's feeling sorry for himself?" Adolfo said. "I bet…"

Mila interrupted him. "And did he apologize?"

"Sort of," Dino said.

"Sort of?"

"He said he was an asshole."

Mila laughed. "Sounds like an apology to me."

"No. No, it doesn't," Adolfo said. "I tell you, he's just feeling sorry for himself. And he wants us to feel sorry for him."

"Adolfo," Mila said, "can't you try to understand what's going on with him?"

Adolfo ignored the question. "Dino," he said, "did Roberto say you should tell me all this?"

"He said it was up to me. So I have. What do you want me to do now?"

"It's up to you."

"Good God!" Mila cried. "'It's up to you, it's up to you!' You two brothers! I'd like to bang your heads together. Talk about stubborn Italians! *Testardo! Testone!*"

She pulled on her woolen cap and stormed out the door. Dino followed, again muttering, "'It's up to you, it's up to you.' Damn! Damn! Damn!" After seeing that Signora Alonzo would be all right for the day, Adolfo, ashamed, ran down the stairs, too, into a piazza covered with two feet of sludge.

At Casa del Popolo, dozens of people milled restlessly around the entrance when Mila arrived, but Alessandro, Vincenzo, Nicolo and Ugo stood guard in front.

"You can't go in there," Nicolo yelled at the crowd of people, some of whom were raising their fists. "The place is flooded. There's nothing to give out. We have nothing!"

Two days after the flood, fear, frustration and anger were spreading in the Santa Croce district, maybe even in all of the city.

"People are saying that there will be an epidemic," Alessandro told Mila. "Look at all the dead dogs and cats in the street. And the garbage!"

"They've heard explosions," Vincenzo said, "and they think the city is going to blow up."

"They've heard that there are escaped prisoners all over," Ugo said. "Murderers. Rapists. And they're armed!"

"And," Nicolo added, "they wonder why the goldsmiths on Ponte Vecchio were warned the night of the flood and no one else. This is not just the Italians who like conspiracies. Many people are blaming the city, the government, for not telling us beforehand."

"And they wonder why the dams weren't fixed long ago."

"And then they want to know why are they so concerned about paintings and statues when they should be taking care of the people?"

"And there are still people dying."

Mila listened to all of these complaints quietly. "Look," she said, "I'm sure there are reasons for all of these complaints, but we don't have time to argue about it. There's work to be done. Let's do it."

Since no one could enter the Casa, what was needed now was to help quiet the Casa's patrons with bread and water. She ordered Alessandro and Vincenzo to go to a bakery she knew in the northern part of Florence and to buy as much bread as they could. Alessandro's Fiat, a few streets away, was water-soaked but, after many attempts, drivable. Nicolo and Ugo were told to go up to Fiesole and find gallons of water.

"What did you do with Franco?" Mila whispered.

"He's still in there," Ugo said. "What can we do?"

In front of the National Library, amid the sodden books, manuscripts, newspapers and periodicals strewn everywhere, Adolfo found Sandro and Enrico in a crowd of library workers. But it soon was more than a crowd. There was a line, a long line that stretched from inside the bowels of the library, out the vestibule and down the steps to trucks that suddenly appeared. One by one, the books and other items were passed, quickly but carefully, from one hand to the next to the next until they were stacked in the trucks.

"This is terrible," Adolfo said. "They're taking all these precious books away and destroying them?"

"No, no," Enrico said. "They're taking them away somewhere to be restored. Well, good luck! How can they ever put these things back in shape? We'd need hundreds, thousands, of more people to help."

But as the day progressed, there were more and more lines, not just with library workers but with hundreds of young people, even many who could not speak Italian.

"What's going on?" Adolfo asked Enrico as he passed along a dripping volume of eighteenth-century verse. "Who are these kids?"

"Don't know. I talked to a couple of them. One was from France, another from Spain. I don't know how they got here so fast. They said they just wanted to help."

The lines grew longer and longer. Adolfo began talking to the young visitors, too, amazed that they would come to Florence on a frigid November day to stand out in the cold and do dirty, back-breaking work.

He noticed a girl who seemed frightened yet still determined. She was tiny, bundled in a cloth coat and long scarf and with blond hair wound on top of her head.

"Hello," he said. "Where are you from?"

"Lucca."

"Ah, that's near my hometown," Adolfo said. "I went there a lot. But that was years ago. Why did you come?"

She passed a mud-soaked book along. "I heard about this and I thought, I have to go there and help."

"Really? That's wonderful!"

"There were other students on the bus coming from Lucca," the girl said. "And I've met boys and girls from Turin and Bologna and Urbino, too."

"All you young people, and you just want to help?"

"Yes. That's all."

Adolfo gently took another book from her. "Thank you. What's your name?"

"Francesca. Francesca Casati. And yours?"

"Adolfo Sporenza. I work at the library."

"Sporenza? Sporenza?"

"It's a pretty common name."

Francesca held on to the next book before passing it on. "I used to date a boy named Sporenza. He was from Sant'Antonio."

"You're kidding! Wait. You said your name was Francesca? The Francesca that Dino talks about? He's my nephew."

"Dino is your nephew? He talks about me?"

"Well, he used to. I think he was writing you a letter. Maybe he didn't finish it. Anyway, you should come over to our place. I know Dino would like to see you."

Dino wanted to make two stops before going to see Roberto, first to Santa Croce and then to the Accademia.

The nave of Santa Croce was still underwater, and priests and monks and workmen were trying to clear away debris. Dino went straight to Michelangelo's tomb and immediately took out a handkerchief and attempted to wipe the marble, but with little success. The tomb was stained a deep blackish brown, residue from the fuel oil. Everything else was stained, too. Machiavelli. Rossini. Galileo. Dante's memorial.

Dino couldn't bear to look at anything else and was about to leave when he saw Tomasso Nozzoli stomping through, clomping on the graves of medieval knights. His face frozen in grief and despair, he carried a long wooden box in his arms. A woman Dino recognized as the principessa's maid followed.

"Signor Nozzoli?"

"Oh, Dino. We're having a funeral for the principessa." Tears dropped on top of the pine lid.

Tomasso said that Father Lorenzo was supposed to have said a Mass for the recovery of the principessa Friday.

"But of course that's when we had the flood. She died last night." He paused for breath. "She seemed fine, and we went out of the room, and when we came back she was gone. Just gone, so peacefully…"

Tomasso had found a dozen boards undamaged by the water in his shop. The boards were short, but so was the principessa, and she didn't need a large coffin. Teressa had washed the principessa's body and dressed it in a bright magenta gown, the one she wore at her last salon. They had lined the coffin with curtains.

They went past the main altar and into the Rinuccini Chapel. Tomasso put the coffin on a pew in front of the Mary Magdalene fresco. Dino thought he heard a baby crying, but knew he must be mistaken.

"*Buongiorno,*" Father Lorenzo said as he entered. "Wait. What has happened?"

Tomasso explained what happened, and the priest embraced him. "I'm so sorry, Tomasso."

The Mass was brief, with both Tomasso and Teressa crying softly. "God bless this lovely woman," Father Lorenzo said at the end, "and keep her with you for all eternity."

Dino slipped away. Leaving the church, and still wondering if there was a baby crying in there somewhere, he made his way up Via Verdi, then Via Fiesolana, then Via degli Allani.

He found workers mopping out the floor of the Accademia, which had not suffered serious damage, and then went to the galleria. Except for the oily residue on the floor, the rooms were not harmed. David still stood imperiously on his pedestal as if defying God and nature as well as Goliath. And The Waking Slave was still emerging from his sleep.

His mass of hair tangled and perspiring profusely even though the room was chilly, Professor Mariotti rushed back and forth from a storage room to put fans in every conceivable place.

"Ah, Dino. We have to get the floor dry. It's still wet."

"The statues weren't damaged?"

"No, thank God. There were only a couple of inches of water because we're higher here. But we have to get the floor dry, we have to get the floor dry, we have to get the floor dry..."

"Are you all right, Professor?"

His eyes were glazed. "Yes, yes. But we have to get the floor dry, we have to get the floor dry, we have to get the floor dry..."

The professor wandered around, looking in vain for more fans. Dino wondered if he would ever be able to teach again.

It was 10 o'clock by the time Dino got to the soup kitchen. He had never seen Father Lorenzo so harried. Even though the temperature inside was not much warmer than outside, he was sweating.

"OK, Sofia, you get the pots on the stove. Claudio, try to find some wood. Amerigo, get the tables ready. They're going to be here for the noon meal any minute even though it's only 10 o'clock. These people are hungry!"

As the others ran about doing their chores, the priest saw Dino standing in the doorway, not knowing what to do.

"Dino! Just the man I was looking for. The military is starting to bring gallons of water into the piazza. Take Sofia and get as many as you can. Then go back and get some more. And more. Tell the soldiers we're feeding the hungry, lots of hungry, and they should give us as much as they can. We need it for the soup. Tell them Father Lorenzo said so."

Dino and Sofia rushed out the door, commandeered the soldiers for water and grinned at each other as they lugged cans and bottles from the trucks to the soup kitchen.

"You know something, Dino," she said, "I've never been so excited in my life!"

"Me, too! Isn't this great?"

"I mean, I felt like I was helping before, but now…"

"I know. This is so great."

"Ah," Father Lorenzo said as they brought in the last cans, "now we can make soup. You see, the miracle of loaves and fishes worked again. Or maybe it was the wedding at Cana. Sometimes I get my miracles mixed up."

Dino doubted that Christ had anything to do with the soup that was even now being cooked for the line of people that had materialized outside the door. Hungry, but subdued, they silently entered and took their bowls to their tables. Hardly anyone spoke, but stared grimly ahead. The *Benvenuto* sign hung in shreds from the ceiling, and the place had never been so quiet.

"Dino," the priest said after the last diner had been served, "take a break. Go see your uncle."

For the first time, Roberto was sitting on, not in, his bed, dressed in a shirt and pants that Dino recognized were Father Lorenzo's. Roberto's thin body shrank inside them. Father Lorenzo must have loaned him a razor, because he was now clean-shaven and the bruises on his face were healing. Someone had also cut back his curly hair.

"Dino!" his uncle said, "tell me. What did you tell Adolfo? And what did he say?"

"I, um, told him that you were getting better."

"And…"

"And that you were sorry for what you've done."

"And what did he say?"

"Adolfo said that he was really sorry, too, and he wants to see you again."

In the dim light, Dino hoped Roberto didn't notice that his ears suddenly became red. He almost expected his nose to grow like Pinocchio.

"Really? He said that?"

"Um, yes."

"That's great. When do you think he'll come here?"

"Roberto, don't you think you could go over there?"

"Over there? I don't know about that. I don't think I can walk that far."

"Roberto, if you wanted to walk that far, I bet you could walk that far."

"I don't know. I'll let you know." Roberto closed his eyes.

Exhausted, and muttering, "'I'll let you know, I'll let you know.' Shit!" Dino returned to the apartment late at night, but Adolfo and Mila still hadn't come back. Signora Alonzo was snoring lightly on the couch. He took off his shoes and collapsed on the hard floor under the window, pulling a blanket over his head. Then the phone rang.

"Dino? Dino! Dino, I've been trying to reach you for days. First there wasn't anything, it didn't even ring, and then I got this strange signal and nothing would happen and today I've been calling and calling but no one answered. Are you all right, Dino? And Adolfo and Mila? Where have you been? Do you have enough food? Dino, should Paolo and I come over there?"

"No, Mama, no. You shouldn't come over. We're all just fine."

"And Dino, what about Roberto? Did you see him again? How does he look? Was his shop damaged in the flood? Is he still with the priest? Is he getting enough to eat? Priests sometimes don't have a lot of food. Dino, say something!"

"Roberto's doing fine, Mama. Just fine."

Piazza Santa Croce after the flood. Photo by Swietlan Nicholas Kraczyna

Chapter Thirty-Five

Sunday, November 13, 1966

By the middle of November, the Arno had returned to normal, but fear spread through Florence every time it rained. Florentines looked to the skies, crossed themselves and returned to shoveling mud and debris and repairing their homes and shops.

International committees raised countless sums of money to salvage the works of art, but something even more significant happened. Thousands of young people, from across Italy, Europe, the United States and even Russia and Japan arrived spontaneously and unannounced to remove mud from the millions of books damaged by the flood. They also helped restore damaged art works and delivered baskets of food to people trapped in their homes.

They became known as gli angeli del fango, *or "The Mud Angels."*

Dino lost his job at Trattoria Eleanora because the place was still closed and Signor Michellini didn't think it would ever reopen. The restaurant was badly damaged by the flood, and Signor Michellini's own home suffered severe damage.

Instead, Dino spent the first days after the flood at Signora Alonzo's apartment. Starting from the front, at the door to the piazza, and working to the back, he needed three days just to shovel out all the gunk and refuse. Municipal trucks eventually hauled away the growing piles from buildings all around the piazza. Then Dino had to wash down the walls, thick with mold. Then he had to clean what furniture was salvageable and throw out what was not.

He went to the Casa and got sheets and blankets and to the market to stock the kitchen shelves. Mila donated dishes, pots and pans. Then Dino went to the *cucina popolare* and brought back one last thing.

"All right, Signora Alonzo," he said as he took her frail hand and led her down the steps from the apartment and back into the home where she had lived for forty years, where she raised three children and where her husband had died. "You're home again."

Signora Alonzo could only whisper *"Grazie, grazie,"* as she gazed around the rooms, the walls clean again and pictures back in their original places. Even the doilies on her little tables had returned. She reached up to hug Dino and seemed about to collapse. He held her until she regained her composure.

"There's something else, Signora." Dino opened the kitchen door, and a small brown puppy bounded out, yelping with glee and almost knocking Signora Alonzo over. She bent down and picked him up, and the puppy promptly licked her face.

"His name is Jambalaya, but you can change it if you want," Dino said. "The mother's name was Elvis and so her puppies were named after Evis Presley's songs." As soon as he said this, Dino knew this was far too complicated for an Italian elderly woman to comprehend.

"Jamba...Jamba... *E' bello!"* Signora Alonzo sank into the faded blue chair that had been her favorite, Jambalaya still licking her face. *"E' bello! E' bello!"*

"I put some milk and pieces of meat in the refrigerator for him, and there's a water dish near the sink," Dino said. "And you'll find some pasta on the shelves if you want to make something for yourself. OK, then, I'll stop by later. I'm going to the *cucina popolare.*"

Dino hadn't been at the soup kitchen for almost a week and was surprised to hear a great deal of hammering, sawing and pounding.

"Dino!" Father Lorenzo said as he opened the door. "Great to see you again! You should see what's going on upstairs. Go, take a look."

The vast space that had housed diners the night of the flood was being transformed. Men, women and a scattering of young people were building partitions throughout the room. Others were hauling in cots, old chairs and dressers.

Dino recognized Gregorio and Nicco from Penny's parties and the Viareggio trip, and the two young women who were trying to put up a wall by nailing a board against a frame.

"Ingrid! Marie! What are you doing here?"

"Dino!" Marie said. "Well, we're just trying to help a little."

"Not very well, as you can see," Ingrid said, trying to straighten out a bent nail. "Gregorio heard about this and told us. There are so many people still homeless, so Father Lorenzo is making little rooms where they can stay until they get back home."

"Nothing fancy, but at least it's dry," Mila said. She paused to suck a thumb she had just struck with a hammer. "Shit! Oh, sorry."

Dino held the board while Ingrid pounded nails. "Where's Penny? Why isn't she here?"

"She went back to England," Marie said.

"No!" Dino said. "She left in the middle of this?"

"She couldn't take it here anymore," Ingrid said, "so she took her Beatles records and her Mary Quant miniskirt and her high white boots..."

"...and her Emilio Pucci dress..."

"...and she flew out Saturday morning."

"I don't understand," Dino said. "I thought she loved Florence."

"I think," Marie said, "she liked the idea of Florence. That it was this wonderful place with all the art and museums and churches. Then she found there was another Florence. She didn't like that at all."

"And," Ingrid said, removing a nail from her teeth, "there was probably another reason. She went to the *carabinieri* office and they confirmed that Raffaele drowned when he jumped from the prison. She was pretty upset about that."

"He couldn't swim," Marie said. "Remember how he would never go in the water at Viareggio?"

Dino didn't remember, but then he had gone to the beach at Viareggio only once. "Well, that's too bad. I guess I never did understand Penny."

"Neither did we," Marie said. "Oops, we better work faster. Our supervisor's coming."

When Dino turned around, he saw a familiar, if unexpected, face. "Roberto!"

"*Ciao*, Dino! Here to help? We can use it."

"Well," Dino said, shaking his uncle's hand, "you seem to have made a good recovery."

"Nothing like work to help the muscles. Father Lorenzo enlisted me. And you know, what Father Lorenzo wants, Father Lorenzo gets."

"So you're helping out here?"

"Not only helping out, I'm in charge! Well, I'm in charge of two teams, including these two great young women. They're doing a fantastic job. But, hey, I've got to help those guys over there. See you later?"

Shaking his head, Dino went back downstairs, where Father Lorenzo put him in charge of guiding diners in and out. The number of diners had tripled since the flood, people who lost their jobs and couldn't afford to buy food, people who lost their homes, people who didn't have much more than the clothes on their backs. Bread was still hard to get, since all the ovens in Florence were damaged, and volunteers had to go to Fiesole where the bakeries were in operation.

"All right, form a line to the right," Dino called as he opened the doors for another group of diners. "No pushing. Everyone will get the same. Carlo, what did I say, 'No pushing.' *Grazie.* All right, make room for Natalie, she's carrying the baby. *Ciao*, Natalie. Little Rico is smiling today. I like it when he smiles. All right, this way. Sofia is waiting for you."

Father Lorenzo looked on with a big grin.

"Dino, I'm so proud of you." He gave him a bear hug and looked into his eyes. "Dino, a couple of months ago, I was a little worried about you. You didn't know that, did you? Well, I just thought the way you hung back, didn't talk much, that maybe you wouldn't get through a crisis or something terrible very well. I guess I shouldn't have worried. You've changed so much in these last months, Dino, and especially since the flood. You can take charge here. You know how to talk to people. You make them feel at home. And besides that, you're getting your uncles back together…"

"Maybe…"

"…you're getting your uncles together. And my God, you saved an old woman's life and then you restored the place where she lives! Dino, whatever else it has done, the flood has helped to make you a man. Really."

A few months ago, Dino would have blushed from his forehead to his neck after such a compliment. Now, he just said, "Thanks, Father," and changed the subject.

"Father, I saw what's going on upstairs. I can never believe how you manage to get these things."

"I suppose I could say that the Lord will provide, but, you know, it takes a lot more than that." He smiled. "Like, for example, knowing where to borrow some cots, if you know what I mean. And lumber. Roberto was great. When I told him about the project, he had some guys go to his woodworking shop and they brought back a huge pile of lumber. And he managed to find some other piles in another woodworking shop."

"You're amazing."

"Dino, remember what I said about how I worried that if Florence had another disaster, there would be a lot more people who were going to be desperate? Well, it's happened. Somehow, we're going to have to find enough people who can help these poor souls."

He put his hand on Dino's shoulder. "And, you know that you're one of them."

"Hope so."

"OK, enough talk," the priest said. "Listen. You never did give me guitar lessons. When all this is over, I'm going to hold you to your promise, you know."

"You're still interested in playing guitar after all this?"

"We're going to get better, Dino. We're going to be all right. Florence has lived through a lot and it will live through this, too. Now, go. Go help Sofia in the serving line."

Sofia looked particularly attractive tonight. Wearing a light blue blouse and dark blue skirt, she poured out soup with a broad smile.

"Hi!" Dino said as he put on an apron. "You look happy."

"Hi to you," Sofia said. "I do? I guess I am."

"Me, too," he said.

With the diners flowing by at a rapid rate, there wasn't much time for conversation. "Want to go for a walk after we've cleaned up?" Dino asked.

"Sure."

But instead of walking along the Arno, they decided to go to the Piazza della Repubblica. Having suffered less damage than other parts of the city, the square on this moonlit evening was again alive with street artists, displays and vendors.

"I love this place," Sofia said. "It always seems like the real heart of Florence."

"I guess it always was," Dino said as they walked past the Column of Abundance. "First a Roman forum, then churches all over, then the Jewish ghetto."

"I can't imagine living in a ghetto."

"I guess Florence has a dark side like everywhere else."

They admired the scarves on one vendor's stand and the cheap souvenirs on another. Dino was going to buy Sofia a bracelet, but remembered that he didn't have any money. Neither did she. She had lost her jobs at the dress shop and the men's hat shop and wasn't needed as a model at the Accademia as often this term.

Dino took her hand. "Are you going to be OK, Sofia?"

"I'll be fine. I've saved up some money and I've always lived on very little. And I can always eat at the *cucina popolare*."

"Looks like we're going to have to skip movies for a while," he said, "now that neither of us is working."

"I can live with that. Remember, I came from Calabria. We didn't have a movie theater in our village."

Dino smiled. "Neither did we."

Dino walked her back to her apartment, and she kissed him gently on the cheek. But she didn't invite him in.

Dino wasn't the only one changed by the flood. When Adolfo brought her home for dinner the next night, Francesca was not the quiet, reserved girl Dino had known in Lucca. Tired but exhilarated, she joined Adolfo in explaining how they had learned to restore ancient books that had been so badly damaged by the flood at the National Library.

"You can't believe how hard this is," Adolfo said.

"First we have to dry out the books," Francesca said. "Page by page! We have to scrape off the mud." She raised her hands to show her dirty fingernails.

"And then wash and disinfect them," Adolfo said.

"Sometimes we use sawdust to dry them out."

"And we have to go so fast," Adolfo said, "because there's always the threat of mold."

"Then we dry them," Francesca said. "We use blotting papers...."

Adolfo interrupted. "We were using green blotting paper, but that did more damage than good. We even hang pages on clotheslines. We're still learning how to do this."

"But we have a lot of help," Francesca said. "Students and young people are coming from all over, France, Germany, England to help. I even met one from Japan."

Dino looked from Adolfo to Francesca and back again, proud and thrilled by the way they had taken on a tedious, never-ending task so enthusiastically.

"Francesca," he said, "do you know what everyone is calling all of you? The *Gli angeli del fango.*"

"The Mud Angels? I like that. At least the mud part is true," Francesca said.

Dino stared at her. This was not the shy Francesca he had known in Lucca. This was a girl, no, a young woman, who was newly poised and confident. He was intrigued. In her own way, she was as fascinating as Sofia. He wanted to get to know this new Francesca.

Later, Dino and Francesca walked along the Arno to the Ponte Vecchio. The street and the old bridge were slowly getting back to normal, but the sides were still littered with garbage, damaged furniture and, here and there, useless Vespas. With no young people lying around singing and laughing, there was no sweet smell spreading from the bridge.

"I wish I could show you some of the museums and churches, Francesca," Dino said, "but most of them are still closed."

"That's all right. I'm too tired at night to go anywhere. I just go back to the convent where they're putting us up and collapse on my bed."

They were silent for a long time, watching a peaceful river that now seemed incapable of doing any harm.

"I'm glad you came to Florence, Francesca," Dino said.

"I am, too, Dino. And I'm sorry for being such a stupid little girl back in Lucca. I shouldn't have written that dumb letter before Christmas last year. I guess I just wanted to see you again, and then when I did, I didn't know what to do about it. I'm sorry, Dino, I really am."

Dino put his hand on her shoulder. "That's all right. Maybe we can go for more walks."

"I'd like that."

"I have a friend, Sofia, that I walk with sometime."

"Oh," Francesca teased, "you have a friend named Sofia? Tell me about her."

"She's just a friend, Francesca. She volunteers at the soup kitchen." He didn't feel it necessary to add that she modeled in the nude for art students and that they almost had a date.

"I'm glad. Really."

"And you? You must have met lots of boys helping with the books."

"A few. There's one, Andrew, who talks to me a lot. He's from London. He's nice. I wouldn't call him a real friend, though."

Dino walked her slowly to the convent. "I can't believe we're being so grown up about all this."

"Maybe," she said, "it's because we have grown up."

Now that he was back on the lumpy sofa, Dino had a hard time going to sleep that night. He thought about Signora Alfonso and Roberto and what Father Lorenzo had said. And then names kept running through his mind. "Sofia…Francesca…Sofia…Francesca…" A few weeks ago, he didn't have any friends, especially girls. Now, he might have two. Maybe his ears weren't so bad after all.

Chapter Thirty-Six

Sunday, November 27, 1966

Although Florence's recovery from the disastrous flood was only beginning, the city celebrated its new life only three weeks later with a gala in the opera house, Teatro Comunale, on November 27.

The floors were still damp and seats were brought in from a movie theater. There was no scenery, but the Maggio Musicale chorus, in costumes lent by La Scala at Milan, sang Monteverdi's 1643 story of love and lust in the age of Nero, L'Incoronazione di Poppea. *At the end, the audience rose to its feet in a standing ovation.*

They could not help but notice the line that floodwaters had left around the theater. It was four feet above the floor.

It had taken three weeks before Dino, with Mila's help, got Roberto and Adolfo together. First, Roberto refused to go to Adolfo's apartment.

"I'm still recuperating," he told Dino, although it was clear that he could cut boards and hammer nails alongside more burly men in Father Lorenzo's project.

Then Adolfo rejected the idea of visiting Roberto.

"He knows where I am."

Finally, in an act of defiance that made Father Lorenzo proud, Dino gave each of them separately an ultimatum. Feet planted apart, hands behind his back, he stood stolidly in front of one uncle and then the other.

"Look," he told Roberto and then Adolfo, "I'm tired of running back and forth between you two. You had a fight, right. But that was years ago. Get over it. You're brothers, for God's sake. Are you going to go through life bearing these grudges? How happy will you be then? You're going to grow old and miserable and kids will be scared to look at you. There are enough grumpy old Italian men like that around. Why do you want to become one of them?"

He paused for breath, but he was just getting started.

"Remember old Signora Franzi and Signora Isadora back in Sant'Antonio? Remember how I was so afraid of them? We all were. They wouldn't even have to do anything, just walk down the street to Leoni's or the church and we'd run and hide. Why? This is what Mama told me once. They had a fight many years ago. Nobody knew what it was about, maybe over a guy or something. Anyway, they refused to talk to one another. And for fifty years they didn't talk to each other even though they lived a street apart. That fight made them bitter old ladies, scaring little kids. And you know what? They both died and went to their graves like that."

He paused again.

"And then there's Rosa and Annabella from the village. They had a fight when they were young girls and didn't speak for years and years. But they finally forgave each other. And now they're best friends. So you can be, too, if you want to, if you would stop being such blockheads."

In each case, Roberto and Adolfo remained silent.

"OK, if that's the kind of a man you want to be, fine. But I'm not going to be a part of it. I'm not going to be a friend to either one of you. There. I've said it."

No one was more surprised by his declaration than he was. He wiped his forehead and put the handkerchief in his back pocket.

The reaction of the uncles was identical. At first, they couldn't believe that this kid, this quiet kid who liked to paint and play guitar and wouldn't harm a fly, would get so riled up. And then they looked down at the floor. And then they looked up at the ceiling. And then both of them put their hands in their pockets and walked away for a while. And when they came back to Dino, they both said the same thing. "OK."

The meeting was arranged for 2 o'clock on a Sunday afternoon in Adolfo and Mila's apartment. Afraid that Roberto wouldn't show up, Dino went to the soup kitchen. He found Roberto sitting on a bench in the back. "Ready?" Dino said as he approached his uncle.

"Ready."

Roberto was still a little weak, so they walked arm in arm. "Whoa!" Roberto said as they went out the door. "Not so fast."

"Just take it slow," Dino said.

In other years on a Sunday, the streets of Florence would be filled with people talking and laughing, enjoying the beauty and history of the city. Now, under leaden skies, Florentines were still stoically shoveling out debris from their homes and shops, putting up windows, repairing roofs. They did this all quietly. God sent them a disaster. They would live through it.

At the apartment building, Dino guided Roberto up the stairs. Adolfo was seated at the kitchen table, Mila stood by the stove. No one said anything for a moment, and then Mila went up to her brother-in-law and kissed him quickly on the cheek. "*Ciao,* Roberto. How are you?"

"I'm fine, Mila."

Neither Roberto nor Adolfo looked at each other. Dino stood at one side, waiting.

Finally, Adolfo made the first move. He got up, walked slowly around the table and took Roberto's hand. "*Ciao,* Roberto."

"*Ciao,* Adolfo."

"Well," Mila said, "how about some coffee, Roberto? And I made some *crostini.* I remember you always liked them."

Mila brought out the plates and poured the coffee. Roberto walked to the window and looked out. Adolfo sat back down. Roberto sat across from Adolfo and they ate in silence.

Exasperated, Mila threw up her hands. "Well," she said, "I'm sure you two have a lot to talk about. I think I'll go to Via dei Neri and see if any more shops are open. I'll see you later." She put on her coat, tied a scarf around her head and headed out the door.

"I better go, too," Dino said. He fled down the stairs.

He knew exactly where he wanted to go, and, as he feared, the music shop was devastated. The window was smashed, and inside, tubas and clarinets, music books and stands cluttered the muddy floor. The Gallinotti guitar was missing.

Next door, boards covered the window of the ceramics shop, but Dino could hear pounding inside. He knocked on the door and after a few more tries, the door opened. Hammer in one hand, Bella in the other, Tomasso Nozzoli greeted the boy.

"Dino!"

"*Ciao,* Signor Nozzoli. How are you?"

Tomasso didn't have to answer. He looked exhausted. Dust and wood chips covered his bald head, his plaid woolen shirt and his blue apron.

"Oh, I'm fine. But I need a break. Come on in."

Remarkably, Tomasso had cleared the broken debris on the floor, set up a couple of new displays and built new shelves along the far wall, all under the watchful eye of Bella, who had crouched on a shelf near the ceiling.

Tomasso told Dino that four boxes of dinnerware had escaped unharmed, and he found more pieces that needed cleaning but were not broken. Some pieces with only small chips or cracks were on a table marked "One-Half Off for a Good Home."

"This is amazing," Dino said.

Tomasso put Bella on the floor and she rubbed Dino's legs. "Well, there's a lot more work to be done, but it will take time. Tourists are starting to come back, and Christmas is only four weeks away, so maybe business will pick up a little."

Dino hesitated. "And you, Signor Nozzoli? Are you feeling better?"

"I get a little better every day. I go up to the cemetery at San Minato two or three times a week to visit the principessa. It's so high it didn't get flooded. I put her next to the prince in the mausoleum. She'll be comfortable there."

"I'm sure she's at peace," Dino said. "And you must have many memories."

"Oh, Dino, Dino, I have much more than that. You can't imagine."

Dino couldn't guess what Tomasso was talking about.

"Dino, the principessa...the principessa...." He paused and brushed his hand over his eyes. "She left me seventy-five million *lire*."

"Seventy-five million..." Dino couldn't comprehend such a large number.

"And that was only part of her estate. She gave most of it to art universities, like the Accademia, and some to galleries, and she said Palazzo Tuttini should be turned into a museum."

"That's wonderful!"

"Yes. Yes, it is. But she left me all this money, Dino. I don't know why she did that."

"She must have loved you very much."

Tomasso pulled out his handkerchief and wiped his eyes again. "And I loved her. I'll always love her. But this money. What am I going to do with it? I don't need any money."

"She didn't leave any instructions?"

"All the will said was this, 'For Tomasso Nozzoli, so that he can do good.' What does that mean? What good can I do? I don't know, Dino, I don't know. I'm just a dumb old soccer player. I run a ceramics shop, and not very well."

"Well, there must be something," Dino said. He began to pace between the ceramic displays. He picked up Bella, stroked her little ears and put her down. He fingered an ornate bowl.

"Tomasso, there are so many people who are in desperate shape now. I see them all the time at the soup kitchen. They don't have clothes, they don't have food, they don't have jobs and they need someone to help them fix up their homes."

"I know. I see them every day around here. Those poor people. I'm lucky I have a place to stay and a shop that brings in a little money."

The big man and the tall boy thought for a long while.

"Wait." Tomasso said. "What did you just say? They need someone to help them fix up their homes?"

"Yes."

"Dino, let's think about this."

"OK."

"Dino, what if we got people together who would help people fix up their homes."

"Who?"

"I don't know. Me, I could do some work, but we'd need a lot more, right?"

"Yes," Dino said. "Well, I could help. I fixed up Signora Alonso's apartment. And I could find some other students." And maybe Francesca and Sofia?

"That's good."

"Oh, my God, Tomasso!" Dino suddenly cried. "Roberto! My uncle! He knows exactly what to do. He owns a woodworking shop at Santo Spirito. Right now he's helping Father Lorenzo. They're converting the second floor of the soup kitchen for people to stay while they don't have homes."

"Really?"

"Sure. And I'm sure Roberto will be looking for work."

They were both so excited now they were practically yelling.

"Wait," Tomasso said. "With all this money, we could pay people...

"...like my uncle, my friends..."

"...and provide jobs!"

"And then," Dino said, "they could buy stuff. Like food, like clothes."

Tomasso waved his arms so wildly that Bella scurried under a shelf. "Wait. What about the people who live in these places? They could fix their places up and we could pay them, too."

"Right!" Dino cried.

"Oh, Dino. This is going to be great! We're really going to do something. We're going to do what the principessa wants us to do."

"You know what, Tomasso? I'm going home right now. Roberto was there when I left and I think he's still there. This is just what he needs. I'll come back tomorrow and we can talk about this some more, OK?"

"OK."

The big man put his arm around Dino's shoulder. "Dino, what would I do without you? You're pretty amazing, you know?"

"Hey, you're the one."

"OK, we're both pretty amazing," Tomasso said.

Dino was about to leave when Tomasso called him back. "Wait, I almost forgot."

He went to the safe, turned the combination and pulled out a small box. "Look what I found. I saved it for you."

Dino recognized it immediately. The broken neck of the Gallinotti guitar.

"Wow. Thanks! I guess this will have to do."

"Well, it's just a reminder. I found it floating outside. You've still got your guitar, right?"

"Yes, but I don't play much anymore."

"Why not?"

"I guess I've got other things to do now."

Dino had said it casually, but when he left the shop, the broken neck of the guitar in his pocket, he realized that it was true. Walking down Borgo dei Greci in the evening light, he came across dozens of people who were still trying to put their lives back together by hammering a door or repairing a window. It would take so long for these proud Florentines to be back to normal.

And then Dino knew that he wanted to be a part of that. Painting and music were fine when he was younger, but he was older now. He was going to be twenty-one next year. As Father Lorenzo said, the flood had changed him. He felt a desire, no, a need, to do something more than paint and write songs. He didn't know how to say it, but he wanted to help people. He didn't know how he was going to do that, maybe becoming involved in Tomasso's grand plan, maybe something else.

He couldn't say he was happy as he watched the people of Florence still trying to dig themselves out, but he could say that he had answered some questions. The flood had indeed changed him. He didn't have to visit The Waking Slave any more. He knew he had taken the first step to get out of the shell that had encased him.

Snow-covered rooftops in a Tuscan village. Photo by Umberto Abate @ Fotolia.com

Epilogue

Christmas 1966

When Rosa and Antonio announced that they were getting married on Christmas eve, two years after their engagement, the first question everyone asked was: Why have you taken so long?

The couple ignored that question, but Rosa quickly answered the second: Where will the reception be?

"We don't want a reception," she said. "We're too old for that. We just want our family and friends together with us."

That meant *Il Gruppo di Cielo.* And what better place than the Cielo itself?

Ezio and Donna readily agreed, and quickly expanded the idea.

"Everyone should stay overnight," Ezio said. "We'll have Christmas eve together, and then Christmas day."

Would there be room? They quickly figured it out. Ezio and Donna would have their room on the first floor, and there were four bedrooms on the second floor. Rosa and Antonio would have one, Lucia and Paolo another, Adolfo and Mila the third and Annabella and Fausta the fourth. The upper floor was still pretty much unfinished, with only a couple of cots, but Roberto and Dino could share it.

"Perfect!" Rosa cried.

More than a month after Roberto and Adolfo had met, Roberto was back in the family, warmly welcomed by Lucia but still tentatively by Adolfo. Roberto had gone back to his woodworking shop and cleaned it out because the flood had wrecked the Santo Spirito area. But he spent most of his time working on Tomasso Nozzoli's project, building and repairing homes for the poor. It now was unofficially known as *gli angeli della casa,* "the angels of the home."

Twice, Adolfo had joined him, arriving the second time unannounced.

"Thought you might like some help," he said.

"Badly," Roberto said. "There's a hammer over there."

For two hours they piled boards, built shelves and repaired a broken wall in an apartment occupied by a family of six off Piazza Santa Croce. Neither said much more than "Hand me the saw" or "I think the stack is high enough." Then Adolfo got ready to leave.

"*Grazie,*" Roberto said.

"Sure," Adolfo said.

Dino took a couple of long walks with Francesca and continued volunteering at the *cucina popolare,* but he and Sofia still hadn't found the time to see a movie, or do anything else. He told Father Lorenzo that with the soup kitchen still caring for so many poor people, he felt guilty about going back to Sant'Antonio for Christmas and the wedding. Father Lorenzo said they would somehow get along without him.

On the morning of December 24, Adolfo and Mila and Roberto and Dino boarded the bus to Sant'Antonio, Adolfo and Mila in one seat and Roberto and Dino behind them. Mila rested her head on her husband's shoulder. Dino read a book. Roberto looked out the window.

They arrived in the village just before the wedding and went directly to the church. Father Sangretto was waiting at the door, and Dino smiled when he saw the priest flanked by two girls in white surplices. Much to his displeasure, Father Sangretto was forced to ask girls to assist at Mass because there were no boys in the village. The girls were the twin daughters of Frederico and Veronica Marsi, who happened to be the parish's biggest donors.

"*Buongiorno,* Father," Dino said.

The priest looked at him sadly. "What a pity," he said.

Dino shook his head and followed the others to the front of the church. Red and white poinsettias decorated the altar, a vase of red carnations stood in front of Saint Anthony and most of the figures were in the *presepio* on the right of the main altar. The Baby Jesus would be placed there at the midnight Mass.

Lucia and Paolo were already in the front row, and Lucia rushed back down the aisle to meet her brothers. "Roberto! Adolfo!" she kept saying over and over. She grabbed their hands and forced them into the pew, Mila and Dino following behind. Belatedly, Lucia kissed and hugged her son and her sister-in-law, but then the organist, a stout old woman who had played for many weddings, sounded the opening chords and everyone faced the entrance.

Rosa had finally chosen something to wear for her wedding, but didn't show anyone until she and Antonio stood at the church door.

"My God," Fausta whispered to Annabella. "She's wearing red! Bright red!"

"She always wears blue. Always."

"And she's wearing a hat! Rosa never wears hat."

The red creation on top of Rosa's head featured a feather that curled down to her shoulder.

Perhaps it was a reflection from her dress, but Rosa was radiant as she strode down the aisle, her arm firmly holding Antonio's. He beamed.

Father Sangretto wasn't pleased that he had to add another Mass to his busy Christmas schedule, and the service was even shorter than usual. Everyone in the congregation recognized what he meant when he said, "Antonio, do you *finally* take this woman, Rosa, as your lawfully wedded wife?"

Antonio agreed, and so did Rosa, and then they kissed and everyone applauded and the happy couple left the church amid a blizzard of confetti as Ezio released a pair of doves.

Decorated with only a few flowers, since it was December, their car led the procession up the hill to the Cielo. A light snow had begun to fall, not unusual for this hilly terrain in December.

"I love it when we can look down on the village covered in snow," Donna said as they arrived at the farmhouse.

Ezio and Donna had trimmed the main room with colorful paper chains and balloons, and a *presepio* stood in the corner. The tiny figure of the Baby Jesus was already in its straw cradle, surrounded by Mary, Joseph, two shepherds, four sheep, three kings and an angel.

"Where on earth did you find that?" Rosa asked. "We had that when I was a little girl here."

"In a box in the tool shed," Ezio said. "No idea how it got there."

Donna brought out the *baccalà,* which had been simmering overnight.

"It's not as good as Rosa's, but I certainly didn't want her to spend her time cooking for us tonight."

Around the table, with logs roaring in the fireplace and snow getting ominously heavier outside, there were toasts to the bride and groom, stories of growing up and tales about the war. Rosa, Donna and Lucia coaxed Antonio, Ezio and Paolo to reluctantly talk about their experiences in the Resistance. Ezio and Donna again recounted how they met in Pietrasanta. Rosa and Annabella remembered how at first they wouldn't speak to each other when they were trapped in the Cielo during the German occupation.

"But then we made up," Rosa said, reaching over to hold Annabella's hand.

"And now we're the best of friends."

The story wasn't lost on Roberto and Adolfo, who looked down at their plates. For their part, they told how they had secretly gone back from the Cielo to the village to get medicine in a futile attempt to save their baby sister's life.

"You made me!" Adolfo said.

"Well, I was older," Roberto said.

"As if I did everything you told me to do."

"No, you were too stubborn."

Mila interrupted. "Still are! Both of you!"

For the first time in years, Roberto and Adolfo smiled at each other.

Then it was time for presents. Rosa and Antonio had insisted that they didn't want any wedding presents, but that didn't preclude Christmas gifts. The group had gotten together and presented them with a letter authorizing a week's stay at Lucca's most elegant hotel.

"And you can take it anytime," Lucia said. "Wait till spring or summer."

Antonio hugged his wife. "Think we can wait that long, Rosa?" She kissed him.

The other presents were small and unsurprising. Pieces of jewelry, a couple of neckties, books. Lucia and Paolo gave Dino not one, not two, but three heavy sweaters, "in case there's a flood again." Ezio and Donna gave everyone a gift box of the products of the farm that they were now selling at stores in the area under the *Prodotto di Cielo* label: wine, grappa, jam, olive oil and honey.

"It's a lot of work," Ezio said, "but it helps, considering my teacher salary."

He had other news. He and Donna were considering opening up the Cielo to tourists during the summer. "There's room," Donna said, "and it would be fun to have visitors from all over Italy, maybe even other parts of Europe."

"Not to mention," Ezio added, "a little extra income."

"Oh," Rosa said, "that would be so nice. The Cielo is such a special place. Other people should be able to come here, to stay here."

"We hope so," Ezio said.

It was almost midnight when everyone decided it was time to go to bed. Rosa and Antonio went first, with much advice and warnings following them up the stairs.

"Just don't be too loud," Ezio told his father. Antonio shrugged and continued.

The others followed into their various rooms, and soon the old farmhouse was dark. With Roberto snoring across the room, Dino lay on his cot trying to make out the heavy dark beams in the ceiling. The wind howled through cracks, and he could hear tree branches snapping just under the window. Yet, under his heavy quilt, he felt warm, safe, secure.

By morning, the snow was still falling heavily, whitening the undulating hills beyond and the olive trees and grape vines nearby. The persimmons on the kaki tree just outside the Cielo's door looked like balls on a Christmas tree, and, down in the valley, Sant'Antonio had the appearance of a tiny toy village.

Rosa and Antonio had made it a point to get up first to avoid any more teasing. "You know," she reminded her new husband, "we spent the night in the same room where I slept when I was a girl and where I stayed during that time in the war."

"Bring back memories?"

"Now I have new ones. The best ones." She put a plate of pastries in front of him and kissed his head.

The others arrived, sleepily, and shared hard bread and coffee. Donna and Ezio began to prepare the main meal in the kitchen and told the others to get out of the way. Annabella and Fausta returned to their room to read romance novels they found near the fireplace. Rosa and Antonio rummaged through a shoebox full of postcards of Florence, Lucca, Siena and Pisa, and he promised her he would take her to every place. Lucia and Paolo coaxed Adolfo, Mila and Roberto to brave the snow and blustery winds and have a snowball fight.

Dino held back and went to his father's grave. He cleared off the marker, sat at the base of a tree and leaned back.

He wished he could talk to the father he never knew. He would have liked to tell him about everything that had happened in the last few years. He wished he could tell him about the Accademia and Father Lorenzo and the people at the *cucina popolare* and Tomasso and the principessa. And the flood. And how people came from all over to help. And maybe Francesca and Sofia.

Dino was the last one back, greeted by the sweet smells of roasted turkey that permeated the entire Cielo.

"Ready!" Ezio called as he turned down the radio playing Christmas music and everyone gathered around the table again.

First, a toast with *prosecco*, which Ezio obtained on a rare trip to Conegliano in the Veneto region. "As soon as I saw this bottle, I knew we had to have some for Christmas." He brought back six bottles.

Then plates of antipasti, salami, Parma ham, *crostini*, olives and artichokes. An hour after that, with more stories occupying the time, Donna brought out a huge bowl of ravioli.

"Remember you gave me these last month, Rosa? I put them in the freezer. They're not as good as fresh, but I swore we would have

Rosa's ravioli for Christmas. I just didn't know we'd have this many guests. And I sure wouldn't try to make them myself."

The roast turkey, arriving yet another hour later, was so tender it fell apart as Ezio carved off one slice after another. And finally, the dessert, *panforte*, which Annabella had made. "Just a small piece for me," she said as Donna cut the sweet bread. "I've gained five pounds just sitting here."

Stuffed, they settled in chairs and benches and on the floor around the fireplace as the wind continued to blow branches against the walls outside. Antonio got out his concertina and led the group in traditional Christmas songs.

Tu scendi dalle stelle
O Re del Cielo
E vieni in una grotta
Al freddo al gelo.
E vieni in una grotta
Al freddo al gelo.

You come down from the stars
O King of Heavens,
And you come in a cave,
In the cold, in the frost,
And you come in a cave,
In the cold, in the frost.

But then Antonio put on his heavy coat, hat and boots. "I'd better go see how the roads are if we're thinking about going back to the village tonight. The snow isn't letting up."

"Dino," Lucia said after he left, "you should have brought your guitar. Then you could play for us, too."

He was standing near the fireplace. Those who had been trapped in the Cielo during the war could not help but remember that it was here that Fausta had given her infamous manifesto defending the Nazis, here where the Contessa who wasn't a countess confessed that she had found a community among the group, and here where Dante, the beloved schoolmaster, had tried to explain why sometimes terrible things happen to innocent people.

Now, standing under his painting of Saint Zita's chapel, Dino was the youngest but also one of the most mature members of *Il Gruppo di Cielo.*

"I don't play the guitar much anymore, Mama," Dino said.

"Really," Lucia said. "Too busy?"

"Sort of. I've got other things to do."

"Oh, oh," Paolo said. "Sounds like a girl to me."

Everyone looked at Dino, expecting a full explanation.

"No," Dino said, "it's not a girl."

"Oh, Dino," Lucia said. "You don't mean…oh my…not a girl… but then…oh, I've heard about boys like that…" She looked at Paolo, who looked confused.

"No, Mama. I said it wasn't *a* girl. I'm thinking about dating two."

"Two!" Paolo whooped.

While everyone else burst into laughter, Lucia wanted details. A few months ago, Dino would have stumbled, become beet red, with his ears burning. Not now.

"Well," he said, putting his arm on the mantel, "you all know Francesca. When the flood happened, she came to Florence to help with the cleanup of the books in the library, and Adolfo brought her home for dinner. Mama, she's changed so much since high school. She's so grown up now, she knows what she wants. I realize that I cared for her a lot, and I still do. And I think she likes me."

"I always liked Francesca," Lucia said. Rosa nodded.

"And then there's Sofia. She's a volunteer at the soup kitchen where I volunteer. She's quite wonderful. We go for walks sometime, and I like her, too. Oh, she's from Calabria."

The reaction to this news varied. Ezio and Donna smiled, Rosa looked perplexed and Fausta muttered, "*Terrone.*"

"Oh, I see." Dino said. "You wonder why I would date someone from Calabria. Well, for one thing she's very beautiful. I know that because she modeled in the life drawing class at the Accademia."

"In the nude?" Lucia exclaimed.

"Yes, Mama, in the nude. That's how models usually model in life drawing classes."

"*Allora*," Rosa said. "So you go out with a girl from Calabria that you see naked in your classroom. *Santa Maria!*"

"Well, Rosa," Dino said, trying not to be condescending, but speaking quietly and firmly, "I wish you could meet Sofia. She could tell you how she grew up in a tiny village, how her mother died in childbirth and her father was killed by the mafia. How she fled first to Naples and then to Rome and then to Siena and finally to Florence. And how she worked as a seamstress in a dress shop and in a men's hat shop before she lost both jobs because of the flood. But she still volunteers almost every day in a soup kitchen among the poorest of the poor."

"*Allora*," Rosa said.

"Oh," Lucia said. "She sounds like a very nice girl. Just like Francesca."

"They're not girls, Mama. They're women. In fact, Sofia is twenty-four."

"But you're only twenty!"

In Italy, even in 1966, it was not considered proper for a young man to date a woman older than he was.

"Mama, four years! It's not a big deal."

Lucia sighed.

"Mama, you'd like her. She's quite wonderful."

"Dino," Paolo said, "remember when Father Sangretto wanted you to a priest? Now you're going out with two women!"

Dino smiled. "I remember. And I remember how I resisted. I guess he was only doing his job, trying to get another boy into the priesthood. But you know, I met another priest in Florence. His name is Father Lorenzo and he runs the soup kitchen where I volunteer. He's amazing, everything I think a priest should be. I mean, I think he's a living saint. I wish I could be just a little bit like him."

"Dino!" Lucia cried. "You mean you're thinking about...but you just said you like those two girls...women."

"Mama, what I've found out is that there are so many paths to follow. Ezio, remember that talk we had last Christmas?"

"Of course," Ezio said.

"You told me not to think so much about what I want to do, where I want to live, but just to see what each day brings. I think that's what I've been doing. I really don't know what I will be doing five, ten years from now. Maybe I'll do something with painting, maybe something with music, maybe something totally different."

Suddenly, Lucia began to cry.

"Mama, why are you crying? What did I say?"

"Dino, you're so grown up now. In four years you've changed so much. I feel like we've lost you."

Dino went over to the rocking chair where Lucia was sitting and put his arm around her.

"No, Mama, you haven't lost me. The only thing I know is that I want to help people somehow, and I don't know where or how that will be. But I do know this. I love Sant'Antonio, and I always will. Last night I was lying in bed and thinking how great this village is and how great you all are. And I love all of you."

Dino said all of this unashamed of his feelings.

There were tears, there were smiles, and there were hugs.

"Dino!" Paolo yelled. "You've said more words in the last ten minutes than you have in the last ten years!"

"*Allora*," Rosa said, smiling. "I keep thinking of you as the little boy drawing pictures on the picnic table."

"There's one more thing I want to say," Dino said. "This morning when I was out for a walk, I looked down at Sant'Antonio and I could see the church through the snow. And I remembered that *Festa di Sant'Antonio* in 1962."

"How could anyone forget that?" Paolo said.

"I've been trying to block it out of my mind," Donna said.

"And I thought," Dino said, "what a great time we had that day. I know I was acting like a stupid sixteen-year-old, because that's what I was..."

"Little Dino," Paolo said.

Dino laughed. "Yes, Little Dino. You know, sometimes in Florence I still think I'm Little Dino. And maybe you still think of me as Little Dino here, too."

"We'll always think of you as Little Dino no matter how old you are," Rosa said.

"No, we won't," Paolo said. "You're really not little anymore."

"Well, it's all right if you do. I don't mind anymore." He kissed his mother and then hugged Paolo.

Just then, Antonio returned from outside, stomping his boots and shaking snow from his hat. "Well, everyone, the road to the village is snowed in. Looks like we're going to be stuck up here for another day or two."

"Wonderful!" Rosa cried.

Ezio put another log in the fireplace, Annabella and Fausta lit some candles, Rosa and Antonio snuggled against a bench, Adolfo and Mila passed around sweaters and blankets, Donna brought out some cookies and Roberto passed around a bottle of grappa. Everyone noticed that he didn't serve himself, but, for the first time, Dino was offered a glass.

"*Buon Natale!*" everyone shouted.

"Isn't this great!" Dino said. "Just great!"

CPSIA information can be obtained at www.ICGtesting.com
Printed in the USA
LVOW111755230312

274512LV00011B/164/P